Françoise Athénais de Rochechouart.
(Marquise de Montespan.)

MADAME DE MONTESPAN
AND LOUIS XIV

BY

H. NOEL WILLIAMS

AUTHOR OF "MADAME RÉCAMIER AND HER FRIENDS"
"MADAME DE POMPADOUR," ETC.

"La jalousie est le plus grand de tous les maux et celui qui fait le moins
de pitié aux personnes qui le causent."—*La Rochefoucauld.*

WITH PORTRAIT

1910

4to Edition published 1903

PREFACE

VOLTAIRE in his *Siècle de Louis XIV.* justifies the space which he devotes to the intrigues of the Court on the ground that the period of which he is treating possesses such extraordinary fascination for the student of history that even the most trivial details can hardly fail to interest his readers. Voltaire's apology might, I venture to think, be in itself a sufficient one for the present volume, were any needed. But this is far from being the case. For Madame de Montespan was something more than the mistress of *le Grand Monarque*, the mother of legitimated princes and princesses, the woman whose blood flows to-day in the veins of half the Royal Houses in Europe ; she was the symbol of her age, the spirit of seventeenth-century France incarnate. In her we find almost all the best and the worst characteristics of the great epoch in French history—an epoch which attained the furthest extremes in both good and evil—its dignity and splendour, its genuine admiration for literature and art, its exquisite courtesy, its light-hearted gaiety, its brilliant wit, side by side with its arrogance and egotism, its senseless prodigality, its flagrant disregard of the moral law, its gross superstition. In studying her life we are studying not her alone, but the whole society of which she was the representative.

PREFACE

Radiant, and joyous, and "beautiful as the day," for twelve long years—years which, by a singular coincidence, are among the most splendid in her country's annals—this woman dominated the whole Court of France, denied political influence by her royal lover, it is true, but denied nothing else, glorying in her dishonour, contemptuously defying the *dévots* and the envious men and women who surrounded her to wrest the sceptre from her grasp. Once indeed, when, for a brief moment, the eloquent pleading of Bossuet prevailed, she received orders to leave Versailles, only to return, a few weeks later, more haughty and more powerful than ever.

But power resting on so frail a foundation as a monarch's guilty passions is seldom permanent, and already her empire, undermined by her own arrogance and capriciousness and the subtle influence of Madame de Maintenon, was tottering to its fall, when, in the autumn of 1680, the revelation of her dealings with the poisoner La Voisin and her fiendish associates came to shatter it to pieces.

Respect for his kingly dignity and consideration for his children combined to force Louis XIV. to preserve the terrible secret, known only to himself and a few trusted advisers, and, to avoid the smallest possibility of its disclosure, Madame de Montespan remained at Court, treated in public by the prince against whose life she had conspired as if she had done nothing whatever to forfeit his esteem, but enduring agonies of mortification, as she saw the power which had once been hers passing slowly but surely into the hands of another. Then, when the Queen was dead and Madame de Maintenon had reached the summit of her ambition, and it became evident that, not content with supplanting her former patroness in the King's affections, the pious lady was determined to inflict upon her those cruel humiliations which Madame de Montespan, in her time, had compelled the gentle La Vallière to endure, the fallen favourite, abandoning the unequal struggle, quitted the Court, to spend the remainder of her days, first, in vain regrets for what she had lost, afterwards, in a sincere and whole-hearted endeavour to atone for her shameful past by a life of penance and good works.

Interesting as is the career of Madame de Montespan, it is rendered all the more so from the opportunity which it affords us of studying those of the two celebrated women whose lives were so closely connected with hers —two women differing as widely from each other as from Madame de Montespan herself ; the one, perhaps next to Jeanne d'Arc the most poetic figure in French history : the other, in spite of all that has been written about her, almost as much an enigma to us to-day as she was to her contemporaries.

Under these circumstances, it is surely a matter for surprise that Madame de Montespan should have been practically ignored by English and American writers and that the fullest account of her to be found in our language should be that given by Miss Pardoe in her " Louis XIV. and the Court of France in the Seventeenth Century," written many years before M. Ravaisson published the result of his researches, and largely based on the marchioness's so-called *Mémoires*, then believed to be genuine, but now quite discredited.

In my endeavour to supply this deficiency and to give

an account at once adequate and strictly impartial of the life of the most famous of Louis XIV.'s mistresses I have traversed a wide field and been at pains to consult not only all the chief contemporary sources of information —the *Mémoires* of Madame de Caylus, Mademoiselle de Montpensier, Saint-Simon, Dangeau, La Fare, Choisy, and Sourches; and the Letters of the Princess Palatine, Madame de Sévigné, Madame de Maintenon, and Bussy-Rabutin, in every case making due allowance for the prejudices of the writer—but a very large number of modern works, particularly those bearing in any way on the Poison Trials. Where so many have been laid under contribution it is somewhat difficult to fairly apportion one's gratitude, and I must therefore confine myself to acknowledging my indebtedness to M. Pierre Clément's *Madame de Montespan et Louis XIV.* (an admirable work, the value of which is, unfortunately, largely discounted by the fact that the author had only a partial acquaintance with the documents which M. Ravaisson has so ably edited); to M. Jules Lair's *Louise de La Vallière et la jeunesse de Louis XIV.*; to the notes of M. Lavallée in his *Correspondance générale de Madame de Maintenon*; to M. Ravaisson's *Archives de la Bastille*; to M. Funck-Brentano's *Le Drame des Poisons*; to M. Floquet's *Bossuet, précepteur du Dauphin et évêque à la Cour*; to M. Loiseleur's *Trois Énigmes historiques*; and to Dr. Lucien Nass's *Les Empoisonnements de Louis XIV.*

H. NOEL WILLIAMS.

LONDON: *July* 1903.

CONTENTS

CHAPTER I

WHEN Louis XIV. lay dying, he sorrowfully acknowledged that he had been too fond of war. He might also
have acknowledged that he had been too fond of women.
Nevertheless, culpable as they undoubtedly were, and deep
as is the stain which they have inflicted on his reputation,
the amours of *le Grand Monarque* at all times present a

certain romantic quality, which is wholly wanting in those of his contemptible successor. Louis XIV. would have scorned to have used his position as king to force his attentions upon any woman whom he had reason to believe was indifferent to him as a man ; he desired to be loved for himself, not for what the accident of birth had made him, and thus even his most evanescent attachments are redeemed by a touch of sentiment.[1]

Again—and here the difference between himself and Louis XV. is even more strongly marked—one must, in justice to him, remember that he never permitted his mistresses, whatever influence they may have acquired over his heart, to have any over his government. "In abandoning our hearts," he says in the *Mémoires* he wrote for the instruction of the Dauphin, "we must remain absolute masters of our minds ; we must make a distinction between the tenderness of a lover and the resolutions of a sovereign, so that the beauty who conduces to our pleasures shall not be at liberty to speak to us concerning our affairs. You know the warning I have given you on different occasions about the influence of favourites ; that of a mistress is far more dangerous."[2]

On the whole, Louis XIV. may be said to have strictly adhered, in appearance at any rate, to the principle here laid down.[3] Neither Mademoiselle de La Vallière, nor

[1] "The late King (Louis XIV.)," wrote his sister-in-law, the Princess Palatine, "was undoubtedly very gallant ; but his gallantry often degenerated into debauchery. At the age of twenty, all sorts and conditions of women found favour in his eyes—peasant girls, gardeners' daughters, maid-servants, waiting-women, ladies of quality—*provided that they were able to make him believe that they loved him.*"

[2] *Mémoires de Louis XIV. pour servir à l'instruction du Dauphin* (edit. 1860), ii. 315.

[3] Charles Perrault relates tnat, one day, in the presence of Le Tellier,

MADAME DE MONTESPAN

Madame de Montespan, nor Mademoiselle de Fontanges, nor any of the numerous ladies who for brief periods held sway over the royal affections, have left the slightest mark upon public affairs; while in regard to Madame de Maintenon—her admirers will pardon our including her in the same category for the sake of argument—it is now generally believed that her influence in affairs of State was very small, and that the story that she was largely responsible for the Revocation of the Edict of Nantes is a myth.

But, at the same time, it must be admitted that, if they had no direct political influence, if they were powerless to remove a Minister who had had the misfortune to displease them, or to plunge the nation into a ruinous war in order to gratify their caprices, indirectly and unconsciously they exercised a good deal, and that of a most pernicious kind. The naïve adoration of Louise de La Vallière, no less than the calculated flattery of Madame de Montespan and her various rivals, went far to confirm Louis XIV. in that fine conceit of his kingly dignity, and to intensify that ingrained selfishness of character which, so long as the splendour of his Court was undiminished and victory attended his arms, rendered him blind to the miseries which his perpetual wars and grinding taxation were bringing upon his realm. When, at length, the *régime*

Lionne, Villeroi, Colbert, and other favourite Ministers and courtiers, the King remarked : " You are all of you here my friends, those of my realm for whom I have the most regard and in whom I place the most confidence. I am young, and women have generally considerable influence over those of my age. I enjoin you all, therefore, that should you remark that a woman, whoever she may be, has acquired ascendency over me and is influencing me in the smallest degree, to immediately apprise me of the fact. I shall only require forty-eight hours to rid myself of her and to set your minds at rest on that score."— *Mémoires de Charles Perrault*, p. 38.

of mistresses came to an end, all the monarch's worst instincts had been developed and his character irrevocably moulded. His so-called conversion was merely a change from one kind of egotism to another; for what is bigotry but egotism in its most subtle and dangerous form?

The first lady to stir the young monarch's pulses was Cardinal Mazarin's niece, Olympe Mancini, the second of the five famous sisters of that name,[1] who made her first appearance at Court in 1657. Mademoiselle Olympe was no beauty—none of Louis XIV.'s early enchantresses were —but Madame de Motteville remarks that " she certainly appeared charming in the eyes of the King, and sufficiently pretty to indifferent people." Anne of Austria seems to have regarded this youthful attachment with complaisance, though the aforementioned chronicler assures us that she could not endure to hear any one speak of the affair as one that might perchance become legitimate. " The greatness of her soul had a perfect horror of such abasement." Another queen — the eccentric Christina of Sweden—who passed through France at this time, was of a different opinion, and declared that "it would be very wrong not to let two young people so admirably suited to one another marry as soon as possible." Nothing, however, came of this affair, for Louis showed no inclination to " abase " himself, and Olympe, who did not want for shrewdness, finding that she had no chance of wearing a crown, " instead of surrendering herself to love," gave her hand to the Comte de Soissons, by whom she had, among other children, a boy named Eugène, destined to become one of the most famous generals of his age and a veritable thorn in the side of his mother's former admirer.

[1] The names of the five were Laure, Olympe, Marie, Hortense, and Marie Anne.

MADAME DE MONTESPAN

After the marriage of Olympe Mancini, the King cast a favourable eye upon a certain Mademoiselle de La Motte d'Argencourt, " who had neither dazzling beauty nor extraordinary intelligence, but whose whole person was agreeable." His predilection for her society became so very marked that both the Queen-Mother and Mazarin became uneasy; and the former, one evening, when Louis had conversed with the young lady rather longer than she considered prudent, rebuked him sharply and openly. The monarch received the maternal reprimand "with respect and gentleness," but it would not appear to have had much effect, for shortly afterwards we hear of him speaking to Mademoiselle de La Motte "as a man in love, who had thrown virtue to the winds," and assuring her that if she would only return his affection, he would defy both the Queen and the Cardinal. The lady, however, from motives either of virtue or policy, declined to entertain his proposals, and Anne of Austria, having pointed out to her son that " he was wandering from the path of innocence," the King was moved to tears, confessed himself in her oratory, and then departed for Vincennes, in the hope that a change of scene might aid him to subjugate his passion. He returned, after a few days' absence, fully determined never to speak to Mademoiselle de La Motte again ; but, " not being yet wholly strengthened," so far departed from his resolution as to dance with her at a ball, with the result that he was on the point of succumbing once more, when the Queen and the Cardinal put an end to the affair by packing the damsel off to a convent at Chaillot, where Madame de Motteville assures us that " she led a life that was very tranquil and very happy."[1]

The next lady to be honoured by the monarch's

[1] *Mémoires de Madame de Motteville* (edit. 1855), iv. 83 *et seq.*

attention was Madame de Beauvais, first *femme-de-chambre* to Anne of Austria. Anquetil describes her as "a woman of experience," and says that she laid her snares for the King in such a way as to render escape impossible.[1] The Queen-Mother, in anger, dismissed her from her service, but soon afterwards reinstated her, as she found it impossible to get on without her. Then we hear of *galanteries* with the beautiful Duchesse de Châtillon, and "a gardener's daughter," and his rejection at the hands of a Mademoiselle de Tarneau, "who had the wisdom to refuse him so much as an interview," which brings us to what may be called Louis XIV.'s first *grande passion*, an affair which was within an ace of having very serious consequences indeed.

Having duly provided Olympe Mancini with a husband, Mazarin introduced to Court the third of the Mancini sisters, Marie by name, whom he withdrew from the Couvent des Filles-de-Saint-Marie at Chaillot, in defiance of the dying request of his sister, Madame Mancini, who had begged him earnestly to make her a nun, "because she had always seemed to her to have a bad disposition, and her late husband, who was a great astrologer, had warned her that this daughter would be the cause of much evil."[2]

---

[1] *Louis XIV., sa Cour et le Régent,* i. 9. Saint-Simon says that gossip credited Madame de Beauvais with being the first lady to prevail over the virtue of Louis XIV. He adds : "I remember her when she was old, blind of one eye and scarce able to see with the other, at the toilette of the Bavarian Dauphiness, where all the Court treated her with extraordinary consideration, because from time to time she went to Versailles, and when there was invariably granted a private audience by the King, who still cherished a great regard for her." In the estimates for 1677, Madame de Beauvais's name appears for a pension of 4000 livres, and in those for 1684 for one of 8000 livres, while in the following year she received a *gratification extraordinaire* of 30,000 livres.

[2] *Mémoires de Madame de Motteville,* iv. 78.

MADAME DE MONTESPAN

At first the King took very little notice of this damsel, which is hardly surprising, as she is described as painfully thin and extremely ugly, with a sallow complexion and "a wide, flat mouth."[1] She improved rapidly in this respect, however, so much so that we find Saint-Évremond—no mean judge, by the way—speaking of her as "a superbly formed creature."

In the spring of 1658 it began to be remarked that Louis XIV. was paying Mademoiselle Mancini an unusual amount of attention, and the young lady herself informs us in her *Apologie*[2] that during a visit of the Court to Fontainebleau "she became assured that she was not hated by the King, who, though very young, had penetration enough to understand that eloquence which, without speaking a syllable, persuades more than all the fine speeches in the world." She adds, with becoming modesty, that at first she was inclined to believe that she was mistaken, until her impressions were confirmed by the extraordinary deference paid her by the courtiers. An

---

[1] *Mémoires de Madame de Motteville*, iv. 83. M. Chantelauze, in his *Louis XIV. et Marie Mancini*, says that it is to Marie Mancini's mouth that allusion is intended in the well-known *cantique*, wrongly attributed to Bussy-Rabutin, which was published in several surreptitious editions of his *Histoire amoureuse des Gaules* :

> "Quem Deodatus est heureux
> De baiser ce bec amoureux
> Qui d'une oreille à l'autre va !
> Alleluia ! "

According to Voltaire, this song was the true cause of Bussy being sent to the Bastille in 1665, and afterwards banished to his estates.

[2] *Apologie, ou les véritables mémoires de Madame M. Mancini, Connestable de Colonne, écrits par elle-même* (Cologne, 1679). The authenticity of this work was at one time disputed, but is now generally acknowledged.

event of the highest importance, however, came at this juncture to interrupt what the writer calls " her ravishing prosperity."

For more than fifteen years and through many strange vicissitudes, Mazarin had steadily pursued his project of marrying Louis to the Infanta of Spain. His object in desiring this union was a twofold one. In the first place, a closer connection between France and Spain would leave the Emperor isolated in Europe and render him practically impotent. In the second, it was more than possible that it might, sooner or later, be the means of giving the crown of Spain to the House of Bourbon, for, as his letters to the French plenipotentiaries at the Congress of Westphalia indicate, the astute Cardinal had made up his mind so to frame the marriage contract that there would be little difficulty in successfully contesting the validity of any renunciation of her rights on the part of the Infanta.

Since 1645, when the Peace of Westphalia was concluded with the Emperor, more than one attempt had been made to make peace on the basis of another Franco-Spanish marriage; but as Philip IV. had no male issue, and the Infanta would have carried with her to France the right of succession to the crown of Spain, the Court of Madrid had hitherto received the Cardinal's proposition with marked coldness. Of late, however, the situation had been greatly modified. In 1657, the Queen of Spain had given birth to a son, an event which placed two lives between the Infanta and the throne, and very sensibly diminished that young lady's matrimonial value; while France had gained great advantages in the field, and it was becoming increasingly difficult for the Spaniards, with troops disheartened by defeat and an impoverished Treasury, to carry on the struggle.

Indirect negotiations were accordingly opened ; but as the Court of Madrid showed its customary vacillation, Mazarin resolved to force it to come to a definite decision, and, with this idea, made overtures to the Duchess of Savoy[1] for the hand of her daughter, Margaret. These overtures were carried so far that a meeting between the two Courts took place at Lyons in November 1658 ; but nothing came of the negotiations, for almost at the same moment as the Savoyards entered the city by one gate, Don Antonio Pimentel, a special envoy from the King of Spain, entered it by another, bringing an offer both of peace and the Infanta. So the poor Duchess of Savoy had to take her daughter home again, carrying with her a written promise that if a treaty for Louis XIV.'s marriage with the Infanta were not concluded by the following May, the young King would wed the Princess Margaret, and a superb diamond necklace given her by the Cardinal, by way of consolation for her disappointment.

Marie Mancini, who had already made up her mind that the crown matrimonial would become her right well, was, of course, overjoyed at the discomfiture of the Italian princess, and while her uncle and Pimentel were busily engaged clearing the way for a treaty between the two belligerent nations, she was no less actively employed in endeavouring to thwart their plans and wean the King from the idea of espousing the Infanta. In this she was all but successful.

After the return of the Court to Paris, Louis's infatuation for the young lady increased in a truly alarming manner, and they were scarcely ever apart. "The King

[1] Christine of France, second daughter of Henri IV. and Marie de Medicis. She married Victor Amadeus I. in 1619, and was left a widow in 1637.

9

never came into the Queen-Mother's presence without Mademoiselle Mancini," writes Madame de Motteville. "She followed him everywhere, and whispered in his ear in the presence of even the Queen herself, undeterred by the respect and decorum which she owed her." [1]

Although, as we have mentioned, the enterprising Marie had few pretensions to beauty, her ready wit and the charm of her conversation more than atoned for her lack of physical attractions. She would appear to have been extraordinarily well-read for a girl of her years, possessing a most intimate knowledge of Italian literature, especially of poetry, and being in the habit of discussing history, politics, and philosophy with Lionne, La Rochefoucauld and Saint-Évremond. "There is nothing that she does not know; there is no book worth reading that she has not read," cried one of her enthusiastic admirers.

The young monarch, though very deeply in love, did not at first evince any desire to gratify Mademoiselle Mancini's ambition; but when he found that his inamorata was "either too proud or too shrewd" to accept a less exalted post, he determined that she should share his throne.

In the meanwhile the progress of this affair was causing the utmost disquietude to the Queen-Mother and Mazarin, all the more so as the preliminaries of peace had been concluded at the beginning of June 1659, and the Cardinal was on the point of setting out for Saint-Jean de Luz to meet the Spanish Prime Minister, Don Luis de Haro, and settle the terms of the definitive treaty. The position was, indeed, a most critical one, for if Louis were to carry his infatuation so far as to decline to marry the Infanta, all the schemes which Mazarin had so carefully built up

[1] *Mémoires de Madame de Motteville,* iv. 143.

would collapse like a house of cards. After vainly remonstrating with his niece, the Cardinal decided to exercise
his avuncular authority, and, a few days before he started
for the South, took the precaution of sending her with
her sisters, Hortense and Marie Anne, to the citadel of
Brouage, near La Rochelle, in charge of their *gouvernante*,
Madame de Venel.

The King, however, was not minded to renounce his
lady-love without an effort. He sent for the Cardinal
and boldly demanded his niece in marriage. Mazarin
replied that he could not take advantage of the honour
which his Majesty wished to do him in a moment of
violent passion ; that he had been chosen by the late King,
and since by the Queen, to assist him with his counsel,
and that having up to that time served him with inviolable
fidelity, he would not now abuse their confidence ; that he
was master of his niece, and " would stab her to the heart
rather than elevate her by so base an act of treachery."
Louis, it is said, went down on his knees in a last
endeavour to melt the Minister's heart, but Mazarin
remained inflexible.

Finding that there was nothing to be hoped for in this
quarter, the King appealed to Anne of Austria, and, the
evening before the day fixed for Mademoiselle Marie's
departure, had a touching interview with his mother,
which lasted an hour, and from which his Majesty
emerged with eyes red with weeping. The Queen had
proved as obdurate as the Cardinal, and had at length
succeeded in inducing her son to sacrifice his inclinations
on the altar of duty.

The separation between the lovers, which took place the
following morning, must have been exceedingly affecting.
The King, with tears in his eyes, insisted on accompanying

MADAME DE MONTESPAN

the young lady to her coach, and it was then that
Marie addressed to him those words of tender reproach :
"Sire, you weep, you love me, and yet you allow me to
go!"[1]

Three days later, Mazarin set out on his journey to the
frontier, in a state of mind far from enviable, for Louis,
ignoring the promise he had given the Queen-Mother,
had refused to abandon his idea of marrying the Cardinal's
niece, and had declared that nothing would induce him to
wed the Infanta. The Minister, therefore, had a double
task before him—on the one hand, to induce the Spanish
plenipotentiaries to agree to the conditions he desired to
impose, and, on the other, to bring his headstrong young
master to reason. He was, moreover, in hourly dread
lest the story of Louis's infatuation should reach Madrid,
in which case it was quite probable that the negotiations
would be promptly broken off.

In the hope of inducing the King to conquer his passion,
the Cardinal kept up an active and voluminous correspondence with him.

CARDINAL MAZARIN *to* LOUIS XIV.

"CADILLAC, *July* 16, 1659.

"Letters from Paris, Flanders, and elsewhere advise
me that you cannot be known to be the same person since
my departure, and that not because of me, but on account
of some one that belongs to me ; that you have entered
into engagements which will hinder you from giving peace

---

[1] The above is the version of the speech which the lady herself gives
in her *Apologie ;* but there are several other renderings—*e.g.* "You
weep and you are master !" (*Mémoires de Madame de Motteville*). "You
love me, Sire, you weep, you are in despair, you are King, and yet I
go !" (Bussy-Rabutin's *Histoire amoureuse des Gaules*).

12

to Christendom and rendering your State and subjects happy by your marriage ; and that if, to avoid so great a calamity, you pass on to make it, the person you espouse will be most miserable, and that through no fault of her own.

" . . . It is said that you are always shut up to write to the person you love, and that you spend in this occupation more time than you did in conversing with her while she was at Court. It is further said that I approve of this and connive at it, in order to satisfy my ambition and hinder the peace.

" It is said that you are at variance with the Queen, and even those who write in the mildest terms say that you avoid her as much as possible. I find, moreover, that the consent I gave, at your urgent request, to an occasional interchange of news between yourself and this person (Marie Mancini) has led to a continual commerce of long letters ; that, in fact, you write to her every day and receive a reply, so that the courier is charged with as many letters as there are days, which cannot be without scandal, nor even without injury to this person's reputation and mine. . . .

" God has established Kings (after matters which concern religion, for the maintenance of which they ought to use every possible endeavour) to watch over the welfare, repose, and security of their subjects, and not to sacrifice them to their private passions, and when such unhappy princes have appeared, they have commonly been forsaken by the divine Providence, and histories are full of the revolutions and miseries they have drawn down on their persons and States. And, therefore, I solemnly warn you not to hesitate any longer, for though, in a certain sense, you are the master to do as you please, yet must you give an account of your actions to God for the saving of your soul, and to the world for the saving of your credit and reputation.

"I conclude all this discourse by declaring to you that if I find not by the answer which I conjure you to send me with all speed that there is reason to hope that you will choose the path that is necessary for your own welfare, for your honour, and for the preservation of your Kingdom, I have no other course open to me but to remit into your hands all the benefits which it has pleased the late King, yourself, and the Queen to heap upon me, and to embark with all my family to go and pass the remainder of my days in some corner of Italy, and pray to God that this last remedy may produce the cure which I desire above all else, being able to say, without exaggeration and without using the term of submission and respect I owe, that there is no tenderness comparable to that which I have for you, and that it will be impossible for me to prevent myself dying of grief should I see you do anything which may blacken your reputation and expose your person and State. . . .

"I believe you know me well enough to credit that what I write comes from the depths of my heart, and that nothing can alter the resolution of which I have spoken save an assurance from you that you will henceforth begin a new course and master the passions to which you are at present enslaved."[1]

The Cardinal's appeal to the young King's sense of

---

[1] *Lettres du Cardinal Mazarin où l'on voit Le Secret de la Négotiation de la Paix des Pirenées, &c.* (À Amsterdam : Chez André Pierrot : 1690), p. 16 *et seq.* Copies of the original letters are preserved in the Bibliothèque Mazarine : *Lettres manuscrites de Mazarin,* vol. iii.

duty was, however, only partially successful. Louis professed his willingness to marry the Infanta, but obstin-
ately refused to break off his connection with Marie
Mancini, and when in August the Court set out for
Bordeaux—the wedding ceremony was to take place at
Saint-Jean de Luz—announced his intention of going to
Brouage to pay the young lady a visit. In great alarm,
Mazarin wrote to the Queen-Mother, imploring her " in
the name of God to do everything possible to prevent this
meeting " ; but, finding that Louis had set his heart on
seeing his lady-love, eventually consented that Madame
de Venel, his niece's *gouvernante*, should bring her charge
as far as Saint-Jean d'Angely. The interview, according
to Madame de Motteville, was full of feeling, and tears
were shed on both sides. Nevertheless, the King continued his journey, and Marie returned to her place of
exile.

The romance continued for some little time longer,
Louis inditing "not letters, but volumes" to his enchantress,
while the Cardinal wrote equally voluminous epistles of
remonstrance, in one of which he assured his Majesty that
" this person had a thousand faults and not a single good
quality to render her worthy of the honour of his kindness."
To which the King sent so curt an answer that Mazarin felt
compelled to implore his forgiveness, and wrote a most
piteous letter to the Queen-Mother, begging her to make
intercession for him with her son.

At length, to the inexpressible relief of the poor
Cardinal, the affair was broken off, not by Louis, but by
the lady herself, who, having come to the conclusion that
the negotiations for the Spanish marriage had gone too
far for her lover to draw back, wrote to her uncle to
inform him that she had decided to follow his counsel and

cease all communication with the King. Louis at first appears to have been deeply mortified by the damsel's conduct, but, in his calmer moments, had the good sense to own that Mazarin in thwarting his passion had acted with courage and discretion.

As for Marie Mancini, she was persuaded by her uncle, who was naturally of opinion that, after what had occurred, it would be dangerous to allow her to remain in France, to accept the hand of a wealthy Italian noble, the Constable Colonna, Prince of Palliano. This union proved anything but a happy one. Colonna became jealous of his wife, and the wife wearied of Colonna. One day, Marie and her sister, Hortense, who had fled from her husband, the Duc de Mazarin,[1] and taken refuge at Naples, disguised themselves as men and made their way to Civita Vecchia, where they embarked in a felucca bound for France ; and, after an adventurous voyage, in which they narrowly escaped being captured, first, by a galley which the enraged Constable had sent in pursuit of them and, afterwards, by a Turkish corsair, landed at Marseilles. The younger sister, hearing that some emissaries of the Duc de Mazarin

---

[1] Armand Charles, Marquis de Meilleraye, who, on his marriage, was created Duc de Mazarin. " He was affected with a species of religious insanity, which showed itself, among other ways, in a modesty of unusual rigour. The great collection of statuary and paintings of which he had become the owner (on the death of the Cardinal) shocked his views, and, armed with a hammer, he went through the galleries, demolishing the statues that offended him by an improper nudity, while Titians and Correggios were smeared over, wherever the dress, or the Magdalens, which the masters had painted, were not such as would be appropriate at a prayer-meeting. Colbert succeeded in checking this destruction, but the collection suffered severely from the piety of its owner. . . . A taste for lawsuits was another of his peculiarities. He was said to have had three hundred and to have lost almost all."— Perkins's " France under Mazarin," ii. 354.

were on their way to intercept her, went to Savoy, whence she proceeded to England and became the mistress of Charles II., who, in the days of his exile, had vainly sought her hand in marriage. Marie set out for Fontainebleau ; but the King was with the army in Flanders, and the Queen, who acted as regent in his absence, hearing of the approach of her former rival, sent an officer to meet her with a *lettre de cachet*, in virtue of which she was carried off to the Abbey of Lys, and later to one at Avency. When Louis was informed of what had been done, he remarked, " Very good."

After a short detention, the princess was released and allowed to proceed to Turin. Here she remained awhile and then made an attempt to re-enter France, only to be stopped at the frontier and sent back to Savoy. She subsequently fell into the hands of her husband and spent the next ten years as a prisoner in various convents in Flanders and Spain, for though she on several occasions contrived to make her escape, she was invariably recaptured. At length, the Constable died, and in 1684 Marie was granted permission to return to the French Court, where, to her intense mortification, she found herself completely forgotten. She appears to have lived for some time in retirement at Passy ; but little is known of her later years, and even the date and place of her death are uncertain.

CHAPTER II

Marriage of Louis XIV. and the Infanta—A question of
etiquette—State entry of the bridal pair into Paris—Personal
appearance and character of the Queen—Marriage of *Monsieur*
and Henrietta of England—Charms of this princess—Attentions
paid her by the King—Jealousy of the Queen and *Monsieur*
—The King, at *Madame's* suggestion, simulates a devotion for
Louise de La Vallière—And falls in love with her—Amiable
character of Mademoiselle de La Vallière—Her disinterestedness
—She becomes the mistress of the King—Vain remonstrances
of the Queen-Mother—Remorse of La Vallière—Her flight
to the convent at Chaillot—The King goes to the convent
and brings her back—The Comtesse de Soissons, the Marquis
de Vardes, and the Comte de Guiche intrigue against La
Vallière—The Spanish letter—The Comtesse de Soissons
persuades Mademoiselle de La Motte-Houdancourt to enter
the lists against the favourite—The King succumbs to her
fascinations—And exiles his rival the Chevalier de Gramont
—Mademoiselle de La Motte demands the dismissal of La
Vallière as the price of her surrender—The King is undeceived by the Queen-Mother—Mademoiselle de La Motte
dismissed from Court—Punishment of the Comtesse de
Soissons and her confederates—La Vallière *maîtresse déclarée*
—Louis XIV. creates her a duchess and legitimates her
daughter.

His ambitious niece having at length had the good taste
to retire from the field, Mazarin pushed on the negotiations for the marriage with all possible expedition.
Owing. however, to the feeble health of the King of Spain,

which rendered a journey to the frontier so late in the year out of the question, it was found necessary to postpone the nuptials till the following April ; and, as a matter of fact, it was not until June 3 that Philip IV., who deemed it indispensable to his own and his daughter's dignity to travel with a retinue which extended for six leagues and required nearly four thousand sumpter-horses and mules to transport their baggage, arrived at Fontarabia, where the Infanta, having formally renounced all rights of succession to the Spanish throne, was married by procuration, Don Luis de Haro acting as proxy for Louis XIV.

Three days later, the two Kings met at the Ile des Faisans,[1] and, kneeling side by side, with a copy of the Gospels between them, solemnly swore to observe the Treaty of the Pyrenees, after which Maria Theresa was formally handed over to her husband, and on June 9 the second marriage took place at Saint-Jean de Luz with great pomp.

Between the house occupied by the Queen-Mother and the church of Saint-Jean a gallery had been erected, a little higher than the street, and along this the royal party made their way, preceded by Mazarin, in full canonicals, the Prince de Conti, and a number of gentlemen bearing blue wands covered with *fleurs-de-lis*. The King was quietly dressed in black and wore no jewels, but the Queen, who was conducted to the altar by *Monsieur*,[2] Louis XIV.'s

[1] The Ile des Faisans is an islet formed by the Bidassoa, about a league from Fontarabia. It was here that the conferences between Mazarin and Don Luis de Haro had been held.

[2] The eldest brother of the King of France was officially styled *Monsieur ;* his wife, *Madame,* and their eldest daughter, *Mademoiselle.* According to Saint-Simon, Gaston d'Orléans, brother of Louis XIII., was the first to regularly bear this title.

brother, was resplendent in the royal robes, and wore the royal crown, entirely composed of diamonds. At the conclusion of the ceremony, which was performed by the Bishop of Bayonne, medals of gold and silver, bearing the portraits of the King and Queen, were distributed among the people.

It is sad to have to relate that the harmony of the day was somewhat marred by a violent dispute between the princesses of the blood and the Princess Palatine,[1] whose pretensions were supported by the Queen-Mother and *Monsieur*, as to whether the latter was entitled to appear at the ceremony with a train to her dress. Since neither party would yield, it was eventually decided to refer the momentous question to the King, who, after a long consultation with the grand master of the ceremonies, gravely announced that no precedent could be found for according so great a privilege to a foreign princess, and that, therefore, the Princess Palatine must remove her train, which, confident of victory, she had already donned. When the Queen-Mother proceeded to acquaint her friend with the royal decision, the lady " gave way to the most passionate grief," and declined to attend the wedding at all.

A few days after the marriage, the Court set out for Fontainebleau, and on August 26, the ceremony having been postponed until that date to allow of fitting preparations being made for their receptions, their Majesties made their famous state entry into Paris by way of the Porte Saint-Antoine.

[1] Anne de Gonzague, second daughter of Charles de Gonzague, Duc de Nevers, and wife of Prince Edward of Bavaria, " Count Palatine," fourth son of Frederick V., Elector Palatine. She must not be confused with her niece, Charlotte Elizabeth, Princess Palatine, the second wife of *Monsieur*.

MADAME DE MONTESPAN

Nearly all the chief contemporary chroniclers have left detailed and glowing accounts of this magnificent pageant, but perhaps the most interesting, having regard to the personality of the writer, is that given by Madame Scarron, the future wife of *le Grand Monarque*, in a letter to her friend, Madame de Villarceaux.

MADAME SCARRON to MADAME DE VILLARCEAUX.

" August 27, 1660.

" I shall not attempt to give you an account of the King's entry. I shall merely say that neither I nor any one else could give you an idea of its magnificence. I do not think that it would be possible to see anything finer, and the Queen must have gone to bed last night sufficiently pleased with the husband of her choice. If any accounts are printed, I will send them to you to-day ; but I myself can relate nothing in order, as I find it very difficult to unravel all that I saw yesterday, during ten or twelve hours.

" The Household of Cardinal Mazarin was not the least gorgeous part of the procession. It was headed by seventy-two baggage-mules ; the first twenty-four with trappings simple enough ; the next twenty-four with trappings finer, richer, and more splendid than the handsomest tapestries that you ever saw, and silver bits and bells ; in short, a magnificent sight which evoked general admiration. Afterwards twenty-four pages went by, followed by all the gentlemen and officers of his Household, a very large number. Next came twelve carriages, each drawn by six horses, and then his guards. His Household took an hour to pass by. Afterwards came that of *Monsieur*. I forgot, in speaking of the Cardinal's,

21

to mention twenty-four horses splendidly caparisoned and themselves so beautiful that I could not take my eyes off them. *Monsieur's* Household appeared after this very mean. Then came the King's, truly royal, for nothing in the world could have been more splendid. You know better than myself of what it is composed, but you cannot imagine the beauty of the horses on which the pages of the royal stables rode ; they came prancing along, and were handled most dexterously. Then came the Musketeers, distinguished by their different plumes ; the first brigade wore white ; the second, yellow, black, and white ; the third, blue and white ; and the fourth, green and white. After this came pages-in-waiting, with flame-coloured surtouts covered all over with gold. Then M. de Navailles, at the head of the light cavalry—all this magnificent ; next Vardes,[1] at the head of the Hundred Swiss ; he wore a uniform of green and gold and looked very well.

"Then . . . No, I think that the gentlemen of quality followed the light cavalry ; there were a great many of them ; all so magnificent that it would be difficult to select any one in particular. I looked out for my friends. Beuvron passed, one of the first, with M. de Saint-Luc. I looked for M. de Villarceaux,[2] but he rode such a restive horse that he was twenty paces past me before I recognised him. I thought him admirable ; he was one of the least richly dressed, but one of the most handsome, while he was mounted on a superb horse which he managed

[1] François René du Bec-Crespin, Marquis de Vardes, son of Henri IV.'s mistress, the Comtesse de Moret, who married *en secondes noces* the Marquis de Vardes. He was a consummate courtier, and likewise a consummate scoundrel. See p. 30 *et seq.*

[2] Louis de Mornay, Marquis de Villarceaux. Madame de Maintenon's references to him are interesting, as he was believed by not a few to be her lover. See p. 86 and note.

perfectly. His brown locks looked beautiful, also, and people cried out in admiration as he rode by. The Comte de Guiche[1] rode all alone, covered with embroidery and precious stones, which sparkled delightfully in the sun. He was surrounded by servants in rich liveries and followed by some officers of the Guards.

"The *Maréchals de France* preceded the King, before whom they bore a brocaded canopy.[2] . . . Next came the Chancellor, wearing a robe and a mantle of gold brocade, surrounded by lackeys and pages in violet satin, bedizened

[1] Armand de Gramont, younger son of Antoine II., Duc de Gramont, and brother of Philibert de Gramont, the hero of Count Hamilton's *Mémoires*. See p. 30 *et seq.*

[2] Four pages of manuscript are missing here, the greater portion of which is presumably devoted to a description of the magnificence of the King and Queen. We will endeavour to supply the omission from the *Gazette de France* of September 3, 1660.

"The King was attired in a suit of silver brocade covered with pearls and adorned with a marvellous number of carnation-coloured and silver ribbons, with a superb plume of carnation-coloured and white feathers clasped by a cluster of diamonds ; his belt and sword were of the richest workmanship. He was mounted on a splendid Spanish horse, a dark bay, with its trappings of silver brocade and its harness sown with precious stones.

"The Queen's pages-in-waiting, in superb liveries, followed. Then came the *calèche* of her Majesty, which might be more fittingly described as a triumphal car. It was covered, inside and out, with gold-wire embroidery, an entirely new invention, on a silver ground, the outside, both front and back, adorned with festoons in relief, all embroidered with gold and silver wire. The canopy, likewise, was embroidered, both inside and out, with the same kind of embroidery, and was supported by two columns encircled with jasmine and olive blossoms, symbolical of Love and Peace. All that part of the *calèche* which is usually made of iron was of silver-gilt, and even the wheels were gilded.

"This marvellous car was drawn by six pearl-coloured Danish horses, whose manes and tails reached to the ground, caparisoned and covered with trappings of the same embroidery, and all of them of such rare

with silver and covered with feathers. In fact, Madame, it would be impossible to witness a more imposing spectacle."[1]

The Queen, who, according to the *Gazette de France*, required no Crown jewels to lend *éclat* to her charms, and whose beauty Madame de Motteville assures us was such that it triumphed over her unsightly Spanish gowns—"an infallible mark of its greatness"—was really a very ordinary-looking young woman indeed, with fine blue eyes and an abundance of fair hair, but with a diminutive figure, heavy features, a dull white complexion, and bad teeth. Moreover, though of a virtuous and kindly disposition and devotedly attached to her husband, she entirely lacked the faculty of pleasing, and was ignorant and bigoted to the last degree. Reared in the most cramping conditions of Spanish etiquette, her every word and action were governed by the most punctilious regard for ceremonial, while her timidity was so great that she was ill at ease in the company of any but her immediate attendants and the Queen-Mother, and positively trembled in the presence of the King. Under these circumstances, it is scarcely a matter for surprise that Louis, unable to derive any pleasure from her society, should have sought amusement and distraction elsewhere. Nor had he long to seek in vain.

At the end of March 1661, *Monsieur* (the Duc d'Orléans)

beauty that no painter could possibly hope to do them justice, and all that one can say is that they were *chefs-d'œuvre* of Nature, made expressly to take part in this pageant.

"The princess [the Queen] was attired in a robe on which gold, pearls, and precious stones made up a brilliant and imposing combination, while her coiffure was resplendent with the Crown jewels, which, however, lent far less *éclat* to her appearance than her own charms."

[1] *Correspondance générale de Madame de Maintenon,* i. 71.

the King's brother, had married Henrietta, daughter of Charles I., who had been brought to France when a child by the faithful Lady Dalkeith and, with the exception of a short visit to England at the time of the Restoration, had resided there ever since, with her widowed mother, Queen Henrietta-Maria. This beautiful and ill-fated princess, whose life and death have been immortalised by Bossuet in his famous oration, was now in her eighteenth year, and one of the most charming of the many charming women who adorned the *Grand Monarque's* Court. "There was about her whole person," says Madame de La Fayette, "a grace and sweetness that won for her a kind of homage which must have been the more pleasant in that it was rendered rather to her personality than to her rank." [1]

The appearance of the bride at Fontainebleau the summer after her marriage lent a new zest to the gaieties of the Court. Every one, we are told, thought of *Madame* and tried to please her, and among her cavaliers no one was more assiduous in his attentions than the King himself. The young girl's unflagging high spirits, lively wit, and contempt for the conventionalities, proved a striking and refreshing contrast to the dull decorum which poor Maria Theresa insisted on observing in season and out of season, and after enduring twelve months of the latter, Louis was in a position to fully appreciate the change. Henrietta, on her part, was far from insensible to the homage paid her by her royal brother-in-law, and can hardly be blamed if she preferred his society to that of the contemptible dandy, her husband, who, according to Saint-Simon, "had all the faults of a woman and none of her virtues." [2]

---

[1] Madame de La Fayette's *Histoire de Madame Henriette d'Angleterre.*
[2] Saint-Simon is, perhaps, too hard on *Monsieur,* who, in spite of his

The intimacy between the monarch and Henrietta soon became so very marked that Maria Theresa, who had the misfortune to be of an exceedingly jealous nature, took umbrage and overwhelmed her husband with tears and reproaches, thereby still further alienating his affection. Finding her remonstrances without avail, she appealed to the Queen-Mother, before whom *Monsieur*, whose vanity was deeply wounded by his wife's preference for Louis, also laid a complaint. Anne of Austria enjoyed nothing so much as an opportunity for exercising over her family the influence which was no longer permitted her in affairs of State. She, therefore, turned a willing ear to the grievances of the neglected wife and husband, and endeavoured to mediate between the two young couples. But her representations only served to make matters worse, and tongues began to wag right merrily.

The King and the young *Madame*, unwilling to relinquish a friendship which both had found so pleasant, but, at the same time, alive to the necessity of putting an end to the dissensions in the Royal Family and to the malicious gossip which they were occasioning, decided that the only thing to be done was for Louis to counterfeit a passion for one of the princess's maids of honour, which, while effectually silencing the voice of scandal in regard to his sister-in-law, would furnish him with a pretext for visiting her apartments as frequently as heretofore. Accordingly, after some little hesitation, a certain Mademoiselle de La Vallière,[1] a very timid and blushing maiden of sixteen,

vanity and effeminacy, had some good qualities, and showed much courage in the field.

[1] She was the daughter of Laurent de La Baume Le Blanc de La Vallière, a brave soldier, who had distinguished himself at the battles of Avein and Rocroi and on the Royalist side during the Fronde. On his

was selected as the object of his Majesty's simulated devotion.

We hasten to acquit *Madame*, who, though an outrageous flirt, was a virtuous woman at heart, of all responsibility for what followed ; indeed, her choice of this innocent child, in place of a finished coquette, is in itself a proof that no harm was intended, and her vexation, if not her remorse, at the *dénouement* of her little plot appears to have been very keen. For the poor maid of honour fell desperately in love with the handsome young monarch who had stooped to honour her with his attentions, nor was it long before Louis, flattered by the flame that he had kindled, returned her passion with all the warmth of an extremely ardent temperament.

In the judgment of Sainte-Beuve, the portraits of Louise de La Vallière can convey but a very inadequate idea of the kind of charm which was peculiarly her own, and it is, therefore, to the writings of her contemporaries that we must turn if we desire to form a just estimate of one of the most poetic figures in French history. Here we shall find a singular unanimity of opinion. "Mademoiselle de La Vallière," says the Abbé de Choisy, who had known her from her childhood, "was not one of those perfect beauties who frequently arouse admiration without kindling love. She was lovable, and that verse of La Fontaine's—

"Et la grâce, plus belle encor que la beauté,"

seems to have been written for her. She had a beautiful skin, fair hair, a winning smile, and a look at once so

death, which occurred in 1654, his widow married Jacques de Courtavel, Marquis de Saint-Rémi, first *maître d'hôtel* to Louis XIV.'s intriguing uncle, Gaston d'Orléans ; and it was at Gaston's little Court at Blois that Louise lived until she was appointed maid of honour to *Madame*.

tender and so modest that it gained one's heart and one's respect at the same moment." [1] Madame de Motteville also praises the sweetness of her face and the amiability of her character ; while that most scathing critic of the ladies of her brother-in-law's Court, Charlotte Elizabeth, Duchesse d'Orléans (Princess Palatine), declares that there was "an inexpressible charm in her countenance," that "her whole bearing was unassuming," and that she was "an amiable, gentle, kind, and tender woman."

What, however, has rendered her personality so irresistibly attractive is that there never has been the least question as to the disinterestedness of her affection. With her Louis XIV. tasted, probably for the first and last time in his life, the happiness so rarely vouchsafed to a monarch of being loved for himself alone. It was the King, not royalty, that Mademoiselle de La Vallière adored, the man rather than the King, and the only favours which she was ever known to ask were not for herself or her friends, but on behalf of people who had been unfortunate enough to incur their sovereign's displeasure.

The watchful Queen-Mother, whose suspicions had been aroused by the fact that her son had ceased to perform his religious duties with his customary regularity, was the first to discover the state of affairs ; but her fears with regard to Louis's connection with *Madame* blinded her to the real danger, and before she had time to interfere, the mischief was done. For the resistance had been short ; the victory fatally easy. Mademoiselle de La Vallière had arrived at Fontainebleau in May ; ere July had run its course, she had become the mistress of the King.

Although unable to save the girl, Anne of Austria did

[1] *Mémoires de l'Abbé de Choisy* (edit. 1888), i. 120.

everything in her power to induce her son to put an end to the intrigue, "representing to him what he owed to God and his kingdom." Louis, however, who on the death of Mazarin, in March 1661, had taken the reins of government into his own hands, no longer tolerated any interference with his authority, and the most that his mother could do was to persuade him to hide his infidelity from the Queen, who was then *enceinte*, until after her confinement.

For six years Mademoiselle de La Vallière held sway over the royal heart ; a lease of power which very few kings' favourites had hitherto been permitted to enjoy. Nevertheless, her reign was far from being an untroubled one, even during the period when his Majesty's passion was at its height. Naturally modest and virtuous, the knowledge of her fault always appears to have weighed upon her mind, and at times caused her the keenest anguish. As long as Louis remained faithful to her, and indeed for some while after he had ceased to be so, love proved stronger than remorse or religion ; but, on the other hand, she was at all times exquisitely sensitive to the least symptom of neglect or displeasure on his part, and more than once the guilty chain which bound her to him was strained almost to breaking-point.

In February 1662 she fled from the Tuileries and took refuge in a convent at Chaillot ; not, as some writers assert, because *Madame* had, in a fit of virtuous indignation, dismissed her from her service, but because she had incurred the grave displeasure of her royal lover owing to her very honourable refusal to enlighten him as to the relations existing between the princess in question and her admirer, the Comte de Guiche. Her flight was quickly discovered, and information brought to the King, who was at the Louvre, giving audience to the Spanish Ambassador. Louis, in great agitation, at once dismissed the diplomatist, and, mounting a horse, and attended only by a single page, started at full gallop for the convent. He found the unfortunate La Vallière in the ante-room—for, the community being at their devotions, she had not yet been admitted to an interview with the superior—lying on the floor, half-dead with cold, fatigue, and despair, and succeeded in persuading her, though not without considerable difficulty, to abandon her intention of taking the vows and return with him to Paris.

Scarcely had the excitement caused by this episode abated, when trouble arose from another source.

The King's passion for La Vallière had naturally excited a great deal of jealousy among the ladies of the Court, and by none was it resented more bitterly than by Olympe Mancini, now Comtesse de Soissons. This designing and unscrupulous woman had contrived to get herself appointed *surintendante* of the young Queen's Household, and, prior to the rise of La Vallière, had recovered much of her former influence over Louis, who, as one writer suggests, was perhaps less diffident with Madame de Soissons than he had been with Mademoiselle Mancini. Deeply chagrined at the loss of the favour from which she had hoped so much, she vowed vengeance on the innocent cause of her disappointment, and having taken counsel with her lover, the scoundrelly Marquis de Vardes, and the Comte de Guiche, already mentioned, a vain and foolish young man, who had never forgiven La Vallière for having once rejected his addresses, resolved to raise a scandal before which she judged the sensitive girl must inevitably succumb.

The plan of the conspirators was to send an anonymous letter, containing a full, true, and particular account of the manner in which his Majesty spent his leisure moments, to the Queen, who, thanks to the exertions of Anne of Austria, was still under the delusion that there was " nothing but mere friendship " between her husband and La Vallière. The letter was written in Spanish, as Maria Theresa was still so ignorant of French that she might have failed to understand it if the vernacular had been employed, and enclosed in an envelope addressed in the handwriting of the Queen of Spain—which Madame de Soissons had stolen from her mistress's apartments—in order to make sure of its reaching its destination unopened.

Fortunately for Maria Theresa and the favourite, the letter fell into the hands of Donna Molina, a Spanish lady in the Queen's service, who, fearing that it might contain some bad news concerning the King of Spain, who was seriously ill, took upon herself the responsibility of opening it, and promptly carried it to Anne of Austria, and, on her advice, to the King. Louis was, of course, much exasperated, but, as the person he employed to investigate the affair was none other than Vardes himself, we can hardly be surprised that the guilty parties should have escaped detection.

Undeterred by the failure of this plot, Madame de Soissons, a few months later, brought forward a rival to La Vallière in the person of a Mademoiselle de la Motte-Houdancourt,[1] one of the Queen's *filles d'honneur*, " who, though no sparkling beauty, had drawn away lovers from the celebrated Menneville (the mistress of Fouquet)." [2]

---

[1] This lady is often confused with the Mademoiselle de La Motte d'Argencourt, already mentioned. Both M. Chéruel, the editor of Saint-Simon's *Mémoires*, and M. de Monmerqué, the editor of the Letters of Madame de Sévigné, have fallen into this error.

[2] Hamilton's *Mémoires de Gramont* (edit. 1888), p. 95.

She very nearly succeeded in drawing away Mademoiselle de La Vallière's as well, for the King fell into the trap prepared for him and pressed his suit with ardour. His passion for the damsel was probably stimulated by the rivalry of the Chevalier de Gramont, the hero of Count Hamilton's *Mémoires*, who, it appears, had never given the lady a thought until he found that she was honoured by his sovereign's attentions, when he straightway concluded that she must be worthy of his. Mademoiselle de La Motte, who had no use for such small fry as the Chevalier when there was a King prepared to fall at her feet, so far from encouraging his addresses, complained of him to her royal admirer; "and then it was that De Gramont perceived that if love renders all things equal, it is not so among rivals," [1] for one fine day he received a peremptory order to retire from Court.

Meanwhile, poor Mademoiselle de La Vallière was plunged in the depths of despair, but Louis, piqued by the resistance of La Motte, who simulated virtue with considerable skill, and by the remonstrances of the Queen's *dame d'honneur*, Madame de Navailles, who was responsible for the good conduct of the maids of honour, and who had gone so far as to put iron gratings before the windows of her charges' apartments, in order to guard against accidents, paid no attention to her reproaches.

At length, Mademoiselle de La Motte, acting on instructions from Madame de Soissons, professed herself ready to surrender, but on one condition—the dismissal of La Vallière. Louis protested, but the lady remained inflexible, and it is quite probable that she would have carried her point had not Anne of Austria, who, though she had no love for the reigning mistress, had still less

---

[1] Hamilton's *Mémoires de Gramont* (edit. 1888), p. 96.

for the intriguing maid of honour, intercepted a letter written by one of Madame de Soissons's friends to La Motte and containing abundant proof that the latter was a mere tool in the hands of the Countess, and laid it before her son. Highly indignant at the way in which he had been duped, the King at once broke off all connection with La Motte, who was shortly afterwards dismissed from the Queen's service for having received the Marquis de Richelieu in her apartments in defiance of Maria Theresa's orders. Three years later, the true story of the Spanish letter came out, and Madame de Soissons was ordered to retire from Court ; while the Comte de Guiche, who had made a full confession of his part in the affair, was sent on foreign service. The third conspirator, Vardes, was already in exile, " expiating some unbecoming words of which *Madame* had complained to his Majesty," and these revelations caused his banishment to be prolonged till 1683.

After the death of Anne of Austria, in January 1666, Louis threw aside the last pretence of concealment, and the deputations from the Parliament and the Courts of Law who came to Saint-Germain to present their condolences to their Majesties were astonished to see the King's mistress among the ladies in attendance on the Queen. As for that unfortunate princess, who had long suffered from all the pangs of jealousy, though they seldom took a more violent form than tears, she appears, after her first burst of indignation was over, to have accepted the situation, and contented herself with dismissing from her service those of her ladies who had been most active in fostering her delusion that the friendship between the King and La Vallière had been of the platonic order. Nevertheless, when, some months later, an opportunity for humiliating her rival presented itself, she did not, as we shall presently see, allow it to slip.

The two lovers had not been separated even for a single day when, in the spring of 1667, the Devolution War broke out with Spain, and Louis XIV. announced his intention of taking the field in person. Before setting out to join the army in Flanders, he resolved to make provision for his mistress and a daughter (Marie Anne de Bourbon) whom she had borne him the previous year,[1] to raise the former to the rank of duchess and to legitimate the latter ; and, accordingly, on May 13, 1667, very much against the wish of "that little violet which hid itself under the grass and was ashamed of being mistress, of being mother, of being duchess,"[2] letters patent were issued to the following effect :

"Louis, by the grace of God King of France and Navarre, to all present and to come greeting :

"The favours which kings exercise in their States being the public recognition of the merit of those who receive them and the most glorious eulogy of those who are thus honoured, we are of opinion that we cannot more effectively give public expression to the peculiar esteem in which we

[1] She had already had two children, a boy, born in 1663, died in 1666, and a daughter, who only lived a few months. Both children had been entrusted to the care of Madame Colbert, who brought them up with her own.

[2] Letter of Madame de Sévigné *to* Madame de Grignan, September 1, 1680. This is probably in allusion to the charming verses of Desmarets :

> "Modeste en ma couleur, modeste en mon sejour,
> Franche d'ambition, je me cache sous l'herbe ;
> Mais si sur votre front je puis me voir un jour,
> La plus humble des fleurs sera la plus superbe."

hold the person of our dear and well-beloved and very loyal Louise de La Vallière than in bestowing upon her the highest titles of honour that a very singular affection, aroused in our heart by an infinity of rare perfections, has suggested to us. And although her modesty has frequently opposed itself to our desire to promote her sooner to a rank proportionate to our esteem and to her good qualities, nevertheless, as the affection which we entertain for her and our sense of justice will not permit us any longer to defer our public recognition of a merit which is so well known to us, nor to refuse any longer to Nature the proof of our affection for Marie Anne, our natural daughter, in the person of her mother, we have acquired the estate of Vaujours, situated in Touraine, and the barony of Christophe, in Anjou, which are two estates equally important on account of their revenues and their tenures.

"But reflecting that there might be something wanting in our bounty if we did not enhance the value of this property by a title which would be at the same time commensurate with the esteem which calls forth our liberality and the merits of the subject on whom it is bestowed; and, moreover, taking into consideration that our dear and well-beloved Louise de La Vallière is descended from a very noble and very ancient house, whose ancestors have given on divers important occasions signal proofs of their great zeal for the well-being and advantage of our State and of their talent and experience in the command of armies . . ."

Then follows the formula for the creation of a duchy, "to be enjoyed by the aforesaid Demoiselle Louise Françoise de la Vallière and, after her decease, by Marie Anne, our natural daughter, her heirs and descendants, both male and female, born in wedlock " ; and the letters conclude with a clause providing that " in the event of the death, without lawful issue, of Marie Anne, our natural daughter, *whom we have declared and do declare legitimate and capable of enjoying all honours and civil rights*," [1] the estates composing the duchy should revert to the Crown.

From these signal marks of the royal favour one would naturally have supposed that time had rather augmented than diminished his Majesty's passion for his mistress. But such was far from being the case. Already a formidable rival had arisen, before whose more opulent charms the star of La Vallière was paling rapidly.

[1] It must not be supposed that in legitimating this child Louis XIV. was guilty of any new departure; the practice was a very old one. So far back as the year 1465, Louis XI. had legitimated his natural daughter by Madame de Sassenage, his queen's *dame d'honneur*, and his example had been followed by more than one of his successors, notably by Henri IV., who had legitimated the numerous children he had had by Gabrielle d'Estrées, Madame de Verneuil, Jacqueline de Beuil, and Charlotte des Essarts, Comtesse de Romorantin. Nor was the custom by any means confined to the issue of Royalty. Under the *ancien régime* the King conferred letters of legitimation very much in the same way as in later times he conferred letters of naturalisation. For their validity, however, it was necessary that the letters should mention the consent of those to whom the child would now be eligible to succeed, and that they should be registered by the Parliament. It should be remarked that not only ordinary natural children but adulterine ones as well might be legitimated.

CHAPTER III

Mademoiselle de Tonnay-Charente—Her praises sung by Loret in *La Muse historique*—Her beauty and wit—Her marriage with the Marquis de Montespan—Dishonourable conduct of their respective parents—*Res angustæ domi*—Madame de Montespan determines to become the mistress of the King—Erroneous views of historians in regard to this matter—She deceives the Queen and La Vallière—Louis XIV. joins the army in Flanders—The Queen orders La Vallière to retire to her estates—French successes in Flanders—The Court sets out to join the King—La Vallière follows in defiance of the Queen's orders—And overtakes the Court at La Fère—Chagrin of the Queen—Pretended indignation of Madame de Montespan—"What! Before the Queen!"—The *garde-du-corps*—Suspicious conduct of the King and Madame de Montespan at Avesnes—La Vallière and Madame de Montespan attend confession together.

In the autumn of the year 1660 there arrived at Court, in the capacity of *fille d'honneur* to Maria Theresa, a certain Françoise Athénaïs de Rochechouart-Mortemart. This young lady, who was the second daughter of Gabriel de Rochechouart, Duc de Mortemart,[1] and of his wife, Diane de Grandseigne, a woman of distinguished piety, " who

[1] The Rochechouarts were an ancient Poitou family, who traced their descent back to the eleventh century, to one Aimery, Vicomte de Rochechouart, Seneschal of Toulouse. The Mortemarts were an equally ancient house, originally from Limousin, whence they passed to La Marche, and thence to Poitou. About the beginning of the thirteenth century the two families intermarried.

had sowed in her heart from her earliest childhood seeds of religion which were never eradicated," [1] was at this time in her twentieth year, and, as she united to beauty of an unusually high order a brilliant if decidedly caustic wit—the "*esprit de Mortemart*" had passed into a proverb—soon came to be regarded as the brightest ornament of the Queen's Household.

The first mention that we have of Mademoiselle de Tonnay-Charente, as she was then called,[2] is in the summer of 1662, when she took part, with a bevy of other young beauties, in a ballet called *Hercule amoureux*, in which Louis XIV. also appeared, doubling the rôles of Mars and the Sun. At the following Christmas, we find her officiating as a *quêteuse* at the Church of Saint-Germain l'Auxerrois,

---

[1] *Souvenirs et Correspondance de Madame de Caylus* (edit. 1889), p. 44. Beyond this we know nothing of her early years, except that she received "an education befitting her rank" at the Couvent de Sainte-Marie at Saintes, which, however, evidently did not include orthography, as the reader will perceive from the following letter, written, in March 1680, in answer to one from the Duc de Noailles, asking her to obtain a post in the Household of the Dauphiness for a M. Tamboneau : "Vous sauest bien que toutte les charges de ches m⁰ la Daufine sont destinées et que mesme ce nesstet [n'était] pas vne aucasion trop favorrable pour mʳ tanbonneau il lan fault chercher daustre et aiseyer de les faires rehusir ie my anploiray auec toute laplication possible ie ne [an illegible word] le moin que vous pour lassurer que dans tous les tans iai souété son auantage et me serest trouée heureuse d'y pouvoir contribuer ditte luy bien tout ce qui peust adousir vn estat aussy facheux que le sien enatant [dant] que l'on puisse le changer. . . ."

[2] Tonnay-Charente was the name of the château where she was born. She was so called to distinguish her from her three sisters : Gabrielle de Rochechouart-Mortemart, married in 1655 to the Marquis de Thianges ; Marie Christine, a nun at the Couvent des Filles Sainte-Marie at Chaillot ; and Marie Madeleine Gabrielle de Rochechouart-Mortemart, Abbess of Fontevrault.

MADAME DE MONTESPAN

at the conclusion of a sermon preached before the King, on which occasion her loveliness evoked such general admiration that the poet Loret was moved to sing her praises in the next number of *La Muse historique*.[1]

> "L'admirable de Mortemar,
> Très-aimable Mignonne, car
> C'est une des plus ravissantes,
> Des plus sages, des plus charmantes
> De toutes celles de la Cour,
> Où l'on void mille Objets d'amour :
> Cette aimable (dis-je) Mignonne
> Si rare et si belle Personne,
> Fit la Quête ce saint Jour-là ;
> Et, comme quelqu'un m'en parla,
> Ce fut, Lecteur, je vous proteste,
> D'un air si doux et si modeste,
> Ou, pour parler plus dignement,
> Avec un si noble agrément,
> Que tout Chrestien, tant fût-il sage,
> Étoit charmé de son vizage,

[1] Jean Loret was born at Charenton about the year 1700. Although he had had but the rudiments of an education, he came to Paris to seek his fortune, and managed to insinuate himself into the good graces of Mazarin, who gave him a small pension. In 1646 he published a volume of burlesque verse, addressed to various distinguished persons of the Court, which met with some success and suggested to him the idea of writing a weekly gazette in which he might relate, in a light and amusing manner, news of a kind to interest the Court and the city. Accordingly, every Sunday, from March 4, 1650, to March 28, 1665, he addressed to his patroness, Madame de Longueville, this gazette in burlesque verses, that is to say, verses of eight syllables. At first, only a few manuscript copies were distributed ; but in 1652 it was printed under the title of *La Muse historique*, and secured a considerable circulation. The complete collection comprises 750 numbers and about 400,000 verses, and forms a mine of valuable information about the doings of Court and town in his day—plays, fêtes, weddings, State functions, and so forth, at most of which Loret, in his capacity as Society journalist, was himself present.

Que l'on dizoit, de main en main,
Plutôt Angelique qu'humain.
O que sa brillante jeunesse
De libertez fut larronesse !
Et que ses propos gracieux,
Et la douceur de ses beaux yeux,
Embellis de clairtez divines,
Firent d'innocentes rapines !
Puis-qu'il est vray qu'en mesme instant,
Cet Objet toûjours éclatant,
Qui de mille amours et la source,
Ataquoit les cœurs et la bource."[1]

The charms which the ingenious Loret celebrated in the above doggerel have been extolled by all the leading chroniclers of the period. Saint-Simon, who, of course, only knew her in her later years, when time and trouble had set their marks upon her, declares that she was "beautiful as the day"; Madame de La Fayette speaks of her as "a flawless beauty"; Madame de Sévigné's letters contain a hundred ecstatic references to that dazzling loveliness which bewitched friend and foe alike; while even the Princess Palatine, who cordially detested her, is fain to confess that she had "beautiful fair hair, fine arms, shapely hands, a very pretty mouth, and a winning smile."

But great as was the renown of her beauty, that of her wit was greater still. "She was always the best of company," says Saint-Simon, "with graces which palliated her proud and haughty manner and were indeed suited to it. It was impossible to have more wit, more refinement, greater felicity of expression, eloquence, natural propriety, which gave her, as it were, an individual style of talk, but delicious, and which, by force of habit, was so infectious

[1] *La Muse historique*, December 31, 1662. We have retained the orthography of the writer.

MADAME DE MONTESPAN

that her nieces and the persons constantly about her, her women and those who had been brought up with her, all caught the style, which is recognisable to-day among the few survivors."[1]

Thus richly dowered by Nature, it would indeed have been surprising if Françoise de Rochechouart[2] had remained long unwed, and on January 28, 1663, after her parents had rejected several distinguished pretenders to her hand, including the Marquis de Noirmoutier, who, if Madame de La Fayette is to be believed, the young lady would have been more than willing to accept as her husband, she married a nobleman from her own province, Louis Henri de Pardaillan de Gondrin, Marquis de Montespan, eldest son of the Marquis d'Antin, and her junior by a year.

Now, there would appear to have been a good deal more mutual affection in this union, from which two children were born,[3] than generally characterised French marriages in the seventeenth century, but any advantage which the young couple might have derived therefrom was counterbalanced by the want of consideration—to employ a mild expression—shown by their respective parents.

It had been arranged that Montespan should receive a dowry of 150,000 livres with this wife. Of this sum, however, the Duc de Mortemart professed himself unable to furnish more than 60,000 at the time of the marriage, but agreed to pay interest on the balance until he could

[1] *Mémoires de Saint-Simon* (edit. 1881), xi. 86.

[2] Historians allude to her generally as *Athénaïs*, but she always signed herself *Françoise*, and was presumably thus addressed.

[3] Louis Henri Pardaillan de Gondrin, Duc d'Antin, born in 1665, and a daughter. Of the latter nothing is known, except that she was alive in July 1774, when Madame de Montespan and her husband were judicially separated.

see his way to discharge his liability. In point of fact, neither principal nor interest was forthcoming. To make matters worse, Montespan lent to his parents, "on a mortgage at five per cent.," the 60,000 livres he had managed to extract from his father-in-law, a proceeding which he soon had reason to regret, for the Marquis and Marquise d'Antin troubled themselves as little about their obligation as did the Duc de Mortemart, doubtless being of opinion that the ties of relationship exempted them from the fulfilment of their promise.

The consequence was that the marquis and his young wife entered upon their married life very seriously handicapped indeed, and before long found themselves deeply in debt. Prudence should have dictated that, under the circumstances, the wisest course would be to renounce the gaieties of the Court and the capital for a time at least, and retire to Montespan's country seat at Bellegarde in the Pyrenees. But the château in question, situated on the summit of the mountains and surrounded by a vast expanse of barren rock, was not at all to the marchioness's taste; and, accordingly, they remained at Court and continued their hopeless struggle to make one livre do the work of two. In order to obtain some relief from their embarrassments, they had recourse to borrowing money, with the inevitable result that they got still deeper in the mire, and amid the undignified annoyances of poverty, or what seemed to her poverty, Madame de Montespan's feeling for her husband changed from affection to indifference, and from indifference to positive dislike.

And so it came about that, as time went on, the young marchioness began to cast envious glances in the direction of La Vallière—La Vallière, who had all the good things of life at her command, who never knew the galling want of money, in whose honour masques and ballets were given, and Lulli composed his most enchanting strains and Benserade his most gallant verses ; while she herself, so immeasurably the favourite's superior in beauty and intelligence, could only by continual pinching and planning maintain a position in accordance with her rank. Would it not be a fair exchange, she asked herself, to surrender that which the Church indeed told her was priceless, but to which the vast majority of the women about her attached so very little value in return for all these advantages—and greater ones besides, for La Vallière was but a poor shrinking creature, who thought only of loving and being loved, and lacked the spirit to acquire that power and influence which might be an abler woman's with very little trouble ?

It was long the fashion among historians, who appear to base their statements chiefly on the authority of Saint-Simon—a chronicler who was not born until 1775, and can, therefore, have been merely repeating the version of the affair which was current in his day—to represent Madame de Montespan as the unwilling victim of Louis XIV.'s desires. One whose work lies before us draws a touching picture of the agony of mind of " the youthful, innocent beauty, fresh from the seclusion of provincial life " when she found that she had had the misfortune to attract the blighting regards of royalty ; of how she entreated her husband to take her away to Guienne and to leave her there until the King had completely forgotten her, and of how Montespan, in fatal confidence, trusted her resistance and refused her petition.

Nothing could possibly be further from the truth. Recent research has established beyond all reasonable doubt the fact that, so far from being the unwilling victim

that so many writers would have us believe, Madame de
Montespan laid her plans for the subjugation of *le Grand
Monarque* with as much deliberation as did Madame de
Pompadour for that of his successor ; and that, as we
shall show when we come to speak of the proceedings
against the Poisoners before the Chambre Ardente, at the
very time when the marchioness was supposed to be
imploring her husband to take her out of the way of
temptation she was, distrustful of the power of her own
charms, actually invoking the assistance of magicians and
witches to enable her to supplant La Vallière in the King's
affections !

Having, therefore, resolved to enter the lists against
the reigning favourite, Madame de Montespan proceeded
to cast about her for the most effective means of com-
passing her end. She quickly perceived that the chief
obstacle to success was the fact that her opportunities for
ingratiating herself with his Majesty were so very limited.
Louis was an indefatigable worker ("He has enough
energy for four kings and one honest man," Mazarin had
once observed), and public affairs and State functions occupied the greater portion of his time, while most of his
leisure was spent either in hunting or in the apartments of
Madame de La Vallière or the Queen. Indeed, the only
occasions on which she could hope to exchange even a
few words with her sovereign were in public, when, of
course, a dozen pair of eyes were on the watch to note
the monarch's slightest movement, a dozen pair of ears
open to catch every syllable that fell from the royal
lips.

After a little reflection, the marchioness came to the
conclusion that the only possible way of securing the

King's favour was by first gaining the friendship and confidence of La Vallière and the Queen, who would, doubtless,
then provide her with the opportunities which she was
at present denied ; and, with this object in view, she
began to pay both ladies assiduous court. Her scheme
was successful beyond her most sanguine expectations.
Neither the duchess nor Maria Theresa had the faintest
suspicion of the lady's intentions—for Madame de
Montespan was most regular in the discharge of her
religious duties, and was looked upon as a perfect model
of propriety—and both were only too pleased to have the
co-operation of so charming and witty a companion in
their far from easy task of entertaining the King. Living
as they did in little worlds of their own, taking but a
reluctant part in the gaieties that went on around them,
supremely indifferent to the *on dits* which were to the
ordinary courtier the salt of life, they had no fund of
small talk wherewith to divert the monarch during the
hours which he spent in their society, and, as Louis was
never at any great pains to conceal his *ennui*, the poor
ladies were painfully conscious of their shortcomings in
this respect. To them, therefore, Madame de Montespan
must have appeared as a kind of godsend, and when, as
the result of her intervention, his Majesty's visits to their
apartments became more and more frequent, their satisfaction knew no bounds. La Vallière cherished the
illusion that, thanks to her friend's help, she was about to
enter upon a fresh lease of favour ; the Queen that she
was gradually weaning her husband from La Vallière.
The marchioness, on her side, was equally pleased with the
way in which matters were progressing, for the King, who
had at first been somewhat diffident in her presence,
through fear, it is said, of her wit, which spared neither

high nor low,[1] had speedily conquered his timidity and now paid her the most marked attention. Such was the position of affairs when, on May 24, 1667, Louis XIV. left Fontainebleau to join the army in Flanders.

No sooner had his Majesty departed than the Queen, greatly daring now that her dreaded lord was no longer at hand to interfere, sent for Madame[2] de La Vallière, and intimated to her that it was her royal pleasure that she should repair to her new estate at Vaujours with as little delay as possible, unless, she maliciously added, she preferred to meditate for a season upon the vanity of worldly things in the seclusion of some convent. Then, having, as she imagined, completely crushed her rival, she departed for Compiègne, while La Vallière, to whom the idea of a sojourn in Touraine, out of reach of all news of her beloved, by no means commended itself, but who, of course, could not follow the Court in defiance of the Queen's express commands, set out for Versailles.

Meanwhile, the French were carrying all before them in Flanders, where, in less than a fortnight, several places, including Charleroi, had capitulated ; the weak Spanish garrisons, behind their half-dismantled fortifications, being powerless to offer any effective resistance. Flattered by these successes, Louis XIV. became desirous of showing himself in his new rôle of conqueror to the Queen and the ladies of the Court and receiving their congratulations. Accordingly, he sent orders for them to follow him, and,

---

[1] Such was the terror which her biting wit inspired that the courtiers were absolutely afraid to pass beneath her windows when they knew the King was with her, lest she should seize the opportunity of turning them into ridicule and injuring them in their sovereign's estimation. They called it "going under fire."

[2] As a duchess, La Vallière was now styled "Madame."

taking advantage of a temporary cessation of hostilities, proceeded to Avesnes to meet them.

In due course, the news that the Court was on its way to Flanders reached poor Madame de La Vallière in her retirement at Versailles, and roused in her as much resentment as her gentle soul was capable of feeling. The bare thought that she, his chosen among women, was to be denied the privilege of acclaiming this modern Alexander seemed to her a punishment too grievous to be borne. Rather than submit to such an indignity she felt that she would cheerfully brave the wrath of a hundred jealous queens. They might exile her to Vaujours ; they might throw her into the Bastille ; they might send her to join her rejected admirer, Fouquet, at Pignerol ; but they should never prevent her from beholding her lover with his laurels thick upon him. Not for one single moment did she hesitate as to the course she should adopt ; a few hours after receiving the news she was following the Court as fast as the horses attached to her coach could travel.

The Queen had reached La Fère, and, having supped, had just sat down to a game of cards—she had, it may be mentioned, a perfect mania for cards and played abominably, much to the satisfaction of her ladies, who won large sums from their royal mistress—when a great commotion was heard outside. Mademoiselle de Montpensier,[1] who was of the party, and to whose *Mémoires* we are indebted for an entertaining account of the little comedy which followed, went to inquire its cause, and was informed that

[1] Anne Marie Louise d'Orléans, Duchesse de Montpensier, daughter of Gaston d'Orléans, Louis XIII.'s brother. She was styled *la Grande Mademoiselle*, to distinguish her from the other *Mademoiselle, Monsieur's* little daughter.

Madame de La Vallière was expected that night. " When the Queen heard this," adds the chronicler, " she appeared deeply mortified."

The following morning, on entering her Majesty's ante-chamber, *Mademoiselle* perceived La Vallière, with two of her friends, who had accompanied her from Versailles, waiting to pay their respects to the Queen. They seemed much fatigued and informed her that they had been travelling all night. After conversing with them for a little while, she passed on into the bedchamber, where she found poor Maria Theresa in a pitiable state of agitation, with tears of anger and mortification streaming down her cheeks. Near her stood three of her ladies, the Princess of Baden, Madame de Montausier [1] and Madame de Montespan, vainly endeavouring to console her, and they all called out in unison on catching sight of *Mademoiselle*, "See the state her Majesty is in ! " Madame de Montespan was especially demonstrative in her sympathy.

The Queen, of course, refused to receive La Vallière, and when, a little later, she went to hear mass at a neigh-bouring church, gave instructions that the door leading to the gallery which had been reserved for the royal party should be locked, in order to prevent the duchess from following her. In spite of these precautions, La Vallière presented herself before her Majesty, as the latter was entering her coach to resume her journey, and made her obeisance. Maria Theresa said nothing at the time,

[1] Julie d'Angennes, youngest daughter of the celebrated Madame de Rambouillet, and wife of Charles de Saint-Maure, Duc de Montausier. She had succeeded Madame de Navailles as *dame d'honneur* to the Queen in 1664, previous to which she had been *gouvernante* to the little Dauphin.

presumably her feelings had temporarily deprived her of the power of speech; but showed her resentment in truly feminine fashion when the Court stopped to dine at noon, by sending word to Villacerf, her *maître d'hôtel*, that "nothing was to be served to the duchess." Villacerf, however, who feared the King a great deal more than he did the Queen, pretended to have misunderstood her Majesty's wishes.

As might be supposed, what they were pleased to consider the outrageous conduct of Madame de La Vallière formed the sole topic of conversation among the Queen's ladies during the day's journey. The Princess of Baden and Madame de Montausier were inexpressibly shocked, while Madame de Montespan exclaimed, " Heaven defend me from being the King's mistress, but, were such a misfortune to befall me, I should certainly not have the effrontery to appear before the Queen ! "

At Guise, where they stopped for the night, La Vallière did not put in an appearance ; and the Queen gave strict injunctions to the officers of her escort to allow no one to depart in the morning before the royal equipage had started, so as to ensure that she should be the first to reach the King.

The favourite, on her part, was equally anxious to be the first to arrive, for thus she would have an opportunity of explaining to Louis how matters stood, before Maria Theresa could have time to lodge a complaint against her. Love, like necessity, is ever resourceful, and La Vallière's, quickened by jealousy and resentment at the treatment she had received, suggested to her a plan of which, under other circumstances, she would never have dreamed.

Next morning, the royal party entered upon the last stage of their long journey; the Queen's coach heading

the *cortège*; La Vallière's following at a respectful distance. Suddenly, the duchess alighted, mounted to the
top of some rising ground, and descried the King's troops
encamped in the distance. Then, hurriedly re-entering
her carriage, she ordered the astonished coachman to take
a short cut across some fields and to drive with all possible
speed.

When the Queen perceived how she had been outwitted
" she threw herself into a fearful passion," and it was only
with the greatest difficulty that her ladies were able to
dissuade her from sending part of her mounted escort to
forcibly arrest the progress of her rival. Her wrath,
however, would probably have been appeased could she
have witnessed the coldness with which his Majesty
received his mistress, who arrived, bruised and shaken,
fully five minutes ere the rest of the Court came up,
only to be met with a laconic "What! Before the
Queen!"

On reaching Avesnes, Louis paid a formal visit to
Madame de La Vallière, who refrained from joining the
Court circle that evening, doubtless through fear of provoking a scene with the enraged Maria Theresa. The
King, however, who, in matters of etiquette, as in all else,
claimed to be the sole arbiter, let it be known that it was
his pleasure that the lady's behaviour should be overlooked,
and accordingly, the following morning, the duchess went
to mass in the Queen's coach and afterwards dined at the
royal table. But it was to her rank, and not to her person,
that these honours were paid, for the days of her ascendency
were already numbered.

During the time the Court remained at Avesnes,
Madame de Montespan shared with her friend, Madame
de Montausier, a suite of apartments close to those of the

King, from which, indeed, they were only separated by a short staircase. On first arriving, a *garde-du-corps* had, as usual, mounted guard before his Majesty's door; but the keen eye of *Mademoiselle* noted, a day or two later, that the man had been removed and placed at the foot of the stairs, presumably to prevent any one ascending; and that this change had no sooner been made than the marchioness frequently excused herself, on one plea or another, from joining the Queen's card-table or accompanying her Majesty in her drives, as she had hitherto been in the habit of doing, and retired to her apartments, and that the King disappeared at the same time and shut himself in his own.[1]

On July 14, the army having resumed its advance, Louis XIV. departed at the head of his troops for Charleroi, while the Court set out on its return to Compiègne. Madame de Montespan, desirous of disarming suspicion until the prize for which she was striving should be fairly within her grasp, showed herself more than ever La Vallière's friend. In the course of their homeward journey, the royal party stopped for a night at Notre Dame de Liesse, where the edifying spectacle might have been witnessed of the two ladies going together to confession. "Who knows," remarks M. Lair, "whether La Vallière, the acknowledged sinner, did not envy the easy conscience with which the young *dame du palais* approached the tribunal of penance?"[2]

---

[1] *Mémoires de Mademoiselle de Montpensier* (edit. Chéruel), iv. 48 *et seq.*
[2] Lair's *Louise de La Vallière et la jeunesse de Louis XIV.*, p. 182.

CHAPTER IV

The King pays a visit to Compiègne—His Majesty keeps
late hours—The Court returns with the King to Flanders—
Incidents of the journey—The Queen receives an anonymous
letter—Louis XIV. joins the Court at Saint-Germain—Change
in his demeanour towards the fair sex—Birth of the Comte de
Vermandois—Suspicion gives way to certainty—" *Un partage
avec Jupiter* "—The Marquis de Montespan refuses to accept
the situation—Opinion of his contemporaries in regard to his
conduct—Stormy interviews between him and the King—He
is supported by his uncle, the archbishop of Sens—An
awkward coincidence—The archbishop defies the King and
threatens to excommunicate both him and Madame de
Montespan—The Marquis de Montespan and Madame de
Montausier—The marquis is imprisoned in For l'Évêque—
He is liberated and retires to his estates—His farewell visit to
the Court—Quarrel between soldiers under his command and
the under-bailiff of Perpignan — Remarkable letter from
Louvois to the Intendant of Roussillon on this matter—
Prosecution of Montespan—He takes refuge in Spain.

MADAME DE LA VALLIÈRE, who was nearing her confinement, returned to her house in Paris;[1] Madame de
Montespan accompanied the Court to Compiègne, there
to await events.

The French successes in Flanders continued, and

[1] The Palais Brion, in the garden of the Palais-Royal. Though
called a palace, it was only a modest one-storied house. Louis XIV.
had given it to Madame de La Vallière in the autumn of 1663, and
here the favourite's first child was born.

Tournai and Douai surrendered to the invaders, after which there was a lull in the operations, and the King seized the opportunity to pay a flying visit to Compiègne, "*afin d'éviter oisiveté*," he tells us in his *Mémoires;* in reality, to prosecute a campaign of a very different kind to that which he was conducting in the Netherlands.

As Louis had omitted to apprise the Queen of his intentions, no arrangements had been made for his reception, and, on his arrival, he found *Mademoiselle* in possession of his apartments. The lady, of course, offered to vacate them; but his Majesty begged her not to do so, protesting that, since he only intended to remain a few days, he could not think of disturbing her, and would content himself with the ante-chamber. This room was immediately below the apartments occupied by Madame de Montespan.

During the King's visit an incident occurred which caused a good deal of wagging of heads among the quidnuncs of the Court.

"One day at dinner," says *Mademoiselle*, "the Queen complained that his Majesty did not retire to rest until a very late hour, and, turning to me, remarked: 'The King did not come to bed last night until four o'clock. It was broad daylight. I cannot conceive what he could have found to occupy him until such an hour.'

"'I was reading my despatches and answering them,' replied the King.

"'But surely you might choose some other time for that,' the Queen rejoined.

"The King turned away his head to hide a smile. I felt very much inclined to smile, too, so kept my eyes steadily on my plate."

After dinner the Queen went for a drive. *Mademoiselle*

and Madame de Montespan accompanied her, as did the King, who was "astonishingly gay."[1]

Louis XIV. decided that the Court should return with him to Flanders, where, since his departure, Courtrai had been added to the list of French conquests, in order to exhibit Maria Theresa to the inhabitants of the towns annexed in her name ; and a few days after the conversation recorded above the Queen and her ladies were once more on the march. Douai was the first town visited, from which they proceeded to Tournai, where the clergy of the cathedral sang a *Te Deum* in honour of her Majesty's arrival, though not, it would appear, with the best grace in the world. While at Tournai, the Queen occupied herself by making a round of the churches and convents, but Madame de Montespan, pleading indisposition, remained nearly the whole time in her apartments.

As the King was anxious to join the army which was about to lay siege to Lille, he judged it best to send back the Court to Arras. This, as it happened, proved a wise decision, for soon after he had quitted Tournai, he had a sharp brush with the enemy, which might have been a serious affair had he been encumbered with the Queen and her *entourage*. The latter, on their side, did not reach Arras without adventures, as a report having been circulated that they were being pursued by the Spaniards, the whole of the sutlers, of whom a great number had followed the Court from the frontier, stampeded, throwing the poor ladies into paroxysms of terror. The alarm, however, turned out to be a false one, and they gained their destination in safety.

The evening of their arrival, the Paris courier brought a letter, in an unknown handwriting, addressed to the

[1] *Mémoires de Mademoiselle de Montpensier* (edit. Chéruel), iv. 51.

Queen. Maria Theresa broke the seals and read it, without making any comment at the time ; but the following night after supper, finding herself alone with *Mademoiselle*, Madame de Montausier, and Madame de Montespan, she suddenly remarked : " I received yesterday a letter, containing certain information, which, however, I refuse to credit. I am advised that the King is in love with Madame de Montespan, and cares for La Vallière no longer ; that it is Madame de Montausier who is conducting this intrigue ; that she is deceiving me, and that the King was with Madame de Montespan in her apartments nearly the whole time we were at Compiègne. In short, they have left nothing unsaid to convince me of the truth of their accusations and to arouse my resentment against her. I do not believe one word of it, and I have sent the letter to the King."

At this totally unexpected confidence the three ladies looked at one another in great embarrassment. *Mademoiselle*, who was the first to recover her self-possession, contented herself by remarking, " Your Majesty has acted wisely." But Madame de Montespan pretended to be furiously indignant, and demanded, with tears in her eyes, how was it possible that any one could imagine that she, who had received so much kindness from her beloved mistress, could be guilty of such base ingratitude ; while the Duchesse de Montausier was equally emphatic in protesting her innocence, and, later on, in referring to some complaints which had reached the Queen with regard to the conduct of another of her ladies, exclaimed : " Since people accuse me of giving mistresses to the King, of what are they not capable of accusing others !" To which the Queen replied that " she was the dupe of no one, though perhaps it was otherwise imagined " ; and, in proof of her assertion, proceeded to overwhelm Madame de Montespan with marks of her favour.[1]

After remaining a few days at Arras, the Court received orders from the King to proceed to Saint-Germain, where, on September 10, Louis joined them. Soon after his arrival, two of Maria Theresa's ladies, Madame d'Armagnac and the Princess of Baden, received orders to retire from Court. No reason was assigned for their disgrace, but it would appear to have been not unconnected with the anonymous letter sent to the Queen. His Majesty was evidently determined to tolerate no interference with his private affairs.

Observant feminine eyes were not slow to remark that since his return from the wars the King's demeanour towards the fair sex had greatly changed. Whereas he had hitherto been exceedingly diffident with the Court beauties, seldom speaking unless they first addressed him, and then usually contenting himself with a grave bow and a brief, if courteous, reply to their questions, he now "began and carried on the conversation like another man."[2] His conquest, or rather what he fondly imagined to be his conquest, of the heart of the haughty Madame de Montespan had inspired him with the belief that henceforth no woman would be proof against his fascinations, and the timid lover of the timid La Vallière was completely transformed.

On October 3, Madame de La Vallière gave birth to her fourth child—a son—who, however, was immediately taken away from her and its existence kept a profound

[1] *Mémoires de Mademoiselle de Montpensier* (edit. Chéruel), iv. 58 *et seq.*

[2] Madame de Longueville *to* Madame de Sablé, September 15, 1667, quoted in Victor Cousin's *Madame de Sablé* (edit. 1854, p. 387).

secret for some months. The poor mother, in ignorance of what fate was in store for him, was in despair ; but the King heartlessly refused to relieve her anxiety until the beginning of the year 1669, when he acknowledged the boy and legitimated him under the title of the Comte de Vermandois.[1]

Meanwhile the suspicions of the Court as to the relations existing between Louis and Madame de Montespan had given way to certainty. In February 1668 Molière's comedy, " Amphitryon," was performed for the first time, in which the audience thought that they detected more than one allusion to the subject which had formed the principal topic of conversation for many weeks past. The lines :

> " Un partage avec Jupiter
> N'a rien du tout qui déshonore,
> Et sans doute il ne peut être glorieux
> De se voir le rival du souverain des dieux "

were generally regarded as a delicate hint to the injured husband to make the best of the situation, and were greeted with a burst of merriment by the assembled courtiers.

If Louis XIV. really flattered himself that Montespan would regard the affair from the poet's standpoint, he was speedily undeceived. The young man was very far from disposed to share with Jupiter, or any one else for that matter, and, in spite of the entreaties of his needy old father, the Marquis d'Antin, who, on hearing of his daughter-in-law's dishonour, exclaimed, " God be praised ! Here is Fortune at last knocking at my door ! " resolutely

---

[1] The Princess Palatine ascribes the King's conduct to the fact that Madame de Montespan had persuaded him that the child was not his, but the Comte de Lauzun's.

declined to accept the rôle of complaisant husband, and proceeded to raise a scandal.

Poor Montespan's contemporaries, with whom, for some reason, he appears to have been anything but popular, do not hesitate to attribute his conduct to the basest motives, and to hint that he would have been complaisant enough had the King been willing to purchase his silence. " He was regarded as a knave and a fool," says Madame de Caylus. " If he had only taken his wife away from Court, the King, although so amorous of her, would have been powerless to exercise his authority against that of a husband. But M. de Montespan, so far from making use of his, thought only of how the occasion might be turned to his own advantage " [1]; while the Princess Palatine assures us that Montespan was "wholly worthless," and gives it as her opinion that " if the King had been willing to pay him a good round sum, he would have been appeased." [2]

Whether this was the case or not,[3] it is certain that Montespan was for several years a veritable thorn in the side of the royal libertine. Not content with "complaining to every one of the friendship of the King for his wife," and telling the lady in pretty plain terms what he thought

[1] *Souvenirs de Madame de Caylus* (edit. 1889), p. 122.

[2] *Correspondance complète de Madame la Princesse Palatine*, ii. 292.

[3] M. Lair, in his *Louise de La Vallière et la jeunesse de Louis XIV.*, mentions a pamphlet of the time which places a more charitable construction upon Montespan's conduct. It contains an account of an imaginary conversation between the Marquis and Lord Castlemaine, the husband of the lady for whom Charles II. had so great a regard. The Englishman takes a philosophical view of his wife's infidelity ; Montespan, on the other hand, is represented as consumed with shame and jealousy. We are inclined to think that this lampoon comes far nearer the truth than the statements of Madame de Caylus and the Princess Palatine.

of her behaviour, he went to Saint-Germain and provoked scenes with Louis himself.

"He used to come very often to see me," says *Mademoiselle*; "he was a relative of mine, and I remonstrated with him. One evening he came and repeated to me an harangue he had delivered to the King, in which he quoted a thousand passages of Scripture, about David and so forth, and ended by making use of very forcible language to induce him to restore his wife and fear the judgment of God. . . . I was at Saint-Germain the following day, and I said to Madame de Montespan, 'Come for a drive with me; I have seen your husband in Paris, and he is madder than ever. I scolded him sharply and told him that if he does not hold his tongue, he will deserve to be locked up.' She replied, 'He is here telling his tales at Court. I am quite ashamed to see that my parrot and he are amusing the mob.'" [1]

Although, as we have mentioned, the old Marquis d'Antin was inclined to regard the affair as a piece of good fortune for his family, and, doubtless, considered his son a fool for his pains, Montespan found a warm supporter in another relative, his uncle, Louis Henri de Gondrin, Archbishop of Sens. This prelate, who had as a young man been notorious for the irregularity of his life, was now almost as remarkable for his austerity, and "charitably desired to protect his family from the sins against which he had failed to protect himself." Accordingly, no sooner was he informed of what had occurred, than he sentenced to public penance a woman of the town, who lived as the marchioness, his niece, was doing, in open concubinage, and caused the publication throughout his diocese of the old canons against the violation of the religious law.

---

[1] *Mémoires de Mademoiselle de Montpensier* (edit. Chéruel), iv. 151.

MADAME DE MONTESPAN

Now, it happened, by a strange and, for Madame de Montespan, a singularly awkward coincidence, that the Court was then at Fontainebleau, which was situated in the diocese of Sens. The consequence was that every one believed that it was the King's new mistress who was being pointed at, and many were the conjectures as to what would follow. The general opinion was that the favourite would demand the disgrace of the rash prelate, and the latter's friends trembled for his safety. Their apprehensions, however, were unfounded ; for although Louis and his mistress tried to carry matters with a high hand, they found more than their match in the archbishop.

In order to punish him for his presumption, the King sent him a peremptory order prohibiting him from leaving the town of Sens. But the archbishop, strong in the justice of his cause, ignored the royal command and, shortly afterwards, paid a pastoral visit to Fontainebleau. On the clergy expressing their astonishment at his hardihood, he replied that no one, not even his sovereign, had the right to prevent him exercising his episcopal functions, and that if the King compelled him by force to return to Sens, he would excommunicate both him and Madame de Montespan. When this was repeated to Louis, he shrugged his shoulders and remarked, " He will be as good as his word."

Madame de Montespan, although boiling with rage at the insult put upon her, shrank from provoking a struggle with ecclesiastical authority, for which, as she well knew, Louis, even in the midst of his irregularities, always retained the most profound respect. She, therefore, decided to leave Fontainebleau, nor did she ever venture to return thither until after the death of the archbishop, which occurred in 1674.

MADAME DE MONTESPAN

While his uncle was engaged in bearding the King, the Marquis de Montespan had turned the whole weight of his wrath upon Madame de Montausier, whose complaisance at Avesnes and Compiègne had contributed not a little to expedite the marchioness's fall—or triumph. The husband of " the incomparable Julie," as the *habitués* of the Hôtel de Rambouillet had been wont to call her, had recently been appointed governor to the Dauphin, an honour which some writers assert he owed to the duchess's recent services, though we prefer to believe that it was in recognition of the admirable courage and presence of mind he had exhibited as governor of Normandy while the plague was devastating that province. A number of ladies had called upon Madame de Montausier to felicitate her upon the distinction which the duke had received, when, suddenly, Montespan entered unannounced and, striding up to the astonished *dame d'honneur*, poured forth a torrent of reproaches, accusing her of stooping to play the degrading rôle of *entremetteuse* in the King's amours, and of deliberately encouraging his wife's misconduct. Then, having relieved his pent-up feelings a little by this outburst, he turned on his heel and quitted the room as abruptly as he had entered it.

When Madame de Montespan and *Mademoiselle*, who had hastened to the duchess's apartments the moment they were informed of what had taken place, arrived on the scene, they found the old lady lying on her bed, trembling with rage and scarcely able to speak. After she had grown a little calmer, she told them that " she thanked God that there had only been women present, for if there had been a man in the room, she felt sure that he would have thrown M. de Montespan out of the window." Madame de Montausier, in fact, seems to have been the principal sufferer by the intrigue, and expiated to the full the share she had taken in bringing it about. She was in bad health at the time, suffering from a nervous affection, the result, if *Mademoiselle* is to be believed, of an encounter with an apparition in a dark passage at the Tuileries, and her mortification at having been so cruelly humiliated before her friends greatly aggravated her complaint. Towards the end of 1669, she resigned her post of *dame d'honneur* and retired from Court, and died two years later at the age of sixty-four.

As Montespan refused to be quiet, the King, losing patience, had him arrested and incarcerated in For l'Évêque, from which, however, he was liberated a few days later on giving an undertaking to retire at once to his estates. He kept his word, but could not resist the temptation of a final parade of his woes, and, accordingly, clothed himself, his children, and his servants in the deepest mourning, and then drove to Court in a coach draped in black, and took leave, with great ceremony, of his relatives and friends. This somewhat theatrical method of inviting public sympathy was not without its effect, especially upon the middle class of Paris, and caused Louis, who, in spite of his despotic ideas, attached considerable value to the good opinion of even the humblest of his subjects, keen annoyance. It is, therefore, scarcely surprising that when, not long afterwards, an incident occurred which afforded him an opportunity of retaliating upon Montespan that he should have hastened to take advantage of it.

In the autumn of 1669, a body of soldiers belonging to a cavalry regiment in which the marquis held a commission had a dispute with the under-bailiff of Perpignan, in the course of which hard words, if not hard knocks, were exchanged. The affair was of very trifling importance, so trifling, indeed, that neither the civil nor the military authorities of the district had deemed it necessary to take any steps to punish the delinquents, and, in all probability, it would have soon been forgotten had not some busybody sent an anonymous letter to Louvois, the Minister for War,[1] acquainting him with what had occurred, and mentioning that the officer in command of the soldiers was the Marquis de Montespan. Thereupon, Louvois, doubtless acting upon instructions from the King, wrote to the Intendant of Roussillon the following letter :

LOUVOIS *to the* INTENDANT OF ROUSSILLON.

"MONSIEUR DE MAQUERON,—I am informed that a scandalous brawl has taken place between the troopers of M. de Montespan's company and the people of the under-bailiff of Perpignan. I am astonished that you should have failed to transmit to me any information in regard to this affair, and must request you to repair, at the earliest possible moment, what can only be the result of an oversight on your part. You must be careful to omit nothing, whether in the informations of the under-bailiff, or in those relating to the disorders committed at Ille, which may help to implicate the commander of the company and the largest possible number of troopers, to the end that they may take alarm and the majority desert, especially the commander, after which it should not be a difficult matter to bring about the ruin of the company.

---

[1] It is, strictly speaking, incorrect to refer to Louvois as War Minister at this period. Michel Le Tellier was still nominally head of the War Office, and remained so until appointed Chancellor in 1677. But since 1666 the latter had practically delegated his duties to his son, for whom some years before he had purchased the survivorship of the post.

If you are acquainted with the names of the troopers who insulted the under-bailiff, they must be arrested at once, in order to make an example of them, and so that you may have from their depositions, at the time of their execution, further proofs and charges against the captain— to endeavour, in some way or other, to implicate him in the informations, to the intent that he may be cashiered with some appearance of justice. If you could contrive that the charges against him are sufficiently grave for the Supreme Council of Roussillon to pronounce some condemnation upon him, it would be an excellent thing.

"You will be able to divine the reasons well enough, however poorly informed you may be of what is going on in this part of the world. I beg you to leave no stone unturned to carry out my wishes in this matter, to give me all the ordinary news in a separate letter written in your own hand, and to return this one to me.

"LOUVOIS.[1]

"AT CHAMBORD, *September* 21, 1669."

The Supreme Council summoned Montespan and the other delinquents before it. None of the defendants, however, put in an appearance, and, on January 10, 1670, judgment went against them by default. We have, unfortunately, no means of ascertaining the punishment nflicted ; but, as the writ issued against one La Grave states that he would be liable to a fine of twenty-five

---

[1] Quoted in Clement's *Madame de Montespan et Louis XIV.*, p. 380. The original of this letter was duly returned to the War Minister, according to his instructions, and no doubt at once destroyed by him ; but the Intendant took the precaution of making a copy of it, a fortunate circumstance, since it affords a highly instructive commentary on the manner in which justice was administered under *le Grand Monarque.*

livres per diem until he obeyed the mandate of the court, it was probably a pecuniary penalty. As for the marquis, he decided that the wisest course was to put the Pyrenees between himself and the King's "justice," and took refuge in Spain, "accompanied by the wife of a councillor of Toulouse, who cherished a regard for him," and whose society, it may be presumed, helped to console him in his exile.

CHAPTER V

Secret of the ascendency of La Vallière—Secret of that of
Madame de Montespan—The ascendency of the latter
coincides with the zenith of the reign of Louis XIV.—Birth
of a daughter—Birth of the Duc du Maine—Secrecy observed
on these occasions—Madame de Montespan brings a demand
for a separation from her husband before the Châtelet—The
court reluctant to grant her request—But eventually does so,
under pressure from the King—Terms of the decree—
Louis XIV. still in dread of the Marquis de Montespan—
Curious correspondence between the King and Colbert in
regard to the marquis.

THE reign of Madame de La Vallière had lasted six years;
that of Madame de Montespan was to endure for just
twice as long. Paradoxical as it may seem, it was to her
very simplicity, her very weakness, far more than to any
of those qualities which have endeared her to posterity,
that La Vallière was indebted for her ascendency. She
was so submissive, so timid, so grateful for every kind
word and look that her royal lover deigned to bestow
upon her, that Louis's passion for her had partaken of the
nature of protection, and he was thus enabled to gratify
his love and his insatiable vanity at one and the same time.
"He reigned where sometimes kings cease to reign, and
commanded in circumstances where even the most imperious
are forced to obey." Not until the convent doors had
closed upon her, not until she was lost to him for ever,

66

did he realise all that he had cast from him. Never again was he to meet with a woman whose only ambition was to be permitted to worship him. Never again was this sublime egotist to be afforded such delightful opportunities for adoring himself under the delusion that he was adoring another.

Madame de Montespan, in nearly every respect the exact antithesis of the woman whom she had supplanted, also strongly appealed to Louis's vanity, though in a different way. "He does not love me," she said one day, in a burst of confidence, "but he thinks it a duty he owes to himself to have the most beautiful woman in his kingdom for his mistress." Here, in this single sentence, in all probability, we have the main secret of that empire which the haughty marchioness enjoyed for twelve years, at first in secret and sparingly, then "thunderous and triumphant," as Madame de Sévigné expresses it, boldly defying the *dévots*, the moralists, and the envious courtiers of both sexes to wrest it from her. If, now and again, clouds covered the sky, they quickly dispersed, and the sun shone forth all the more radiantly for its temporary eclipse.

The period of her ascendency, it is interesting to note, almost exactly coincides with the zenith of the age of Louis XIV. ; the era when the Monarchy reached its giddiest height, and noble and prelate cringed before the King as before the vicegerent of the Almighty ; when the armies of France marched from victory to victory, and Europe, amazed and paralysed, trembled at Louis's frown. The era, too, when Molière and Racine composed their masterpieces, when Mignard painted his finest portraits, and Bossuet delivered his most eloquent orations. And those who gaze to-day upon Picquart's wonderful

MADAME DE MONTESPAN

engraving, and contemplate that cascade of sunny curls, those exquisite features, that haughty and imperious air, are fain to admit that of that most splendid epoch Madame de Montespan is no unworthy representative, and to recall the words of an enthusiastic historian, "*Voilà la reine, la vraie reine, une majesté digne de Louis XIV. !*"

In the early spring of 1669 Madame de Montespan set the seal upon her dishonour by giving birth to the first of the seven children she bore the King,[1] a daughter, who, however, only lived three years, and at Saint-Germain, on March 31, 1670, a son, the future Duc du Maine, made his entrance into the world. On both occasions the utmost secrecy was observed, the Duc du Maine, immediately after he was born, being wrapped up in a shawl and confided to the care of the King's favourite, the Comte de Lauzun, who carried him concealed beneath

[1] Here is the list :

1. A daughter, born in 1669 (probably in March) ; died at the age of three.
2. The Duc du Maine, born March 31, 1670 ; married March 19, 1692, to Mademoiselle de Bourbon-Charolais ; died in 1736.
3. The Comte de Vexin, born June 20, 1672 ; died in 1683.
4. Mademoiselle de Nantes, born June 1, 1673 ; married in 1685 to the Duc de Bourbon ; died in 1743.
5. Mademoiselle de Tours, born in 1674 ; died September 15, 1681.
6. Mademoiselle de Blois, born June 1677 ; married February 1692 to the Duc de Chartres (the future Regent) ; died in 1749. The daughter of Madame de La Vallière, whom Louis XIV. legitimated in 1667, and who, in 1680, married the Prince de Conti, was also called Mademoiselle de Blois.
7. The Comte de Toulouse, born in 1678 ; married in 1728 to Mademoiselle de Noailles, widow of the Marquis de Gondrin ; died in 1737.

his cloak to a coach which was waiting in the park to take them to Paris.

In the following July Louis XIV. caused a demand for a separation *de corps et de biens*, formulated by Madame de Montespan, to be brought before the Châtelet. The reasons adduced were the wasting of their common property by the marquis, domestic discord (*mauvais ménage*), and ill-treatment of the marchioness by her husband. The machinery of the law, however, worked even more slowly in the seventeenth century than in our own day, in addition to which the Châtelet was not unnaturally reluctant to commit the iniquity demanded of it; and it was not until four years later (July 7, 1674), and after considerable pressure had been brought to bear upon the members of the court by the King and his Ministers, that the desired separation was pronounced by the *procureur-général*, Achille de Harlay, assisted by six judges.

"The said dame de Montespan," ran the wording of the decree, "is and will remain separated from the property and habitation of her husband, whom we have prohibited from any longer cohabiting with or approaching her." The marquis was also ordered to restore the dowry of 60,000 livres he had received with his wife, and to provide her with alimony to the amount of 4000 livres, "payable quarterly, and in advance." On appeal, however, it was decided that the *dot* should not be repayable until after Montespan's death, when, in the event of his wife having predeceased him, it was to revert to their two children ; while the marchioness, with a great show of magnanimity, surrendered her alimony in favour of her offspring, "never having had any intention of causing by her demand for a separation the breaking-up of the establishment of the said lord her husband, but, on the contrary, being desirous of contributing as far as possible to maintain the dignity of his household, and to provide his said children with an education befitting their rank."

The decree of separation which Louis had succeeded in wringing from the reluctant Châtelet was far from assuring him peace of mind. What difficulties subsequently arose we cannot tell; but some correspondence which passed between his Majesty and his faithful Minister, Colbert, in the spring of 1678, proves that the King was convinced that it was still in the power of the man whom he had so cruelly injured to avenge his wrongs. In May of that year, the Marquis de Montespan had come to Paris in connection with a lawsuit which he was prosecuting before the Parliament. Louis, however, evidently considered his presence in the capital highly suspicious, and we find him writing to Colbert as follows:—

Louis XIV. *to* Colbert.

"Camp at Diense,
"*May* 17, 1678.

"I omitted to tell you before I left that as M. de Montespan is in Paris, it would be well to keep him under observation. He is a madman capable of any extravagance. I desire you, therefore, to note what he is doing, what people he mixes with, and what conversation he holds. In a word, keep yourself thoroughly well informed as to his movements, and if anything which you consider of importance occurs, let me know."

To which the Minister replies:—

70

MADAME DE MONTESPAN

Colbert *to* Louis XIV.

"SCEAUX, *May* 24, 1678.

" I received yesterday, Sire, Your Majesty's communication of the 17th, and I have executed without delay the commands which Your Majesty has been pleased to lay upon me on the subject of M. de Montespan. In reference to this matter, I think it right that you should be informed that about three or four years ago I received instructions from you to expedite the decision of an action which he was bringing before the Parliament, so as to deprive him of that reason, or pretext, for remaining in Paris. I executed Your Majesty's order ; his action was adjudicated upon, and he took his departure, as I was given to understand.

" About a fortnight ago, I went to see the Archbishop of Sens, in reference to the Abbey of Lys,[1] which Your Majesty has been pleased to bestow on my sister. As I was leaving his house, M. de Montespan accosted me and begged me to recommend a second time to M. de Novion [2] a lawsuit of his which was then going on, and the decision of which he was awaiting ere retiring to his province. But I did not comply with his request, as I considered that I ought not to meddle in his affairs without instructions.

" If Your Majesty deems it advisable that the Sieur de Novion should make use of this expedition, perhaps he (Montespan) will then take his departure. However, I will execute Your Majesty's commands."

The King's rejoinder, scribbled in the margin of Colbert's letter, was brief and to the point :—

[1] An abbey of the Benedictine Order, near Melun.
[2] First President of the Parliament of Paris.

MADAME DE MONTESPAN

Louis XIV. *to* Colbert.

"Camp at Nuder,
"*May* 28, 1678.

"You may give the judge a hint to finish M. de Montespan's business, so that he may take his departure sooner."

Doubtless, Colbert lost no time in giving the desired hint to the presiding judge; doubtless, too, that functionary did all in his power to oblige his royal master. But the action in question seems to have been a somewhat complicated one, and dragged on, as lawsuits have a way of doing; while, in the meantime, rumours of a disquieting nature must have reached Louis, for in the middle of June Colbert received another letter.

Louis XIV. *to* Colbert.

"Saint-Germain-en-Laye,
"*June* 15, 1678.

"I am informed that M. de Montespan is indulging in indiscreet talk. He is a madman whom you will do me the pleasure to have closely watched; and, in order that he may no longer have any pretext for remaining in Paris, see Novion, so that the Parliament may hasten.

"I know that Montespan has threatened to see his wife. As he is capable of it, and as the consequences might be alarming, I count on you to take care that he does not make a scene.

"Do not forget the details of this matter; and especially see that he leaves Paris at the earliest possible moment." [1]

[1] Quoted in Clément's *Madame de Montespan et Louis XIV.*, p. 248 *et seq.*

CHAPTER VI

Singular conduct of Madame de La Vallière—Probable explanation—Reasons which induced Louis XIV. to compel her to remain at Court—"*Chez les Dames*"—Cruel humiliations inflicted on La Vallière—She flies to the Couvent de Sainte-Marie at Chaillot—Unsuccessful attempts of the Comte de Lauzun and Maréchal de Bellefonds to induce her to return—Her message to Louis XIV.—The King sends Colbert to Chaillot—La Vallière returns—Relief of the King—Pretended delight of Madame de Montespan—Opinions of *la Grande Mademoiselle* and Madame de Scudéry on the situation—Opinion of Bussy-Rabutin—The King insists on La Vallière accompanying the Court to Flanders—Curious instructions of Louvois to the Intendant of Dunkerque.

AND what of Madame de La Vallière?

The part played by Louise de La Vallière in the interval between the triumph of Madame de Montespan and her final retirement to the Carmelites in April 1774 seems, at first sight, well-nigh inexplicable. Remembering her exquisitely sensitive nature, remembering how passionately she had loved the King, one would naturally have expected that the moment all doubt as to the relations between Louis and Madame de Montespan had been set at rest she would have seized the first opportunity to retire from Court.

Madame de La Vallière did nothing of the kind. She remained on the stage where she had so long filled the

73

principal rôle ; she made no change in her mode of life ; she continued to assist, with a smile on her lips, if with anguish at her heart, at ballets, fêtes, and other amusements of the Court, seemingly indifferent to the fact that these diversions were no longer organised in her honour, but in that of another. Nay, she did more than that. She lived on what were, to all appearance, terms of the closest intimacy with her successful rival, occupying apartments communicating with hers at the Tuileries, riding in the same carriage,[1] and even standing sponsor to one of her illegitimate children.[2]

What is the explanation of her conduct ?

By far the most feasible one that we have been able to discover is that given by the lady's biographer, M. Jules Lair. He says :

"The King held La Vallière bound by a tie far stronger than that of a woman's passion for a man—the love of a mother for her son. The little boy born at Saint-Germain in 1667 was not recognised until February 1669. No provision, moreover, was made for his future until the end of the year, when the King at length decided to confer upon him the office of Admiral of France, vacant by the

---

[1] François Maucroix, canon of Rheims, who was at Fontainebleau in August 1670, relates the following incident in his *Mémoires :* "M. Barrois and myself, having noticed his Majesty's carriages standing in the Oval Court, waited nearly an hour, and at length saw the King enter his *calèche*. Madame de La Vallière stepped in first, the King next, and then Madame de Montespan. All three sat on the same seat, for the *calèche* was a very large one. La Vallière seemed to me very pretty, and stouter than I had imagined her to be. I thought Madame de Montespan extremely beautiful ; her complexion was particularly admirable."—*Mémoires de Fr. Maucroix*, ii. 33.

[2] To Mademoiselle de Nantes, afterwards Duchesse de Bourbon, baptized December 1673 (see p. 100, *note infra*).

presumed death of M. de Beaufort.[1] Madame de La Vallière's fortune was always more apparent than real. The income derived from Vaujours was very small. Many of the inhabitants were miserably poor, and the duchess was so kind-hearted that far from putting pressure upon her vassals, she interceded for them. Besides, this estate had been settled upon her daughter to the exclusion of her son."[2]

That is, in all probability, the reason why the discarded mistress remained at Court ; that is why she continued on terms of apparent amity with the woman who had deceived and supplanted her. Unable herself to make any provision for her little son, she recognised that his future must entirely depend upon the good pleasure of his royal father, and, rather than prejudice his interests, she made up her mind to endure what to her sensitive nature must have seemed little short of purgatory.

But why, it may be asked, did Louis desire her to remain ? Why did he compel this woman, whom he had loved, or imagined he had loved, for six long years, to allow herself to be bound, so to speak, to the chariot wheels of her triumphant rival ? The question is answered by Bussy-Rabutin in a letter to Madame de Montmorency: " He required a cloak for his relations with Madame de Montespan." [3]

Louis did not attempt to conceal from himself the fact that his intrigue with Madame de Montespan stood on a

[1] François de Vendôme, Duc de Beaufort. He had been sent at the head of a French force to succour Candia, which was besieged by the Turks, and was killed in a sortie on the night of June 25, 1669. His body was never recovered, and for some time an idea seems to have prevailed that he was not dead, but a prisoner in Turkey.

[2] Lair's *Louise de La Vallière et la jeunesse de Louis XIV.*, p. 206.

[3] *Correspondance de Roger de Rabutin* (edit. Lalanne), i. 380.

very different plane from that with La Vallière. In the
latter case, he had injured no one but poor Maria Theresa;
in the former, he had cruelly wronged a member of his
own nobility, and one, too, who was very far from inclined
to suffer in silence. We have seen that so late as the
summer of 1678, four years after Madame de Montespan
had been judicially separated from her husband, the King
had still reason to dread the vengeance of the marquis.
How much greater, then, must have been his fears while
Montespan's wounds were still fresh, and while he was
still in possession of all the rights which the French law
gave to the principal party in the marriage contract! At
all costs Louis felt that the intrigue must be disguised
until a decree of separation had been obtained and the
marquis disarmed or, at least, deprived of his most dangerous weapons. And so, to avoid public scandal, Madame
de La Vallière remained publicly the King's mistress, and
when his Most Christian Majesty desired to visit Madame
de Montespan, he always made a rule of passing through
the apartments of the *maîtresse déclarée*, which, as we have
mentioned, communicated with them. Soon the Court
had a *mot* to describe the situation. Whenever the King
went ostensibly to visit Madame de La Vallière, it was
said that he had gone " *chez les Dames,*" implying that he
had gone to see one lady in order to see the other.

Nothing is more typical of that coarseness and utter
indifference to the feelings of others which underlay the
polished courtesy of which we read so much than Louis's
treatment of his discarded mistress, whose only fault had
been that she had loved him too well. Madame de
Montespan, either because she had reason to fear that a
day might come when La Vallière would regain her
ascendency over the royal heart, or more probably because

hers was one of those natures which take a cruel delight in adding insult to injury, and are always more vindictive towards those who they themselves have wronged than towards those who have wronged them, from the very first resented her continuance at Court, and never lost an opportunity of exercising her biting wit at the fallen favourite's expense ; while Louis, far from remonstrating with his mistress, would appear to have ably seconded her. " The Montespan woman," says the Princess Palatine, " derided La Vallière in public, treated her abominably, and obliged the King to do likewise." How intolerable the situation must have been the following incident will serve to show.

One day Louis was passing through the duchess's apartments *en route* for those of Madame de Montespan, carrying in his arms a favourite toy spaniel. Observing his ex-mistress gazing wistfully after him, he turned and tossed the little dog towards her, exclaiming contemptuously, " Here, madame, is company for you ! "

At length matters came to such a pass that La Vallière's fortitude entirely gave way, and on the night of Shrove Tuesday 1671, while a grand ball was in progress, she repaired to her apartments, exchanged her gorgeous dress for a simple grey gown, and fled from the Tuileries for the second time, on this occasion taking refuge at the Couvent de Sainte-Marie, at Chaillot, leaving behind her a letter directed to the King, informing him of her intention.

Louis's conduct on learning of La Vallière's flight showed how greatly times had changed. He did not now, as he had eight years before, throw himself on horseback and gallop to the convent to assure the poor fugitive of his undying affection and to entreat her to return ; he did not even postpone his departure for Versailles, which had been fixed for the following evening, but set out at the appointed time in company with Madame de Montespan and *Mademoiselle*.   However, on reflection, he decided that he ought not to allow the day to pass without doing something to mark his sense of the ingratitude with which he doubtless considered La Vallière had treated him ; and so, after they had proceeded a short distance, he began to weep incontinently.   Madame de Montespan promptly followed suit, as did *Mademoiselle*— " to keep the others company," she tells us—and thus they continued all the way to Versailles.[1]

But La Vallière, considered as the cloak wherewith to cover his relations with Madame de Montespan, was far too useful a person for his Majesty to dispense with her services just then ; and, accordingly, he despatched his favourite, the Comte de Lauzun, to the convent to bring her back.   The duchess, however, curtly refused to listen to him, and Lauzun was compelled to return to Versailles and report the failure of his mission.   A second ambassador, Maréchal de Bellefonds,[2] a worthy man and an intimate friend of the fugitive, proved no more fortunate, although La Vallière, aware of the sympathy which he felt for her, spoke to him with greater freedom.   She charged him to tell the King that " she would have quitted the Court after having lost the honour of his favour, had she been able to make up her mind never to see him again ;

---

[1] *Mémoires de Mademoiselle de Montpensier* (edit. Chéruel), iv. 260.

[2] Bernardin Gigault, Marquis de Bellefonds (1630–1694). He served with distinction in Spain, Italy, Flanders, and Holland, and was made *Maréchal de France* July 8, 1668. In 1670, and again in 1673, he was sent as Ambassador Extraordinary to the Court of St. James's, and he commanded the French army in Holland in the campaign of 1684.

that her weakness had been so great that she was scarcely in a fit state to dedicate herself to God ; that it was, however, her desire that the remains of the passion that she still entertained for him might serve as her penance ; and that, after surrendering to him her youth, it was not too much to devote the rest of her life to the care of her salvation."

When Bellefonds faithfully reported this message to the King, the latter began to weep afresh, but managed to sob out a request that Colbert should attend him. On the arrival of his trusted Minister, Louis ordered him to proceed at once to Chaillot and not to return without the lady, authorising him to employ force if no other means would serve his purpose. Colbert, however, preferred to trust to diplomacy, and when he reached the convent and was admitted to the duchess's presence, drew so lively a picture of the King's distress that La Vallière's tender heart was touched, and she agreed to accompany him, on the understanding that his Majesty would permit her to retire from Court if she persisted in her resolution to do so.

Louis, we are told, received the duchess with great emotion. He conversed with her for nearly an hour, and wept once more, this time presumably with relief at recovering this very convenient screen for his double adultery. Madame de Montespan was even more demonstrative, running to meet her victim with open arms and with tears—" of what kind ? " asks Madame de Sévigné, very pertinently—streaming down her cheeks. The marchioness had been rather pleased than otherwise on first hearing of La Vallière's flight. Truth to tell, she was becoming somewhat weary of the precautions to which the King's dread of a public scandal had compelled her to submit for the past three years, and was impatiently looking forward to the time when she would be able to stand forth " thunderous and triumphant " as *maîtresse déclarée*. With La Vallière gone, it would be out of the question for Louis any longer to conceal the intrigue, and her acknowledgment must follow as a matter of course. She had, therefore, suggested to her lover that, since the lady was so very anxious to remain at Chaillot, it might be as well to allow her to do so, and when he took a different view of the matter, high words had ensued.[1] Finding Louis firm, however, the favourite was shrewd enough to take her discomfiture in good part, and even to outdo his Majesty in the warmth of the welcome she accorded the unfortunate duchess.

The latter's conduct in this affair was generally condemned by the gossips of the Court. " Every one," says *Mademoiselle*, " considered that La Vallière had behaved in a very ridiculous manner ; that she ought to have remained in the convent or have made favourable terms with the King, instead of returning like a fool. Although the King wept, he would have been very pleased to have got rid of her at that time." [2] For Louis, on the other hand, the Court, or at least the feminine portion of it, seems to have had nothing but praise. " The Duchesse de La Vallière," writes Madame de Scudéry to Bussy, " has resumed her place at Court. I cannot refrain from expressing to you my opinion that the King acts in a most commendable manner, even towards his *quitteries*, as the Maréchal de La Meilleraye remarks. He treats those whom he has once loved with a consideration which your fine gentlemen would not show towards a woman

[1] Madame de Montmorency *to* Bussy-Rabutin, February 25, 1671.
[2] *Mémoires de Mademoiselle de Montpensier* (edit. Chéruel), iv. 261.

whom they had ceased to care for, although she might be as faithful as the Duchess has been." [1]

But Bussy, an infinitely shrewder judge of human nature than his fair correspondent, saw the other side of the shield. " You will never induce me to admit," he answers, " that the King deserves praise for having treated his discarded mistresses with kindness. What he has done has been with no idea of compensating them for the injury they have suffered through his desertion ; and I even go so far as to maintain that it is to suit his own convenience and for political reasons that he has made La Vallière return." [2]

The cynical count had accurately gauged the situation. Shortly after La Vallière had resumed her fetters, Louis XIV. gave orders for one of those military promenades to Flanders with which he was wont to gratify his martial instincts when there was no actual fighting on hand ; and the Queen, the Royal Family, and a number of the most favoured courtiers prepared to follow the troops. The duchess was among those who were honoured by a " command " from his Majesty, but, surmising the motive which had prompted the invitation, she requested permission to decline. The King, however, insisted on her accompanying the Court, and the poor lady had no option but to obey. The following letter, written by Louvois to Robert, the Intendant of Dunkerque, will explain why Louis was so anxious for the presence of " our very dear and well-beloved cousin, the Duchesse de La Vallière."

" *March* 7, 1761. You must prepare the room marked V for Madame de Montespan ; make a door

[1] Madame de Scudéry *to* Bussy-Rabutin, March 6, 1671.
[2] Bussy-Rabutin *to* Madame de Scudéry, March 13, 1671.

there at the place marked I, and a passage to enable her to pass into the room marked Q, which will be suitable for her wardrobe.

" Madame de La Vallière will occupy the room marked Y, in which you must make a door at the place marked 3, and a passage *to enable her to pass under cover into Madame de Montespan's room*."[1]

No wonder poor La Vallière sighed for the humble cell of the convent !

[1] Quoted in Rousset's *Histoire de Louvois*, i. 311.   The original letter is preserved in the Archives of the French War Office.

CHAPTER VII

Madame de Montespan seeks a guardian for her children by Louis XIV.—Madame Scarron (Madame de Maintenon) is recommended to her—Widely divergent views as to the character of this lady—The probable truth—Her romantic history—Her birth in the prison at Niort—Hardships of her early years—Her marriage with the poet Scarron—Madame de Montespan obtains a pension for her after her husband's death —She refuses to accept the charge of the children unless commanded to do so by the King—Difficulties of her post— Subterfuges to which she is compelled to resort to conceal the nature of her occupation—The house in the Rue de Vaugirard —Precautions observed there—Madame Scarron's disappearance from society causes much astonishment—Relations between her and Madame de Montespan—Louis XIV.'s early antipathy to Madame Scarron—It disappears on a closer acquaintance— His visits to the Rue de Vaugirard—Madame Scarron returns to society—Louis XIV. desirous of legitimating the children of Madame de Montespan—Difficulties in the way of such a step —Anxiety of the King—A convenient precedent—Legitimation of the Duc du Maine, the Comte de Vexin, and Mademoiselle de Nantes—Illness of the Duc du Maine— Madame Scarron takes him to a doctor at Antwerp—Her letter to Madame de Montespan—Madame Scarron and her charges established at Court.

THE children of Madame de La Vallière had, as we have mentioned, been confided to the care of Madame Colbert, the wife of Louis XIV.'s faithful Minister, who had brought them up with her own; and when, in the spring

of 1669, Madame de Montespan gave birth to her first
child by the King, she and her lover began to look about
for some lady who could be trusted to perform a similar
service for the new mistress.

A Madame d'Heudicourt, a confidante of the favourite,
to whose complaisance Madame de Montespan had been
not a little indebted during the early days of her intrigue
with the King, expressed her willingness to undertake the
responsibility. But Madame d'Heudicourt was a born
intrigante and, according to Saint-Simon, "beautiful as the
day"; and the marchioness knew by experience how very
dangerous it was to put one's friends too much forward
when one's lover happened to be of a susceptible nature.
She, therefore, courteously declined the lady's offer, and
resolved to seek for some one who was a stranger to the
Court and its wicked ways. Well would it have been for
Madame de Montespan had she been content to trust her
ally!

Madame d'Heudicourt, who would appear to have
taken the refusal of her offer in very good part, now
suggested that possibly a friend of hers might serve the
favourite's purpose. This was a Madame Scarron, the
widow of the author of *Virgile travesti* and other poems
in burlesque verse, which had enjoyed a great vogue in
their day, who, since her husband's death, eight years previously, had been living in the Rue de Saint-Louis on a
small Court pension. Madame de Montespan had often
met this lady at Madame d'Heudicourt's and at the
Hôtel d'Albret, and had been favourably impressed by
her manner and conversational powers. What was more
to the present purpose was that Madame Scarron had the
reputation of being both discreet and trustworthy; that
she possessed, in a pre-eminent degree, the art of rendering

herself serviceable to all whom she approached, taking care of her friends' houses in their absence, superintending their entertainments, and nursing them with care and devotion when they were ill, and that, though she had none of her own, she was noted for her love of children and her skill in their management. She seemed, in short, exactly the kind of person who was required, and Madame de Montespan lost no time in authorising Madame d'Heudicourt to approach her on the subject.

Few characters in history have been the subject of more blind adulation, on the one hand, or more unscrupulous calumny, on the other, than has Madame de Maintenon, to give Madame Scarron at once the title by which she is known to fame. By her admirers, she is represented as "a sort of courtly Jeanne d'Arc, divinely appointed to convert a licentious King from the error of his ways." By her detractors, a scheming hypocrite, who passed from a youth of secret vice to a middle age of ostentatious piety, because she foresaw that, in her own case, religion and virtue were the safest cards to play, and who, after basely betraying her benefactress, contrived to bewitch a superstitious monarch into humiliating subjection to her. Up to about the middle of the last century the latter view predominated; but in recent years the current of opinion has set in strongly in the opposite direction, and more than one important " Life " has appeared, which, whatever other merits they may possess, can certainly not have the smallest claim to be considered impartial studies. What, then, is the truth?

The truth would seem to lie midway between these two extremes. Madame de Maintenon merits neither the shameful aspersions of her enemies nor the extravagant praises of her friends. Her character was a singularly complex one, in which the two most prominent traits were intense religious conviction and worldly prudence pushed to the verge of unscrupulousness. That she was ever the mistress of Villarceaux or any one else we do not for one moment believe, in the first place, because the charge rests on very unsatisfactory evidence,[1] and, in the second, because it is entirely opposed to the consistency of her character. " Every trustworthy record," says Mr. Cotter

[1] Both Saint-Simon and the Princess Palatine affirm in the most positive manner that Madame de Maintenon was Villarceaux's mistress. But, as the former chronicler was not yet born, and the latter was living in Germany at the time the intrigue was supposed to be going on, and both are well known to have been bitterly hostile to the lady in question, their testimony is of little value. What, at first sight, appears to be evidence more worthy of attention is contained in a letter written by the famous courtesan, Ninon de Lenclos, to Saint-Évremond, then living in retirement in England, and dating probably from the last years of Ninon, who died in 1706. " Scarron was my friend ; his wife's conversation gave me infinite pleasure, but I found her too *gauche* for love. As for details, I know nothing, I saw nothing, but I often lent my yellow room to her and Villarceaux." (*Causeries d'un Curieux*, ii. 588, by M. Feuillet de Conches, who possessed the original letter.)

M. Geoffroy, in his *Madame de Maintenon d'après sa Correspondance authentique* (p. 7), throws doubt upon the authenticity of this letter; while M. Lavallée (*Correspondance générale de Madame de Maintenon*, p. 81) regards it " as a Parthian shaft launched by the old courtesan, abandoned by all and disgusted with everything, against the witness of her debauchery, risen through her virtue to the height of consideration and greatness," and quotes a sentence from another of Ninon's letters which is in direct contradiction to the first : " Madame de Maintenon was virtuous in her youth through weak-mindedness. I wished to cure her, but her fear of God was too great." We may add that if there really was a *liaison* between the lady and Villarceaux, it is rather strange that the latter, who was a gentleman rather given to boasting about his conquests, should never have avowed the fact, but, on the contrary, complained to his friends of his want of success.

MADAME DE MONTESPAN

Morison in his brilliant little *étude*, "proves that Madame de Maintenon moved in a plane that diverged at right angles from the path which leads to sins of the flesh. It was not that she resisted such temptations; she was not aware of them. It was her favourite maxim that an irreproachable behaviour is also the cleverest in a worldly sense. She acknowledged that a wish to stand well with the world and win its esteem was her master passion, and that 'she *hated* everything that could expose her to contempt.' Setting aside her religious principles, of which none but the uncandid will dispute the persistency, it is evident that in her cool, sedate mind the impulses in question found no place. Her lips were never touched with fire, and no flame, holy or unholy, ever burned in the depths of her heart."[1]

On the other hand, to maintain, as her enthusiastic admirers insist on doing, that her whole conduct was dictated by the purest and most disinterested motives, that her sole object was the salvation of Louis XIV., will not bear the test of investigation for a moment. That she ardently desired to pluck the monarch as a brand from the burning for his own sake is beyond question, but that she appreciated to the full the material advantages which the post of keeper of his Majesty's conscience would confer is no less certain. The motives which guided her in this matter, as in every action of her life, were two, and two which are generally considered to be utterly incompatible—worldly advancement and eternal salvation. She would seem, in short, to have been of opinion that there were exceptions to the Scriptural precept concerning the impossibility of serving two masters, and that she might hold to the one without necessarily despising the other.

[1] Cotter Morison's *Madame de Maintenon*: an *étude*, p. 23.

MADAME DE MONTESPAN

Françoise d'Aubigné, afterwards Madame Scarron, and later Madame de Maintenon, came of an ancient family originally from Anjou, the most distinguished member of which was her grandfather, the famous old Huguenot, Théodore Agrippa d'Aubigné, "for whom nothing was too hot or too cold," and who wielded sword and pen with equal facility. This accomplished old gentleman had a most unworthy son, Constant by name, who, not content with wasting his substance in riotous living, committed various crimes, in consequence of which he passed a considerable part of his life in gaol. In the year 1635 he was serving a term of imprisonment at Niort, and here, on November 27, his second wife,[1] Jeanne de Cardillac, a brave and devoted woman, who had obtained permission to share his punishment, gave birth to Françoise.

The little girl had a miserable childhood, the hardships of which were never effaced from her mind. Her mother brought her to Paris, where they lived in extreme poverty, Madame d'Aubigné squandering what little money she possessed in hopeless lawsuits. After a time, an aunt, Madame de Villette, took compassion on the poor child, gave her a home, and instructed her in the rudiments of the Protestant faith, to which she became firmly attached. In 1643 Constant d'Aubigné was liberated, and he, with his wife and children, sailed for Martinique with the idea of retrieving their fortunes. Their hopes were not realised, however, and when, two years later, Constant had the good taste to die, his family found themselves totally

---

[1] He had married for the first time in 1611, and, eight years later, "having surprised his wife in company with the son of an advocate, had killed the latter with thirty blows of a poniard and his wife with seven, after first making her pray to God." (Letter of Anne de Rohan to the Duchesse de Trémoille, quoted in Lavallée's Introduction to *Correspondance générale de Madame de Maintenon*, p. 3.)

unprovided for. They returned to France, where Madame d'Aubigné resumed her litigation, while Madame de Villette again took charge of Françoise, who was now twelve years old, tall for her age and giving promise of great beauty.

But the child was not permitted to remain long under her aunt's hospitable roof, for another relative, a Madame de Neuillant, a bigoted Catholic, obtained a royal order to have the charge of the little girl made over to her, in order to remove her from Calvinist influences. This good lady, who appears to have been about as unpleasant a representative of her sex as one might expect to meet in the course of an ordinary lifetime, was not only a bigot but a miser, and obliged the unfortunate Françoise to dress like a peasant-girl and perform the most menial offices. She also adopted various harsh measures to induce her to abjure her religion, but without success ; and it was not until the girl had been sent to the Ursuline convent in the Rue Saint-Jacques, and had been privileged to hear two learned divines argue the chief points at issue between the Churches for her special edification, that she decided to embrace the faith of which she afterwards became so distinguished an ornament.

On leaving the convent, Françoise went to live with her mother, who was occupying a single small room in the Rue des Tournelles, and supporting herself chiefly by needlework. Shortly afterwards she made the acquaintance of the poet Scarron, who, though barely forty years of age, was a helpless cripple, " having only the use of his right hand, his eyes, and his tongue," but whose buoyant humour no amount of physical suffering could suppress.

La belle Indienne, as Scarron styled the girl, in allusion to her sojourn in Martinique, who, in addition to her good looks, was the possessor of a ready if somewhat precocious wit—no mean recommendation in those days— soon became a great favourite with the jovial little poet and his circle, which included some of the most brilliant figures in the gay world of Paris. When, in 1651, Madame d'Aubigné died, Scarron sent for Françoise, and, for once in a way, forcing himself to be serious, pointed out the dangers which surrounded her now that she was alone in the world, and offered either to pay for her admission into a convent or the protection of his own name.

The young lady's choice was soon made. She had at Scarron's and elsewhere seen something of the good things that life had to offer, and consequently had no desire to immure herself in a convent. Her strong religious views made her shrink from the idea of relinquishing her honour in order to obtain them, but, handicapped as she was by her poverty and her antecedents, she knew well that she could never hope for a husband such as she might reasonably have looked for had her lines been cast in more pleasant places. Scarron, poor fellow, was only half a man, it is true, but half a man is better than no man at all, and she had had abundant proof of how kind a heart beat in that pain-wracked body. She therefore decided that it was better to be a nurse than a nun, and the marriage contract was duly drawn up. When the notary, according to custom, asked Scarron what he brought his bride, the wit replied, " Immortality ! The names of the wives of kings die with them ; that of Scarron's wife will live for ever." The poet little suspected when he made this grandiloquent speech how strangely it was to be verified, although it is not as the wife of the author of *Vergile travesti*, but of a very different personage, that Françoise d'Aubigné is remembered by posterity.

MADAME DE MONTESPAN

This strange union lasted eight years, during which the young wife nursed her suffering husband with unremitting care and tenderness, superintended his dubious finances with a skill which reflected infinite credit on her business capabilities, and so impressed his companions with her worth and dignity that one of them remarked that if he were offered the choice of speaking in an unbecoming manner to her or the Queen-Mother he would rather do so to the latter. Scarron died in 1660, leaving behind him little save debts, for, in spite of his wife's skilful management, he had been too incorrigible a spendthrift ever to save a sou. Françoise was then twenty-five, tall and well-made, with, according to Madame de Scudéry, " a smooth, beautiful skin, light, pretty chestnut hair, a well-shaped nose, a sweet, modest expression, and the finest eyes you could wish to see." She had, of course, again to face the world without resources, but now she had made wealthy friends, who extended their hospitality to her until she succeeded in obtaining the renewal in her favour of a small pension which Scarron had received from the Queen-Mother. When Anne of Austria died this, of course, ceased, and an appeal to the King's generosity was at first unsuccessful. At length, however, another pension was granted her, mainly, it appears, through the intercession of Madame de Montespan.

Madame Scarron met Madame d'Heudicourt's proposal with admirable diplomacy. She was in straitened circumstances ; the offer was a tempting one from a pecuniary point of view, and, therefore, not to be lightly refused. But she was quick to perceive that there would be a vast difference in her position if, by the exercise of a little tact, she could contrive to be employed by the King instead of

only by his mistress.   By obtaining the command of Louis
to take charge of the child she would bring herself into
immediate connection with the King ; by declining to do
so, unless commanded by him, she would enhance the
apparent value of her services, and, in fact, place him
under an obligation.   She accordingly replied that with
Madame de Montespan's child she could have no concern,
but that if the little girl were indeed the King's, and his
Majesty would lay his commands upon her, she would be
ready to accept the responsibility.   The favourite, anxious
to get the matter settled, raised no objection, and Madame
Scarron, having been summoned to Saint-Germain, and
formally requested by Louis to accept the post, entered
upon her duties at once.

     She speedily found that the position was very far from
being a sinecure, and, indeed, nothing but her indomitable
courage and innate talent for dissimulation could have
enabled her to fill it with success.   " If this step was the
beginning of Madame de Maintenon's singular good
fortune," says her niece, Madame de Caylus, "it was
likewise the beginning of her difficulties and embarrassments."   The most absolute secrecy was one of the
stipulations insisted upon.   The children—for a boy, the
future Duc du Maine, was born the following year—
were at first placed, each separately with their nurses, in
small houses in the environs of Paris.   Madame Scarron
was enjoined to give them the most assiduous care, and
never to allow a day to pass without paying them a visit ;
but, lest suspicion should be aroused, she was forbidden to
live with them or make any change in her mode of life.
She has herself related the subterfuges to which she was
compelled to have recourse in order to baffle the curiosity
of her friends.

MADAME DE MONTESPAN

"This strange kind of honour (the charge of the children) cost me endless annoyance and trouble. I was compelled to mount ladders to do the work of upholsterers and mechanics who might not be allowed to enter the house. I did everything myself, for the nurses did not put their hands to a single thing, lest they should be tired and their milk not good. I would go on foot and in disguise from one nurse to another, carrying linen or food under my arm. I would sometimes spend the whole night with one of the children who was ill in a small house outside Paris. In the morning, I would return home by a little back gate, and, after dressing myself, would go out at the front door to my coach, and drive to the Hôtels d'Albret or de Richelieu, so that my friends might perceive nothing, or even suspect that I had a secret to keep. I became very thin, but no one divined the reason."[1]

Suddenly, towards the end of the year 1672, Madame Scarron withdrew from society altogether, and went into the strictest retirement. Madame de Montespan's first two children were growing up, and a third had just appeared upon the scene ; and these circumstances necessitated a new arrangement. The favourite, accordingly, purchased a large, rambling house in the then remote quarter of the Rue de Vaugirard, standing some little way back from the street, and surrounded by a garden shut in by high walls. Here, Madame Scarron established herself with the children and their nurses, living in good style, but discouraging visitors, and devoting herself exclusively to her charges' education. The most elaborate precautions were taken to prevent people whom it was impossible to altogether exclude from obtaining the slightest inkling of the real occupation of the mistress of the house. But, as

[1] *Correspondance générale de Madame de Maintenon,* i. 146.

there was always a danger that some chance caller might catch sight of a nurse or hear one of the children crying, she brought with her the infant daughter of Madame d'Heudicourt, in order that her presence might serve to cover that of the others.

Madame Scarron's disappearance from Paris society, in which she had occupied so prominent a place, caused the greatest astonishment among her friends. "As for Madame Scarron," writes Madame de Coulanges to Madame de Sévigné, who was then in Brittany, " her mode of life is astonishing. Not a single soul has any communication with her. I have received a letter from her, but I take care not to boast about it, for fear of being overwhelmed with questions."[1] All kinds of rumours were flying about, for the most part highly detrimental to the reputation of the lady in question. Some of these reached the Rue de Vaugirard, and caused the worthy *gouvernante*, to whom the good opinion of the world was as the breath of life, the keenest mortification.

To add to her troubles, she now frequently found herself at odds with Madame de Montespan. The latter's arrogance and capriciousness seemed to increase with her favour, and rendered her at times almost unbearable. Of course, she did not dare to venture near the house, but she was perpetually sending for Madame Scarron, interfering with her arrangements for the education of the children, finding fault with her on the slightest pretext, and flying into the most violent passions. The elder woman's reputation for piety was a fruitful source of discord between them, as the marchioness saw in it only a tacit reproach to her own immoral life. This was especially the case when she happened to be *enceinte*. " In

[1] Madame de Coulanges *to* Madame de Sévigné, December 2, 1672.

God's name," she wrote to her, on one occasion, when summoning her to Court, "do not make any of your great eyes at me!" Far from being grateful to the *gouvernante* for the care she bestowed upon the children, and the unceasing vigilance which alone enabled her to preserve the secret of their existence, she made it the subject of untimely pleasantry. One day, a fire broke out in the house which sheltered the little family. Madame Scarron, fearing that she might be forced to call in the neighbours to her assistance, and thus run grave risk of discovery, despatched a mounted messenger to the Court with a letter informing Madame de Montespan of the state of affairs ; whereupon that lady sent word that "she was glad to hear about the fire, as it was a sign of good luck for the children." [1]

Nevertheless, life in the Rue de Vaugirard was not without its compensations, for it was there that the sorely-tried widow was enabled to sow the first seeds of that great fortune which she was one day to reap.

At first Louis XIV. was rather repelled than attracted by his children's *gouvernante*. He disliked clever people —they made him painfully conscious of his own deficient education—and the *habituées* of the Hôtels de Richelieu and d'Albret, in whose salons Madame Scarron had been a bright and shining light, plumed themselves on being the successors of the *précieuses* of the Hôtel de Rambouillet. It was the fashion at Court to make game of these cliques; and Madame de Montespan, in spite of the fact that in her earlier and more reputable days she had derived great pleasure from their gatherings, was particularly fond of turning them into ridicule for the diversion of the King. Moreover, Madame Scarron's cold and reserved manner

---

[1] Languet de Gergy's *Mémoires sur Madame de Maintenon*, p. 130.

impressed Louis far from favourably, and for some time he never spoke of her to Madame de Montespan except as "*Votre belle esprit*" (Your learned lady).

But this did not last long. As he was much attached to his children, the monarch not infrequently paid surreptitious visits to the Rue de Vaugirard, and when he knew her better and studied her more closely, his prejudices gradually melted away. He could not but be touched by the devoted care which she lavished on her charges. No mother could possibly have been more patient, more tender, more solicitous in every way for their welfare. Their slightest troubles seemed to awaken an answering chord in her heart, their most insignificant ailments occasioned her the deepest distress, and when the eldest child died, she wept for her as bitterly and mourned for her as long as if she had been her own daughter. He discovered, too, that this demure and unobtrusive woman possessed qualities which he had never even suspected— a sound common-sense, which appealed strongly to his eminently practical mind, a quiet humour which was not altogether an unwelcome change after the boisterous gaiety of his mistress, and conversational powers which both surprised and delighted him. He found his way with increasing frequency to the house, and the oftener he came, the longer he stayed, and the more reluctant he was to take his leave.[1]

At the beginning of December 1673, Madame Scarron

---

[1] It is to this period, if to any, that the *essai de séduction* mentioned by so many writers belongs. The belief that Louis attempted to storm this impregnable fortress of virtue in later years prevails no longer. The letter containing the famous passage, "*Je le renvoie toujours affligé, jamais désespéré*," which even historians like Henri Martin cite as authentic, is an impudent forgery of La Beaumelle.

returned to society as abruptly as she had quitted it twelve months before. "We supped again yesterday, with Madame Scarron and the Abbé Testu, at Madame de Coulanges's," writes Madame de Sévigné to her daughter. "We talked a great deal, and you were not forgotten. We took it into our heads to escort Madame Scarron home at midnight, to the farthest end of the Faubourg Saint-Germain, a long way beyond Madame de La Fayette's, almost as far as Vaugirard, and quite in the country, where she lives in a large, handsome house, with a large garden, and beautiful and spacious apartments. She has a coach, men-servants, and horses, dresses quietly, but elegantly, in the style of a woman who associates with persons of rank ; she is amiable, handsome, good-natured, and free from affectation ; in a word, a charming companion."

The explanation of the lady's sudden reappearance in Paris society was that there was no longer any secret to guard. Louis XIV. was about to acknowledge the children of Madame de Montespan.

The King had been anxious to take this step for some time past. His motive was not, as might be supposed, a sentimental one—the feeling that he could not well refuse to the reigning mistress what he had already conceded to the discarded La Vallière. It was a far graver reason. In the eyes of the French law the children in question belonged not to the King, but to the husband of Madame de Montespan, and Louis had grounds for believing that the latter, who was still breathing forth fire and slaughter, contemplated taking measures to enforce his rights. Were he to do so, the courts would be compelled to entertain his suit, and although it might be possible to bring sufficient pressure to bear upon the judges to induce them to

decide against the marquis, the case could not fail to pro-
voke a terrible scandal, which would certainly not be confined within the borders of France. The prospect of
being called upon to engage in litigation with one of his
own subjects over so very delicate a matter was hardly
such as the monarch who aspired to be the arbiter of
Europe could afford to regard with equanimity. Besides,
to do him justice, Louis was much attached to these
children—in fact, the Duc du Maine seems to have been
his favourite child—and the possibility of having to surrender them filled him with alarm. He, therefore, resolved to forestall Montespan and legitimate them.

At first sight it would appear to have been a simple
matter enough for the King to issue letters of legitimation.
Had he not done so in favour of Madame de La Vallière's
children, and no man had said him nay? But, in the
present case, where the mother was a married woman, the
situation was far more complicated. To name the mother
would be to reduce the affair to a farce, since the children
it was proposed to legitimate were legitimate already,
inasmuch as the Marquis de Montespan, their father in
the eyes of the law, had never repudiated them. On the
other hand, no precedent could be found for omitting the
name of the mother. Henry IV., the legitimator *par
excellence*, had invariably named them. Not that the
astute Béarnais had ever found himself in a like predica-
ment, for though Gabrielle d'Estrées and Jacqueline de
Beuil, the respective mothers of César de Vendôme and
Antoine de Moret, had been married women, their unions
had been merely nominal ones, contracted for the convenience of his Majesty and subsequently annulled.
Henri, therefore, in both instances, had been able to
declare, with more or less good faith, in the letters patent:

MADAME DE MONTESPAN

"We know that the marriage was void and was never consummated, as is proved by the decree of nullity which has since been pronounced." But Madame de Montespan had two children by her husband, who bore his name and whose legitimacy had never been questioned, and her marriage had not been dissolved. In consequence, it was impossible to name the mother. The only solution of the difficulty would have been for La Vallière to have allowed her name to appear in the document. The duchess's complaisance, however, stopped short of acknowledging the sons and daughters of her rival as her own.

For months Louis racked his brains to discover some way out of the imbroglio, but to no purpose, and at the beginning of the year 1673 the approaching birth of another child came to add to his anxiety. At this moment, a totally unexpected coincidence provided him with the means of severing the Gordian Knot.

The young Duc de Longueville,[1] killed at the passage of the Rhine, had left a will in which he bequeathed a considerable part of his fortune to a natural son, who was generally believed to be the fruit of an intrigue between the deceased nobleman and the wife of the Maréchal de La Ferté, although the document in question contained no mention of any lady, and, at the same time, requested his mother, the celebrated Madame de Longueville, to use her

---

[1] Charles Paris d'Orléans, popularly believed to be the son of La Rochefoucauld. He was a very gallant young gentleman indeed, and his untimely death, Madame de Sévigné tells us, caused "an infinite number of ladies to weep." Had he lived a little longer, he would in all probability have ascended a throne, as, on the motion of John Sobieski, the Polish Diet had resolved to depose the feeble and imbecile Michael Viecnowiski and offer the crown to the nephew of the Great Condé, and deputies from Poland were actually on their way to the French camp at the time when the duke fell.

influence with the King to obtain the legitimation of the little boy. The duchess, who had been passionately attached to her son, at once approached his Majesty on the subject, and, as may be supposed, was accorded a very gracious reception. Nothing, indeed, could have been more opportune for Louis. Here, without any action on his own part, was the chance of establishing the very precedent he had been vainly seeking. No one could possibly suspect him of any ulterior motive in granting the last request of a gallant soldier, a prince of the blood, cut off in the flower of his youth in the service of his king and country ; and no one could blame him if he chose to follow what would henceforth, no doubt, be a common practice. Accordingly, on September 7, 1673, letters patent were issued legitimating Longueville's son, under the name of the Chevalier d'Orléans, *without naming the mother*, and duly approved by the Parliament. Three months later (December 20, 1673) the gentlemen of the long robe were called upon to register a similar document, of which the preamble, a very brief one, was as follows :—

"Louis, by the grace of God, etc. The affection with which Nature inspires Us for our children and many other reasons which serve to considerably augment these sentiments within Us compel Us to recognise Louis Auguste, Louis César, and Louise Françoise."[1]

The first was named Duc du Maine ; the second, Comte de Vexin ; the third, Demoiselle de Nantes. "Nothing more could have been done for the children," remarks

[1] The last child had been privately baptized two days previously, the godfather being one Thomas Dandin, a priest, and the godmother, Louise de La Vallière, after whom the little girl was named, and who thus, by a supreme act of self-abnegation, admitted as her godchild the daughter of the man whom she had loved so passionately and the rival who had supplanted her in his affections ! When the officiating priest

MADAME DE MONTESPAN

M. Lair ; "but for the mother what a difference between these letters and those of 1669, in which 'the singular merits of our well-beloved Louise de La Vallière' were so loudly proclaimed ! The haughty Montespan had to rest content with that 'many other reasons.'"[1]

In spite of their acknowledgment by their royal father, the children continued to occupy the house in the Rue de Vaugirard for some months longer. "We have seen the Duc du Maine," writes Madame de Sévigné to her daughter on January 5, 1674, "but he has not yet visited the Queen ; he arrived in a coach and saw only his father and mother." The explanation of the delay in bringing them to Court was that Louis preferred to wait until the action for a separation, which was still dragging its weary length along, had been decided in Madame de Montespan's favour, before flaunting the fruit of their intrigue in the face of the world. Public opinion drew a nice distinction between the conduct of a lady whose husband had forfeited his legal rights and one who was still, nominally at any rate, under marital authority.

In the meanwhile, the little Duc du Maine was seized

---

demanded of the sponsors the names of the parents, there was no answer, and, after an embarrassing pause, he passed on to the next question.

It is interesting to compare these surreptitious proceedings with the pomp which marked the baptism of Henri IV.'s daughter by Gabrielle d'Estrées in 1696. "After pages bearing torches came guards, Swiss, drums, trumpets, and violins ; then Maréchal Matignon bearing a taper, the Duc d'Epernon a basin (silver-gilt), the Duc de Nevers a vase, the Duc de Nemours a towel, the Duc de Montpensier the cradle, the Prince de Conti the infant, wrapped up in a silver cloth lined with ermine, the train being six yards long and borne by Mademoiselle de Guise."—Bingham's *Marriages of the Bourbons*, i. 238.

[1] Lair's *Louise de La Vallière et la jeunesse de Louis XIV.*, p. 282.

with convulsions, as the result of which one of his legs contracted to such an extent that he was no longer able to walk. The King was much concerned, and the whole Faculty of Paris exhausted their skill in their endeavours to find a remedy, but without success. As a forlorn hope, it was decided to send him to a doctor at Antwerp, who was a specialist in cases of this kind, and was reported to have effected some marvellous cures ; and, accordingly, in April 1674, he set out for Flanders under the care of Madame Scarron, who received instructions to assume the name of the Marquise de Surgères, and to give people to understand that the duke was her son. From Antwerp she writes to Madame de Montespan as follows :—

MADAME SCARRON *to* MADAME DE MONTESPAN.

"*April* 20, 1674.

"The doctor visited the prince yesterday. He is just such a man as you have been told, very kind and natural in his manner, with nothing of the quack about him. Nevertheless, I confess to you, Madame, that I find it difficult to put any faith in him ; still one must follow his instructions.

"I am suffering in anticipation all that this poor child will have to endure. You will be able with justice to reproach me now with being too fond of him. To conclude, the doctor pretends that it is nothing but weakness, and that reassures me. The prince said to him, 'At all events, Monsieur, I was not born like this ; neither my mamma nor my papa are lame.'"

The Antwerp treatment, which, as will be gathered from the foregoing letter, was of the heroic order, was far from being a success, and the little duke returned to Paris if anything rather worse than when he left. On July 7 the much-desired separation was at length pronounced by the Châtelet, and a fortnight later the Duc du Maine, the Comte de Vexin, and Mademoiselle de Nantes, having been formally presented to the Queen, were definitely established at Court together with their *gouvernante.*

CHAPTER VIII

Serious illness of Louise de La Vallière—On her recovery she
determines to take the veil—Her visits to the Carmelite
convent in the Rue Saint-Jacques—She resolves to enter that
community—The Carmelites agree to receive her—She applies
to Bossuet to overcome the objections of the King and Madame
de Montespan—Interview between Bossuet and the favourite
—Madame de Montespan sends Madame Scarron to La
Vallière to dissuade her from her resolution—La Vallière's
reply—Opinion of the Court ladies on the matter—The King
gives his consent to La Vallière entering the Carmelites—
Bossuet's letter to Maréchal de Bellefonds—La Vallière's
farewell to the world.

LOUISE DE LA VALLIÈRE was spared the pain of witnessing
the final triumph of her rival. Three months before she
had quitted the Court for ever.

Towards the close of the year 1669 or the beginning of
1670 the duchess was taken suddenly ill. The nature of her
malady does not appear to be known, and it is quite conceivable that, as her biographer, M. Lair, suggests, it was
not due to natural causes. Whatever it may have been,
it was very serious, and for some days her life was despaired
of. While she lay " like a poor criminal on the scaffold
waiting until the preparations for his execution had been
completed," [1] she suffered in anticipation all the torments
of the lost, and determined, if she were spared, to begin a

[1] *Réflexions sur la miséricorde de Dieu*, Twenty-fourth *réflexion*.

new life. Accordingly, on her recovery, she consulted her confessor as to the steps it would be necessary for her to take to give effect to her resolution. The divine in question, who, like the majority of fashionable *directeurs*, was of an accommodating disposition, offered to accept her professions of penitence and admit her to the sacraments. But La Vallière " declined this hasty absolution, which could assure her only a false peace of mind " ;[1] and, after some months spent in vainly endeavouring to discover a more effectual means of easing the pangs ot conscience, decided that the only possible way in which she could hope to make reparation for her sin was by taking the veil.

In thus renouncing the world she felt that she would be injuring no one. The King had long ceased to love her, and regarded her merely as a convenient screen for his intrigue with Madame de Montespan. Her little boy had at length been recognised and provided for; while her daughter, Mademoiselle de Blois, would actually benefit by her retirement, since, in that case, Vaujours would revert to her. As for her mother and her other relatives, she owed them nothing; they had regarded her fall with complaisance, if not with a warmer feeling, and had been only too ready to profit by the bounty of her royal lover.[2]

It was in pursuance of this resolution that, on Shrove Tuesday 1671, Madame de La Vallière fled to the Couvent de Sainte-Marie, at Chaillot; and though, in deference to Louis XIV.'s wishes, she ultimately consented to return to Court, she was none the less determined to seek the seclusion of the cloister as soon as she could prevail upon the King to give his consent.

[1] *Réflexions sur la miséricorde de Dieu*, Eighth *réflexion*.
[2] Lair's *Louise de La Vallière et la jeunesse de Louis XIV.*, p. 273.

In the meanwhile, she resolved to seek for a convent which would be ready to receive her when she had obtained the permission she so much desired. Mademoiselle de Montpensier, to whom she had confided her intention, advised her not to take the veil, but to enter as a boarder at the Couvent de la Visitation, another convent at Chaillot. This was a very fashionable form of retreat in those days, and was much affected by ladies who were devotionally inclined, or whose relatives deemed that a period of seclusion from the world and its temptations might not be without its advantages. Such were, of course, amenable to most of the rules of the convent so long as they remained beneath its roof, but, on the other hand, were at liberty to return to a mundane life at any time. La Vallière, however, animated by a spirit of sincere remorse, was in no mind to be content with half measures. As in love she had sought nothing but love, in penitence she desired nothing but pardon, and the more thorough her expiation, the greater she considered would be her chance of obtaining peace in this world and salvation in the next.

Now, it had happened that, on several occasions, the duchess had visited incognito the Grand Couvent of the Carmelites in the Rue Saint-Jacques, and had been much impressed by the air of quiet happiness which pervaded its inmates, notwithstanding that the life to which their vows condemned them, with its serge and sackcloth, its midnight vigils, its macerations, and servile duties, was regarded by the world as little better than death itself. In the course of one of these visits, a friend who accompanied the ex-favourite accidentally addressed her by name. Instantly the manner of the nuns, which until then had been friendly and unconstrained, changed to one of frigid reserve ; "every lip was closed and every eye averted." Far from resenting their behaviour, La Vallière esteemed them the more on that account, and forthwith resolved to choose their convent in preference to a less strict community.

The reputation of the Carmelites stood so deservedly high that the duchess did not dare to address her request directly to them. The Order required that candidates for admission to their convents should be of unblemished virtue, and this rule was most stringently enforced. She, therefore, took counsel with her friend, Maréchal de Bellefonds, and begged him to enlist the good offices of his aunt, Judith de Bellefonds (in religion Mère Agnès de Jésus)—who had been for many years an inmate of the establishment in question, and had filled the office of prioress in 1649—to induce the community to make an exception in her favour. Mère Agnès promised her assistance, with the result that, after a good deal of hesitation, it was decided to receive the penitent ; and, at the end of October 1673, the marshal wrote informing her that she would be admitted whenever she desired.

La Vallière did not at once avail herself of the permission accorded her. She was unwell at the time, and the Prioress of the Carmelites, on learning of this, advised her to wait until she had fully recovered her health before entering on a life so very different from that to which she had been accustomed. Moreover, she was extremely doubtful as to whether the King and Madame de Montespan would permit her to carry out her resolve. Not only was her presence, as we have said, necessary as a screen for the lovers, but her choice of such a very austere Order might not unreasonably be regarded as a reflection upon the reigning mistress, so much more culpable than poor La

Vallière, by reason of her double sin. The legitimation or Madame de Montespan's children in December of that year removed the first obstacle, but strengthened the second, since the proud mother was now, to all intents and purposes, *maîtresse déclarée*.

In her perplexity, the duchess, on the suggestion of Bellefonds, turned for advice and assistance to Bossuet. This great man, whose extravagant views on the subject of kingly authority have unfortunately blinded many to the true nobility and disinterestedness of his character, and led them to accuse of ambition and sycophancy one whose whole life is a protest against such insinuations,[1] had come to Court in 1662 as preceptor to the Dauphin,[2] and had already made several distinguished converts. In his relations with his penitents he observed the happy mean between those confessors who, to borrow his own words, " in their unfortunate and inhuman complaisance, place cushions beneath the elbows of sinners and seek coverlets for their passions " and those who " bring hell continually before them and fulminate nothing but anathemas." Eloquent yet simple, gentle yet inexorably firm, a thorough man of the world, a profound judge of the human heart,

[1] If Bossuet was ambitious, why, asks M. Clément very pertinently, did he remain content all his life with third-class bishoprics like Condom and Meaux, when there was no position in the Church to which he might not have aspired ?

[2] Here is what Nicolas Colbert, Bishop of Luçon, wrote to his brother, in recommending Bossuet for the post : " He preaches an austere morality, but one that is thoroughly Christian. Those who know him say that he lives in accordance with the precepts he lays down. He has always appeared to me to have much intelligence, and I know that he is a high-principled man. His face does not belie him, for it is very intellectual. In manner, he is unassuming, pleasant, and courteous. In short, I know nothing of him but what is good." Quoted in Clément's *Madame de Montespan et Louis XIV.*, p. 56.

he exercised in the confessional an influence which few members of his Church have wielded either before or since. "How many in that Court," remarks one of his biographers, "received from the great bishop counsel, light, hope, consolation, new life ? "[1]

It is an error to suppose, as more than one writer has, that it was on Bossuet's advice that Madame de La Vallière first conceived the idea of entering the Carmelites ; she would appear to have fully made up her mind to take this step some time before she consulted the bishop. But, on the other hand, there can be no question that he both confirmed her in her resolution and did much to remove the difficulties which lay in her way.[2] Perceiving that if Madame de Montespan could be induced to give her consent, that of the King would not be difficult to obtain, he consented, at the duchess's request, to treat with the favourite on her behalf. The reception he met with was not an encouraging one. "Madame de La Vallière has constrained me to speak on the subject of her vocation to Madame de Montespan," he writes to Maréchal de Bellefonds. "I said what was necessary, and made her understand, so far as I could, how wrong it would be to hinder her in her good intentions. There is no great objection to her retirement, but it seems that the idea of the Carmelites is alarming. She has done all she could to cover this resolution with ridicule. I trust that by-and-by a different feeling will prevail in regard to it."[3]

[1] Abbé Pauthe's *Madame de La Vallière. La morale de Bossuet à la Cour de Louis XIV.*

[2] Bossuet is also said to have assisted her in the composition of her famous *Réflexions sur la miséricorde de Dieu*, which she wrote on her recovery from the illness of which we have spoken.

[3] Letter of December 25, 1673.

To the exhortations of the good bishop Madame de Montespan responded by despatching Madame Scarron and her prudent counsels to the penitent. The *gouvernante* did everything in her power to induce La Vallière to abandon her intention of taking the veil, and suggested that she should enter the convent as a benefactress until she had assured herself that her strength would be equal to observing its regulations. Thus she could serve God in peace and quiet without taking any step which she might hereafter have cause to regret. Madame Scarron might have added that, as such a proceeding was common enough, it would cast no reflection upon La Vallière's successor in the royal favour.

The duchess curtly replied that what was proposed would not be penance at all, since it would involve nothing more trying than a separation from her friends ; and when Madame Scarron proceeded to enlarge upon the hardships and privations which were imposed upon the regular members of the Carmelite community, answered that for some months past she had been sleeping on the bare ground, wearing sackcloth, and habituating herself to all the austere practices of the nuns in the Rue Saint-Jacques. Many years afterwards, Madame Scarron, then Marquise de Maintenon, instanced the replies of La Vallière on this occasion as an edifying example of the effects of grace. Whether she appreciated the sincerity of the duchess's conversion so well at the time is very doubtful. It is more than possible that she shared the opinion of the majority of the Court ladies, voiced by Madame de Sévigné in a letter to her daughter : " Madame de La Vallière talks no more about retiring ; it is enough to have announced her intention. Her waiting-woman threw herself at her feet to dissuade her from doing so.

MADAME DE MONTESPAN

Could she resist such an appeal ? "[1] Almost at the same time the same writer was exalting the piety of Madame de Montespan's sister, Madame de Thianges, " who had left off rouge,[2] covered her neck, and was the very pink of modish devotion."[3]

At length the persistence of La Vallière and the representations of Bossuet triumphed ; Madame de Montespan withdrew her objections ; the King gave a reluctant consent, and the duchess set about her preparations for departure. " I send you a letter from the Duchesse de La Vallière," writes Bossuet to Belle-fonds, " which will show you that, by the grace of God, she is going to carry out the intentions that the Holy Spirit has implanted in her heart. The whole Court is edified and astonished at her tranquillity and cheerfulness, which increases as the time draws nearer. Indeed, there is something so heavenly in her mind that I cannot think of it without a continual thanks-giving. The strength and humility which accompany all her thoughts are surely the mark of the Finger of God, the work of the Holy Spirit. Her affairs have been arranged with a wonderful ease ; she breathes nothing save penitence, and without being alarmed at the austerity of the life which she is about to embrace, she looks forward to the end with a hope which causes her to forget the suffering. I am both delighted and dumbfounded by

[1] Madame de Sévigné *to* Madame de Grignan, December 15, 1673.

[2] This was the usual outward sign of devotion in those days. As soon as a lady had resolved to embrace religion, she publicly announced her intention by appearing with her natural complexion. No one ever doubted the sincerity of a person who was prepared to undergo so terrible a mortification.

[3] Madame de Sévigné *to* Madame de Grignan, January 5, 1674.

her conduct ! I talk and she acts ! The words are mine, the deeds are hers ! When I dwell upon these things, I enter into her longing for silence and retirement. I cannot utter a single word but what sounds like my own condemnation." [1]

April 21 was the day fixed for La Vallière's retirement to the Carmelites. The Court was then at Fontainebleau : that beautiful spot, which had been the scene of her fall, was to be the scene also of her final farewell of the world. On the 18th she timidly submitted to the King a list of pensions which she wished to bestow : two thousand *écus* to her mother, Madame de Saint-Rémi, two thousand livres to her married sister, Madame de Hautefeuille, and a hundred livres to each of her servants. She also gave some souvenirs—rings, bracelets, and so forth—to her personal friends ; the remainder of her jewellery she divided between her son and daughter.

Two days later the duchess began her farewell visits, "like a princess taking leave of a foreign Court." Etiquette, of course, demanded that she should bid adieu to the King; moreover, that the interview should be in public. It was a trying moment for both. Egotist though he was, Louis was deeply moved, and made no attempt to restrain his tears. The woman, however, showed herself stronger than the man. Fearing some useless return of tenderness, La Vallière made a profound reverence and retired.

From the King's apartments she proceeded to those or the Queen. She had resolved, in spite of the remonstrances of her friends, that as her sin had been public, her penance should be public too, and now, throwing herself at her Majesty's feet, she implored her forgiveness for the

[1] *Œuvres complètes*, xi. 19 ; Letter of April 6, 1674.

humiliations she had inflicted upon her and the wrong she had done her. And the good Queen, who had long since forgiven her, raised her up, and, embracing her, assured her once more of her pardon.

In the meanwhile, the touching nature of these adieux had begun to disquiet Madame de Montespan, who, accordingly, pounced upon the penitent ex-favourite, and, with many expressions of sympathy, carried her off to her own apartments, where, it is interesting to note, La Vallière partook of her last meal at the Court. The following morning the duchess was present at the King's mass, and Louis, as on the previous day, was unable to restrain his emotion ; indeed, an hour later the observant courtiers remarked that his Majesty's eyes were still red with weeping. On leaving the chapel, La Vallière entered a coach that was in waiting and set out for Paris. Her two children accompanied her, while some of her friends and relatives followed in another carriage. A great crowd had assembled to witness her departure, and the ex-favourite, who was attired in a ravishing toilette, bowed and smiled to all her acquaintances with as much unconcern as if she were bound upon some pleasure trip, instead of on her way to what those about her regarded as a living death.

At the gate of the Carmelites she was received by the prioress. " My mother," said the duchess to her, " I have made all my life such a bad use of my will that I am come to surrender it into your hands, once and for all." Desiring, as far as possible, to anticipate her vows, she then demanded, as a special favour, permission to at once assume the dress of a nun, and, her request having been granted, hastened to exchange the costly gown which she was wearing for the coarse robe of the convent. The same evening she cut off her hair. This essentially feminine sacrifice soon got noised abroad, and convinced even the sceptics that the world had seen the last of Louise de La Vallière.[1]

[1] Lair's *Louise de La Vallière et la jeunesse de Louis XIV.*, p. 291 *et seq.*

CHAPTER IX

Madame de Montespan " thunderous and triumphant "—Her
magnificence—Extraordinary consideration shown to her—
Infatuation of the King—Complaisance of Maria Theresa—
Madame de Montespan obtains the dismissal of the Queen's
maids of honour—The Queen compelled to ask favours of
Madame de Montespan—Madame de Montespan declines to
accept a present of jewellery from the King—Letter from
Louis XIV. to Colbert on this subject—The King builds the
Château of Clagny for Madame de Montespan—Madame de
Sévigné's description of its gardens—The cost of its con-
struction.

AND at Versailles, Fontainebleau, and Saint-Germain, La
Vallière's triumphant rival, her husband disarmed, her
children legitimated, stood forth in the full blaze of her
shameless glory.   No Court of modern times has surpassed
in splendour that of *le Grand Monarque ;* no favourite, not
excepting even Madame de Pompadour, has excelled
Madame de Montespan in prodigal magnificence.   If
Louis XIV. denied his mistress political influence, he
denied her nothing else, and princely châteaux, gorgeous
equipages, costly jewellery, and resplendent toilettes made
their appearance at the first semblance of a wish as at the
wave of some magician's wand.   Madame de Sévigné has
described to us that wonderful robe of " gold upon gold,
with a double gold border, embroidered with one sort of
gold blended with another sort, which makes up the

divinest stuff ever invented by the wit of man."[1]   And
on another occasion she writes : " Madame de Montespan
was dressed entirely in *point de France ;* her hair arranged
in a thousand curls, the two from her temples hanging
very low upon her cheeks ; black ribbons on her head,
with the pearls of the Maréchale de l'Hôpital,[2] and, in
addition, diamond clasps and pendants of the greatest
beauty ; three or four jewelled pins ; no coif ; in a word,
a triumph of beauty that threw all the Ambassadors into
admiring wonder."   When she travelled, a number of the
royal guards were invariably told off to escort her.   She
passed through the provinces in a six-horse coach, followed
by another coach, also drawn by six horses, in which sat
her waiting-women, while a train of baggage-waggons,
sumpter-mules, and men-servants on horseback brought
up the rear.   When she entered a town, the municipal
authorities waited upon her to pay their respects, and
governors and intendants offered her their homage.   If
she had been Queen of France, she could not have been
treated with greater consideration.

The Queen, indeed, was relegated to quite a secondary
position.   Louis XIV. spent nearly the whole of his time
in Madame de Montespan's society, and even transacted
business with his Ministers in her apartments.   She and
her children generally dined with him in his cabinet, on

---

[1] It was the gift of an accomplished courtier, Langlée by name, a
great authority on matters of dress, jewellery, and furniture, and one of
the most successful gamesters of his day, and was sent to Madame de
Montespan anonymously.

[2] " Larger than those of the Queen," says Mademoiselle de
Montpensier.   Maréchale de l'Hôpital appears to have sold them to the
King.   She had offered them in 1659, in exchange for the post of
dame d'honneur to the future Queen.   Her offer was not accepted,
however, and the Duchesse de Navailles was appointed.

which occasions no one but the Dauphin and *Monsieur*
were allowed to enter, and he drove about with his mistress
seated by his side, while his unfortunate consort followed
in another carriage. When Versailles was finished, the
Queen was allotted eleven rooms on the second floor ;
Madame de Montespan twenty on the first. The Queen's
train was borne by a simple page ; Madame de Montespan's by a *pair de France*, the Duc de Noailles.[1]

Poor Maria Theresa, however, had long since recognised the utter futility of remonstrance and had found
consolation for the loss of her husband's affection in
devotional exercises and works of charity. So resigned
did she eventually become that when one of her ladies
happened to report that the King was casting tender glances
at some new beauty, she would shrug her shoulders and
remark, " That is Madame de Montespan's affair."

It was fortunate for her that she had succeeded in
schooling herself to complaisance, for it had already

[1] Anne Jules de Noailles (1650–1708), at this time aide-de-camp to
the King. According to Mellot (*Mémoires politiques et militaires*), he
saved Louis's life at the siege of Valenciennes in 1674. The King was
standing in a place much exposed to the fire from the town, and Noailles
besought him to move out of danger. Louis reluctantly consented, and
scarcely had he done so, when a cannon-shot struck the very spot on
which he had stood. In May 1689 Noailles was appointed Governor
of Languedoc, with orders to extirpate Protestantism, and earned
unenviable notoriety by his persecution of the unfortunate Calvinists.
He was made *maréchal de France* in 1693, and served with considerable
distinction in Spain. Saint-Simon represents the duke in an odious
light ; while that arch-calumniator the Princess Palatine accuses him
of being the father of Madame de Montespan's youngest daughter,
Mademoiselle de Blois. His wife (*née* Marie Françoise de Bournonville),
by whom he had no less than twenty-one children, was a very clever
and charming woman, and one of Madame de Montespan's most intimate
friends.

become apparent that the favourite had it in her power to make things exceedingly unpleasant for the first lady in the land. On her marriage, Maria Theresa had been given twelve maids of honour, and this arrangement continued until 1673, when Madame de Montespan came to the conclusion that to allow so many charming young ladies about the Queen was to throw temptation in the King's way, and, accordingly, induced his Majesty to make the misconduct of one of the damsels an excuse for dismissing them *en bloc* and supplying their places with twelve *dames du palais*, whom the marchioness, we may presume, took care should be as elderly and unprepossessing as possible.

On another occasion, a Spanish lady in the Queen's service had the misfortune to offend the haughty sultana, and the latter having complained to the King, Louis gave orders for the delinquent to be sent away. Maria Theresa, however, addressed herself to her rival and implored her, as a personal favour, to intercede with his Majesty and obtain permission for the lady to remain, a request to which the marchioness was graciously pleased to accede. "The Queen is overjoyed," writes Madame de Sévigné, "and declares that she will never forget the obligation under which Madame de Montespan has placed her."

A letter from Louis XIV. to Colbert, who served as the medium for the King's correspondence with his mistress during his absence with the army, will convey some idea of the lengths to which the monarch's infatuation carried him. Shortly before setting out for the campaign of 1674, Louis had offered to make Madame de Montespan a present of some magnificent jewellery which had come into the market ; but the lady had replied that she could not think of accepting so costly a gift. His Majesty,

charmed by her self-denial, determined that she should not
be the loser thereby, and wrote to Colbert as follows :—

Louis XIV. *to* Colbert.

"Camp near Dôle,

"*June* 9.

"Madame de Montespan absolutely refuses to accept
the jewellery ; but, in order that she may not lose by that,
it is my wish that you have a little casket made, to contain
the articles which I am about to specify, so that I may
have something to lend her at any time that she may
require. This may appear extraordinary, but she is not
inclined to listen to reason at the present moment.

"The casket must contain a pearl necklace, and I wish
it to be of fine quality; two pairs of ear-rings, one of
diamonds, which must be fine ones, and one of other stones;
a case with diamond fastenings ; a case with fastenings
of different kinds of stones, which must be removable
two at a time. I require stones of different colours, so
as to allow of them being changed. I shall also want a
pair of pearl ear-rings.

"You must also procure four dozen studs, in which the
central stones must be removable, while the outer circle
must consist of small diamonds. You must have the
stones prepared accordingly.

"I tell you this in good time, in order that you may
have ample leisure to have it made, and that every care
may be taken to have everything as beautiful and perfect
as possible. I shall be able occasionally to make use of
this jewellery myself for another purpose, if it is properly
made, for this casket will always be at hand for me to take
from it anything that I may judge suitable.

"It will be necessary to go to some expense over this ;

but I am quite prepared for it, and it is my wish that
the work should not be done hurriedly. Send me word
what steps you are taking in the matter and when you are
likely to have everything ready." [1]

Madame de Montespan's reluctance, or pretended reluctance, to accept the present we have just spoken of was
no doubt prompted by the fact that his Majesty was about
to make her one of a different kind, beside which the
most costly specimens of the jeweller's art would have
appeared hardly worthy of notice. In the autumn of
1665, with the idea of enlarging the park surrounding
his father's little hunting-lodge, which was soon to be
transformed into the magnificent Château of Versailles,
Louis XIV. had purchased from the governors of the
Hospice des Incurables at Paris the estate of Clagny.
Here he built for Madame de Montespan a little pleasure-
house; but, when she was taken to see it, the lady
was dissatisfied, and contemptuously remarked that it
was only fit for an opera-girl. Thereupon, his Majesty
immediately gave orders for it to be pulled down, and
commissioned the famous architect Mansart to design a
splendid palace in its place. "Your son has transmitted
to me the plan for the house at Clagny," writes Louis to
Colbert, at the end of May 1774. "I have no answer to
send you at present, as I wish to ascertain what Madame
de Montespan thinks about it." A few days later, the
divinity having in the meanwhile condescended to approve
of Mansart's efforts, the King writes again : "I have
told your son to send you the plan for the house at
Clagny, and to inform you that, after having examined it
with Madame de Montespan, we both approve of it, and

[1] Quoted in Clément's *Madame de Montespan et Louis XIV.*, p. 221.

120

that it must be begun at once ; I believe that they have
already commenced building. Madame de Montespan is
most anxious that the garden should be planted this
autumn. Do everything that will be necessary to oblige
her in this matter, and let me know what steps you have
taken to do so."

Anything more beautiful than this château it would be
difficult to conceive. In shape it was somewhat similar to
that of Versailles, having two wings at right angles to the
main buildings, and, like Versailles, faced east and west.
On the ground-floor was a gallery, 210 feet long and
25 feet broad, adorned with pictures representing various
scenes in the Æneid, and groups in relief, and terminating,
on one side of the house, in a magnificent orangery paved
with marble, and, on the other, in a chapel, in the decoration
of which the most famous artists of the day had been
employed. The centre of the *rez-de-chaussée* was occupied
by a spacious salon surmounted by a dome, and the
grand staircase had been constructed on an entirely novel
plan.[1]

What, however, seems to have aroused the most admiration were the gardens, which Madame de Montespan had
been so anxious to have planted, and the laying-out of
which had been entrusted to Le Nôtre.[2] When Le Nôtre
received the commission, he represented to the King that

[1] Cimber and Danjou's *Archives curieuses de l'histoire de France; Vie
de J. B. Colbert*, vol. ix. p. 28. *Livre de tous les plans, profils, et éléva-
tions du Chasteau de Clagny*, par Jules Hardouin Mansart (Paris, 1680,
fol.). The British Museum possesses a copy of the latter work, a very
rare and valuable one.

[2] André Le Nôtre (1613–1670). He designed the majority of the
most beautiful gardens of his time, including those of Vaux-le-Vicomte
(the ill-fated Fouquet's château), Chantilly, Fontainebleau, Sceaux,
Saint-Cloud, Versailles, and the Tuileries. In 1775, Louis XIV.

the grounds of the château were not extensive enough to enable him to accomplish anything out of the common, so Louis acquired, at great expense, the adjoining estate of Glatigny, and this, when united to Clagny, gave the celebrated gardener full scope for his genius. Madame de Sévigné, who visited the château in August 1675, thus describes the result :—

"The gardens are finished. You are well acquainted with Le Nôtre's style. He has left a little shady wood remaining, which has an admirable effect, and has planted a grove of orange-trees, tall enough to afford some protection from the sun, in large tubs. It is divided into walks and alleys, bounded on both sides by palisades, all ablaze with tuberoses, roses, jessamine, and pinks. This flowery fence serves to conceal the tubs in which the orange-trees are planted, and thus gives one the impression that they are growing out of the ground ; and the appearance of a natural orange-grove in our climate is assuredly the most beautiful, the most surprising, the most enchanting novelty that can be imagined."[1]

All this magnificence was, of course, not obtained without vast expense. The accounts, which have fortunately been preserved, show that the estates of Clagny and Glatigny cost 405,502 livres, and the construction of the château and its dependencies, including the gardens, 2,456,218 livres, 7 sous, 8 deniers, which gives a total of

having ennobled him and given him the Cross of Saint-Michel, wished to give him a coat-of-arms as well. Le Nôtre replied that he had one already, and that it consisted of three snails surmounted by a cabbage-head. "Sire," added he, "can I forget my spade ? How dear ought it not to be to me, since it is to it that I am indebted for the favours with which your Majesty honours me !"

[1] Madame de Sévigné *to* Madame de Grignan, August 7, 1675.

2,861,728 livres, 7 sous, 8 deniers, or over half a million sterling in money of to-day.[1]

On Madame de Montespan's death, in May 1707, Clagny reverted to the Duc du Maine. From him it passed to his eldest son, the Prince de Dombes, and thence to the latter's brother, the Comte d'Eu, who sold it in 1766 to the Dauphiness Marie Josèphe. When, in the following year, the Dauphiness died, Louis XV. gave orders for it to be pulled down.

[1] Le Roi's *Histoire de Versailles,* i. 8.

CHAPTER X

Louis XIV. heaps favours upon Madame de Montespan's relatives and children—*La Grande Mademoiselle* and her suitors—The Comte de Lauzun—Anecdotes about him—He incurs the enmity of Madame de Montespan—*Mademoiselle* conceives a violent passion for him—And determines to marry him—An amusing courtship—Diplomacy of Lauzun —" *C'est vous !* "—Lauzun accepts *Mademoiselle's* offer of her hand—And induces her to make a donation in his favour of the bulk of her property—*Mademoiselle* writes to the King —The King's reply—Interview between *Mademoiselle* and Louis XIV.—The King gives his consent to the marriage— *Mademoiselle* and Lauzun announce their approaching union —Astonishment of the Court—Indignation of the Royal Family—Opposition of Louvois and other Ministers— Madame de Montespan uses her influence to stop the marriage—The King withdraws his sanction—A painful scene —Despair of *Mademoiselle*—Lauzun is arrested and sent to Pignerol—Probable reason for the King's harsh treatment of him—His rigorous imprisonment—*Mademoiselle* endeavours to procure his release—Pretended sympathy of Madame de Montespan—*Mademoiselle* offers to settle some of her wealth on the Duc du Maine in return for Lauzun's pardon—Interview with the King—Extravagant demands of Madame de Montespan—*Mademoiselle* compelled to acquiesce—Lauzun's consent required—Madame de Montespan and Lauzun meet at Bourbon—Lauzun obdurate—He is imprisoned at Chalon-sur-Saône—Second meeting between him and Madame de Montespan—He consents to her conditions and is liberated —But refused permission to return to Court.

As might be expected, the King's bounty was far from being confined to Madame de Montespan herself; honours and riches were showered upon her relatives and her children.   Her father, the Duc de Mortemart, was made governor of Paris; her brother, the Duc de Vivonne, general of the galleys, governor of Champagne, and *maréchal de France*;[1] one of her sisters, the Marquise de Thianges, was granted a pension of 9000 livres and a *gratification* of 6000 livres; another, Gabrielle de Roche-chouart, a nun of Poissy, who had only pronounced her vows four years before, was made abbess of Fontevrault, to the disgust of the nuns and "the astonishment and affliction of the Pope."[2]   As for the children, the Comte de Vexin was hardly out of the nursery before his royal father made him abbot of both Saint-Denis and Saint-

---

[1] He was one of the batch of marshals appointed in July 1675 after the death of Turenne—"the small change for Turenne," the witty Madame Cornuel called them.   His appointment, if we are to believe the following story, which the Abbé de Choisy relates in his *Mémoires*, was entirely due to the intervention of his sister : "The King had drawn up with Louvois the list of those whom he intended to honour with the bâton of *maréchal de France;* and, after doing so, went to visit Madame de Montespan, who, while rummaging in his pockets, came upon this list, and, not finding the name of M. de Vivonne, her brother, flew into a rage worthy of her.   The King, who could not, and dared not, oppose her to her face, stammered, and said that M. de Louvois must have forgotten to put it down.   'Send for him this moment!' cried she, in an imperious tone, and reprimanded him as he deserved.   Louvois was sent for, and the King having suggested to him very kindly that doubtless he had overlooked Vivonne, the Minister accepted the responsibility and acknowledged the error that he had not committed.   This time Vivonne was placed on the list ; the lady was appeased, and contented herself with reproaching Louvois for his negligence in a matter which touched her so closely."—*Mémoires de l' Abbé de Choisy* (edit. 1888), ii. 33.

[2] Three dispensations were required : the first, because she was not yet twenty-five ; the second, because she had not worn the veil for five years ; and the third, because she had changed her Order.

Germain-des-Prés, in spite of vigorous remonstrances from the Vatican, and even talked of giving him the Abbey of Cluny as well, though this establishment was the chief of its Order and its superior had always been an ecclesiastic; but the little count's early death prevented this scandal. His elder brother, the Duc du Maine, as an earnest of what he might expect when he arrived at man's estate, was appointed captain of the Hundred Swiss, colonel of a regiment which henceforth bore his name, and governor of Languedoc. Nor did his good fortune, even as a boy, by any means end there.

We have mentioned, in speaking of the birth of the little duke, a certain Comte de Lauzun, who took charge of the child immediately he was born and carried him off in a coach to Paris. By a singular coincidence, it was to the misfortunes of this same nobleman that the Duc du Maine was indebted for the fact that before he was twelve years old he found himself the possessor of immense wealth.

Mademoiselle de Montpensier, *la Grande Mademoiselle*, was at this time the richest heiress in Europe; indeed, as her mother, Marie de Bourbon, heiress of the House of Montpensier, had died in giving her birth, she may be said to have had the rôle of *demoiselle à marier* from infancy. Seldom has any lady had so many suitors of exalted rank. The Emperor Ferdinand III., Philip IV. King of Spain, Alfonso VI. of Portugal, Charles II. of England (then, however, a king without a kingdom),[1] *Monsieur*, Louis XIV.'s brother, the Dukes of Savoy, Lorraine, and

[1] Charles II. was very anxious indeed to get possession of Mademoiselle's wealth, in order to aid him in recovering his crown, and even promised "to sacrifice his conscience and his salvation for her"; in other words, embrace the Roman Catholic faith. The princess, however, had no mind to risk her fortune in what she considered a hopeless struggle,

Neuburg,[1] and the Comte de Soissons, prince of the blood, were all, at one time or another, pretenders to her hand; while it is quite possible that, but for the prominent part taken by her father and herself in the wars of the Fronde, she might have had the chance of becoming Queen of France.[2] *Mademoiselle*, however, seems to have been impervious to them all, with the exception of the Emperor, whose proposals she was not allowed to entertain, as they did not happen to accord with the views of the wily

and, in spite of the exhortations of the devout Duchesse d'Aiguillon, "who pressed her terribly to marry Charles if he would become a Catholic, saying that she would be responsible to God for the salvation of his soul," sent him about his business.

[1] In 1653 the Duke of Neuburg sent his Jesuit confessor to *Mademoiselle* with proposals of marriage. The Jesuit showed the princess a portrait of the duke, saying, "He is the best man in the world ; you will be extremely happy with him. His first wife, who was a sister of the King of Portugal, died of joy on his return from a voyage." However, the duke's offer was declined.

[2] In the spring of 1652 her father sent her to relieve Orléans. She entered the town clad in complete armour, like a second Jeanne d'Arc, and compelled the Royalists to raise the siege. She afterwards took an active share in the defence of Paris ; and while the Battle of the Faubourg Saint-Antoine was in progress, threw herself into the Bastille and turned the cannon of the fortress on the King's troops, thereby forcing them to retire, and saving the beaten army of Condé from annihilation. When Mazarin, who with the Queen-Mother and the young King was watching the fighting from a place of safety, saw the first gun discharged, he exclaimed : "*Voilà un coup de canon qui a tué un mari!*" meaning that by that act *Mademoiselle* had effectually destroyed all chance she might have possessed of marrying Louis XIV. Two days later, the Princess exhibited great courage and humanity in saving Lefèvre, the provost of the merchants, and other Royalists from the fury of the mob, which, exasperated by Condé's defeat, would otherwise have massacred them in cold blood. In fact, throughout the war *Mademoiselle* played a very heroic, if at times a slightly burlesque, part.

MADAME DE MONTESPAN

Mazarin; and she was approaching her fortieth year, still unwed, and, to all appearance, likely to remain so, when she fell violently in love with the Comte de Lauzun, a man many years younger than herself.

A cadet of a noble, but impoverished, Gascon family, Lauzun, who, as his father was still alive, was then known as the Marquis de Puyguilhem, had come to Court about 1658, where he quickly succeeded in insinuating himself into the good graces of Louis XIV., who gave him a regiment of cavalry, and soon afterwards raised him to the rank of general and created for him the post of colonel-general of dragoons. La Fare says of Lauzun that he was "the most impudent little man that had been seen for a century," [1] and certainly the stories related about him go far to bear out this dictum. Take the following, for example :—

[1] *Mémoires du Marquis de la Fare* (edit. 1884), p. 94. Saint-Simon has left us an interesting portrait of Lauzun, which certainly does not depict him in a very favourable light : "A small, fairish man, well made in figure, haughty in countenance, which was full of intelligence and imposing, though the face was not agreeable in youth, as I have been told by his contemporaries ; full of ambition, caprices, and oddities ; jealous of every one ; always anxious to get beyond the goal ; content with nothing ; unlettered, without any adornment or charm of mind ; naturally quick to take offence, solitary, morose ; a perfect noble in all his habits ; malicious and malignant by nature even more than from jealousy or ambition ; an excellent friend, when he was a friend, which was rare, and a good relation ; a ready enemy, even to those who did not interfere with him ; cruel to defects and in discovering cause for and applying ridicule ; extremely brave and at the same time dangerously rash ; a courtier equally insolent, sarcastic, and base to servility ; a master of all the resources of industry, intrigue, and villainy to attain his ends ; and, in addition to all this, dangerous to the Ministers, feared by every one, and full of cruel shafts of wit, which spared no one."—*Mémoires du Duc de Saint-Simon* (edit. 1881), xx. 39.

MADAME DE MONTESPAN

Lauzun was enamoured of the Princesse de Monaco,[1] whose heart he fondly imagined was his, and his alone, when one fine day it came to his knowledge that the lady was carrying on an intrigue with Louis XIV., and that, that very evening, Bontemps, the King's confidential *valet-de-chambre*, was to conduct her muffled in a cloak, so as to avoid recognition, by way of a private staircase, to a door which communicated with his Majesty's apartments. Lauzun, who was of a very jealous nature, was highly indignant at his mistress's perfidy, and forthwith determined to see whether he could not devise some plan to thwart her intentions. Accordingly, he made a reconnaissance, which resulted in the discovery that almost immediately opposite the door by which the princess was to be admitted there was a large cupboard, used by the servants to keep their brushes, brooms, and so forth, through the keyhole of which it was possible to command a view of all who came in or went out. Here, some little time before the hour appointed for the rendezvous, he concealed himself, and, with his eye glued to the keyhole,

---

[1] Catherine Charlotte de Gramont, sister of the celebrated Philibert de Gramont, and wife of Louis I., Prince de Monaco. Leaving her consort to the enjoyment of his miniature sovereignty, she lived a gay life at the French Court, where she was renowned for the rapid succession of her lovers, every one of whom was regularly hung in effigy by the prince in the avenue leading to his palace at Monaco, with a label round his neck for the information of passers-by. The number became so great that strangers flocked from far and near to admire the spectacle, and at length Louis XIV. felt constrained to interfere. He ordered the prince to remove the effigies ; but the latter turned a deaf ear to his suzerain's commands and continued to add to his collection, until Louis, finding that his threats were vain and the scandal on the increase, had recourse to conciliatory methods, and promised that a strict guard should be kept over the princess, upon which understanding his Highness consented to do as he was required.

awaited developments. After he had been on the watch
for a few minutes, his patience was rewarded by seeing
the King come out, put a key in the door, and go back
again. No sooner had he disappeared, than Lauzun
emerged from his hiding-place, double-locked the door,
put the key in his pocket, and retreated to the shelter of
his friendly cupboard. In due course, Bontemps and the
lady arrived, and the former was much puzzled on finding
that the key was not in the door according to arrangement. He began to look about, to see if by any chance
it had been placed elsewhere, but, failing to discover it,
knocked, at first very gently, then louder, and presently
the King came to the door. Bontemps asked him to let
them in, as the key was not in the lock. Louis replied
that he had himself put it there only a few minutes before,
and essayed to open the door, which, however, resisted
his efforts. His Majesty was furious and was for breaking
it open, but desisted on reflecting that the noise would
inevitably bring other people to the spot and thus compromise the princess. Eventually, he and Madame de
Monaco "had to say good-night to one another from
opposite sides of the door," to their intense mortification
and the huge delight of Lauzun, who had, of course, been
an unseen witness of the whole of the little comedy.[1]

Another of Lauzun's exploits, of which Madame de
Montespan herself was the victim, was characterised by
even greater audacity, but was, unfortunately for him,
destined to be followed by very serious consequences.

Not long after the marchioness became Louis XIV.'s
mistress, Lauzun had begged her to use her influence with
the King to obtain for him the post of Grand Master of
the Artillery—an appointment which the monarch had

[1] *Mémoires de Saint Simon* (edit. 1881), xix. 175.

already promised him, but which he had not yet confirmed, as Lauzun had foolishly broken the pledge of secrecy under which it had been given—and this the lady had promised to do. Being somewhat doubtful of her sincerity, however, he persuaded one of her *femmes-de-chambre*, who was in love with him, to conceal him in the favourite's apartments, in a place where he could overhear every word that passed between Madame de Montespan and the King. "A cough, the slightest movement," says Saint-Simon, "would have been sufficient to betray this rash person, and then what would have happened?" But his lucky star was in the ascendant, and he was enabled to learn all he wanted to know, and subsequently to effect his escape undetected, having had a very practical demonstration of the truth of the old proverb which warns us that listeners never hear any good of themselves.

Enraged beyond measure at the duplicity of the woman whom he had imagined to be his friend, Lauzun took the first opportunity of inquiring of her, "with an engaging smile and a profound reverence," if he might flatter himself that she had condescended to remember her promise to plead his cause with the King. The favourite assured him that she had kept her word, and actually had the effrontery to tell him the arguments she had advanced to insure success. Thereupon, Lauzun entirely lost his temper and, seizing her by the wrist, repeated to her word for word the conversation she had had with the monarch, and wound up by overwhelming her with taunts and reproaches.

Madame de Montespan was so overcome with astonishment and dismay that she was unable to utter a single word in reply, and had no sooner reached the Queen's apartments, whither she was bound when met by Lauzun, and where Louis XIV. was awaiting her, than she fainted away, to the great consternation of his Majesty. When she came to herself, she related to her royal lover all that had passed, and expressed her firm conviction that Lauzun must be in league with the Evil One, since in no other way could he possibly have obtained such an accurate account of the conversation they had had about him. The haughty favourite never forgave Lauzun for his insulting conduct towards her on this occasion,[1] and the events which we are about to relate provided her with an opportunity of gratifying her malice to the full.

Mademoiselle appears to have cast a favourable eye

[1] Lauzun's imprisonment in the Bastille, to which he was sent a few days later, was as a punishment for his insolence to the King, and not to Madame de Montespan, as some writers state. Saint-Simon says : "When Puyguilhem (the title which he then bore) found that he was not to have the Artillery, the relations between him and the King became very strained. This could only last a few days. Puyguilhem, having the *grande entrée* (the right of entering the King's private apartments at the same hours as the First Gentlemen of the Bedchamber and the high Court officials), watched for a *tête-à-tête* with the King, and summoned him audaciously to keep his promise. The King replied that he no longer felt called upon to do so, since he had only given him the promise under the pledge of secrecy, and that pledge he had failed to keep. Thereupon Puyguilhem walked away a few steps, turned his back on the King, drew his sword, broke the blade with his foot, and shouted furiously that he would never again serve a prince who had so shamefully broken his word. The King, in a transport of rage, did perhaps at this moment the finest action of his life. He turned instantly, opened the window, and flung out his cane, remarking that he should be sorry to strike a man of quality, and left the room. The next day Puyguilhem, who had not dared to show himself in the meantime, was arrested and taken to the Bastille."—*Mémoires du Duc de Saint-Simon* (edit. 1881), xix. 173.

Lauzun's imprisonment was a very brief one, and, through the intercession of his friend, the Marquis de Guitry, he was not only restored to favour, but made captain of the King's bodyguard.

upon Lauzun as early as the year 1660, when, in referring
to Madame de Monaco's (then Mademoiselle de Gramont)
tendresse for the Count, she writes that " other people had
the same taste—perhaps too many for the welfare of the
personage in question " ; but it was not until some years
later that she became " convinced that he was the only
man capable of sustaining the dignity of the position
which her rank and fortune could confer—the only person,
in short, worthy of her choice."

The details of the courtship, as related by *Mademoiselle*
in her entertaining *Mémoires*, are intensely amusing.
Lauzun, though of course overjoyed at his extraordinary
good fortune, was far too shrewd to allow the princess to
suspect his real feelings. At first, he affected to believe
that her interest in him was such as a sovereign might
take in a subject, and invariably treated her " with a
respect so submissive that he would never even approach
her unless she had taken the precaution to make the first
advances." This was very gratifying to *Mademoiselle's*
vanity, for, though a virtuous and kind-hearted woman,
she had an overweaning idea of her own importance, and
her predilection for the count's society began to excite
remark. Then, when it was no longer possible for him to
pretend to misunderstand her, Lauzun assumed the airs of
the pensive, melancholy bachelor, who was as yet a complete stranger to the tender passion, and played the part
so adroitly that the lady became more infatuated than ever.
She tells us how, on one occasion, she rose at daybreak,
in order to watch her gallant ride past her windows at
the head of his regiment ; how, on another, at a review,
when Lauzun, hat in hand, was addressing the King, she
implored his Majesty to request the count to cover himself, as, the weather being damp, she was fearful lest he

should take cold ; and how, on a third, she held him in conversation for the space of five hours.

At length, she confided in him that she was desirous of bestowing her hand upon one whom she fondly loved, and whom she had every reason to believe reciprocated her passion, but whose "elevation of soul" was his only qualification for so great an honour. Would he advise her to brave the disapproval of the world and follow the dictates of her heart, or wed where she could not give her affection ? Modesty, she added, forbade her to tell him the name of her beloved, but she would write it upon a sheet of paper, leaving a blank space at the bottom for his reply, and enclose it in an envelope, which she would hand him in the course of the evening. When Lauzun opened the letter, the words " *C'est vous* " met his eye.

Of course the cunning adventurer protested that he was overwhelmed by the honour which the princess proposed to do him, painted in glowing terms his own unworthiness, hinted at the possible displeasure of the King, whose regard, he assured her, no consideration on earth could induce him to forfeit, the opposition of the Royal Family, and so forth ; all of which objections, as he foresaw, only served to confirm *Mademoiselle* in her resolution, for she was one of the most obstinate women who ever breathed, and eventually he consented to become her husband. If he had behaved with becoming diffidence during the courtship, he showed himself wonderfully wideawake to his own interests as soon as the matter was settled, and not only persuaded the infatuated princess to promise to obtain for him the title of Duc de Montpensier, but to make a donation in his favour of the bulk of her immense estates, including the principality of Dombes and the county of Eu.

MADAME DE MONTESPAN

But before the marriage could take place, the King's sanction was required. *Mademoiselle* had not the hardihood to seek a personal interview with her cousin, but wrote him instead a long letter, requesting permission to wed her Lauzun. His Majesty returned a very gracious, if somewhat evasive, answer, assuring her of his affection and of his unwillingness to stand in the way of her happiness, but begging her to think well over the matter, and to do nothing in haste. A few days later, *Mademoiselle*, encouraged apparently by the "gracious air" with which the King had regarded her and her lover when he happened to observe them conversing at the Tuileries, laid wait for Louis as he was retiring to rest, and urged her demand with so much warmth and eloquence that the King gave his consent, advising her at the same time " to keep her project a secret till the moment of its execution."

Now if *Mademoiselle* and Lauzun had been sensible enough to follow this advice, all would have been well; for had the marriage once taken place, nothing short of a Papal decree could have set it aside. But alas! "the princess being intoxicated with love, and the count with vanity,"[1] they not only decided to proclaim their approaching union to the world, but to defer its consummation until arrangements could be made to celebrate it with becoming pomp and magnificence.

This publicity and delay ruined everything. The announcement that "*Mademoiselle—la Grande Mademoiselle — Mademoiselle*, daughter of the late *Monsieur—Mademoiselle*, grand-daughter of Henri IV.—Mademoiselle d'Eu—Mademoiselle de Dombes—Mademoiselle de Montpensier—*Mademoiselle*, cousin-german to the King —*Mademoiselle*, the only match thought worthy of

[1] *Mémoires du Marquis de La Fare*, p. 96.

135

Monsieur," [1] was about to bestow her hand upon a simple gentleman, caused the most unbounded astonishment at Court, where, as Sismondi observes, the conquest of a province or the downfall of a monarchy would have caused less sensation. The Royal Family were furiously indignant at the idea of such a *mésalliance*. *Monsieur*, whose hand *Mademoiselle* had recently rejected, remonstrated with the King in the strongest terms, and declared that to allow such a marriage to take place in the Louvre, a privilege which the lovers had requested, would be to dishonour the memory of Henri IV. The Prince de Condé announced his intention of attending the ceremony —in order to blow out the bridegroom's brains as he left the church. Even the Queen, who seldom interfered in matters which did not immediately concern herself, added her voice to the general clamour of disapproval, and, according to *Mademoiselle*, spent the whole of one night dissolved in tears. Louvois, too, Lauzun's most bitter enemy, was active in the same direction, and, in company with several Ministers and noblemen, waited upon the King, and represented to him that the proposed marriage could not fail to be most injurious to his reputation, not only in France but in foreign countries as well, since every one would believe that he did not hesitate to sacrifice his nearest relatives to make the fortunes of his favourites. Finally, Madame de Montespan, eager to avenge the affront of which mention has already been made, and persuaded, it is said, by Madame de Maintenon, whose interests at this time marched with her employer's, that, supported by the immense wealth of *Mademoiselle*, Lauzun's influence might clash with her own, threw her weight into the opposition scale, and thus disposed of any lingering

[1] Madame de Sévigné *to* Madame de Grignan, Dec. 15, 1670.

scruples that Louis might have entertained about retracting the promise he had given to his cousin.

The result was that on December 18, 1670, two days before the date fixed for the ceremony, a messenger was despatched to the Luxembourg—where he found the bride-elect superintending the preparation of her future husband's apartments—with a request that she would repair at once to the Tuileries. When she arrived, the King informed her that he was inconsolable at what he felt compelled to announce to her, but that public opinion was accusing him of sacrificing his cousin to the interests of his favourite ; that such a report would injure his reputation at Foreign Courts, and that, therefore, he could not allow the affair to proceed.

Poor *Mademoiselle*, bathed in tears, threw herself at the King's feet, declared that, if he persisted in depriving her of her Lauzun, she asked nothing better than to be allowed to die there upon the spot, and used every argument she could think of to induce him to relent. But, though his Majesty was so touched by her grief that he, too, went down upon his knees, and remained in that position for three-quarters of an hour, mingling his tears with hers, he was obdurate.

When the unhappy lady at length realised that nothing would shake the King's resolution, and that her lover was indeed lost to her, her agony of mind was pitiable to behold, and found vent in "tears, cries, lamentations, and the most violent expressions of grief."[1]   Her distress,

---

[1] Letter of Madame de Sévigné *to* Madame de Grignan, December 20, 1670. The Abbé de Choisy relates that he was at the Luxembourg when *Mademoiselle* returned from her interview with the King, and that she came in "looking like a Fury, with dishevelled hair, and menacing heaven and earth with her fists." On the way thither, she had, in her rage, broken the windows of her coach.

however, if we are to believe the testimony of that rather malicious chronicler, Madame de Caylus, would appear not to have been without its humorous side. "She took to her bed," says the writer in question, "and received visitors like a disconsolate widow, and I have heard Madame de Maintenon relate that she kept crying out in her despair, ' He should be there ! He should be there ! ' that is to say, ' he should be in my bed,' for she pointed to the vacant place." [1]

But, alas for *Mademoiselle*, a worse trial was in store for her! In the following November, Lauzun was suddenly arrested and conveyed to the Bastille, and thence to Pignerol, where he was kept a close prisoner for ten years, without any reason whatever being assigned for his detention.

This affair caused all the more astonishment at Court as, since the rupture of his marriage, Louis XIV., as if anxious to compensate the count for his disappointment, had loaded him with favours. Voltaire ascribes the arrest to the fact that the King had discovered that a secret marriage had taken place between him and *Mademoiselle;* but this cannot have been the cause, for even if there was such a marriage, of which no satisfactory proof exists, it could not have been celebrated until after Lauzun's release, as when that event took place, *Mademoiselle* was urging the King to withdraw his prohibition. The reason given by Saint-Simon and La Fare appears far more probable.

Both of these writers attribute it to a *rapprochement* between Louvois and Madame de Montespan, the former of whom had long been bitterly jealous of Lauzun on account of his favour with his sovereign and his popularity

[1] *Souvenirs et Correspondance de Madame de Caylus* (edit. 1889), p. 79.

with the army ; while the latter had far from satisfied the grudge she bore the count by the share she had taken in preventing his marriage, and had lately become still further incensed against him owing to some very indiscreet language he had used about her in the presence of her royal lover. "Together," says Saint-Simon, "they managed to arouse the King to a remembrance of the broken sword and the insolence of having so soon afterwards, and while still in the Bastille, refused for several days the post of captain of the bodyguard ; they made him consider Lauzun as a man who was beside himself, and had inveigled *Mademoiselle* till he was almost on the point of marrying her and securing her immense fortune ; in short, as a very dangerous person, on account of his audacity, and one who had taken into his head to gain the devotion of the troops by his magnificence, by his services to the officers,[1] and by the manner in which he lived with them while in Flanders, which caused them to adore him. They made it a crime on his part to remain on terms of friendly intimacy with the Comtesse de Soissons, who had been driven from Court and suspected of criminal offences. They probably laid other things to his charge of which I never heard,[2] judging from the barbarous treatment that they finally succeeded in meting out to him."[3]

Saint-Mars, the governor of Pignerol, a creature of Louvois,[4] caused to be prepared for the unfortunate count's reception a gloomy dungeon, above the door of which the

[1] *Mademoiselle* tells us that Lauzun was in the habit of distributing money among the poorer officers, saying that it came from the King.

[2] La Fare says that Madame de Montespan assured the King that she went in fear of her life so long as Lauzun was at liberty.

[3] *Mémoires du Duc de Saint-Simon* (edit. 1881), xix. 177.

[4] This Saint-Mars was afterwards made governor of the Bastille, and held that office from 1698 to 1708.

prisoner is said to have traced the well-known verse from
Dante :—

"Lasciate ogni speranza voi ch'intrate."

Here, without books or writing materials, or indeed any
means of alleviating the monotony of his life, Lauzun had
ample leisure for reflecting upon his past indiscretions.   In
response to his complaints, Louvois wrote that he had
given orders that he was to be treated " with all the respect
due to his birth and rank."   But, notwithstanding this
assurance, the rigour of his imprisonment does not appear
to have been mitigated ; and when, on one occasion, permission was granted to his brother and sister to visit him
for the purpose of discussing some urgent family affairs,
we find the War Minister sending instructions to the
governor that they were not to be allowed to give him
any writing-paper, to converse with him in a low tone, or
to speak of any matters unconnected with the business in
hand—" and, above all, not of Mademoiselle de Montpensier "—on any pretence whatever.[1]

As may readily be imagined, *Mademoiselle* was inconsolable for the long and harsh imprisonment of her lover,
and made every possible effort to deliver him.   She used
to go very frequently to see Madame de Montespan—of
whose responsibility for Lauzun's misfortunes she does
not, strange to say, seem to have entertained any suspicion
—and pour her woes into her ear, declaring that there was
no sacrifice she was not prepared to make in order to
procure his release ; and, eventually, the favourite decided
to endeavour to turn the poor lady's devotion to the

[1] Delort's *Histoire de la détention des philosophes et des gens de lettres,
précédée de celle de Fouquet, de Pellisson, et de Lauzun,* i. *passim.*   Clément's
Madame de Montespan et Louis XIV., p. 35 *et seq.*

profit of her eldest son, the Duc du Maine. Accordingly, she affected great sympathy and would often observe, " Think of everything you can do to please the King, that he may grant you what you have so much at heart." *Mademoiselle* repeated this to some of Lauzun's friends, who were of opinion that the best way to please the King or Madame de Montespan—which was, of course, much the same thing—was to lead them to suppose that she would be willing to settle some of her wealth on the Duc du Maine.

After some further discussion, one of the party, named Baraille, was deputed to go to Madame de Montespan with a proposal to that effect from *Mademoiselle*, and met with a very encouraging reception. The next day, the princess herself visited the marchioness, who thanked her warmly, and assured her that her interests were dearer to her than her own, but advised her not to say anything about Lauzun to the King, " until they had adopted those measures which might lead to the accomplishment of her wishes." " I must," she added, " explain to the King the views you entertain for M. du Maine, and your desire to please his Majesty. Thus you will be united more closely to him without saying a word about M. de Lauzun. He may perhaps be as desirous of setting him free as you yourself are, but you know how many people dislike and fear him. They are always on the alert to speak ill of him the moment they perceive that the King displays the slightest compassion for him. But, as soon as he can say, ' My cousin has proposed these measures ; I can refuse her nothing,' you will be able to arrange matters with him, and no one will know that M. de Lauzun is at liberty until the order for his release is sent."

The princess willingly agreed that Madame de Montespan

should inform the King of her intentions with regard to the little duke, which she, accordingly, did the following evening at the Queen's ; whereupon his Majesty, who seemed highly pleased, as well he might be, took *Mademoiselle* aside, expressed his conviction that her affection for him could alone have dictated the generous offer of which the marchioness had just informed him, said a great many other amiable things, and concluded by assuring her that he should neglect no opportunity of showing her marks of his friendship.

Madame de Montespan was, of course, delighted at the step which *Mademoiselle* had taken, and determined to lose no time in inducing her to take a still more decided one. She, therefore, proposed that the princess should make a deed of gift of the principality of Dombes, the county of Eu, and the duchy of Aumale in favour of her son. The cool insolence of such a proposition will be understood when we mention that the revenues of Dombes and Eu alone were estimated at upwards of 200,000 livres ; that *Mademoiselle* had settled all three properties on Lauzun, together with the duchy of Saint-Fargeau and the beautiful estate of Thiers in Auvergne, at the time of their proposed marriage, and that it would be necessary to get him to renounce them before she would be able to dispose of them in favour of the Duc du Maine. The princess felt that she could not bring herself to comply with such a demand, and, therefore, replied that Madame de Montespan had misunderstood her ; that she had never had the least intention of making a conveyance of any of her estates to the little duke, but only of appointing him her heir. To which the favourite curtly rejoined that it was the King's pleasure that the matter should be arranged in the manner which she (Madame de Montespan) had indicated.

MADAME DE MONTESPAN

After a good deal of haggling, *Mademoiselle* was informed that, unless she could see her way to do what was required of her, the consequences might be exceedingly unpleasant, and the Bastille was hinted at. Alarmed by these threats, and convinced that the King would never consent to her lover's release on any other terms, she finally yielded.

For the validity of the affair, as we have already said, Lauzun's renunciation of the gifts of *Mademoiselle* was necessary; and, accordingly, in the spring of 1681, it was given out that his health had broken down, and that his physicians had prescribed for him a course of the waters of Bourbon. Thither he was conducted under a strong escort, and was met by Madame de Montespan, who had made the journey under a similar pretext. The marchioness offered him his liberty in return for his signature to a contract of renunciation ; but Lauzun indignantly refused, and was once more incarcerated, this time in the Château of Chalon-sur-Saône.

In September of the same year, Madame de Montespan again visited Bourbon, where she lost her little daughter, Mademoiselle de Tours. The favourite and Lauzun had a second interview ; and this time the unfortunate count, whose sojourn in his new prison had doubtless been made as unpleasant as possible, with the view of bringing him to reason, expressed his willingness to do as she desired.

Mademoiselle appears to have been given to understand that, in return for the sacrifice she was making, Lauzun would be permitted to return to Court, and that the King would, in all probability, waive his objection to their marriage. But once they had obtained what they wanted, Madame de Montespan and Louis troubled themselves very little about their part of the bargain, and the latter not only refused to hear of a marriage, but directed that Lauzun was to be given the choice of residing in one of four towns—Nevers, Amboise, Tours, and Bourges—and to remain within its walls during his Majesty's pleasure. It was not until two years later that *Mademoiselle* succeeded in obtaining permission for him to return to Paris, on condition that he would pass his word not to approach the Court. He was eventually, however, restored to favour, in recognition of her services to the English Royal Family at the Revolution of 1688, and made duke and *pair de France*. La Bruyère said of Lauzun that no man ever dreamed as he lived, so extraordinary was his career.

CHAPTER XI

ON June 4, 1675, a crowd of distinguished people invaded
the little church of the Carmelites of the Rue Saint-

Jacques. Among them might have been seen the Queen ; *Monsieur*, the King's brother ; his second wife, the out-spoken Princess Palatine ; the future Queen of Spain, his daughter by the ill-fated Henrietta of England, destined like her mother to a sudden and mysterious end ; the beautiful Duchesse de Longueville, herself a penitent these twenty years past ; Mademoiselle de Montpensier, and Madame de Scudéry. They had come, drawn thither either by sympathy or curiosity, to witness the final act in the long tragedy of Louise de La Vallière—the taking of the veil. The ex-favourite's novitiate had expired two days before, and the following evening she had pronounced her vows in the chapter-house of the convent, taking the name of Sœur Louise de la Miséricorde.

The ceremony began ; mass was said by the chaplain of the Carmelites, the Abbé Pirot ; and then Bossuet entered the pulpit and preached an eloquent and moving sermon from the text, " *Et dixit qui sedebat in throno : 'Ecce nova facio omnia'* " ("And He who sat upon the throne said : 'Behold, I make all things new' ").[1]

" Madame," he began, addressing the Queen, " it will be without doubt a grand spectacle when He who sitteth upon the throne whence the universe is ruled—He who can do as readily as He saith, inasmuch as by the Word of His Mouth He can do all things—when He shall from the height of His throne, at the end of the world, make known that He reneweth everything, and when, at the same time, we behold all nature changed into a new world for God's elect. But when, in order to prepare us for these marvellous changes to come, He works secretly in the hearts of men by His Holy Spirit, changing, re-newing, moving them to their very depths, filling them

---

[1] *Apocalypse*, ch. xxi., v. 5.

with aspirations hitherto unknown, such a change is no
less wonderful, no less astonishing. And truly, Christians,
there can be nothing more marvellous than these changes
we behold. What have we seen, and what do we see?
What formerly, and what now?   There is no need for me
to dwell upon them ; the things speak for themselves.

"... Come then and marvel with me at these great
changes worked by the Hand of God.   Nothing of the old
form remains ; all is changed without ; and within the
change is greater still ; while I, to celebrate these pious
novelties, I break a silence of so many years, and a voice
long a stranger to the pulpit is heard once more."

Then he showed the errors of a soul forgetful of
its Creator, wholly absorbed in itself. He showed it
enamoured of things as perishable as "the flower that the
sun withers, the vapour that the wind carries away" ; a
slave to the senses, greedy of riches, fallen insensibly into
the snares of avarice, or, perhaps, like Alexander the
Great, devoured by ambition, thirsting for fame, desirous
of making a noise in the world in life and after death.
Then, having exposed the utter hollowness of the things
to which the world attaches so much importance, and the
folly of those who love the praise of men rather than the
glory of God, he drew the picture of a soul acknowledging its fault, abandoning little by little all that it
had held most dear, and surrendering itself wholly to
God.

"And you, my sister," he concluded, turning towards
the gallery where La Vallière sat beside the Queen,
"descend, approach the altar ; victim of penitence, approach to consummate your sacrifice. The fire is kindled ;
the incense is prepared ; the sword is drawn ; the sword is
the Word that separates the soul from itself to attach it

wholly to God. The sacred pontiff [1] awaits you with that mysterious veil that you demand. Envelop yourself in that veil; live hidden from yourself as well as from the world; and, assured of God, escape from yourself, go out from yourself, and take so lofty a flight that you will only find rest in the essence of the Father, the Son, and the Holy Spirit." [2]

While the congregation was still under the spell of the great preacher's eloquence, Madame de La Vallière descended from the gallery, pale as death, but far more composed than some of those who were watching her. With a firm step she approached the altar, knelt down, kissed the ground, and received the black veil, which had been presented by the Queen and blessed by the Archbishop of Paris, from the hands of the prioress.[3] When the funereal pall was seen to cover the penitent, a shiver ran through the assembly, and many burst into tears.

But the eyes of Sœur Louise de la Miséricorde were dry !

"Behold, I make all things new !"

When Bossuet had chosen these words for his text, Louise de La Vallière's conversion was not the only one which he had in mind. He believed, or at least he hoped, that two other sinners had seen the error of their ways and had definitely resolved to begin a new life.

[1] Harlay de Chanvallon, Archbishop of Paris.
[2] *Chefs-d'œuvre oratoires de Bossuet* (edit. 1844), iv. 583 *et seq.*
[3] And not from those of Maria Theresa, as so many writers have stated.

MADAME DE MONTESPAN

Madame de Montespan, extraordinary as it may appear, in view of what we have already related, and still more extraordinary in view of what we shall hereafter have occasion to relate, was very punctilious in the discharge of her religious duties. "Great glutton and gourmand as she was," says Saint-Simon, "nothing in the world could have induced her to neglect the regulations of the Church in regard to the fasts of Lent and the Ember Days, and she left the King to go and recite some prayers every day"; while Madame de Caylus assures us that she fasted so rigidly in Lent as actually to have her bread weighed. When one day the Duchesse d'Uzès expressed her astonishment at such scruples, the favourite exclaimed, "What, Madame! Is it necessary for me, because I commit one sin, to commit all the others as well?"[1] Hitherto no obstacle had been placed in the way of her performing her Easter devotions; but when on Maundy-Thursday 1675 she applied to a priest at Versailles, the Abbé Lécuyer, for absolution, it was curtly refused.

The marchioness, highly indignant, complained to the King, who at once summoned the curé of the parish to which Lécuyer was attached to the château, and ordered him to admonish his subordinate. The curé, however, respectfully yet firmly justified the priest's action, declared

---

[1] The Dauphin, when he grew up, had very similar scruples, apropos of which the Princess Palatine relates the following story: "One day the Dauphin brought Raisin, the actress, to Choisy, and hid her in a mill, without giving her anything to eat or drink; for it was a fast-day, and the Dauphin thought there was no greater sin than to eat meat on a fast-day. After the Court had departed, he gave her for supper some salad and bread toasted in oil. Raisin laughed at this very much, and told several persons about it. When I heard of it, I asked the Dauphin what he meant by making his mistress fast in this manner. 'I had a mind,' he answered, 'to commit one sin, not two.'"

that what he had done had his full approval, and declined to interfere.

In great perplexity, Louis thereupon consulted Bossuet,[1] whom he held in the highest esteem, and with whom he frequently had long conversations in regard to the education of the Dauphin. The bishop proved true to the oath which he had sworn at his consecration, "*Si mon roi conseil me demande, bon et loyal je le lui donnerai*," and, without a moment's hesitation, replied that, " under the circumstances, an entire and absolute separation was an indispensable condition of being admitted to participate in the Sacraments."

Now Louis XIV. had been brought up by his mother, Anne of Austria, to regard the rites and ceremonies of the Church with an almost superstitious reverence, and it is said that during the whole of his life he only failed to hear mass twice. Thanks to the excessive indulgence of his confessor, he had up to this time, like Madame de Montespan, been permitted to communicate; but the knowledge of his utter unworthiness to approach the Holy Table had troubled him sorely, and there is reason to believe that on at least one occasion he had communicated *en blanc*, that is to say, with unconsecrated wafers. Moreover, the scandal of the life he had so long been living had lately been brought very forcibly home to him by Madame de La Vallière's renunciation of the world and by the sermons of the eloquent Bourdaloue.

The celebrated Jesuit had preached at the Court during

---

[1] Père de La Chaise, who had just been appointed confessor to the King, was also called into consultation. But the worthy Father, anxious to stand well with both sides, excused himself from expressing an opinion, on the plea that " it behoved him to remain silent in the presence of a bishop."

that Lent and the preceding one, and had not hesitated to exhort the dissolute monarch to repentance in the strongest terms. " Ah, Christians ! " cried he one day, " how many conversions would not your single example produce ! What an attraction would it not be for certain sinners, discouraged and fallen into despair, could they but say to themselves : ' There is that man whom we have seen wallowing in the same debauchery as ourselves, there he is, converted and submissive to the will of God ! ' " Then, addressing himself directly to the King, the fearless preacher continued : " Truth is what saves kings, and your Majesty seeks it, loves them who make it known to him, can have nothing but contempt for those who hide it from him, and, far from resisting it, will esteem it glorious to be conquered by it."

Such being the case, Louis was fain to admit that Bossuet was in the right; and the bishop, following up his advantage, pleaded so earnestly and so forcibly for a separation that the King yielded, sent an intimation to Madame de Montespan that it was his desire that she should retire to her house in the Rue de Vaugirard in Paris, and authorised Bossuet to visit her there and do all in his power to induce her to consent to the complete severance of their guilty connection.

The favourite, though furious at what she deemed the pitiable weakness of her royal lover, understood his character too well to believe that any arguments that she might make use of would, in his present state of mind, be of the slightest avail, and, accordingly, quitted Versailles that very day for Paris, where, the same evening, Bossuet visited her, " muffled in a grey cloak."

One can well imagine the reception he encountered. "She overwhelmed him with reproaches," says his secretary, the Abbé Le Dieu; "she declared that it was ambition that had prompted him to obtain her dismissal; that he aspired himself to dominate the King's mind." Then, finding the bishop quite unmoved by her furious denunciations, she changed her tone; strove to win him to her side by flattery and promises; "dangled before his eyes the highest dignities of Church and State"; vowed that she would make of him a second Mazarin, if such were his wish, provided only he would consent to be blind, or at least to be silent, in regard to her relations with the King. All was in vain. To her promises, as to her insults, Bossuet replied by urging her to make reparation for her grievous sin, and the terrible scandal of which she had been the cause, by consenting to do as Louis required, and living henceforth a reputable and Christian life; and, at length, after several further interviews had taken place between them, the marchioness, either because she was for the moment really penitent, or more probably because, confident of her ability to recover her empire over the royal heart before many months had passed, she had decided that her best course was to humour the King, surrendered at discretion.

In the meanwhile, Louis, a prey to conflicting emotions, had shut himself up in his private apartments, where for a whole month he denied himself to all save his Ministers —who, indeed, were only admitted when their business was such as to brook no delay—and Bossuet. The latter saw him daily, and remained closeted with him for hours at a time, applying himself, with unremitting zeal, to the task of comforting his disconsolate master and confirming him in his virtuous resolutions. The Abbé Le Dieu relates that one day the contrite monarch happened to pay a visit to the Dauphin's study at the moment when, by a singular coincidence, Bossuet was delivering, for the benefit of his royal pupil, a homily on the subject of the temptations which beset kings and the dire consequences of yielding to them. Louis took a seat, begged the bishop to proceed, and listened with great attention till he had finished, when he exclaimed, " My son, avoid these shameful passions, these miserable entanglements, and take good care never to follow my example in this respect. I would have given my right arm to be cut off—here, in an ecstasy of remorse, he extended it towards the young prince—to have had strength to resist such a deplorable weakness ! "[1]

The submission of Madame de Montespan, of course, greatly simplified Bossuet's task; and, on April 17, Louis XIV. communicated at the parish church of Versailles, while the marchioness, now believed to be in a state of grace, was permitted to follow his example in Paris. A month later, the King announced his intention of taking command of the army in Flanders, where a fresh campaign was about to open.[2] Before setting out, he authorised Madame de Montespan to remove from Paris to Clagny; and, the day before his departure, visited her twice, to take what was believed to be a final farewell of his ex-mistress. In proof of his edifying intentions, the interviews took place in a cabinet with a glass door, through which it was possible to see them " from head to foot," as Madame de Scudéry wrote to Bussy-Rabutin. The lady adds that "the conversations were long and

[1] MSS. fragments of the Abbé Le Dieu, quoted in Floquet's *Bossuet, précepteur du Dauphin et évêque à la Cour*, p. 497.

[2] According to M. Floquet, Bossuet had neglected no opportunity of inflaming his sovereign's warlike ardour, in the hope that ambition and the thirst for military glory might serve to divert his mind from the more culpable passion.

sorrowful." [1] The following day, when on the point of starting for Flanders, Louis solemnly assured the Queen, Bossuet, Père de La Chaise, and the curé of Versailles that all was at an end between him and Madame de Montespan.

But the battle was not yet won. The King and the marchioness had both professed the most sincere contrition, had both given repeated assurances that the scandal should never be renewed, and the lady was no longer at the Court. But human nature is deplorably weak—a violent passion, as poor Mademoiselle de Fontanges afterwards reminded Madame de Maintenon, is not got rid of as easily as a soiled garment—and Clagny was but a stone's throw from Versailles. To regard what had occurred, as some of the *dévots* insisted on doing, as a great victory for religion and morality seemed to persons of common-sense the purest chimera. When, at the conclusion of his course of sermons, Bourdaloue had gone, according to custom, to take leave of the King, Louis had said to him, "Father, you will be pleased with me; I have sent Madame de Montespan to Clagny." "Sire," the outspoken Jesuit had replied, "God would have been far more pleased if Clagny were forty leagues from Versailles." [2] And Madame de Scudéry wrote to her friend, Bussy-Rabutin : "The King and Madame de Montespan have parted, loving each other, so it is said, more than life. They say that she will return to Court, but will not reside in the château, and will never see the King except in the Queen's apartments. I doubt it, or at least I doubt that it will continue thus, for there would be great danger of love recovering its supremacy." To which

[1] Madame de Scudéry *to* Bussy-Rabutin, May 15, 1675.
[2] Languet de Gergy's *Mémoires de Madame de Maintenon.*

the sage Bussy answers: "One does not gain the victory over love save by running away from it."

The danger which was so clearly seen by Bourdaloue, by Madame de Scudéry, and by Bussy-Rabutin was equally apparent to Bossuet. "Pray to God for me, I beseech you," he writes to Maréchal de Bellefonds; "pray to Him to deliver me from the heaviest burden which can be laid upon a man, or to put to death all that is earthly within me, so that I may act through Him alone. Thank God, throughout the whole of this matter I have not once thought of myself. But that is not enough; one ought to be a St. Ambrose, a true man of God, altogether or another world, whose every act might preach, whose every word were an oracle of the Holy Spirit, whose whole conduct were heavenly. God chooses that which is of no account to confound that which is; but to do this one ought not 'to be'; that is to say, one ought to be nothing whatever in one's own eyes, emptied of self, wholly filled by God." [1]

Never for a single moment did he relax his efforts to finish the good work he had so well begun. The King, on setting out to join the army, had expressed a desire that Bossuet should correspond with him during his absence in Flanders; and the bishop joyfully acceded to his sovereign's request and wrote frequently, exhorting him to remember "the promises which he had given to God and man," and encouraging him in his resolution to lead a life which should henceforth be above reproach. For nobility of thought and dignity of language, combined with respectful firmness, the following letter, we venture to think, has seldom been surpassed :—

[1] *Œuvres complètes,* xi. 24 ; Letter of June 20, 1675.

MADAME DE MONTESPAN

"Sire,—The Day of Pentecost, on which your Majesty
has resolved to communicate, draws near. Although I
doubt not that you are thinking seriously of your promise
to God, as you have commanded me to remind you of it,
I feel that at this season it is especially incumbent upon
me to do so. Remember, Sire, that there can be no true
conversion unless you labour to eradicate from your heart
not only the sin itself but its original cause. True conversion does not content itself with destroying the fruits
of death, as Scripture saith, that is to say, sins ; but it
goes down to the root, which will infallibly cause them to
revive if it is not plucked out. This is not the work of
a day, I admit ; but the longer and more difficult this
work is, the greater the need to labour at it. Your Majesty
would not consider yourself assured of a rebel town as long
as the author of its sedition retained its credit there. In
like manner, your heart will never be at peace with God
as long as this violent passion, which has for so long
estranged you from Him, continues to reign there.

" Nevertheless, Sire, it is this heart which God demands.
Your Majesty is acquainted with the terms in which He
commands us to give it wholly and entirely to Him ; you
have promised me to read and re-read them frequently.
I send you again, Sire, other words of this same God,
which are not less urgent, and which I entreat your
Majesty to place beside the first. I have given them to
Madame de Montespan, and they have caused her to shed
many tears. And assuredly, Sire, there is no more just
cause for tears than the knowledge that one has pledged
to a human being a heart that God claims for himself.
How difficult it is to withdraw from so unhappy and fatal

an entanglement ! Nevertheless, Sire, it must be done, or there can be no hope of salvation. Jesus Christ, whom you are about to receive, will give you the strength, as He has already given you the desire.

"I do not ask, Sire, that you should stamp out all in a moment a flame so violent ; that would be to ask the impossible. But, Sire, strive to subdue it little by little ; fear to maintain it. Turn your heart towards God ; think often of your obligation to love Him with all your strength, and of the unhappy condition of a heart which, in attaching itself to a human being, is thereby rendered incapable of giving itself wholly to God, to whom it belongs.

"I trust, Sire, that the many great interests which every day tend to occupy your attention more and more will do much towards effecting your cure. People speak of nothing but the splendour of your troops and of what they are capable of effecting under so great a commander ; and I, Sire, the while, I think in secret of a war far more important, and of a victory far more difficult that God puts before you.

"Meditate, Sire, upon those words of the Son of God; they would seem to have been uttered for great kings and conquerors : ' What shall it profit a man,' saith He, ' if he gain the whole world and lose his own soul ? and what can recompense him for so terrible a loss ? ' What will it profit you, Sire, to be redoubtable and victorious without, if you are vanquished and a captive within ? Pray then to God that He may set you free. I pray to Him for that incessantly with my whole heart. My anxiety for your salvation redoubles daily, because I see every day more clearly the perils which beset your path.

"Sire, grant me a favour: order Père de La Chaise to

send me word of the state which you are in. I shall be content if I learn from him that distance and occupation are beginning to have the beneficent effect that we had hoped for. You have now a precious opportunity. Far removed from temptations and occasions for sin, you are in a position more tranquilly to consult your needs, form your resolutions, and regulate your conduct. May God bless your Majesty! May God give you victory, and, with victory, peace both within and without! The more your Majesty gives your heart in sincerity to God, the more you put all your trust and confidence in Him, the more will He protect you with His All-powerful Arm.

"I visit Madame de Montespan as frequently as possible, in compliance with your Majesty's commands. I find her fairly resigned; she occupies herself largely with good works, and she seems to me to be much affected by the truths which I lay before her, which are the same as those of which I have spoken to your Majesty. May God impress them on both your hearts, and perfect His work, so that all the sorrows, the sufferings, and the exertions which you have undergone in order to subdue yourselves may not be in vain.

"I say nothing to your Majesty concerning Monseigneur le Dauphin. M. de Montausier is sending you a faithful account of his state of health, which, thank God, is perfect. The instructions which your Majesty gave on leaving are scrupulously carried out, and it appears to me that Monseigneur le Dauphin is more than ever determined to profit by what your Majesty has said to him. God, Sire, will bless your Majesty, provided you are faithful to Him.

"I am, with profound respect and submission, Sire,

MADAME DE MONTESPAN

your Majesty's most humble, obedient, and faithful subject and servant,

" J. Bénigne,

" *Anc. èv. de Condom.*"[1]

On Whit-Sunday, Louis duly communicated in the camp at Latines, " *avec beaucoup de marques de piété,*" writes Pellisson, who was a witness of the ceremony.[2] The same day Madame de Montespan also performed her devotions ; and we learn from Madame de Sévigné that " her life was exemplary," and that she was dividing her time between superintending the workmen who were putting the finishing touches to Clagny and playing *hoca*[3] with *Monsieur* at Saint-Cloud ! At the beginning of June, one of her children, the Comte de Vexin, was taken ill with fever, and the marchioness, who, whatever her faults may have been, was certainly a most devoted mother, insisted on nursing him herself, and scarcely left his side for a whole week. The Court, delighted to have an excuse for visiting Clagny to see for itself how the ex-favourite was bearing her disgrace, flocked to inquire after the little invalid, and Madame de Montespan complacently remarks, in a letter to her friend, the Duchesse de Noailles, that it was very evident that "the majority of people had retained a great regard for her." Among the visitors was the Queen, who spent half an hour in the sick-room and then persuaded the anxious mother to drive with her to Trianon. Poor Maria Theresa, it may be added, seems to have entertained no doubts whatever as to the sincerity

---

[1] Formerly Bishop of Condom. It was thus that Bossuet signed himself from the time of his resignation of the see of Condom till his appointment to that of Meaux.

[2] *Lettres historiques de Pellisson* (edit. 1729), ii. 276.

[3] *Hoca* was a game of hazard introduced into France by Mazarin.

of the lady's repentance. She and the marchioness had had, a few days after the King's departure, an interview of two hours duration at the Carmelites in the Rue du Bouloi, and had parted " seemingly very much pleased with each other."[1]

Absence, La Rochefoucauld tells us, while proving fatal to minor passions, serves as a stimulus to great ones, just as the wind which extinguishes a candle fans a fire into a blaze. If Bossuet believed that " distance and occupation were beginning to have the beneficent effect he had hoped from them " ; if the Queen was convinced of Madame de Montespan's good faith, there was a person at Versailles, a grave, silent, austere man, the very last in the world one would have thought capable of playing the rôle of inter-mediary in an illicit love affair, who, had he chosen to speak, could very speedily have undeceived them. During his absence in Flanders, Louis XIV. had, as usual, kept himself in constant communication with the Comptroller-General, Colbert; but the letters which passed between the monarch and his favourite Minister in the course of that summer were by no means confined to affairs of State.

Louis XIV. *to* Colbert.

> " Camp at Gembloux,
> "*May* 28, 1675.

" Madame de Montespan sends me word that you have given orders for the purchase of some orange-trees (for Clagny), and that you never fail to consult her wishes.

---

[1] Madame de Sévigné *to* Madame de Grignan, May 29, 1675.

It was the Duchesse de Richelieu, the Queen's *dame d'honneur*, a lady devoted to the interests of Madame de Montespan, who had brought about this reconciliation, and " had received such kind and affectionate letters from the King that she was more than repaid for what she had done."

MADAME DE MONTESPAN

" Continue to follow the instructions I have given you in this matter, as you have done up to the present."

Louis XIV. *to* Colbert.

" Camp at Latines,
" *June* 5, 1675.

" I see by the letter you have sent me that the Assembly of the Clergy has begun very well. Do everything in your power to induce them to finish soon.

" Continue to do whatever Madame de Montespan may wish, and let me know what orange-trees have been brought to Clagny, for she informs me that there are some there, but I do not know what kind they are."

Louis XIV. *to* Colbert.

" Camp at Latines,
" *June* 8, 1675.

" The expense is excessive,[1] and I perceive by this that, in order to please me, nothing is impossible for you. Madame de Montespan informs me that you are acquitting yourself admirably in the matter about which I sent you instructions, and that you are constantly inquiring if there is anything which she desires. Continue to do so on all occasions.

" She also tells me that she has been to Sceaux, where she spent a pleasant evening. I have advised her to go one day to Dampierre, and have assured her that Madame de Chevreuse and Madame Colbert will give her a hearty welcome. I am sure that you will do the same. I shall be very pleased if she can find something to amuse her,

[1] The expense of the construction of Clagny.

161

and the ladies in question are well qualified to divert her.
See that my wishes are carried out.

"I am well persuaded that you will know what steps to
take in order to provide her with facilities for amusement."

LOUIS XIV. TO COLBERT.

"CAMP ON THE HEIGHTS BEFORE HUY,
"*June* 15, 1675.

"I am very pleased that you have purchased some
orange-trees for Clagny. Continue to procure the finest,
if Madame de Montespan so desires."

The tone of these letters, and still more the evidence
which they contain that a clandestine correspondence was
being carried on between Louis and the ex-favourite, are
hardly consistent with the former's declaration that all
was at an end between him and Madame de Montespan,
and, in point of fact, the flame of the monarch's guilty
love, far from being quenched, was about to burn more
ardently than ever.

At the beginning of July, Louis wrote to Bossuet,
giving him renewed assurance of his virtuous intentions,
and asking whether, in view of their altered relations
it might not be possible for Madame de Montespan to
return to Court and resume her duties as *dame du palais*
to the Queen. The prelate, as might be expected, hastened
to reply that such a concession, besides being contrary to
all the laws of the Church, would be to invite an inevitable
relapse, and could by no means be permitted.

Finding Bossuet inexorable, Louis applied to his confessor, Père de La Chaise, who had accompanied him to
Flanders " to give him heart against heart." The prudent

Jesuit answered that of course he, an humble priest, could not possibly, on his own responsibility, sanction an arrangement upon which a bishop had just imposed his veto, but that he would consult the Archbishop of Paris (Harlay de Chanvallon)—a very accommodating divine indeed, it may be observed—who might conceivably be disposed to take a more lenient view of the matter. The outcome of the correspondence which passed between the confessor and the metropolitan was that, a few days before the date fixed for Louis XIV.'s return from Flanders, Bossuet learned, to his inexpressible sorrow and mortification, that Madame de Montespan was re-established at Versailles, the archbishop and Père de La Chaise having consented to her return " because the King had given his word of honour that he would do nothing but what was right."[1]

Although in despair at the discovery that his worst fears were about to be confirmed, Bossuet, nevertheless, resolved to make one last effort to prevent a renewal of the terrible scandal which had so long disgraced the Court. Accordingly, when Louis, " intoxicated by his recent triumphs, forgetful of the solemn promises and protestations made by him at the hour of departure, and greedily impatient, after a separation of three or four months, to once more behold his mistress, warned to be at Versailles at the precise moment of his return," stopped to change horses at Luzarches, the first person he caught sight of was the austere bishop advancing to meet him, pale but determined. The King did not give him time to speak.

[1] *Œuvres d'Antoine Arnauld* (edit. 1785), v. 722. It is hardly surprising that the archbishop should have been so complaisant, since he kept a mistress of his own, a certain Madame de Bretonvilliers, whom the wits of Paris called " *La Cathédrale.*" For a further account of the amours of this prelate see *Correspondance de Bussy-Rabutin*, v. 39 and appendix ; *Revue rétrospective*, vol. i. 165.

"Say nothing to me, Monsieur ; say nothing to me !" he stammered, visibly embarrassed and reddening with annoyance. "I have given my orders; they must be obeyed."[1]

Louis continued his journey to Versailles, where the whole Court was, of course, simmering with excitement. Which of the combatants was to conquer—the bishop or the marchioness, duty or passion, right or wrong? To the Scudérys, the Sévignés, and the Bussy-Rabutins it was all as diverting as a comedy by Molière. Its suspense was speedily relieved. Madame de Caylus tells us that it was the general opinion among the ladies that Madame de Montespan ought not to appear before the King without some preparation on both sides, and that it would be advisable for their first meeting to take place in public, "in order to guard against the inconveniences of surprise." So it was arranged that his Majesty should visit Madame de Montespan in her apartments, but, to leave no further room for scandal, that several ladies of the highest rank and the most unblemished virtue should be present at the interview. We will let the chronicler relate the sequel in her own words :—

"The King came, accordingly, to Madame de Montespan's apartments, as had been decided; but he gradually drew her into the embrasure of a window, where they whispered together for a long time, wept, and said what is usually said in such cases. Finally, they made a profound reverence to these venerable matrons, and withdrew into an adjoining room ; and thence came the Duchesse d'Orléans[2] and afterwards the Comte de Toulouse."[3]

[1] Floquet's *Bossuet, précepteur du Dauphin et évêque à la Cour*, p. 511.
[2] Madame de Montespan's youngest daughter, born in June 1677 ; she married the Duc de Chartres, afterwards Regent.
[3] Madame de Montespan's youngest son, born in July 1678.

MADAME DE MONTESPAN

Madame de Caylus concludes, with obvious malice : " It seems to me that one can still detect in the character, the physiognomy, and the whole person of the Duchesse d'Orléans traces of this combat between love and religion."[1]

[1] *Souvenirs et Correspondance de Madame de Caylus* (edit. 1889), p. 46.

CHAPTER XII

Madame Scarron at Court—She is divided between the claims of religion and self-interest—Her confessor, the Abbé Gobelin, assures her that it is her duty to remain with Madame de Montespan's children—She consents to do so with pretended reluctance—Relations between her and Madame de Montespan, at first friendly, soon become strained—The children the principal cause of the differences between them—Madame Scarron complains to her confessor of Madame de Montespan's treatment of her—" Pray to God to guide my plans "—She purchases the Château of Maintenon, and takes the name or her property—She resolves on the conversion of Louis XIV. and the discomfiture of the favourite—Her resolution apparently the result of a *rapprochement* between her and the devout party —To satisfy her conscience, she begins by warning Madame de Montespan of the error of her ways—She remonstrates with Louis XIV.—The King a witness to a violent scene between her and Madame de Montespan—Her conduct at the time of Madame de Montespan's temporary disgrace—She takes the Duc du Maine to Baréges—Honours paid to them on the journey—Scene of enthusiasm at Bordeaux—Madame de Maintenon corresponds with Louis XIV.—The antagonism between her and Madame de Montespan an open secret at Court—Consideration shown her on her return to Versailles —" Atys is too happy ! "

WE left Madame Scarron, with her charges, established at Court, a position which, of course, brought her into daily intercourse with Madame de Montespan and afforded her increased opportunities for confirming the excellent impression she had already made upon the King. The worthy *gouvernante's* translation from the Rue de Vaugirard to Versailles had not been accomplished save at the cost of a severe struggle between her religious convictions and the dictates of worldly prudence. She could not disguise from herself that her position was hardly one that was consistent with professions of exalted piety, for the specious argument that she was sacrificing her repose and her reputation in order to bring poor neglected children up in a Christian manner, wherewith she would appear to have quieted her conscience during the past four years, no longer served her : now that her charges had been acknowledged, a dozen ladies of high rank would have been only too delighted to undertake the responsibility. At the same time, there was not a courtier at Versailles more determined to push his fortunes by pleasing his sovereign than this devout widow, and the practical side of her nature revolted at the thought of rejecting so excellent an opportunity of advancement.

Madame Scarron was much assisted in her task of reconciling the conflicting claims of religion and self-interest by her judicious choice of a confessor. This was a certain Abbé Gobelin, one of those intelligent *directeurs*, in whom the seventeenth century was so prolific, who endeared themselves to the fair ladies who sought their advice by invariably counselling them to do what they perceived that they wished.[1] In the present instance, the

[1] Bourdaloue, who, in later years, declined the honour of directing Madame de Maintenon's conscience, was very severe upon the fashionable lady's confessor of this type, " who seems to have received a mission from God for one soul alone, to whom he devotes all his attention ; who several times a week regularly passes several hours with her, either in the confessional or elsewhere, in converse of which no one can divine the subject or conceive the utility."

holy man, who, doubtless, had a very nice appreciation of the value of Court favour, and was fully alive to the advantage of having a friend so near the person of the King, assured Madame Scarron that it was her duty to remain with Madame de Montespan's children, however painful it might be ; and the lady consented to do so, with secret relief, but with much apparent reluctance.

" I know not how long I shall remain here," she writes to the abbé on first arriving at the Court. " But I am resolved to conduct myself like a child, to strive to acquire a profound indifference for all my surroundings, and for the mode of life to which I am compelled to conform, to detach myself altogether from what troubles my repose, and to seek God in everything that I do. Please remember that I am remaining at Court in accordance with your desire, and that I shall leave the moment you counsel me to do so."[1]

In spite of her efforts to convince herself that she was doing violence to her feelings by remaining at Court, it is probable that Madame Scarron would have been well content with her lot but for her relations with Madame de Montespan. For a few weeks matters went smoothly enough between the two ladies. The favourite was delighted to have at her beck and call a person so amiable, so charming, and so eminently serviceable, and seemed as if she could not see enough of her. Every evening Madame Scarron would go to the marchioness's apartments, at the hour when the King usually took his leave, and remain, conversing with the sultana, while the latter made her preparations for retiring for the night, and frequently accompanied her in her drives and visits to Paris. But soon quarrels arose. The children were the

[1] *Correspondance générale de Madame de Maintenon,* i. 195.

principal bone of contention. As was only to be expected, the little ones were far more attached to their *gouvernante*, who had tended them with so much care and devotion ever since they could remember, than to the mother of whom they had seen so little, and showed their preference in the naïve manner peculiar to the young. Madame de Montespan, who could not bear to occupy a subordinate position, even in the affections of a child, was annoyed, and her annoyance took the form of constant interference with the *régime* of the nursery. She would invade the children's apartments at all hours, stuff the poor infants with unwholesome food, scold the nurses, and, when Madame Scarron ventured to remonstrate, fly into the most ungovernable passions.

" Madame de Montespan and I have had to-day a very sharp altercation," writes the *gouvernante* to her confessor, " and, as I am the party that suffers, I have wept much, while she gave her own version of it to the King. I confess that I find it extremely difficult to remain in a position in which I may have mischances like this every day, and that it would be very sweet to resume my liberty. Over and over again I have wished to be a nun, and the dread of repenting of it has made me pass through many states of feeling that a thousand persons would call a vocation. For several months I have been dying to go into retirement, but the same fear hinders me from doing so. This is a very cowardly kind of prudence, and my life is consumed in strange agitations. Think of it before God, I implore you, and reflect a little upon my need for repose. I feel that I can assure my salvation here, but I should be more certain of it elsewhere. I cannot believe that it is God's will that I should put up with Madame de Montespan. She is incapable of friendship, and I cannot do without that : she cannot endure my opposition without hating me ; she represents me to the King just as she pleases and causes me to lose his esteem. He regards me as an eccentric kind of woman, who must be humoured, and I dare not speak directly to him, as she would never forgive me ; and, even if I were to speak, my obligations to Madame de Montespan would prevent me from saying anything against her. Thus I can find no remedy for my sufferings. Meanwhile, death is approaching, and you and I shall deeply regret so much wasted time."[1]

Other letters in much the same strain follow, in one of which she complains that "the children are being killed under her very eyes (presumably by over-indulgence) and that she is powerless to prevent it " ; and in another that she is "perishing away visibly and has the saddest fits of depression." As time goes on, however, we begin to notice a change in the tone of her letters. She still complains bitterly of her hard fate, still offers to resign her post the moment her confessor thinks it advisable, but she is evidently possessed by some great resolution. "*I beg of you to ask God to guide my project for His glory and for my salvation.*" And again : "*Pray to God to guide my plans.*"[2]

Now, what was this project, these plans, for which Madame Scarron—or rather Madame de Maintenon, as we must now call her, since, at the beginning of the year 1675, she had purchased the Château of Maintenon,[3] and, in accordance with the custom of the time, taken the name

---

[1] *Correspondance générale*, i. 220 ; Letter of September 13, 1674.

[2] Letters of March 6 and 29, 1675.

[3] The Château de Maintenon, situated in what is now the department of Eure-et-Loir, fourteen leagues from Paris, ten from Versailles, and four from Chartres, had been built by Jean Cottereau, *trésorier des finances*, under Louis XII. and François I. Louis XIV. did not, as stated by several writers, make Madame Scarron a present of this property. She

of her property—was inviting her confessor's prayers ? Nothing less than the conversion of Louis XIV. and the discomfiture of Madame de Montespan !

There can be little doubt that in the interval between Madame de Maintenon's arrival at Court and the time at which the above passages were written a *rapprochement* of some kind had taken place between the lady and the devout party, of which Bossuet and the Duc de Montausier, the Dauphin's governor, were the recognised chiefs. In the eyes of these worthy men the King's incontinency was a far greater calamity for his realm than the widespread misery and want that his continual wars and reckless expenditure were bringing upon the wretched peasantry ; indeed, it is not improbable that some of them were inclined to attribute these evils to the Divine wrath at his Majesty's disregard of the Seventh Commandment rather than to their true cause. If only Louis could be induced to reform his ways and lead a virtuous life, all would be well : the King's enemies would submit, peace would be restored, trade and agriculture would revive, and the country become prosperous and happy once more. But how was this to be brought about ? The King's confessor had remonstrated so far as he dared, Bourdaloue, Bossuet, and Mascaron [1] had preached some very outspoken sermons, but Madame de Montespan's empire still remained unshaken. Why not assail the monarch on the

bought it herself, partly with a sum of money given her a few months before by the King in recognition of her services to his children, and partly with her own savings. On her death, Maintenon passed into the possession of the Noailles family, to whom it still belongs.

[1] In 1669, Mascaron had drawn upon himself rebuke and temporary disgrace by a bold sermon on the observance of the Seventh Commandment. Six years later, he appears to have again incurred the royal displeasure by attacking another of Louis XIV.'s weaknesses—desire for

side which he had himself weakened? Why not try what effects moral sentiments in the mouth of a pretty woman might have? Madame de Maintenon, though verging on forty, still retained much of her early beauty, the sincerity of her religious convictions was beyond dispute, her condemnation of unchastity notorious. Where would it be possible to find any one better qualified to play the rôle of female missionary and wean Louis from the arms of the syren who had so long bewitched him into those of Mother Church? Who first suggested this project to Madame de Maintenon we cannot tell; but certain it is that the proposal, strongly appealing as it did to both sides of her character, met with a very favourable reception, and that before she had been many months at Court she found herself definitely committed to the task of saving the King's soul—and making her own fortune.

It must not be supposed that Madame de Maintenon deliberately set herself to undermine the position of the woman to whom she owed so much—the woman concerning whom she had written to the Abbé Gobelin, " My obligations to Madame de Montespan hinder me from saying anything against her "—without experiencing some qualms of conscience. But, with that remarkable skill for reconciling contradictions which is, perhaps, the most interesting trait in her character, she had devised a sure and certain way of quieting any scruples that might be likely to trouble her and shielding herself against the reproaches of her benefactress.

military glory. " I performed my devotions to-day,' writes Madame de Maintenon to the Abbé Gobelin (March 3, 1675), " and heard a fine sermon from Père Mascaron. He expressed himself rather too warmly on the subject of conquerors, and told us that a hero was a robber, who did at the head of an army what thieves did alone. Our master (the King) was displeased at what he said."

MADAME DE MONTESPAN

She would begin, she resolved, by warning the marchioness of the error of her ways and solemnly adjuring her to repent and lead a godly life. If her appeal were successful, well and good ; if not, she would have done all that loyal friendship and Christian charity had the right to expect from her, and would be free to speak to the King when occasion offered. She would, doubtless, be accused of ingratitude, of duplicity, of ambition, but the armour of religious zeal would, she felt confident, be proof against all such insinuations.

An opportunity to say a word in season to her erring sister was not long in forthcoming.

The favourite used sometimes to go to Paris and spend a few days in her house in the Rue de Vaugirard, on which occasions Madame de Maintenon generally accompanied her. Languet de Gergy relates that during one of these visits the two ladies were out walking together, when Madame de Montespan entered a church and, after reciting some prayers, approached the confessional. " Madame de Maintenon," continues the chronicler, " was transported with joy. ' There,' said she to herself, ' is the door of conversion standing open.' On leaving the confessional, Madame de Montespan heard mass and communicated, and Madame de Maintenon had no doubt whatever that her conversion was sincere and that she had given the confessor convincing assurances of her changed disposition. But what was her astonishment when, on returning to the house, she beheld Madame de Montespan making preparations for her return to Court ! Thereupon, unable to restrain her zeal, she said to her, ' What ! are you going, Madame, straight from communicating to deliberately throw yourself into certain danger of offending God !' Madame de Montespan wept a great deal, but her tears were those of weakness, not of penance." [1]

After this incident, Madame de Maintenon evidently considered herself at liberty to speak to the King. She has herself related the manner in which she first approached his Majesty on this very delicate subject :—

"When I found myself sufficiently established in the King's favour to speak freely to him, I had the honour, on a certain Apartment-day,[2] to promenade with him, while the others were occupied with cards and various amusements. As soon as I was out of earshot of the rest, I said to him : 'Sire, you are very fond of your Musketeers ; they give you a great deal of occupation and amusement every day. What would you do if some one were to tell you that one of those Musketeers of whom you are so fond had carried off another man's wife and was actually living with her? I am sure that this very evening he would leave the Hôtel des Mousquetaires and would not be allowed to sleep there, however late it was.'" "The King," adds Mademoiselle d'Aumale, "took her remonstrance in very good part, laughed a little, said that she was right, but it did not have any effect upon him at the time."

It seems not improbable that Louis XIV. informed his mistress of what the *gouvernante* had said to him, for soon afterwards we find Madame de Maintenon writing to the Abbé Gobelin : " Terrible scenes are taking place between

[1] Languet de Gergy's *Mémoires sur Madame de Maintenon*, p. 167.

[2] Three times a week, from six till ten o'clock in the evening, the King's apartments were thrown open to the whole Court. These days were called "Apartment-days." Etiquette was to a large extent laid aside on these occasions ; the King, for the time being, became a private individual, and every one was at liberty to amuse themselves as they pleased, with cards, music, or conversation.

MADAME DE MONTESPAN

Madame de Montespan and myself. Yesterday the King
was a witness of them."

The King had, indeed, surprised the two ladies "in a
crisis the most violent that could be imagined," hot with
the ardour of battle, almost, in fact, on the point of blows,
and had inquired what was the matter. Madame de
Maintenon recovered her calm on the instant, curtseyed,
and answered, "If your Majesty will be pleased to pass
into the next room, I shall do myself the honour of
telling you." Louis did as she requested ; Madame de
Maintenon followed him ; Madame de Montespan,
choking with rage, allowed them to go. The *gouvernante*
then unbosomed herself to the King, declared that the
injustice, harshness and cruelty of Madame de Montespan
were more than she could bear, and that she must crave
his permission to resign her post and retire from Court.
The monarch, in great alarm at the prospect of losing
so admirable a guardian for his children and a lady
in whose conversation he had begun to take so lively
a pleasure, endeavoured to make excuses for his mistress,
asserted that Madame de Maintenon was mistaken in sup-
posing her to be intentionally unjust, and added, "Have
you not often perceived how her beautiful eyes fill with
tears when she hears of a touching and generous action ? "
Finally, Madame de Maintenon, who, of course, had not
the least intention of being taken at her word, and,
perhaps, saw in the remark about the "beautiful eyes"
a delicate hint that the corn was not yet ripe for the
sickle, magnanimously consented to remain, but, at the
same time, contrived to let the King see that it was solely
out of deference to his wishes that she was willing to
overlook the conduct of Madame de Montespan.[1]

[1] *Souvenirs de Madame de Caylus* (edit. 1889), p. 61.

Madame de Maintenon's hopes rose high when, at the following Easter, Madame de Montespan received orders to retire from Court, though, doubtless, she would have been better pleased if the credit of the favourite's discomfiture had belonged to her instead of to Bossuet. However, she was too sincere in her desire for the King's salvation not to do what she could to second the bishop's efforts; and, accordingly, we find her writing to the Abbé Gobelin: "You will hear it said that I saw the King yesterday; fear nothing; I consider that I spoke to him as a Christian and a true friend of Madame de Montespan." [1]

When this letter was written, Madame de Maintenon was on the point of starting for Baréges, in the Pyrenees, in charge of the little Duc du Maine, who, it was hoped, might benefit by a course of the waters. Their journey presented a curious contrast to that of the previous year to Antwerp. Then, they had travelled incognito; now, it resembled a royal progress. "The King himself could not have been better received," writes the *gouvernante* to Madame de Montespan; "everywhere honours and endless acclamations. You would have been enchanted, Madame, and you cannot conceive the lengths to which the love of this people for their King, and all that belongs to him, carries them." [2]

In the face of the abject servility to the throne which characterised all classes at this period, it was, indeed, hardly to be expected that any nice distinctions would be drawn between the legitimate and the legitimated offspring of Jupiter; and in every town through which they passed the travellers were greeted with the utmost

[1] *Correspondance générale de Madame de Maintenon*, i. 268.
[2] *Ibid.*, i. 278.

enthusiasm. At Poitiers, they were "nearly stifled with caresses." At Cognac, the government of which Madame de Maintenon had lately obtained for her shiftless and pretentious brother, Charles d'Aubigné, a company of little boys, armed and uniformed like the Musketeers, came out to meet them, and formed themselves into a guard of honour for the little duke, much to the delight of the latter. At Blaye, the Duc de Saint-Simon [1] gave them "a magnificent reception," and the aldermen of Bordeaux came, bringing with them a splendid barge, propelled by forty oars. In this, the Duc du Maine, his *gouvernante*, and their suite embarked, and proceeded down the Garonne to the city, were they were welcomed with trumpets, violins, discharges of cannon, and cries of "*Vive le Roi !*" from the multitudes which lined the banks. On landing, they were received by Maréchal d'Albret, the Governor of Guienne; and the municipal authorities presented an address, for which the little Duke returned thanks in person. This ceremony over, they entered a carriage, and, followed by a long stream of others, proceeded at a walking pace, through cheering crowds, to the house which had been prepared for their reception. [2] No wonder Louis XIV. felt that he was not as other men when such honours were paid to the fruit of his irregularities !

While in the Pyrenees, Madame de Maintenon, under the pretext of allaying the King's anxiety in regard to his little son's health, wrote "full and frequent" letters to his Majesty, and there can be little doubt that these epistles, which the first Napoleon greatly preferred to

---

[1] The father of the author of the famous *Mémoires*, who was born on January 15 of that same year.

[2] *Correspondance générale de Madame de Maintenon*, i. 276.

those of Madame de Sévigné,[1] exercised no inconsiderable influence upon the lady's fortunes, and, as her biographer, the Duc de Noailles, remarks, "ended by entirely gaining for her the confidence and friendship of the monarch."[2]

Madame de Maintenon's return was awaited with impatience by the Court; for it would appear that the antagonism between her and the favourite was now an open secret, and that it was the general opinion in well-informed circles that highly interesting developments might be looked for in the near future. "I must give you a little peep behind the scenes that will surprise you," writes Madame de Sévigné to her daughter. "The perfect friendship between *Quantova*[3] and her travelling friend (Madame de Maintenon) has been converted for the past two years into the most inveterate enmity. It is an acrimony, an antipathy, like that between black and white. You ask whence it proceeds? From the friend's pride, which makes her revolt against the orders of *Quanto*. She does not love to obey; she is willing to comply with the wishes of the father (the King), but not

[1] Nisard, in his *Histoire de la Littérature Française*, says that Napoleon compared the letters of Madame de Sévigné to "snow eggs, with which a man could surfeit himself without overloading his stomach."

[2] *Histoire de Madame de Maintenon*, i. 505.

[3] The names *Quantova* or *Quanto*, generally the latter, employed so frequently by Madame de Sévigné to indicate Madame de Montespan, are, according to a writer in *L'Intermédiaire des Chercheurs et Curieux* (vol. xviii. p. 488), in allusion to the favourite's passion for play and to her habit of demanding in Italian, "*Quanto?*" (How much do you stake?). The custom of giving sobriquets known only to the parties interested had, in the seventeenth century, passed from diplomatic to private correspondence, the object being to baffle indiscreet curiosity. The surnames or sobriquets employed by Madame de Sévigné had been invented by her and her correspondents, and were, of course, only used by them, since they alone held the key.

with those of the mother. It is to oblige him that she has undertaken this journey, and not in the least to gratify her."[1]

The *gouvernante* and her charge arrived at Versailles at the beginning of November. Their visit to the Pyrenees had been so far successful that the little duke, though he was still very lame, and, indeed, continued so to the end of his life, was now able to walk without assistance. The King was greatly delighted, and expressed his sense of the obligation under which Madame de Maintenon had placed him so very warmly that Louvois, who had hitherto scarcely deigned to notice her existence, thought it incumbent upon him to pay her a visit of congratulation; while when she went to sup with Madame de Richelieu that evening, she found herself treated with the most extraordinary deference by the ladies who were present, " some kissing her hands and others her gown," if Madame de Sévigné was correctly informed.[2]

Not long after her return, a little incident occurred which still further strengthened the growing conviction that a new star had arisen in the sky of Versailles. One day, in the presence of a number of people, Louis XIV. happened to ask Madame de Maintenon what was her favourite opera. " *Atys*,"[3] was the reply. " *Atys* is too happy!" rejoined the King, quoting a line from the opera in question, but in a tone which caused the courtiers standing by to exchange meaning smiles.[4]

[1] Letter of August 7, 1675.

[2] Letter of November 10, 1675.

[3] An opera by Quinault and Lulli, the Gilbert and Sullivan of that day. They collaborated in a number of operas.

[4] The Duc de Noailles's *Histoire de Madame de Maintenon*, i. 513.

CHAPTER XIII

The Queen and Madame de Montespan visit Louise de La
Vallière at the Carmelites—Madame de Montespan's conversa-
tion with La Vallière—Madame de Montespan goes to Bourbon
—Honours paid her on the journey—Servility of Louise's
brother, the Marquis de La Vallière—M. Morant's barge—
Meeting between the King and Madame de Montespan at
Saint-Germain—The favourite's position appears invulnerable
—"A scent of fresh game in the land of *Quanto* "—Madame de
Soubise—Scandalous conduct of the King—" The star of
Quanto begins to wane "—Madame de Ludres a pretender to
the royal heart—Her adventure with Charles IV. of Lorraine
—The sovereignty of Versailles trembling in the balance—
Birth of Mademoiselle de Blois—Madame de Ludres is
discarded—And cruelly humiliated by her triumphant rival—
Madame de Montespan's favour apparently more firmly estab-
lished than ever—Madame de Maintenon again takes the
Duc du Maine to the Pyrenees—Letters of the Duc du Maine
to Madame de Montespan—The Court accompanies the King
to Lorraine—Louis XIV. enters Flanders—Taking of Ghent
—Madame de Montespan visits the King at Oudenarde—
Birth of the Comte de Toulouse—Diplomatic illness of Père
de La Chaise—Louis XIV. refused absolution.

THE year 1676 was almost as fertile in incident as its
predecessor. In the middle of April, Louis XIV. left
Versailles to join the army, and, a few days later, Madame
de Montespan started for Bourbon for a course of the
waters. Before doing so, however, she paid two visits
to the Carmelites in company with the Queen, who had

apparently forgiven the favourite for the deception she had practised upon her the previous year. Madame de Sévigné has left us an interesting account of one of these visits :—

" *Quanto* set on foot a lottery and collected everything that could be useful to the nuns. This caused great amusement in the community. She conversed a long time with Sœur Louise de la Miséricorde (Madame de La Vallière), and asked her whether she was as happy there as was generally reported. ' No,' replied she, ' I am not happy, but I am contented.' *Quanto* talked to her a good deal of the brother of *Monsieur* (the King), and inquired if she had no message to send him and what she should say to him for her. The other, in the sweetest tone and manner possible, though perhaps a little piqued at the question, replied, ' Whatever you please, Madame, whatever you please.' Fancy this to be expressed with all the grace, spirit, and modesty which you can imagine. *Quanto* afterwards wished for something to eat, and gave a four-pistole piece (about forty livres) to purchase the ingredients for a sauce, which she made herself, and ate with a wonderful appetite. I tell you the simple fact without the least embellishment." [1]

Madame de Montespan's journey to Bourbon was almost as triumphant as that of her son to Baréges twelve months before. She had a coach-and-six for herself another for her waiting-women, two *fourgons*, six mules, and ten or twelve servants on horseback. In all, her suite consisted of forty-five persons, exclusive of the royal guards who invariably escorted her on these occasions What must have been the feelings of the ragged, starving peasants who had been requisitioned by the authorities

[1] Madame de Sévigné *to* Madame de Grignan, April 29, 1676.

of the various districts to repair the roads along which
she was to pass, as the haughty favourite and her *entourage*
swept by? At every town and village at which she
stopped the utmost deference was paid her, and every day
a courier from the army brought her a letter from the
King. When she reached Bourbon, she found that the
Marquis de La Vallière (the brother of Louise) had given
orders for addresses to be presented to her by all the
towns within his jurisdiction! The marchioness, however, had the good taste to decline this compliment, and
the servile La Vallière was compelled to countermand the
order.

During her stay, which lasted about a month, the
favourite, always lavishly generous, distributed large
sums of money in charity, presented the hospital with
twelve beds, and enriched the Capuchin convent in the
town. She also "received visitors with courtesy," among
them Madame Fouquet, the wife of the disgraced *surintendant*, who came to implore her good offices to obtain
her husband's release or, if that were not possible, permission to share his imprisonment.

At the beginning of June, Madame de Montespan set
out for Fontevrault, where she intended to spend the
remainder of the time until the King's return with her
sister, the abbess. As her journey for the greater part of
the distance was to be by water—along the Allier from
Moulins to Nevers and thence by the Loire to Tours—
the Intendant, M. Morant, obligingly provided a gorgeous
barge, "upholstered in crimson damask, and decorated
with a thousand monograms and pennants of France and
Navarre." This little attention is believed to have cost
the gallant Intendant at least a thousand crowns; but, as
the favourite wrote a most enthusiastic description of

it to the King, it no doubt proved a judicious investment.

Louis XIV. and the marchioness both reached Saint-Germain, where the Court then was, on the same day (July 8), and it at once became apparent that absence had not diminished the King's passion for his mistress. "The friend of *Quanto* arrived about an hour before *Quanto*, and while he was conversing with his family, word was brought him of her return. He ran to meet her with great precipitation, and remained with her a considerable time. The whole evening was dedicated to pure and simple *friendship*. The friend's wife (the Queen) has wept bitterly."[1] For once poor Maria Theresa's fortitude had forsaken her.[2]

The weeks went by, and the favourite appeared invulnerable. "Never was the sovereign power of *Quanto* so firmly established," writes Madame de Sévigné. "She feels herself superior to all opposition, and has no more fear of her little sluts of nieces[3] than if they had been turned to charcoal. She appears entirely delivered from the fear of shutting up the wolf in the sheepfold. Her beauty is extraordinary, her dress equal to her beauty, and her gaiety to her dress."[4]

But what is this? A fortnight later, Madame de Sévigné writes again, and now she has a different tale to

[1] Madame de Sévigné *to* Madame de Grignan, July 10, 1676.

[2] The Queen was not the only person who viewed his Majesty's conduct with displeasure, for the next day Madame de Maintenon wrote to her confessor : "Yesterday I had a violent headache and feel quite prostrated."

[3] The daughters of Madame de Thianges, with one of whom it was reported that Louis XIV. was in love. The elder married the Duc de Nevers and the younger an Italian nobleman, the Duke Sforza.

[4] Letter of August 7, 1676.

tell. "There is a scent of fresh game in the land of *Quanto*, but no one can tell exactly where. The lady whom I have mentioned to you has been named ; but, as the people of this country are esteemed deep politicians, perhaps it is not there either. One thing, however, is certain, namely, that the gallant (the King) is gay and quite himself, and the demoiselle (Madame de Montespan) sad, embarrassed, and sometimes tearful." [1]

The "fresh game" in question was Anne de Rohan, Princesse de Soubise, *dame du palais* to the Queen, very beautiful, very discreet, and very greedy. She loved the King out of love for her husband, a very complaisant old gentleman indeed, nearly forty years her senior, who, unlike the poor Marquis de Montespan, had not the smallest objection to share with Jupiter, so long as Jupiter was prepared to make it worth his while. He was rarely seen at Court, was wholly occupied in the management of his estates, and never appeared to entertain the slightest suspicion of his wife's infidelity. After collecting for him all the honours, dignities, and hard cash she could lay her hands on, Madame de Soubise, her object accomplished, retired from the field, though, if Saint-Simon is to be believed, there were occasional returns to favour, extending over a period of several years.

Thanks to the discretion of the Princess and the complaisance of her friend, the Maréchale de Rochefort, "a lady," says Saint-Simon, "of experience in this *métier*," who obligingly permitted her apartments to be used as a rendezvous, this affair was never more than suspected at the time, and on September 2 we find the omniscient Madame de Sévigné writing again : "The vision of

[1] Letter of August 24, 1676.

MADAME DE MONTESPAN

Madame de Soubise has passed quicker than a lightning-flash; they have made it all up again. I am told that the other day at cards *Quanto* had her head resting familiarly on her friend's (the King) shoulder, and it was believed that this affectation meant 'I am higher in favour than ever.'"

The conduct of his Most Christian Majesty at this juncture must have afforded a highly interesting study for the moralist. He had evidently reassured Madame de Montespan that she alone possessed his heart, while he would appear to have been taking every day a keener pleasure in the society of Madame de Maintenon, who had lately returned from a three weeks sojourn at her château, whither the King had despatched Le Nôtre to lay out the gardens, and "whose favour was extreme." At the same time, he was carrying on his intrigue with Madame de Soubise, and it was darkly hinted that he had relations which were rather more than friendly with two other young beauties, Madame de Louvigny [1] and Mademoiselle de Rochefort-Théobon.[2]

Madame de Montespan was soon undeceived. "The star of *Quanto* begins to wane," writes Madame de Sévigné on September 11; "there are nothing but tears, unfeigned vexation, affected cheerfulness, sulks; at last, *ma chère*, it is all over. Every one is now upon the watch, conjecturing and divining, and faces are thought to shine like stars that, but a month ago, were deemed unworthy to be compared with others. But the cards go merrily on, while the fair one keeps to her apartments. Some tremble, others rejoice, some wish things to remain

[1] Marie Charlotte de Castelnau, Comtesse de Louvigny. Her husband afterwards became Duc de Gramont.

[2] Lydie de Rochefort-Théobon, afterwards Comtesse de Beuvron.

as they are, the majority desire a dramatic change ; in a word, we are all eyes and ears for what the most clear-sighted report." And on the 30th of the same month : "Every one believes that the friend (the King) loves her no longer, and that *Quanto* is embarrassed between the consequences which might follow the return of favours and the danger of no longer enjoying them— the fear that they are being sought in some other quarter. On the other hand, the rôle of friend does not content her ; so much beauty as she still has and so much pride are not easily relegated to the second place. Jealousies are keen. Have they ever stopped anything ? " Then, on October 15 : "Had *Quanto* retired into private life at Easter the year she returned to Paris, she would have been spared the mortification which she now endures ; it would have been sensible to adopt that course ; but human weakness is great ; one wishes to make the most of one's beauty, and this economy brings ruin rather than riches."

At the beginning of the following year a new and very formidable pretender to the royal heart appeared upon the scene. This was a certain Isabelle de Ludres, a lady from Lorraine, *fille d'honneur* to the Princess Palatine, the second *Madame*. Her contemporaries describe her as a very beautiful woman and very witty, but with a disagreeable voice and a strong German accent.[1] When she was quite a young girl she had attracted the notice of the susceptible Charles IV., Duke of Lorraine, who fell so madly in love with her that he sent away his mistress, Beatrix de Cusance, who died of grief shortly

[1] Madame de Sévigné relates how, when taking a sea-bath for the first time, the lady cried out, " *Oh, Matame te Grignan, l'étranze sose t'être zettée toute nue dans la mer !* "

afterwards, and determined to make her his duchess. However, before the date fixed for the nuptials he transferred his affections to another damsel, a Mademoiselle de Nanteuil, and announced his intention of espousing her instead. The fair Isabelle, who had a number of very passionate letters from the duke in her possession, and was by no means inclined to surrender the crown matrimonial without a struggle, prepared to oppose the marriage ; but, on being threatened with a prosecution for *lèse majesté*, a capital offence in those days, thought better of it and resolved to try her fortune at the French Court, where she made a number of conquests, including Madame de Montespan's brother, the Duc de Vivonne, the Chevalier de Vendôme, and the young Marquis de Sévigné, and, finally, Louis XIV. himself.

The progress of this affair was interrupted by the King's departure for the army at the end of February ; but his Majesty had paid the lady such very marked attention that Bussy-Rabutin wrote to his friend, Président Brulart, that it was the general opinion that Madame[1] de Ludres was about to become *maîtresse en titre*. The excitement at Court as the time for Louis's return drew near was almost painful in its intensity ; the war was entirely forgotten ; nothing else was talked of but the

---

[1] Though unmarried, she was styled *Madame*, in virtue of a canonry which she held in Lorraine. When she became the King's mistress, a wit wrote :

> " La Vallière étoit du commun,
>   La Montespan de la noblesse,
>   La Ludre étoit chanoinesse.
>   Toutes trois ne sont que pour un :
>   C'est le plus grand des potentats
>   Qui veut assemble les États."
>
> —*Manuscrit Maurepas*, iv. 57.

prospects of the rival mistresses. Who could find time to think about the fate of Europe when the sovereignty of Versailles was trembling in the balance?

The stars in their courses fought for Madame de Montespan. When the monarch arrived, he found a fresh pledge of the marchioness's affection awaiting him in the shape of a little daughter, afterwards Mademoiselle de Blois;[1] and this circumstance probably decided the day in the elder woman's favour. Anyhow, Louis fell at his old mistress's feet again, and Madame de Ludres was discarded, the King offering her the sum of 200,000 livres by way of compensation for her disappointment, which, however, was declined.

Finding herself restored to favour, Madame de Montespan turned like a Fury upon her vanquished rival and overwhelmed her with cruel taunts and insults. "She would like to strangle her," writes Bussy-Rabutin to Madame de Montmorency, "and makes her life unbearable." From another source we learn that, in the presence of the King, the marchioness invariably alluded to the poor woman as "that rag," and treated her so shamefully that at length she resigned her post as *fille d'honneur* to *Madame* and retired from Court. Four

---

[1] Born at Maintenon, May 4, 1677. Madame de Montespan had gone thither with the *gouvernante* immediately after the King's departure, in order to hide her condition from the inquisitive eyes of the Court, and remained there until within a week of his Majesty's return. The two ladies would appear to have been on very amicable terms at this time, their hostility to Madame de Ludres being no doubt a bond of sympathy between them. Nevertheless, Madame de Maintenon, "who did not spare exhortations and remonstrances," refused to undertake the charge of the future Duchesse d'Orléans, who was accordingly brought up secretly in the house in the Rue de Vaugirard, as was the Comte de Toulouse, born the following year.

years later, she accepted from Louis a pension of 2000 crowns and a present of 25,000 livres—"in consideration of her services" ran the brevet—a proceeding which seems to lend colour to the cynical Bussy's insinuation that her refusal of the royal generosity in 1677 was merely a ruse to convince his Majesty of the disinterestedness of her affection and win him back.

As for Madame de Montespan, she believed herself so secure that she became more haughty and arrogant than ever. Never, in fact, had her position seemed more unassailable, never had the King's passion appeared more ardent than after this infidelity. "Oh! my daughter, what a triumph at Versailles! What redoubled pride! What a re-entry into possession! I was in her room for an hour. She was lying on her bed, decked out, with her hair dressed, resting for the *médianoche*.[1] She launched shafts of contempt at poor Io (Madame de Ludres), and scoffed at her having had the audacity to complain of her. Imagine all that an ungenerous pride could suggest to her in her hour of triumph, and you will not be far from the mark."[2] Then: "*Quanto* and her friend are together longer and more eagerly than ever. The ardour of their first years has returned, all obstacles are banished, all restraint removed, which persuades us that never was empire seen more firmly established." And, a little later: "Madame de Montespan was the other day covered with diamonds; the brilliance of so blazing a divinity was

---

[1] A meat supper which was served at midnight on fast-days. There appears to have been considerable diversity of opinion among the devout as to the lawfulness of this meal. The Abbé Gobelin allowed Madame de Maintenon to partake of it; the Queen's confessor strongly disapproved of the practice.

[2] Madame de Sévigné *to* Madame de Grignan, June 11, 1677.

more than one could bear. The attachment seems stronger than ever; they are all eyes for one another; never has love been known to recover its ground like this."[1]   It was her last triumph, dazzling but short-lived, and destined to be followed by years of bitter anguish.

Towards the end of June, Madame de Maintenon again took the Duc du Maine to Baréges. To judge by the letters she wrote to the Abbé Gobelin during her absence, she was evidently in a very despondent mood, desirous of abandoning the struggle and retiring from Court. "It is impossible for me to sacrifice my life, my liberty, my health, and my salvation." "I am passing my life in agitations which deprive me of all the pleasures of the world and of the peace which is necessary to serve God." "I am passionately desirous of leaving the Court." Whether she was really so anxious to retire from the field as she wished her confessor to believe is doubtful; in any case, the latter does not appear to have had much difficulty in persuading her to remain, but then it was always part of her rôle to pose as a martyr.

While in the Pyrenees, the little Duc du Maine, who was a charming and affectionate child, kept up an active correspondence with his " *belle Madame,*" as he styles his mother. Madame de Montespan, who, to give her her due, loved her children dearly, could have little dreamed as she read these letters of the ingratitude with which in after years the writer was to repay the care and tenderness she lavished upon him.

[1] Madame de Sévigné *to* Madame de Grignan, July 2, 1677.

MADAME DE MONTESPAN

THE DUC DU MAINE *to* MADAME DE MONTESPAN.

"*June* 1677.

"*Ma belle Madame*,—I do not cease thinking of you during the journey. If you could but know how I long to come to you, you would not be able to prevent yourself from sending to fetch your little *mignon*; for you are so kind to me that I ask you for everything that I want. Adieu, *ma belle Madame*, I love you with all my heart."

THE DUC DU MAINE *to* MADAME DE MONTESPAN.

"BARÉGES, 1677.

"I am very delighted, *ma belle Madame*, to find that you remember your little *mignon*. You know how fond I am of receiving letters, and I am delighted to have one from your beautiful hand, and all full of caresses. I am going to write one to the little de Rochefort,[1] but I have begun by writing to you, because my heart tells me many things to say to you. I beg you, Madame, to see that the King does not forget the *mignon*."

THE DUC DU MAINE *to* MADAME DE MONTESPAN.

"I have received a letter from the King which has transported me with joy; it is the most condescending that could be imagined. I shall not do as you did, when, at Maintenon, you burned one from him. Far from doing that, I shall keep it as long as I live, and be very proud to have a letter from his Majesty in my desk. Adieu, Madame, I love you passionately."

[1] Son of Maréchale de Rochefort, Madame de Soubise's obliging friend.

MADAME DE MONTESPAN

THE DUC DU MAINE *to* MADAME DE MONTESPAN.

"For a long time, Madame, I have longed to have a little timepiece, like the one you have, and I should like it to come from your hand, for then I shall prize it a thousand times more. If you could send it in a little parcel, I should be delighted. Believe, Madame, that my heart is yours, and that you can make of it all that you please."

THE DUC DU MAINE *to* MADAME DE MONTESPAN.

" Although the King has done me the honour to write to me, Madame, I have not failed to read your letter with very great pleasure. I shall strive to add to the joy which you feel in regard to what you have been told about me, and what you have written to me encourages me to do well, as I desire nothing so ardently as to be in your good graces. For the rest, I thank you very humbly, *ma belle Madame*, for your kindness to my nurse ; she is a woman whom I love much.

" Madame de Maintenon has told me that you have brought her to Fontainebleau ; I am very pleased, and I beg you not to forsake her. I have another favour to ask you, which is that I may not wear petticoats any longer."

THE DUC DU MAINE *to* MADAME DE MONTESPAN.

" I was very pleased, Madame, at receiving your time-piece, since it is a proof of your affection and kindness to me ; I was so delighted all the morning that I could not eat any breakfast. My affection for you, Madame, increases more and more every day, and I take the liberty of telling you of it to show you that I am not ungrateful. I beg you, Madame, to tell the King that the *mignon* loves him more than life."

THE DUC DU MAINE *to* MADAME DE MONTESPAN.

" I am going to give you all the news of the house to amuse you, Madame, and I shall write much better when I think that it is for you. Madame de Maintenon spends all the day in spinning, and, if she were allowed, she would spend all the night as well, or in writing. I read the life of Cæsar on the journey here, that of Alexander at Baréges, and yesterday I commenced that of Pompey. Madame de Maintenon had a headache yesterday, and did not get up except for mass. M. Le Ragois [1] is taking the waters; they did not agree with him the first day, but he is pleased with them now. M. Fagon [2] scalded me yesterday in the little bath; I hope that he will be more moderate another time, and that I shall not cry so much. I bathe in the bath on the days when the weather is cool, and in my room when it is warm. Lutin is very lazy, and in Madame de Maintenon's bad books. I am very pleased with Marcine; Valentin and des Aubiers are very attentive. I have made a friend of Ance, because he has the honour to be one of yours. I am satisfied with Clément. Marotte is a good girl, and waits very well. La Couture does not like lending me Madame de Maintenon's dresses when I have a mind to disguise myself as a girl. I have received the letter which you wrote to your dearest little *mignon;* I am delighted with it, Madame, and I shall do my best to obey you."

[1] The Abbé Le Ragois, the little duke's tutor. He was the author of several historical works.

[2] Guy Crescent Fagon, afterwards chief physician to the King.

MADAME DE MONTESPAN

The Duc du Maine *to* Madame de Montespan.

" You can well believe, Madame, that I shall experience a joy inconceivable on seeing you again. I ask your pardon, Madame, for writing you so short a letter, but the heat has so exhausted me that I cannot write any more. I have, however, sufficient strength left to beg you very humbly, Madame, to tell the King that I am the most obedient of his servants."

The Duc du Maine *to* Madame de Montespan.

" *Ma belle Madame,*—I am overwhelmed with delight at what you have said in the letter which you have done me the honour to write to me about the journey. I beg you very humbly to let me know what day I must start to return to Court. I shall not speak to you of anything else to-day, because I have it so much at heart that I cannot find sufficient words to express myself."

The Duc du Maine *to* Madame de Montespan.

" At Ville-Dieu, on the Road from Baréges.

" The road which remains for me to travel appears very long ; for I am very impatient to see the Court again, and especially the King and yourself, whom I love with incomprehensible tenderness."

The Duc du Maine *to* Madame de Montespan.

" Tarbes, *September* 15, 1677.

" You have written me a letter with which I am delighted, Madame, and since you order me to ask for some reward, I entreat you, Madame, to allow me to leave off petticoats. I am starting to come to you."

MADAME DE MONTESPAN

THE DUC DU MAINE *to* MADAME DE MONTESPAN.

"RISQUÉ,[1] *September* 16, 1677.

"I left Bagnères on Tuesday, Madame, and slept at Tarbes, and to-day I travel as far as Aire. My joy will be complete when I see you, Madame ; but it has already begun. I am the man whom you love most in the world."[2]

Unfortunately, none of the letters written by Madame de Montespan to the Duc du Maine during his visit to the Pyrenees have been preserved ; but, four years later, when the little duke, then eleven years old, had begged to be allowed to accompany the King and the army to Strasbourg, his mother wrote to him as follows :—

MADAME DE MONTESPAN *to the* DUC DU MAINE.

"FONTAINEBLEAU, *September* 23, 1681.

"If I were capable of feeling any joyful emotion,[3] I should have experienced it on seeing the manner in which the King has received your proposal to go to the war ; he was so pleased that he spoke of it to everybody, and I do not doubt that if you had been here he would have taken

[1] Riscle (Gers).

[2] The little duke also wrote a letter to the King, which is of interest, as showing that the correspondence between Louis XIV. and Madame de Maintenon, which had commenced during the lady's previous visit to the Pyrenees, had been resumed : " The letter which you have done Madame de Maintenon the honour to write to her, Sire, has made me jealous, for I set such great store by the marks of your regard that I cannot permit you to bestow them on others. What *la belle Madame* (Madame de Montespan) writes me will encourage me to sustain the reputation which I flatter myself I have gained, as nothing is more precious to me than the approval of your Majesty."—*Correspondance générale de Madame de Maintenon*, i. 347.

[3] Madame de Montespan had just lost her little daughter, Mademoiselle de Tours, who died at Bourbon, September 15, 1681.

you with him. For myself, who value your reputation above all things, I should have consented without pain to your undertaking a journey in which your health would have been endangered, to enjoy the pleasure of hearing you praised by every one, and of seeing you do something to prove that you possess courage and ambition worthy of the son of a hero. I say nothing to you of other matters, in regard to which you will feel like me ; but it is, nevertheless, well that you should know that you are happily spared that intermingling of blood which is ordinarily the fate of people of your position (*i.e.* natural children), and that from whichever side you regard yourself, you will find nobility, courage, and intellect. It is a singularity very advantageous; but one that also obliges you to turn it to good account.

"I do not speak to you of my grief; you are naturally too good not to have experienced it yourself. As for Mademoiselle de Nantes,[1] she has felt it as deeply as if she were twenty, and has received the visits of condolence, which the Queen, Madame la Dauphine, and all the Court have paid her, with marvellous grace. Every one admires her ; but I confess I have paid too dearly for these praises to have derived any pleasure from them. Every place where I have seen that poor little one (Mademoiselle de Tours) affects me so deeply that I am very glad to undertake a journey which in itself is the most disagreeable that can be conceived, in the hope that the distraction will diminish to some extent the *vapeurs* which have not left me since the loss which we have sustained. I much fear that we shall have started before your letters arrive."

"I am writing to M. le Marquis de Montchevreuil [2] to

---

[1] Her eldest daughter, then eight years old.
[2] The Duc du Maine's *gouverneur*.

take what steps he deems advisable for your return ; but I believe you will be a little less anxious to do so when you know that the King will not return for six weeks. In the event of your arriving before, you will find the Hôtel de Longueville [1] ready to receive you." [2]

On February 7, 1678, Louis XIV. left Versailles, with the Queen, Madame de Montespan, and part of the Court, to join the army which was advancing on Lorraine. This movement was, however, merely a feint to divert the attention of the allies from the real object of the campaign, which was the siege of Ghent.

" The King," said his ill-fated sister-in-law, Henrietta, on a certain occasion, " is not a person calculated to render happy even those whom he wishes to treat with the greatest kindness"; and, indeed, Louis's conduct in compelling his mistress, who was again *enceinte*, to follow him, in the depth of winter, along roads where the cumbersome coaches of the time sunk almost to their axletrees in the mud at every few yards, seems to have been little short of barbarous. The despatches which

[1] "The Hôtel du Maine was situated in the Rue Saint-Thomas du Louvre. It was the Hôtel de Longueville, so famous in the time of the Fronde and the Duchesse de Chevreuse. Mesdames de Montespan and de Maintenon stayed there when they came to Paris. This hôtel has now been pulled down, and the street no longer exists."—*Correspondance générale de Madame de Maintenon*, ii. 210, note.

[2] *Correspondance générale de Madame de Maintenon*, ii. 209. Commenting on this letter, M. Lavallée says : " Of all the letters which I have had to examine in arranging the correspondence of Madame de Maintenon none have astonished me more than this. It affords a very strange testimony to the morals and ideas of the Court of Louis XIV. Every one aided and abetted the Great King's adulteries ; no one made any distinction between legitimate children and bastards ; and his mistresses, far from blushing for their position, openly gloried in it, and explained the situation naïvely to their children."

Saint-Pouange, one of Louvois's agents, who accompanied the troops, sent to his chief furnish us with some interesting details concerning this strange journey, which the egotistical monarch doubtless regarded as a great privilege for his Court, but which the latter must have looked upon with very different feelings :—

"*February* 9, *Provins.*—The King arrived at four o'clock this afternoon, having only started at seven o'clock in the morning. The roads are in such a terrible condition and so rough that most of the carriages belonging to the Court had great difficulty in getting here. The coaches containing the *dames du palais* are frequently delayed. The King read this evening, at Madame de Montespan's, while they were playing bassette, part of the despatches you sent me."

"*February* 13, *Fère-Champenoise.*—Madame de Montespan had another attack of fever [1] last night, and it is said that she did not leave this morning until ten o'clock, when she started for Sezanne. She is better now."

"*February* 15, *Vitry.*—You will have gathered from the letters I sent you yesterday that Madame de Montespan's health was much improved. She has to-day taken medicine, which is having a beneficial effect." [2]

"*February* 18, *Commercy.*—Madame de Montespan is very well, and during the march to-day has been riding in the Queen's coach." [3]

[1] On the previous day, Louis XIV. himself had written to Colbert that "Madame de Montespan had just had '*le quatrième accès de fièvre,*' but that it would not prevent her continuing her journey."

[2] At Vitry, the municipal authorities presented to the King "four dozen bottles of Rheims wine"; to the Queen, "twenty-six pounds of preserved fruit and eight hundred dried pears"; and to Madame de Montespan, "a basket of dried pears ornamented with bows of ribbon."

[3] Rousset's *Histoire de Louvois*, vol. ii. pt. i. p. 488, note. The

MADAME DE MONTESPAN

Meanwhile the advance into Lorraine had produced the effect which Louis and Louvois had anticipated, and discomforts suffered by the unfortunate ladies of the Court during this campaign seem to have been trifling compared with those they were compelled to undergo on a similar expedition in the autumn of 1680. Fléchier, the future Bishop of Nimes, who accompanied the Court in his capacity as *lecteur* to the Dauphin, thus describes his experiences in a letter to his friend, Mademoiselle Deshoulières :—

" *Stenay, November* 6.—Yesterday was a day of adventures for the Court. Up till then the journey had passed without any incident, unpleasant or otherwise. We had been travelling for some days along roads that continuous rain had ruined. The equipages reached Thionville with considerable difficulty, and the following day's march proved longer than had been anticipated, either because the King was compelled to go out of his way to visit one of his strongholds or because they had taken into account only the distance to be covered and not the difficulties of the route. The King started at daybreak, and the Queen some time afterwards. On the march the wind rose and the rain redoubled. The coaches became separated, according as they were well or badly horsed. The carts overturned, and the drivers used terrible language. In the midst of this confusion, people dined as they could. Finally, as the day was drawing in and the rain still continued, the majority of people gave up all hope of reaching our destination. The King, after having made the round of the fortifications of Longwy, wished to go to the village of Longuyon, where his quarters were ; but the night overtook him, his guides misled him, and he found himself, with a troop of courtiers, in the midst of a wood, soaked with rain and as muddy as a postilion, a few leagues from Luxembourg, where the Spaniards have a strong garrison. The King deliberated whether he should sleep in the wood, as no one was able to show him the way. But some guards, after searching about on all sides, at length discovered the road and lighted some fires of straw ; and by this means the King gained his quarters at eight or nine o'clock at night. The Queen had not yet arrived, which caused the King great uneasiness. He waited some time, and then, as no news came, he and all the courtiers remounted their horses to go and meet the princess, whom they found two leagues off, guided by some peasants, who were lighting straw to show the way, for the officers had been unable to follow, and, as it had been impossible to foresee that the day's march would occupy such a long time, no one had drawn off the troops which had been covering Ghent, while the greater part of the garrison had been withdrawn for service elsewhere. Accordingly, on arriving at Metz, a fortnight from leaving Versailles, the King, after reviewing his troops, turned to the north, and marched rapidly towards Flanders. Stenay was reached on February 27, and here the army and the Court separated; the former, with the King riding at its head, continuing its march to Ghent, which Maréchal d'Humières with some 40,000 men was already preparing to invest; the latter proceeding to Lille by way of Cambrai and Arras.

The reduction of the famous Flemish city proved an easy task, for it was only defended by 500 Spaniards, and the inhabitants were indisposed to render the soldiers any assistance; and on the night of March 10 the Queen and Madame de Montespan were roused from their slumbers at Cambrai to receive the news of its surrender.

"Your courier," writes Villacerf, first *maitre d'hôtel* to the Queen, to Louvois, "brought the news of the taking of Ghent at midnight." The Queen was in bed and asleep, as was also Madame de Montespan. I woke them up to receive the news and to give them the King's letters. It would be impossible to imagine a more lively joy than they evinced. . . I will inform you regularly of all that passes at our little Court, though, according to appearances, there will be nothing of importance to relate.

taken the precaution to procure torches. The Queen was weeping, and continued to weep until the next day. You can well understand that they had a tolerably unpleasant night. Both the gentlemen and the ladies slept on straw. Madame de Montespan had great difficulty in obtaining a wretched mattress for Mademoiselle de Nantes, whom she had brought with her."—Delacroix's *Histoire de Fléchier*, p. 228.

The Queen is lodged at the Archbishop's palace; Madame de Montespan is the only other lady there. (Evidently the Archbishop of Cambrai was a very liberal-minded prelate.) I find the Queen rather better tempered than on previous expeditions. If she were younger, I should be encouraged to hope that her disposition might change." [1]

To Villacerf had been allotted the post of guardian of the seraglio, a position which was not at all to his taste, for, in a subsequent letter to the War Minister, he remarks: "It is a strange thing to have the charge of women; I shall praise God when you have relieved me of it."

On arriving at Lille, Madame de Montespan announced her intention of going to Oudenarde, whither the King had proceeded after the fall of Ghent, to offer his Majesty her felicitations in person; and, in spite of the remonstrances of poor Villacerf, who had been charged not to let her out of his sight, but who was, of course, unable to leave his royal mistress, set off, accompanied by the Comtesse de Soissons, now restored to favour. After spending a couple of days with her lover, the marchioness returned to Clagny, where, on July 4, she gave birth to her seventh and last child by the King, a boy, who was subsequently legitimated, under the title of the Comte de Toulouse, as was the little daughter born the previous year.

An incident, which was in all probability not without its effect upon the subsequent relations of Louis XIV. and Madame de Montespan, marked the monarch's return from this campaign. "The King," writes the Marquis de Sourches, "being still violently enamoured of Madame

[1] Rousset's *Histoire de Louvois*, vol. ii. pt. i. p. 495.

201

MADAME DE MONTESPAN

de Montespan, and returning to Versailles, after the
taking of Ghent and Ypres, some days before Easter, in
the year 1678, Père de La Chaise, his confessor, remained
behind at Lille, asserting that he was unwell, either
because such was really the case, or because he did not
wish to give absolution to the King, who, in spite of all
his remonstrances, declined to break off his connection
with Madame de Montespan. In the absence of his
confessor, the King sent for Père de Champy (Jesuit),
who, after a lengthy interview with him, refused to hear
his confession, as he was unwilling to give him absolution,
and, nevertheless, contrived to speak so sensibly that the
King, very far from being offended at his refusal, was
very pleased with him, and spoke of him highly to everybody." [1]

[1] *Mémoires du Marquis de Sourches*, i. 89.

CHAPTER XIV

Generosity of Louis XIV. to Madame de Montespan—
Her income, nevertheless, insufficient for her expenditure—
The King makes her a grant of the proceeds of the tobacco
monopoly—But withdraws it at the entreaty of Colbert—He
arms several vessels as privateers to operate for her benefit—
Madame de Montespan one of the most reckless gamblers
known to history—The age of Louis XIV. remarkable for its
passion for play—Madame de Sévigné's description of the
gambling at Versailles—Enormous sums won and lost by
Madame de Montespan—An all-night *séance* at bassette—
The King pays Madame de Montespan's losses—And forbids
bassette to be played any more—Madame de Montespan as a
philanthropist—She founds the Hôpital des Vieillards at
Saint-Germain-en-Laye — Her munificence to the general
hospital in the same town—She persuades the King to found
a convent for the Ursuline nuns at Saint-Germain—She
builds a home for little orphan girls at Fontainebleau—And
completes the dome of the church of the Oratorian monastery
at Saumur—Her patronage of men of letters—She causes
Corneille's pension to be restored to him—She suggests the
appointment of a royal historiographer—But causes Pellisson
to be dismissed for having given a verdict against her in a lawsuit—Racine and Boileau read fragments of their contemporary
history to the King and Madame de Montespan—Racine's
outrageous flattery of Louis XIV.—La Fontaine dedicates his
second collection of fables to Madame de Montespan—The
favourite presents him to the King—She protects Quinault
and the composer Lulli—Ingratitude of Madame de Montespan's literary *protégés*.

THE immense sums spent upon the construction of
Clagny, the recommendations to Colbert to spare no

expense to gratify Madame de Montespan's caprices, the
magnificent jewels and toilettes with which she dazzled
the eyes of the most splendid Court in Christendom, the
almost regal state observed by her in her journeys to
Bourbon and elsewhere show that the lady must have
had little cause to complain of the liberality of her royal
lover ; and, indeed, it is hardly possible to conceive that
any favourite of modern times could have been the object
of more lavish generosity.   We have, unfortunately, no
means of ascertaining even approximately the total
amount she received from the King, since, unlike
Madame de Pompadour, she appears to have kept no
accounts, probably considering such bourgeois calcula-
tions beneath her dignity ; but it must have been something truly colossal.   In the spring of 1677 within the
space of fifteen days, Colbert placed at her disposal,
" according to instructions received from his Majesty
previous to his departure for the army," 97,500 livres ;
and there can be no doubt that this was only one of
many similar sums paid to the lady, in addition to her
regular allowance.   What this was during the years of
her favour is not known ; but from the time of her
retirement from Court in 1691 until 1707 she was in
receipt of a *monthly* pension of 100,000 livres,[1] and it
is, therefore, reasonable to suppose that it was a very
munificent one.[2]

---

[1] In 1707 it was reduced by two-thirds on account of the impoverished state of the Treasury.

[2] A separate allowance was made Madame de Montespan for the
support of her children.   In 1677 we find that a pension of 150,000
livres was paid to her " for the maintenance and education of the Duc
du Maine, the Comte de Vexin, and the Demoiselles de Nantes and de
Tours, natural children of his Majesty, together with their domestics,

MADAME DE MONTESPAN

But great as was the generosity of the King, it seems to have been insufficient to meet Madame de Montespan's expenditure; and, accordingly, we find her having recourse to various expedients for increasing her income. Thus, in 1674, she persuaded Louis to make her a grant of the revenue arising from the recently established tobacco monopoly,[1] though she was not permitted to enjoy it for long, as Colbert, at the risk of mortally offending the haughty favourite, protested so strongly that the King ordered her to surrender it. Four years later, the Treasury was called upon to provide the necessary capital for the lady to indulge in what in those troublous times often proved a highly lucrative form of speculation. On April 16, 1678, Colbert writes to the Intendant of Rochefort, informing him that the King had given a vessel called *Le Hardi* to Madame de Montespan and the Comtesse de Soissons to be fitted out as a privateer, and directing him to have it equipped with "stores, cannon, arms, powder, rigging, and the apparatus required." Similar instructions had already been sent to the Intendant of Brest; and, three weeks later, a third vessel was ordered to be fitted out for the same purpose. By the express desire of Madame de Montespan, the sailors to man these ships were to be chosen in her own province. To the favourite's great disappointment, the Peace of Nimeguen was concluded before *Le Hardi* and her consorts were ready for sea; but the lady evidently did not abandon the idea, since in 1697 she appears as part-

train, suite, and equipage"; while eight years later she was granted no less a sum than half a million " for the maintenance of the Duc du Maine and the Demoiselles de Nantes and de Blois," the eldest of whom was only fifteen years of age.

[1] This tax on its establishment only produced 500,000 livres. Twenty years later it had risen to 1,600,000 livres.

owner of another piratical craft. "If you can form any idea of the profit accruing to Madame de Montespan from her share in this armed vessel," writes the Comte de Toulouse's secretary to a shipowner at Brest, "I beg of you to let me know, so that I may send word in advance to Fontevrault, where she is now staying, and from which she is constantly writing to inquire if there is any news, as she concludes that it can hardly be less than a million livres.[1]

That Madame de Montespan should have been occasionally in need of money is scarcely surprising, when we reflect that not only was she prodigal in the extreme, but one of the most reckless gamblers of which history has any record.

The France of Louis XIV. was remarkable for its passion for play, and if the vice was not quite so widespread as in the eighteenth century, the stakes were infinitely higher. "Play without limit and without regulation," said Bourdaloue, in one of his sermons, "which is no longer an amusement, but a business, a profession, a trade, a fascination; a passion, nay, if I may say so, a rage and a madness, which brings inevitably in its train the neglect of duty, the ruin of families, the dissipation of fortunes, the mean trickery and knavery which result from greed of gain, insanity, misery, despair.[2]

The games most in fashion were lansquenet, hombre, bassette, reversi, trou-madame, and hoca, the last a species of hazard, which is said to have been introduced into France by Mazarin. It was, from all accounts, a game which lent itself very easily to trickery, and about

[1] Quoted in Clément's *Madame de Montespan et Louis XIV.*, p. 395.
[2] Hurel's *Les Orateurs sacrés à la Cour de Louis XIV.*, ii. 54.

1678 it was made illegal, for in that year the Marquis de Seignelay writes to La Reynie, the Lieutenant of Police : " His Majesty intends to speak so strongly to M. de Ventadour about the hoca that goes on at his house that there is no room for doubt that it will put an end to this kind of thing in the future."[1] Nevertheless, hoca continued to be played, for in March 1682 we hear of Madame de Montespan losing 50,000 écus, " which greatly displeased the King "; while six years later, two *grandes dames*, the Comtesse de Rothelin and Madame de Reuilly, were exiled, the former to Champagne and the latter to Abbeville, for disobeying the royal edict.

All the Royal Family—including even the devout Queen, who invariably lost her money, because, as the Princess Palatine observes, she never seemed able to remember the rules of any game—were devoted to play ; and in this respect the Court set a deplorable example to the rest of the country. Madame de Sévigné has left us a lively picture of the gambling which went on of an afternoon at Versailles :—

" At three o'clock the King, the Queen, *Monsieur*, *Madame*, *Mademoiselle*, the Princes and Princesses, Madame de Montespan, all her suite, all the courtiers, all the ladies—in a word, all what is called the Court of France, assemble in that fine apartment of the King which you know. All is furnished divinely, all is magnificent. One knows not what it is to feel hot, and it is easy to pass from one room to another without the slightest crush. A game at reversi gives form to the assembly and makes every one sit down. The King is with Madame de Montespan, who holds the cards ; *Monsieur*, the Queen, and Madame de Soubise ; Dangeau and company,

---

[1] Quoted in Clément's *La Police sur Louis XIV.*, p. 84.

Langlée and company are at different tables. A thousand louis are thrown on the baize ; they use no other counters. I saw Dangeau[1] play and could not help observing how awkward others appeared in comparison with him. He thinks of nothing but the game; gains where others lose ; never throws a chance away ; profits by every mistake ; nothing escapes or distracts him ; in short, his skill defies fortune. Thus two hundred thousand francs in ten days, a hundred thousand écus in a month, are added to his receipt-book.

"The pools are of five, six, and seven hundred, and the larger of a thousand or twelve hundred louis. To begin with, each person pools twenty: that makes a hundred; and the dealer afterwards pools ten. The person who holds the knave of hearts receives four louis from the others ; and when anyone tries for the pool and fails to take it, he pays in sixteen. They talk incessantly. 'How many hearts have you ? I have two ; I have three ; I have one ; I have four.' Dangeau is delighted with this chatter; he discovers the cards they have in their hands, draws his conclusions, and is guided in his play by

---

[1] Philippe de Courcillon, Marquis de Dangeau (1638–1720), soldier, diplomatist, poet, courtier, diarist, and gambler. Although successful in all these varied rôles, he is now best remembered by his *Journal*, which, in spite of the ridicule poured upon it by Voltaire, who had a grudge against the author, is a work of great value, "the necessary complement, if not the counterpart, of the *Mémoires* of Saint-Simon." Fontenelle relates an amusing story of Dangeau's versatility. "Having, one day at Saint-Germain, asked a favour of the King, Louis promised to grant it on condition that, during a game of cards in which he was about to take part, he should put his request into verse, confining himself to exactly a hundred lines. At the conclusion of the game, at which he had appeared to be no more occupied than usual, he recited his hundred lines to the King, fairly counted." La Bruyère has drawn Dangeau's portrait in his *Caractères*, under the name of Pamphilus.

their indiscretions. I observed with pleasure his great skill and dexterity."

Pools of a thousand or twelve hundred louis, equivalent to between four and five times as much in money of to-day, might, one would imagine, have been sufficient to satisfy the cupidity of even the most inveterate of gamblers; but such play was the merest bagatelle to what went on in private. "Dancing has now gone out of fashion," writes the Princess Palatine to one of her German friends. "Here, in France, as soon as people get together, they do nothing but play lansquenet; the young people no longer care about dancing. . . They play here for frightful sums, and the players seem bereft of their senses. One shouts at the top of his voice; another strikes the table so violently with his fist that the whole room resounds; a third blasphemes in a manner to make one's hair stand on end; all appear beside themselves; and it is horrible to watch them."[1]

During the early years of her favour, the years when she exercised undisputed sovereignty over the King's heart, Madame de Montespan's gaming would appear to have been kept within bounds, at least we can find no mention of anything very remarkable in the records of her contemporaries. But when the passion of her royal lover was on the wane—when, on the one hand, the Soubises, the Louvignys, and the Ludres began to appear upon the scene, while, on the other, the subtle influence of Madame de Maintenon was slowly but steadily increasing—then it was that the haughty sultana sought distraction from her jealousy and mortification in gambling orgies which would seem absolutely incredible were they not vouched for by a score of witnesses.

[1] *Correspondance complète de Madame, Duchesse d'Orléans*, i. 15.

MADAME DE MONTESPAN

During the campaign of 1678, Saint-Pouange writes from Lille to Louvois: "The day before yesterday, M. de Langlée, who kept the bank, lost 2700 pistoles,[1] of which Madame de Montespan and Madame la Comtesse de Soissons won a considerable part."[2] Some months later, we learn that the lady is "winning coups at bassette which amount to a million livres, and that she grumbles when people refuse to accept her wagers."[3] Then, on January 13, 1679, the Comte de Rébenac informs the Marquis de Feuquières: "Madame de Montespan's gambling has reached such a pitch that losses of 100,000 écus are common. On Christmas Day she lost 700,000 écus; she staked 150,000 pistoles on three cards and won."

The climax, however, seems to have been reached at the beginning of the following March, when an all-night *séance* was held in Madame de Montespan's apartments, and the players staked as if they had the coffers of the State behind them. "The last mail informs me," writes the Marquis de Trichateau to Bussy-Rabutin, "that, on the night of Monday to Tuesday, Madame de Montespan lost four hundred thousand pistoles playing against the bank, which, however, she eventually won back. At eight o'clock in the morning, Bouyn,[4] who kept the bank, wished to stop; but the lady declared that she did not intend to go to bed until she had won back another hundred thousand pistoles which she owed him from a

---

[1] The pistole was worth from 10 to 11 livres.

[2] Rousset's *Histoire de Louvois*, vol. ii. pt. i. p. 495.

[3] Madame de Montmorency *to* Bussy-Rabutin, December 9, 1678.

[4] A wealthy financier of the time. Dangeau describes him as a "coarse brute," and says that he had at one time served a long term of imprisonment for embezzlement.

previous occasion. *Monsieur* only left Madame de Montespan's apartments in time to attend the King's *lever*. The King paid thirty thousand pistoles which *Monsieur* and Madame de Montespan still owed to the other players." [1]

As a result of this scandalous night, Louis XIV. interdicted bassette as he had already interdicted hoca; but, doubtless, lansquenet, reversi, and trou-madame [2] afforded Madame de Montespan and her associates ample scope for their energies, even if means were not forthcoming for evading the royal edict.

But, if Madame de Montespan squandered money on her pleasures with almost criminal recklessness, she was at the same time extremely generous—splendidly, lavishly generous; and some of the fruits of her good works endure to this day. At first this benevolence may have proceeded from mere ostentation, but in her later years, as we shall see, it was prompted by far worthier motives.

In 1670 the Queen had founded, conjointly with a society of charitable ladies, a hospital at Saint-Germain-en-Laye, which took the name of the Hôpital de la Charité. In 1678 Madame de Montespan founded, in her turn, a hospital, called the Hôpital des Vieillards, and four years, later, acquired in the neighbouring valley of Fillancourt, for 17,000 livres, a site, which she presented to the hospital, for the construction of additional buildings.

[1] The Marquis de Trichateau *to* Bussy-Rabutin, March 6, 1679.

[2] Trou-madame was a game of hazard, somewhat similar to hoca, played with thirteen little balls on a board containing thirteen pockets.

Finally, in December 1688, we find her buying sixty perches of land in the same place, "for the use of the said hospital," on which a new hospital and a church were erected. The constructions of 1682 and 1688 are still in existence. About the same period, the marchioness enlarged the general hospital at Saint-Germain, founded by Louis XIV. in 1681,[1] and its registers state that for many years, when, owing to the ruinous expenditure which the wars against the Coalition entailed, the institution received hardly any assistance from the State, Madame de Montespan contributed in the most generous fashion to its support; indeed, but for her timely help, it is very probable that it would have been compelled to close its doors altogether.[2]

The foundation of the Hôpital des Vieillards and her splendid liberality to the general hospital were not the only benefits which Saint-Germain received from Madame de Montespan. In 1681[3] the Marchioness persuaded Louis XIV. to found a convent for the Ursuline nuns in the same town, and no doubt herself contributed liberally to its support. Here is the brevet constituting her *fondatrice* :—

[1] The hospital possesses an agreement between her and two master-masons, which provides for the construction of a large ward, at a cost of 4500 livres.

[2] M. Clément (*Madame de Montespan et Louis XIV.*, p. 411) says that one of the hospital registers contains a number of receipts for sums given by Madame de Montespan between 1687 and 1707. A deed of July 3, 1697, gives her the title of *fondatrice*, and another of July 26, 1710, speaks of her as "benefactress of this institution," and states that she was in the habit of auditing the accounts. The hospital for old men founded by Madame de Montespan in June 1678 was incorporated with the general hospital in 1803.

[3] She had then ceased to be the King's mistress.

MADAME DE MONTESPAN

" SAINT-GERMAIN-EN-LAYE,
" *March* 28, 1681.

" To-day, March 28, 1681, the King being at Saint-Germain-en-Laye, his Majesty having approved the proposition and very humble supplication which has been made to him by the dame Marquise de Montespan, *surintendante* of the Queen's Household, to establish a convent for the Ursuline nuns at Saint-Germain-en-Laye, for the instruction of young girls in the fear of God and the occupations and employments of their sex, his Majesty has caused his letters patent to be despatched, whereby he has granted and given to the Ursuline nuns of the town of Saint-Denis the hotel belonging to his Majesty called the Hôtel des Fermes, situated at Saint-Germain, and the sum of 30,000 livres, on the conditions stated by the present brevet.

" And his Majesty, wishing to treat favourably the said dame de Montespan, desires and understands that she shall enjoy all the rights, honours, advantages, and privileges belonging to the *fondatrice* of the said monastery; that she shall assume that position and be recognised as such by the said nuns in the same manner as in the foundation of other establishments of the said Ursulines. His Majesty likewise desires that the said nuns shall confer on the said dame de Montespan all the necessary powers and privileges, since the said monastery has only been founded on the express condition that the said dame de Montespan should be its *fondatrice*, and not otherwise ; and, in testimony of his will, his Majesty has granted the present brevet, which he has been pleased to sign with his own hand, and cause it to be countersigned

213

by me, Councillor, Secretary of State and of his orders
and finances.

"Signed : LOUIS and (lower down) COLBERT."[1]

Fontainebleau also benefited by Madame de Montespan's liberality. Here, in November 1686, the marchioness "having learned that there were many young
orphan girls and others living in idleness, want, and, for
the most part, without shelter, and being moved with
compassion for the misery of these poor children," built
a home, called the Hôpital de la Sainte-Famille, in the
Rue de La Rochefoucauld, on a site which had been
given by the King, who, in addition, made an annual
grant to the institution of 4500 livres. The Hôpital de
la Sainte-Famille accommodated sixty little orphan girls,
who received instruction in "religion, writing, sewing,
and the making of lace."

Another generous act on the part of the marchioness
was the completion, in 1695, of the dome of the church
attached to the Oratorian monastery of Notre Dame des
Ardilliers at Saumur, which had been begun forty years
before by Abel Saurien, *surintendant des finances.* She
also enlarged the monastery."[2]

Of Madame de Montespan's other benefactions, notably
of the hospice which she founded at Oiron in 1703, we
shall speak later on.

Speaking one day of the conversational powers of the
Mortemart sisters, the Abbé Testu remarked : "Madame
de Fontevrault converses like one who talks, Madame de
Thianges like one who dreams, Madame de Montespan

[1] Clément's *Madame de Montespan et Louis XIV.,* p. 413.
[2] *Ibid.,* p. 414.

like one who reads." This dictum seems a little strange
in view of the fact that Madame de Montespan's education, to judge by the orthography of her letters, must
have been decidedly neglected, while the Abbess of Fontevrault was an excellent classical scholar, and published
translations of both Plato and Homer.[1] But, whatever
may have been the favourite's literary attainments, there
can be no question but that she had a genuine admiration
for the great writers of her time, and did everything in
her power to further their interests. When Corneille, in
his old age, was deprived of his pension, it was Madame
de Montespan who caused it to be restored to him. It
was Madame de Montespan, again, who introduced
Racine into the immediate *entourage* of Louis XIV., and
it was she who first suggested the idea of having a history
of *le Grand Monarque's* reign written by a royal historiographer, who was to accompany the King on his campaigns
and to be given special facilities for acquiring materials
for his work. Louis readily assented, such a proposition
being indeed very soothing to 'his vanity, and Pellisson
was appointed. For a time things went smoothly enough;
but, unfortunately, Pellisson, besides being an historian,
was also a *maître des requêtes*, and, in that capacity, found
himself one day called upon to give judgment in a lawsuit in which Madame de Montespan was one of the
parties. Rightly or wrongly, he decided against the lady,
and straightway lost his post, which was henceforth shared
by Racine and Boileau.

The two poets were high in favour with Louis XIV.,
and used frequently to be summoned to his private
apartments to read fragments of their contemporary
history to the monarch and his mistress. Neither of

[1] See p. 332 and note.

them was exactly a Tacitus, but, as both were consummate flatterers, their lack of the historic faculty was no doubt overlooked. Racine, indeed, carried his flattery of royalty to lengths which nowadays would be considered absolutely ludicrous, though, according to his latest biographer, M. Larroumet, he believed that in so doing he was performing a most praiseworthy action. " In his eyes, the King was the representative of God on earth, and flattery as much a duty as prayer to God." He not only flattered Louis in conversation and in his works, but in public ceremony. In 1678, in his capacity as Director of the Academy, he terminated a discourse, wherein a eulogy of the King held the chief place, by the following declaration : " All the words of our language, all the syllables, should appear precious to us as so many instruments to be used for the glory of our august protector." And in 1685, on a like occasion : " Happy those who have the honour to approach the person of this great Prince, *the wisest and the most perfect of all men !* " [1] Even Louis XIV., with his insatiable appetite for flattery, found some difficulty in digesting this last piece of adulation. " I am very pleased," said he to Racine. " I should have praised you more if you had praised me less." [2]

Madame de Montespan also patronised La Fontaine, who had certainly made a bold enough bid for her favour.

[1] Boileau's brother, the Abbé Boileau, pressed Racine very closely as a flatterer. One day, he proposed to the Academy that the word *bonheur* (good fortune) should be proscribed from panegyrics of Louis XIV., " because his fortune is his own work, the result of his industry, of his genius, which foresees and provides for all emergencies, &c. &c." It was disparaging to a prince, he said, whose success was owing to himself, to speak of his good fortune.

[2] M. Larroumet's *Racine*, p. 112.

In 1678 he dedicated to her his second collection of fables, in verses which fairly outstripped the limits of flattery. Here are the closing lines :—

"Sous vos seuls auspices ces vers
Seront jugés, malgré l'envie,
Dignes des yeux de l'Univers.
Je ne me mérite pas une faveur si grande :
La Fable en son nom la demande.
Vous savez quel crédit ce mensonge a sur nous ;
S'il procure à mes vers le bonheur de vous plaire,
Je croirai lui devoir un temple pour salaire :
Mais je ne veux des temples que pour vous." [1]

Curiously enough, the very first fable in the book, *Les Animaux malades de la peste*, is one of La Fontaine's most biting satires on the injustice of the great; but this did not prevent the favourite from presenting the author to the King, who is, of course, the lion of the fable, nor the King from according him a very gracious reception and bestowing on him a purse of gold. The story goes that the absent-minded poet, who had intended to beg his Majesty's acceptance of a copy of his work, forgot to bring the book, and, what is still more strange, forgot to take away the purse of gold !

Another of the marchioness's *protégés* was the poet Quinault, and she also protected the composer Lulli, who collaborated with Quinault in so many operas. In 1671 she interfered on Lulli's behalf in the quarrel between him and the Abbé Perrin over the control of the Opera, a step which was very fortunate for that

---

[1] *Fables choisies*, &c. (À Paris, chez Denys Thierry, 1678), iii. 7. The British Museum possesses a copy of this edition, formerly the property of King George III. It was also to flatter Madame de Montespan that La Fontaine composed the fable entitled, *Les Dieux voulants instruire un fils de Jupiter ;* "the son of Jupiter" being the Duc du Maine.

institution, but very much the reverse for poor Perrin, who died in want some years later.

Madame de Montespan's literary *protégés* were not conspicuous for their gratitude. In 1677, Quinault satirised the marchioness in the opera of *Isis*, wherein she figures as Juno, pursuing with vengeance the unfortunate Isis (Madame de Ludres), whom Jupiter (Louis XIV.) changes into a cow to protect from her wrath. As soon as Mademoiselle de Fontanges appeared upon the scene, La Fontaine transferred his allegiance to her;[1] while "the haughty Vasthi" of Racine's *Esther* is obviously the poet's former patroness.[2]

[1] See p. 189.
[2] This tragedy was produced at Saint-Cyr, January 26, 1689.

CHAPTER XV

Magnificent New Year's gifts received by Madame de Montespan in 1679—"The King on the brink of a deep precipice" —Mademoiselle de Fontanges becomes mistress of Louis XIV. —The King resolves to break finally with Madame de Montespan—Madame de Montespan leaves Saint-Germain for Paris—But returns and is appointed Superintendent of the Queen's Household—And apparently resigns herself to the situation—The favour of Mademoiselle de Fontanges becomes public—Arrogance and ostentation of the new mistress—She is made a duchess—Fury of Madame de Montespan—Singular relations between Louis XIV. and Madame de Maintenon—The King creates for her the post of second *dame d'atour* to the Dauphiness—Her favour increasing rapidly, in spite of Louis's passion for Mademoiselle de Fontanges— Explanation of this apparent enigma—Illness of Mademoiselle de Fontanges—She loses her beauty, and with it the King's affection—Madame de Montespan returns to the field—A triangular duel for possession of the royal heart—Madame de Sévigné on the situation—Increasing ascendency of Madame de Maintenon—Futile efforts of Madame de Montespan to check it—Total discomfiture of Mademoiselle de Fontanges —Madame de Montespan and Madame de Maintenon face to face.

THE year 1679 opened to all appearance most auspiciously for Madame de Montespan. To judge from the magnificence of the New Year's gifts which she received, her empire must have seemed more assured than ever. "This year's presents have made a great sensation,"

writes Madame de Scudéry to Bussy-Rabutin, "*Monsieur*
has given Madame de Montespan a gold salver exquisitely chiselled, with a border of emeralds and diamonds,
and two golden goblets with the lids encrusted with
emeralds and diamonds.   This present is said to have
cost ten thousand écus.   The Queen and all the *dames du
palais* have also given her presents.   I have not heard
whether she has made them any, with the exception of
the Princesse d'Harcourt, to whom she has given a hair-
shirt, a scourge, and a prayer-book adorned with diamonds.
Madame de Maintenon has given her a little book, encrusted with emeralds, entitled *Les Œuvres de M. le Duc
du Maine*.[1]   It is a collection of all the pretty things he

---

[1] Its correct title was *Œuvres diverses d'un auteur de sept ans*. Only
a very few copies were printed, of which the Bibliothèque Nationale
possesses one, and it was preceded by a dedication from Madame de
Maintenon to Madame de Montespan, the work of Racine. The book
contained a number of the little duke's letters. Some of these have
already been given in a previous chapter. Here are some others, written
to Madame de Montespan during her absence with the army in 1678 :—
   " *Saint-Germain, February* 7, 1678.—I am inconsolable, Madame,
at not having seen you leave to-day. The King did me the honour to
notice me as he was coming out of chapel ; I was delighted at the little
nod he gave me, but grieved at his departure, and, for you, Madame,
very disappointed that you did not appear grieved. You were beautiful
as an angel. Adieu, *ma belle Madame*.—LE MIGNON."
   " *February* 1678.—*Monsieur's* little daughter is becoming a little more
lively. Madame de Maintenon has told me to teach her to play
billiards and shuttlecock. I flatter myself that I am acquitting myself
very well, and I am very satisfied with her ; I can see that she is doing
her best to imitate the most skilful players. It is not the will that she
needs ; it is her slowness, which causes her to spend an hour in making
her stroke ; she tries very hard. Adieu, *ma chère enjant*."
   " *February* 17, 1678.—I shall try to deserve the praises that the King
bestows on me by increasing every day the esteem which you say he has
for me ; and when it will only be a question of pleasing you, I shall do
the same, as I love you to excess."

has said since he came into the world." Madame de Scudéry does not say anything about the King's present to the favourite; but it is safe to presume that it was at least equal in magnificence to that of *Monsieur*.

But soon the scene changes once more. At the beginning of March, we find Madame de Maintenon imploring the Abbé Gobelin "to pray and to have prayers said for the King, who is on the brink of a deep precipice." [1] This "deep precipice" was the heart of Marie Angélique d'Escorailles de Roussille, Demoiselle de Fontanges, a young beauty of eighteen summers and maid of honour to *Madame*, who supplies us with the following details :—

"I had a *fille d'honneur* named Beauvais.[2] She was a very honest creature. The King became enamoured of her, but she remained virtuous. Then he turned his attention to the Fontanges girl, who was also very pretty, but without any intelligence. At first he said, laughing: 'Here is a wolf who will not eat me up'; and forthwith fell in love with her. Before she came to me, she had dreamt all that was to befall her, and a pious Capuchin had explained her dream to her. She told me all about it herself before she became the King's mistress. She dreamt that she had ascended a high mountain, and having reached the top, she was dazzled by an exceedingly bright cloud; then she found herself in such profound darkness that she awoke in an agony of fear. She told her confessor, who said to her: 'Be on your guard. That mountain is the Court, where some great distinction

---

[1] *Correspondance générale de Madame de Maintenon*, ii. 47.

[2] Uranie de La Cropte-Beauvais, daughter of La Cropte-Beauvais, equerry to the Prince de Condé. She appears to have been in love at this time with the young Comte de Soissons, who married her in October 1680, in spite of considerable opposition from his mother and other members of his family.

awaits you. It will, however, be of short duration. If you abandon God, he will abandon you, and you will fall into eternal darkness.' . . . The Fontanges girl was a silly little creature, but with a warm heart, and beautiful as an angel from head to foot. She was terribly senti-mental and loved the King passionately in the style of a heroine of romance."[1]

Like most of *le Grand Monarque's* affairs of the heart, this intrigue was most carefully disguised at first; never-theless, the secret was very quickly penetrated by Madame de Montespan, who remonstrated with her fickle lover in her usual violent manner, but to no purpose. As Holy Week was approaching, and, with it, his annual access of devotion, his Most Christian Majesty bethought him of making a kind of compromise with Heaven. In order to be free to indulge his passion for his new mistress with an easy conscience, he resolved to break finally with his old one. At the same time, with the idea of tempering the wind to the shorn lamb, he decided to promote the latter to the coveted post of Superintendent of the Queen's Household, at present occupied by the Comtesse de Soissons. Madame de Montespan had endeavoured to prevail upon the King to appoint her to this office some years before, but Louis had had the good taste to spare his unfortunate consort this last humiliation. Now, however, that his illicit connection with the lady had ceased, the former objections would disappear, and the

---

[1] If Bussy-Rabutin is to be believed, the subjugation of the impres-sionable monarch had been deliberately planned by the young lady's relatives, "who, seeing her beauty and grace, and having more regard for their fortune than for their honour, clubbed together to fit her out for Court, and to provide her with means corresponding to the position she was about to enter."

appointment would, moreover, serve the purpose of pro-
claiming to the world that all was at an end between
them.

On March 15, Madame de Montespan suddenly left
Saint-Germain, where the Court then was, and proceeded
to Paris, where she remained a week.   It was the general
opinion that her departure was occasioned "by the
jealousy which she had conceived for Mademoiselle de
Fontanges "; but, as we shall explain in a subsequent
chapter, it had a far graver significance.

A letter from the Marquis de Trichateau to Bussy-
Rabutin contains some interesting details in regard to the
little Court revolutions now in progress :—

"The King has fasted three days, performed his
devotions, and touched the sick.[1]   Madame de Montespan has had many conferences with Père César (her
confessor).   On Wednesday (March 21) she returned to
Saint-Germain, where she attended *Tenebræ*, standing the
whole time behind the King's chair.   The Queen sent to
ask her to attend her at communion.   On Friday she
returned to Paris, and on Saturday she went to Maintenon, returning to Saint-Germain-en-Laye on the following Tuesday, where everything went on as usual, save
that the King did not see her except in the presence
of Monsieur.   Wednesday, the Comtesse de Soissons
received the King's command to resign her post (as
Superintendent of the Queen's Household).   The

---

[1] Those suffering from King's Evil.   The *Gazette de France* states
that in Holy Week 1684, Louis XIV. touched and distributed alms to
900 people.   The King said to each person, "The King touches thee ;
may God heal thee !" The virtue of the royal touch in the seventeenth
century was not supposed to be confined to the King's Evil.   John
Aubrey writes in his "Miscellanies" : "Arise Evans had a fungous

princess in question was at Chaillot, in a little house
which she has there. M. Colbert was continually passing
to and fro. In the evening she spoke to the King at the
Queen's, who complimented her highly on the satisfaction
which she had given her. She replied with all the respect
imaginable, and, finally, she has accepted two hundred
thousand écus, and Madame de Montespan has in this
way become Superintendent of the Queen's Household,
and is no longer mistress."[1]

Not a little to the surprise of the Court, Madame de
Montespan seemed resolved to accept the situation with
a good grace. "All is very quiet here," she writes to
her friend, Maréchal de Noailles ; " the King only comes
into my apartments after mass and after supper. It is
much better to see each other seldom with pleasure than
often with embarrassment."[2] Nevertheless, we learn from
Madame de Scudéry's letters to Bussy-Rabutin that,
although the ex-favourite appeared resigned to her fate
in public, she was reported to be shedding bitter tears in
the privacy of her apartments, and that there had been
a long and heated conversation between her and the
King in the Orangerie at Versailles, during which the

nose and said it was revealed to him that the King's hand would cure
him. And at the first coming of King Charles II. into St. James's
Park he kissed the King's hand and rubbed his nose with it, which dis-
turbed the King, but cured him. Mr. Ashmole told it me."

[1] *Correspondance de Bussy-Rabutin*, iv. 344. A brevet of April 11,
1679, accorded to Madame de Montespan "the same honours, rank,
precedence, and other privileges which Duchesses enjoy." The most
important privilege was that of being seated in the royal presence. It
should be noted that she did not receive the *title*, as Mademoiselle de
La Vallière and Mademoiselle de Fontanges did. So long as her
husband lived, she was compelled to remain "*marquise*."

[2] Quoted in Clément's *Madame de Montespan et Louis XIV.*, p. 251.

latter was heard to remark that "he was being tormented over much and was weary of it."[1]

As for Mademoiselle de Fontanges, little was seen or heard of her for some months. "Never have the King's amours been carried on more secretly than this Fontanges affair," writes Bussy to Trichateau, on August 3. "It is not even known where she is lodged, though it is believed to be above the King's apartments." He expresses his opinion that this privacy cannot last much longer, and a few weeks later we hear that the King is "desperately in love"; that workmen are being employed day and night preparing a magnificent suite of apartments for the reception of the new sultana,[2] and that the latter is likely to obtain "all the favours which the other two enjoyed, and more besides."

Gradually Mademoiselle de Fontanges began to take a more prominent place at Court, where she astonished every one by her arrogance and ostentation. She drove about in a magnificent coach drawn by eight horses (Madame de Montespan had been content with six); she presented herself at the King's mass on New Year's Day, "extraordinarily adorned with diamonds, over a dress made from the same material as that of her Majesty";[3] she passed in front of the Queen without curtseying to or even taking the slightest notice of her. Honours and riches were showered upon her and her relatives. She was created a duchess, with a pension in proportion to her

[1] Letters of Madame de Scudéry *to* Bussy-Rabutin, June 18 and September 25, 1679.

[2] One night, the painters, on going away, left the doors open, and two tame bears belonging to Madame de Montespan, which were allowed to roam about at will, got in and did a great deal of damage. Next day it was said that the bears had avenged their mistress.

[3] Letter of Bussy *to* La Rivière, January 15, 1680.

rank ; one of her sisters was appointed Abbess of Chelles, just as Madame de Montespan had been made Abbess of Fontevrault ; another received on her marriage a dowry of 400,000 livres from the King ; people hastened to solicit her good offices with his Majesty ; and the capricious La Fontaine, who only a year before had dedicated to her predecessor in the royal favour his second collection of *Fables*, addressed to her an " Epistle " in which he styled her " *digne présent des cieux* " and besought her to present his verses " *au dompteur des humains.*" [1]

Bitterly mortified though she undoubtedly was at the triumphs of her rival, Madame de Montespan for a time contrived to disguise her feelings, and " the two sultanas," as Bussy calls them, appeared to live on amicable terms. On New Year's Day, 1680, Mademoiselle de Fontanges made magnificent presents to the ex-favourite and all her children ; and two months later the new divinity appeared at a ball at *Monsieur's* house, at Villers-Cotterets, " in great brilliance and adorned by the hands of Madame de Montespan." [2] But when, at the beginning of April, Mademoiselle de Fontanges was created a duchess, the haughty woman could restrain herself no longer. " Madame de Montespan is enraged," writes Madame de Sévigné to her daughter, in the same letter in which

[1] Here are the opening lines :—

> " Charmant objet, digne présent des cieux,
>   (Et ce n'est point langage du Parnasse),
> Votre beauté vient de la main des dieux ;
>   Vous l'allez voir au récit que je trace.
> Puissent mes vers mériter tant de grâce
>   Que d'être offerts au dompteur des humains,
> Accompagnés d'un mot de votre bouche,
>   Et présentés par vos divines mains."

[2] Letter of Madame de Sévigné *to* Madame de Grignan, March 6, 1680.

she announces the elevation of the new favourite ; " she wept bitterly yesterday. You can imagine what a martyrdom this is to her pride." And the marchioness adds: " It is rendered still more bitter by the high favour which Madame de Maintenon enjoys." [1]

Nothing, indeed, is more curious, at first sight, than the relations which existed between Madame de Maintenon and Louis XIV. during the period when the latter was believed to be the slave of Mademoiselle de Fontanges. One would naturally have supposed that, while engaged in this intrigue, the monarch would have had but little inclination for the society of a lady whose reprobation of unchastity was so notorious, and who had not hesitated to remonstrate with him on his connection with Madame de Montespan, rather late in the day, it is true, but none the less warmly. The very reverse was the case. When, at the end of the year 1679, the Household of the Dauphiness-elect (the Dauphin was betrothed to Marie Anne of Bavaria, and the marriage was to take place in the following February) was chosen, it was announced that a second *dame d'atour* was to be appointed, and Madame de Maintenon was nominated. The appointment of a second *dame d'atour* was an entirely new departure, and no one doubted that the idea had originated with the King, with the object of placing in an independent position the lady whose companionship was evidently becoming more and more necessary to him. From that moment the progress of the ex-*gouvernante* in her sovereign's good graces was rapid in the extreme, notwithstanding the fact that for some months longer Louis's passion for Mademoiselle de Fontanges remained at a high temperature. " Madame de Maintenon grows daily

[1] Madame de Sévigné *to* Madame de Grignan, April 6, 1680.

more in favour," writes Madame de Sévigné, on March 30, 1680. "Nothing now but perpetual conversations between her and the King, who gives all the time he used to bestow on Madame de Montespan to Madame la Dauphine." And a fortnight later: "His Majesty frequently spends two hours at a time in Madame de Maintenon's apartments, conversing in so friendly and natural a manner as to make it the most desirable spot in the world."

The explanation of this apparent enigma was, as a matter of fact, a very simple one. Mademoiselle de Fontanges was merely a pretty doll, whose beauty gratified the King's senses, but with whom he had not a thought or taste in common; who was, indeed, so ignorant that her lover "seemed quite ashamed whenever she opened her lips in the presence of a third person."[1] From her childish caprices and vapid chatter Louis turned with a sense of positive relief to the society of Madame de Maintenon, whose natural charm was heightened by contrast with the youthful *maîtresse déclarée*. In her he found a woman "always modest, always mistress of herself, always reasonable,"[2] and who joined to these rare qualities the attractions of wit and conversation; who, in short, opened to him, as Madame de Sévigné aptly expresses it, a new country—the intercourse of a sincere and unreserved friendship, in which he experienced every day a keener pleasure.

At the beginning of the year 1680, Mademoiselle de Fontanges bore her royal lover a child, who, however, only survived a few days. Owing to the unskilfulness of the surgeons who attended her, and who, it may be

[1] *Souvenirs et Correspondance de Madame de Caylus* (edit. 1889), p. 29.
[2] *Ibid.*

mentioned, received a fee of no less than 100,000 livres
for their services, her confinement proved all but fatal;
and though she recovered sufficiently to return to Court,
it was not long before her health began to give way; and
with the decline of her health her beauty waned also.

This was Madame de Maintenon's opportunity, and we
may be sure she did not fail to take advantage of it.
Religious arguments, which would have had but small
effect upon Louis so long as his mistress retained her
dazzling loveliness, presented themselves in a very different
light when, in place of the brilliant girl who had once
bewitched him, he found a pale, sickly woman, no longer
strong enough to follow him on his royal progresses to
Flanders and elsewhere or to take her former part in the
gaieties of the Court. She had always bored him, had this
poor, silly child without an idea in her pretty head beyond
dress and luxury; now that she no longer appealed even
to his senses, he became absolutely indifferent to her. So
conscience and inclination joined hands, and slowly but
surely Mademoiselle de Fontanges dropped out of his life.

No sooner did she perceive that the star of her rival
was beginning to wane, than Madame de Montespan's
hopes revived, and she returned to the field, " horse, foot,
and artillery"; and for some weeks a sort of triangular
duel was waged for the possession of the royal favour
between her, Mademoiselle de Fontanges, and Madame
de Maintenon; the first striving to recover what she had
lost, the second, to retain the sceptre which was slipping
from her grasp, the third, to push the advantage which
she had lately gained still further; while every move in
the game, every phase of the struggle, was watched with
almost breathless interest by the lynx-eyed courtiers, as
the correspondence of the time abundantly testifies.

"I have just heard," writes Bussy to Trichateau, on May 18, "that the day the King left for Saint-Germain, as he was entering his coach with the Queen, some angry words passed between him and Madame de Montespan about the perfumes which she always uses, and which make his Majesty ill.[1] The King spoke to her at first with courtesy, but as she replied with a good deal of tartness, his Majesty grew warm. For my part, I do not think that she will remain long at Court. When lovers, after having broken with one another, do not remain friends, they generally go to the other extreme." The next day Trichateau reports that the King had given Mademoiselle de Fontanges "unmistakable proofs that he finds her worthy of his love," and that he evidently regarded her recent illness "as a wound received in his service." Then, on the 25th of the month, Madame de Sévigné writes: "The other day there was a sharp quarrel between the King and Madame de Montespan. M. Colbert endeavoured to bring about a reconciliation, but could with difficulty prevail upon his Majesty to partake of *médianoche* with her, as usual. It was only on condition that every one else should be admitted."

From the same writer we glean some highly interesting information with regard to the fortunes of the third candidate for the monarch's favour :—

"*June 5.*—The credit of Madame de Maintenon still continues. The Queen accuses her of being the cause of the separation between her and Madame la Dauphine.

---

[1] Anne of Austria had used perfumes to excess, and the King when a boy had imbibed a strong antipathy to them. He declared that this weakness on the part of his mother was responsible for the violent headaches to which he was subject, and would not allow his personal attendants to use scent of any kind.

The King has comforted her for this disgrace. She goes to visit him every day, and their conversations are of a length which give rise to numberless conjectures."

" *June* 9.—Madame de Maintenon's favour is constantly increasing, while that of Madame de Montespan is visibly declining."

" *June* 20.—I am told that the conversations between his Majesty and Madame de Maintenon are becoming more frequent and more prolonged ; that they last from six o'clock until ten ; that the daughter-in-law (the Dauphiness) occasionally pays her a short visit ; that she finds them each sitting in an easy chair ; and that they resume the thread of their conversation as soon as she leaves. My friend (Madame de Coulanges) informs me that no one any longer approaches the lady but with fear and respect, and that the Ministers render her the same homage as other people."

" *June* 30.—I have had a letter from Madame de Coulanges in which she tells me that the other day the King spent three hours in Madame de Maintenon's apartments, the lady being indisposed with a headache ; that Père de La Chaise visits her ; that Mademoiselle de Fontanges is continually weeping because she is no longer beloved, and that the most splendid establishments are powerless to soothe her grief."

At the beginning of July, it would appear that a cabal had been formed by Madame de Montespan, " who was ready to die with mortification at the influence obtained by wit and conversation," against the ex-*gouvernante*, and that rumours reflecting upon that lady's early career were floating about, for Madame de Sévigné inquires of her daughter, " Could she (Madame de Maintenon) suppose that people would always remain in ignorance of the first

volume of her life?"[1] while Madame de Maintenon herself writes to her brother : " They are enraged against me,
and, as you say, will stop at nothing in order to injure
me. If they fail, we shall laugh at them ; and if they
succeed, we shall suffer with courage."[2]

Finding that her attempt to discredit her rival with
the King was unlikely to succeed, Madame de Montespan,
if we are to believe Madame de Caylus, next endeavoured
to inspire his Majesty with a passion for her niece, the
beautiful Duchesse de Nevers, "in order to preserve the
royal favour in her own family."[3] Madame de Caylus
is one of those chroniclers whose statements, especially
where their enemies are concerned, it is usually wise to
accept with reservation ; but, in the present instance, the
charge seems to be confirmed by a passage in a letter of
Madame de Sévigné : " The King went the other day
to Versailles with Madame de Montespan, Madame de
Thianges, and Madame de Nevers, who was so covered
with flowers that Madame de Coulanges says, 'Flora is a
fool to her.' *Mon Dieu!* how dangerous such a jaunt
would be to a man who had anything of the libertine in
his composition ! "

But the intrigue, if intrigue there really was, failed of
its purpose ; and the same letter informs us that " people
were amazed at the degree of favour which Madame de
Maintenon was enjoying, and that no friend could show
more regard to another than did the King to her."[4]

A few days later, the King and Queen set out on a
royal progress to Flanders, and both Madame de Montespan

[1] Letter of July 7, 1680.
[2] *Correspondance générale*, ii. 114.
[3] *Souvenirs de Madame de Caylus* (edit. 1889,, p. 67.
[4] Madame de Sévigné *to* Madame de Grignan, July 17, 1680.

and Madame de Maintenon accompanied the Court. As for poor Mademoiselle de Fontanges, she was far too unwell to stand the fatigues of the journey, and sorrowfully wended her way to Chelles, to pass the time until the Court's return with her sister, the abbess. Madame de Sévigné jests at her discomfiture : " You have been diverted by the person who was wounded ' in the service ' (of the King)," she writes to her daughter. " She is so much so that she is believed to be qualified for admission to the Hôtel des Invalides." And in another letter : " Madame de Fontanges has started for Chelles. She has four coaches drawn by six horses, her own has eight. All her sisters are with her, but there was an air of gloom over the whole party which inspired pity ; the fair one pale and wan, changed with loss of blood and overwhelmed with grief, despising 40,000 écus a year and the *tabouret*,[1] which she has, and wishing for health and the King's heart, which she has lost."[2]

Some weeks later, we hear of her at the consecration of her sister as Abbess of Chelles, on which occasion she was so ill that she came to the ceremony " in a *robe de chambre*, a mob-cap, and a shawl," and went back to bed immediately it was over.[3] She reappeared at Versailles at the end

---

[1] The stool on which a duke or duchess was allowed to sit in the royal presence.

[2] Letters of July 14 and July 17, 1680.

[3] Letter of Madame de Scudéry *to* Bussy-Rabutin, August 28, 1680. Madame de Sévigné relates an amusing anecdote in connection with this ceremony. The splendour of the ritual, the exquisite music, the incense, and the number of bishops who officiated, so impressed a good country lady that she could not help exclaiming, " Surely I am in Paradise ! " Whereupon a wag, who sat near her, remarked, " Pardon me, Madame, but there are not so many bishops there."—Letter of September 17, 1680.

of August, to meet the King on his return from Flanders, but if she had anticipated any return of tenderness on the part of her quondam adorer, she was speedily undeceived, as Louis treated her with marked coldness and paid her nothing but formal visits, lasting a few minutes.

The total discomfiture of poor Mademoiselle de Fontanges left Madame de Montespan and Madame de Maintenon face to face ; and the Court, believing that the critical moment had arrived, was fairly bubbling over with excitement. But, little as the quidnuncs of Versailles suspected it, the contest was already decided. During the King's absence in Flanders events had occurred which had effectually extinguished any chance which Madame de Montespan might have possessed of recovering her ascendency.

CHAPTER XVI

ABOUT the year 1673, the penitentiaries of Notre-Dame informed the police authorities that the majority of the

women who had confessed to them for some time past
accused themselves of poisoning some one.   This warning,
strange to say, does not appear to have made much impression upon the police, and even the famous case of
Madame de Brinvilliers, the prelude to the terrible drama
which was about to send a shudder through Europe, left
them still unmoved.   They evidently inclined to the
belief that the crimes of this fiendish woman were merely
such as from time to time occur even in the most law-
abiding communities, and were not to be regarded as in
any way typical of the state of public morality.

   In September 1677, fourteen months after Brinvilliers
had expiated her crimes in the Place de Grève, information was received that a note had been found in the confessional of the Jesuit church in the Rue Saint-Antoine,
revealing a plot to poison the King and the Dauphin.
This would seem to have been a false alarm, as no evidence was subsequently forthcoming that any such thing
was contemplated, but it had the effect of rousing the
police to activity, and the sleuth-hounds of the law were
at once set to work.

   The recently-created post of Lieutenant of Police
was, fortunately for the ends of justice, filled by an official
whose name deserves to be held in honour for all time,
one Gabriel Nicolas de La Reynie, a man of great ability
and spotless integrity, and absolutely fearless in the discharge of his duties.   If he had been slow to move,
very possibly because he had not been allowed a free
hand, he now showed himself indefatigable in his efforts
to sift the matter to the very bottom, and in the following
December caused the arrest of a certain Louis de Vanens,
who had formerly held a commission in the army and was
on terms of intimacy with many distinguished people at

MADAME DE MONTESPAN

Court, Madame de Montespan among the number. The papers seized on him and on his mistress, a woman called Finette, brought to light a gang of alchemists, coiners, and magicians whose ramifications extended into all classes of society. It was an important capture, as, in addition to his manipulation of the coin of the realm, Vanens was subsequently found to be hand in glove with the Poisoners, and there can be little doubt that he had taken part in bringing about the death of Charles Emmanuel II., Duke of Savoy, who had died under highly suspicious circumstances in June 1675;[1] but towards the close of 1678 it was followed by two arrests, which enabled La Reynie to lay his hand upon an infinitely more dangerous association.

An advocate in small practice, Maître Perrin by name, came to Desgrez, a smart detective officer who had distinguished himself in the Brinvilliers affair, and told him that on the previous day he had been dining in the Rue Courtauvilain with a certain Madame Vigoureux, the wife of a ladies' tailor ; that among the company, who were very merry, was a woman called Marie Bosse, a well-known *devineresse* or fortune-teller ; that this Marie Bosse in her cups had begun to boast of the profits of her trade and of the grand people she numbered among her clients, and had wound up by remarking, "*Another three poisonings, and I shall be able to retire with my fortune made !*" The majority of the company, he added, had laughed heartily, believing that the woman's words were merely a drunken jest, but he had seen, by the angry looks which his hostess

---

[1] The principal agent in causing the Duke's death was Charles II.'s friend, Count de Castelmelhor, whom the Duchess of Savoy (*née* Marie de Nemours) honoured with her affection. Vanens was believed to have been one of his accomplices.

had darted at the speaker, that there was something serious in them.

Desgrez was evidently of the same opinion, for he immediately despatched the wife of one of his archers to Marie Bosse, with a trumped-up story about a cruel husband whom she desired to get rid of. The *devineresse* fell headlong into the trap prepared for her; told the woman to call again, and, when she did so, gave her a phial of liquid, which her pretended client promptly handed to the police. The phial was found to contain a deadly poison; and Marie Bosse and Madame Vigoureux were forthwith arrested.[1] An Order in Council of January 10, 1679, instructed La Reynie to proceed against these women and their accomplices; and, two months later, the police effected another capture, the importance of which can hardly be overestimated—that of Catherine Deshayes, the wife of Antoine Monvoisin, a peddling jeweller of Villeneuve-sur-Gravois.

This woman, usually known as La Voisin, was one of the greatest criminals known to history, and the state of affairs which her trial and that of her accomplices brought to light the most appalling that the imagination can possibly conceive. "Human life is publicly trafficked in," wrote the Lieutenant of Police. "Death is almost the only remedy employed in family embarrassments; impieties, sacrileges, abominations are common practices in Paris, in the surrounding country, in the provinces."

It was the failure of her husband, who had a shop on the Pont-Marie, that had first led La Voisin "to devote herself to cultivating the powers that God had given her," as she expressed it. She was skilled in cheiromancy, and appears to have made a profound study of physiognomy,

---

[1] Ravaisson's *Archives de la Bastille,* iv. 157.

an elaborate treatise on which was found among the papers seized at her house. She was also an expert psychologist, and thus was able to give a real foundation to her sorcery.

Belief in magic and witchcraft was at this period well-nigh universal ; even such men as Bossuet were firmly persuaded of the efficacy of sorcery, while those who openly expressed their incredulity were looked upon as little better than atheists. Not only the common people, but the bourgeoisie and the nobility were as ignorant and as grossly superstitious as in the Middle Ages.[1] As La Voisin's fame spread, people of all sorts and conditions flocked to her house—youths barely out of their teens begging her for some charm to soften the hearts of their mistresses or to bend the opposition of some stern parent ; women of mature years, whose lovers had neglected them for fresher charms, seeking her aid to compel their faithless paramours to return to them ; impatient heirs to inquire when they might hope to inherit the fortunes they coveted ; young wives anxious for the demise of elderly husbands. Well did La Fontaine write of her :—

> " Une femme à Paris faisait la pythonisse :
> On l'allait consulter sur chaque évènement :
> Perdait-on un chiffon, avait-on un amant,
> Un mari vivant trop au gré de son épouse,
> Une mère fâcheuse, une épouse jalouse,

[1] See Dr. Lucien Nass's *Les Empoisonnements sur Louis XIV.*, chap. i. Superstition was, of course, equally prevalent in other countries. M. Ravaisson says that about this time a performing horse, such as may now be seen in almost any circus, was burnt alive by the Inquisition in Spain " as a pupil of the devil " ; while a man named Brioche, an exhibitor of marionettes, so astonished the simple Swiss that they wanted to burn him as a magician, and he had great difficulty in escaping the hands of the executioner.

MADAME DE MONTESPAN

Chez la devineresse on courait
Pour se faire annoncer ce que l'on désirait."[1]

No expense was spared by the sorceress in order to impress her clients. She was accustomed to deliver her oracular sayings clothed in a magnificent robe, the skirt of which was edged with the finest *point de France*, and a cloak "of crimson velvet studded with 205 two-headed eagles of fine gold and lined with costly fur.[2] Even her shoes were embroidered with golden two-headed eagles."

La Voisin's principal assistant was a man called Lesage, who was her lover, or rather one of her lovers, for she was noted for her gallantry.[3] His real name was Adam Cœuret, and he appears to have been at one time a wool merchant,[4] but soon abandoned that prosaic calling for the more profitable one of a magician. He had a remarkable talent for jugglery, by means of which he duped not only the people who came to avail themselves of his art, but even the witches with whom he worked. One of his favourite tricks was to write his clients' requests to the "Spirit"—as the devil was called—in notes, which he then enclosed in balls of wax and pretended to throw into the fire. Some days later he would give them

---

[1] According to M. Ravaisson, La Fontaine was at one time on friendly terms with La Voisin.

[2] M. Funck-Brentano's *Le Drame des Poisons*, p. 118. The author, who has the bills of the maker in his possession, says that the cloak and robe, which were specially woven for her, cost 15,000 livres, and that the mere weaving of the eagles on the cloak cost 400 livres.

[3] Among those upon whom she bestowed her favours were André Guillaume, the *exécuteur de la haute justice*, who had executed Madame de Brinvilliers and narrowly escaped having to perform the same office upon La Voisin herself, the Comtes de Cousserans and de Labatie, and the architect Fauchet.

[4] Voltaire says that he had been a priest, but this is incorrect.

back the notes, saying that the "Spirit," who had received them through the flames, had returned them.

A far more terrible coadjutor was the infamous Abbé Guibourg, the sacristan of Saint-Marcel at Saint-Denis, who claimed to be an illegitimate offshoot of the Montmorency family and had formerly been chaplain to the Comte de Montgommery. At the time of his arrest he was about seventy years of age; his face was red and bloated with drink; "prominent blue veins formed a network on his cheeks," and he was afflicted with a most horrible squint. Such was the monster whose name will ever be associated with the unspeakable abominations of the "black mass." [1]

La Voisin, like all the sorceresses, practised medicine, and had besides an intimate knowledge of poisons.[2] She soon found, as she confessed to La Reynie, that the majority of those who came to consult her wished "to be ridded of some one," but at first she hesitated to assist them to obtain their object, probably through fear of the consequences if she were detected; it could hardly have been from any qualms of conscience. Her hesitation, however, did not last long, and once embarked upon this horrible traffic she found it so lucrative that she seems to have devoted nearly the whole of her time to it.

---

[1] The "black mass" will be found fully described in the *Introduction* to volume iv. of M. Ravaisson's *Archives de la Bastille*; in M. Funck-Brentano's *Le Drame des Poisons*; or in M. Huysmans's *Là-bas*. For reasons which the reader will no doubt appreciate, we refrain from describing it here.

[2] Dr. Lucien Nass, in his learned work, *Les Empoisonnements sur Louis XIV.*, treats exhaustively of the poisons then in vogue. Arsenic, it appears, was, as it continued to be till the end of the eighteenth century, the "King of Poisons"; but opium and antimony were also largely used, and La Voisin is believed to have frequently employed a preparation made from hemlock.

MADAME DE MONTESPAN

In spite of the notoriety which they enjoyed, La Voisin, La Bosse, La Vigoureux, and their fellow-sorceresses, of whom the most formidable was a woman called Françoise Filastre, were very careful to conceal the real nature of their operations. Their art apparently consisted in drawing horoscopes, cheiromancy, clairvoyancy, the cure of nervous maladies, the vending of aids to beauty, and so forth, which accounts for the fact that their nefarious practices remained so long unsuspected.

As may readily be imagined, the consternation of the authorities on discovering that such frightful crimes were rampant in their midst was unbounded; and their alarm was intensified by the fact that at this period the ignorance of pathology and chemistry was such that even the ablest physicians were, as a rule, incapable of detecting traces of poison in a corpse. The King shared the general horror and indignation, and gave orders that no stone should be left unturned to bring the criminals to justice, and in order to avoid the cumbersome procedure of the ordinary courts, and at the same time to ensure greater secrecy, it was resolved to entrust the matter to a special commission, composed of the *élite* of the Councillors of State, presided over by Louis Boucherat, afterwards Chancellor, with La Reynie and Bazin de Bezons of the Academy [1] as examining-commissioners. [2]

[1] Elected in 1643, at the age of twenty-six, on the death of Chancellor Séguier. He was the first Academician to deliver an address at his reception.

[2] The names of the other judges were Louis de Breteuil, formerly Comptroller-General; Daniel Voisin; Gaspard de Fieubet; Michel Le Pelletier; Pomereu de La Bretesche, afterwards Intendant of Brittany; Bernard de Fortia, formerly Intendant of Auvergne; d'Argouges; André Le Fèvre d'Ormesson, afterwards Intendant of Lyons; and Antoine Turgot, a very learned person, who subsequently wrote an account of the proceedings in Latin verse.

MADAME DE MONTESPAN

This court was called the Chambre Ardente, not, as several writers have supposed, because it had power to condemn persons to the stake, but because in former days tribunals specially constituted to deal with extraordinary crimes sat in a chamber hung with black and lighted by torches and candles.[1]

The procedure was as follows :—

The persons arrested [2] were, on the requisition of the *procureur-général*, brought before La Reynie and Bezons, who, after examining them, drew up a detailed report to be submitted to the court. The court then decided whether there was sufficient evidence to justify a remand. If there was, they issued a warrant to that effect, and the trial followed in due course. When all the witnesses had been heard, the *procureur-général* proceeded to sum up in favour of acquittal or condemnation, the accused was heard for the last time, and the court pronounced judgment, from which there was no appeal. It was not necessary for the judges to be unanimous ; a bare majority was sufficient to decide the fate of the prisoner.

In order to understand more readily what we shall presently relate, it will be as well for the reader to bear in mind two facts : first, that as the examinations conducted by La Reynie and Bezons were in private, their colleagues had no knowledge whatever of what took place beyond the official report which was subsequently submitted to them ; and, secondly, that the commissioners in question would appear to have received private instructions from the

---

[1] *Le Mercure galant*, April 1679, p. 336.

[2] They were arrested by *lettre de cachet;* that is to say, by roya warrant. The Chambre had no power to arrest any one on its own authority. Owing to this circumstance, as we shall see, more than one person managed to effect his escape.

King that in the event of anything of unusual importance occurring, as, for instance, the denunciation by one of the prisoners of a person of high rank, they should communicate with him *before* laying the evidence before the court.

The Chambre Ardente met for the first time on April 10, 1679, in the hall of Arsenal. From that date until July 21, 1682, when it was dissolved, it held 210 sittings, after having been suspended, for reasons which will be explained, from October 1, 1680, to May 19, 1681.

"The Chambre Ardente," says M. Funck-Brentano, "deliberated on the fate of 442 accused persons and ordered the arrest of 367 of them. Of the arrests, 218 were sustained. Thirty-six persons were condemned to the extreme penalty, torture ordinary and extraordinary [1]

[1] There were two kinds of *question*—the *preparatory*, which was inflicted on the accused during examination to make him admit the crime with which he was charged ; and the *preliminary*, to which persons condemned to death were subjected, in order to oblige them to reveal their accomplices. The *preliminary* consisted of two parts, the *ordinary* and the *extraordinary*, the latter being, as a rule, twice as severe as the former. As for the methods of torture in vogue, these varied in different parts of France. At Autun boiling oil was used ; in Normandy the thumb-screw ; while in Brittany fire was applied to the feet. But in Paris the *question aux brodequins* (the "boot") and the *question à l'eau* (the water torture) were generally employed. The "boot" was used in England and Scotland, but the *question à l'eau* seems to have been peculiar to France. The method of operating was as follows : Cords were attached to the victim's arms and feet, and fastened to iron rings in the walls of the torture-chamber, in such a way that he was suspended in the air in a horizontal position. Enormous quantities of water were then introduced into the stomach through a funnel placed between the teeth. This, rapidly accumulating within the body, occasioned the most terrible agony. Madame de Brinvilliers was subjected to this punishment.—See Bingham's "Bastille" and Rousse's *Justice criminelle*.

and execution; two of them died a natural death in gaol; five were sent to the galleys; twenty-three were exiled; but the majority had accomplices in such high places that their cases were never carried to an end." [1]

The first person of any note to be compromised by the confessions of the prisoners was Madame Philbert, the wife of the fashionable flutist of that name. Before wedding the musician, she had been the consort of a wealthy wholesale tradesman called Brunet, who was passionately fond of music and kept open house for all who were able to gratify his tastes in that direction. The fascinating Philbert soon became one of the most frequent guests, a sort of *ami de famille*, in short, though his relations with Madame appear to have been rather more than friendly. For some time matters went on with great satisfaction to all parties concerned, the flute-player delighting the husband with his dulcet strains and making love to the wife, and might have continued thus for an indefinite period had not the unsuspecting Brunet, in an evil hour, offered his daughter, plus a handsome *dot*, to the musician. The latter, who, like Bohemians all the world over, spent his money as fast as he earned it, was by no means unwilling to espouse so well-dowered a young lady, and after consulting apostolic notaries, who informed him that, for a consideration, it would be possible to obtain canonical letters which would enable him to wed with a clear conscience, accepted M. Brunet's offer. Madame Brunet, however, was by no means disposed to surrender her lover, and having vainly endeavoured to turn him from his purpose, sought out La Voisin, whom she assured that " if she had to do penance for ten years, it was necessary that God should

---

[1] *Le Drame des Poisons,* p. 132.

carry off Brunet, her husband, for she could not endure to see Philbert, whom she loved to distraction, in the arms of her daughter." Whether La Voisin undertook this case or not is uncertain ; if she did, she must have bungled it, for it was her fellow-sorceress, Marie Bosse, who, for the sum of 2000 livres, provided the lady with the means of obtaining her freedom.

Brunet dead, the flute-player's feelings towards the daughter underwent a change, and, " on the advice of his friends," he decided to wed the widow, which he accordingly did, the King himself signing the marriage-contract.

On May 15, 1679, the Chambre condemned Madame Philbert to be hanged and her body to be cast into the flames. A request to be allowed to see her husband and children for the last time was refused. The flute-player, who had meanwhile surrendered to take his trial, was acquitted of all complicity in the affair, and, on his release, became a greater favourite with the ladies than ever ; so much so, we are told, that he was positively embarrassed by their attentions.[1]

The rigorous sentence passed upon Madame Philbert aroused in La Reynie and other lovers of justice hopes which, unfortunately, were not destined to be realised. The flute-player's wife had had no friends among the judges ; no one was interested in saving her from the penalty of her crime, but it was far otherwise when the wives of the gentlemen of the long robe—ladies with whom they had danced, and dined, and supped, and possibly made love to—began to appear before the court.

A fortnight after the execution of Madame Philbert, a certain Madame de Poulaillon, an extremely pretty young woman, scarcely more than a girl, was arraigned. Her

[1] *Archives de la Bastille*, v. 367.

case presented all the elements necessary for a domestic comedy, or tragedy, in the seventeenth century—a young and foolish wife, an elderly and wealthy husband, and a needy and unscrupulous lover, one La Rivière by name, who was a natural son of the Bishop of Langres, but had the impudence to style himself the " Marquis de La Rivière." Madame de Poulaillon had been in the habit of supplying the gallant, " who had a wonderful talent for getting money out of ladies," with funds,[1] until her husband became suspicious and cut down the handsome allowance he had hitherto been in the habit of making her. Madame thereupon proceeded to sell the plate, the furniture—" the big gilded bed, upholstered in English watered silk "—and even Monsieur's clothes. Poulaillon retaliated by stopping the allowance altogether and bought his wife's gowns himself, all of which the lady promptly sold or pledged and handed the proceeds to her lover.

With the reduction of supplies the ardour of the *soi-disant* marquis perceptibly cooled, upon which Madame de Poulaillon, in despair of losing him altogether, determined to get the inconvenient husband out of the way. Her first idea was to have him kidnapped, but, failing to find any one to carry out her plan, she had recourse to Marie Bosse, whom she interviewed in the Carmelite church in the Rue du Bouloi—a strange place for such negotiations! The young woman pleaded for something which would do the work at once ; but the sorceress, who favoured more gradual methods, because in

[1] The rôle of *homme entretenu* was then quite the accepted thing among young men of fashion, and excited neither astonishment nor disgust. The custom had, indeed, become so widespread that Bourdaloue felt compelled to denounce it from the pulpit.

that case suspicion was less likely to be aroused, persuaded her to exercise patience. So it was decided to employ arsenic. The wretched husband's shirts were to be washed in arsenic;[1] arsenic was to be put in the *lavements* then in general use;[2] arsenic was to be mixed with his soup and with his wine. Four thousand livres was to be paid to the sorceress for her deadly concoctions, and the conspirators went home well satisfied with their day's work. Poulaillon, however, was warned by an anonymous letter—possibly there had been an unseen listener to the conference in the Carmelite Church—and the plot came to nothing. A like result awaited a subsequent attempt on the part of the lady to have her husband murdered by hired bravoes, who, after agreeing to do as she desired, came to the conclusion that it would be equally profitable and a good deal safer to inform Poulaillon, who thereupon very sensibly shut his wife up in a convent and laid an information before the Châtelet.[3]

[1] The poisoned shirt was one of the most diabolical of these hags' inventions. For its effects, see Dr. Lucien Nass's *Les Empoisonnements sur Louis XIV.*, p. 38 *et seq.*

[2] The *lavement intoxiqué* is believed to have been used with deadly effect in numbers of cases. Dr. Lucien Nass thinks that there can be no doubt that many of the apothecaries of Paris were in league with the Poisoners.

[3] As soon as he learned of the arrest of Madame de Poulaillon, the fascinating La Rivière, who was the cause of all the trouble, fled to Burgundy, where he made the acquaintance of Bussy-Rabutin and his widowed daughter, Madame de Coligny, who lived with him. Learning that the widow was "richly left," the rascal consoled her to such good purpose that she signed a promise in her blood to marry him "whenever it should please him." La Rivière waited until Bussy had departed on a visit to Paris, and then called upon the lady to fulfil her engagement; and when the count returned he found that he had gained a son-in-law. Having, during his visit to the capital, picked up a good deal of

MADAME DE MONTESPAN

The evidence against Madame de Poulaillon was so damning that the *procureur-général* had no hesitation in demanding the extreme penalty—torture and death. But, alas for justice! The prisoner was so very pretty, and exhibited during her trial such extraordinary fortitude and so much contrition, that the judges were touched, and, after deliberating together for four hours, decided to commute the death-sentence upon which they had at first agreed to one of banishment from Paris.

Some excuse might possibly be made for the reluctance of the court to condemn Madame de Poulaillon, inasmuch as her murderous designs had failed; but no such plea was available in two other cases—those of Mesdames de Dreux and Leféron—which came before the Chambre in the following spring.

Madame de Dreux was the wife of a *maître des requêtes*, and is described as a lady of great beauty and "of infinite charm and distinction." She was proved to have poisoned at least three persons; to have offered La Voisin "2000 écus, a ring, and a diamond cross" to make away with her husband, and to have endeavoured to put an end to Madame de Richelieu, the wife of one of her lovers, by sorcery. Nevertheless, the judges, with two of whom, it is interesting to note, the lady claimed relationship,

information about the gentleman in question, he was naturally furious, and threatened "to beat the life out of La Rivière with his cane"; but the latter prudently kept out of his way. In process of time disillusion came to the love-lorn Madame de Coligny, or rather "Marquise" de La Rivière, and she and her father appealed to the Châtelet to dissolve the union, on the ground of some irregularity in the marriage-contract. The husband resisted, however, and would only consent to surrender his conjugal rights on condition of receiving a handsome allowance, on which he lived in luxury for the rest of his days.—*Archives de la Bastille*, v. 161, note; *Correspondance de Bussy-Rabutin*, iv., appendix.

contented themselves with admonishing her. Madame de
Dreux took this admonition so much to heart that no
sooner had she been set at liberty, than she applied to a
sorceress called La Joly, "an abandoned woman, who carried
on an extensive business (*i.e.* in poisoning and sorcery),"
for poison to get rid of a lady upon whom M. de Richelieu
had cast a favourable eye. Fortunately for the intended
victim, La Joly was arrested before her client had found
an opportunity of carrying out her design, and, as a result
of her admissions, a fresh warrant was issued against
Madame de Dreux, who, however, was warned in time,
doubtless by one of the friendly judges, and contrived to
effect her escape. A year or two later she was allowed
to return to Paris, on condition that her husband should
be responsible for her future conduct.[1]

A miscarriage of justice hardly less scandalous than the
above was perpetrated in the case of Madame Leféron,
who also belonged to judicial society, being the wife of
the president of the first court of *enquêtes*, "an excellent
judge and a good and disinterested man." Madame
Leféron had already passed her fiftieth year when she
conceived a violent passion for a young gentleman named
De Prade, a member of the profession of which the
"Marquis" de La Rivière was so distinguished an ornament, and determined to substitute him for the worthy
president with as little delay as need be. With this
end in view, she consulted La Voisin, and at the beginning of September 1669 found herself free to marry
again. "Madame Leféron," said La Voisin on the day
of her execution, "came to me overwhelmed with joy at
being a widow, and when I asked her if the phial of liquid
had taken effect, she replied, 'Effect or not, he is done

[1] *Archives de la Bastille*, vi. 207 note, 460 and 465.

for (*creve*)." [1] Shortly afterwards she married De Prade; but, inasmuch as she very quickly discovered that the young man cared only for her money, their wedded life was a brief and stormy one, and it is probable that the new husband would have shared the fate of his predecessor had he not had the good fortune to discover his wife's amiable intentions towards him and leave France. Although not a shadow of doubt existed as to this woman's guilt, the only punishment awarded her was banishment from Paris and a fine of 1500 livres!

In the meanwhile, the affair had begun to assume alarming proportions. The operations of the sorceresses had by no means been confined to the city; the Court was equally besmirched, and members of the noblest families in France were implicated. Among them may be mentioned the famous Maréchal de Luxembourg; the Comtesse de Soissons (Olympe Mancini), Louis XIV.'s first love; her sister, the Duchesse de Bouillon (Marie Anne Mancini); the Princesse de Tingry, *dame du palais* to the Queen; the Marquise d'Alluye, the Comtesse du Roure, the Comte de Clermont-Lodève, the Comtesse de Polignac, the Marquis de Cessac, the Marquis de Feuquières, and Maréchale de La Ferté, the lady whose reputed offspring had provided the King with the precedent which enabled him to legitimate the children of Madame de Montespan. In several cases, notably in that of the Comtesse de Soissons, Louis XIV., in order to avoid scandal, warned the culprits that their misdeeds had been brought to light and thus gave them time to effect their escape, though it is only fair to say that he punished them himself by declining to allow them to

---

[1] *Procès-verbal d'exécution de La Voisin, Archives de la Bastille,* **vi. 181.**

return to Court or Paris and, when the charges against them were very grave, even to recross the frontier; but Maréchal de Luxembourg, the Duchesse de Bouillon, and one or two others were compelled to stand their trial.

Luxembourg, in all probability, owed his arrest to the malice of Louvois, who hated the hunchback general almost as much as he had formerly hated Turenne. When he learned of the decree which had been launched against him by the Chambre, the marshal sought an audience with the King, and then, after spending an hour with Père de La Chaise, went to the Bastille and surrendered himself. If we are to believe the reports which were current and which have been handed down to us by Madame de Sévigné, the hero of so many hard-fought fields behaved in anything but an heroic manner on this occasion, weeping, wringing his hands, crying out that he had forsaken God and that God was now forsaking him, and so forth. " *Ce n'est pas même une femme*," writes the lady contemptuously; " *c'est une femmelette.*"

The marshal's trial supplies some welcome comic relief to the grisly drama before us. Apart from an unfounded charge of poisoning a commissioner from the War Office who had just taken his receipt for a large sum of money for the payment of the troops, which resulted in the witnesses being promptly sent to the galleys for perjury, the accusations brought against him were ludicrous to the last degree, though probably they were not so regarded at a time when belief in sorcery was so prevalent. He had, it appears, employed the magician Lesage to beg the "Spirit" to bring about his son's marriage with the daughter of his enemy Louvois (this, doubtless, partially accounted for the War Minister's persecution of the marshal); to enable him to gain battles to efface the memory of his failure to relieve Philipsburg in 1676; "to do something" to the disadvantage of Maréchal de Créqui; to remove his wife[1] and the governor of a province whose office he coveted; and to cause that his steward, who had offended him, should be hanged. All these requests and a number of others were carefully written down by the marshal on sheets of paper and handed to Lesage, who made them up into little balls, covered them with wax, and then pretended to throw them into the fire, whence, he assured his distinguished client, they would be duly transmitted to the infernal regions.[2]

There was no evidence that either Luxembourg or Lesage had taken any steps against the persons mentioned in the former's requests; they had been content to leave everything to the discretion of the "Spirit," and after remaining fourteen months in the Bastille—part of the time being passed, according to Voltaire, in "a kind of dungeon six and a half feet long"—the marshal was released and eventually restored to his offices.

A strong touch of comedy likewise marked the examination of the Duchesse de Bouillon, "who went and asked La Voisin for a little poison to get rid of a tiresome old husband that she had, and a nostrum to enable her to espouse a young man with whom she was in love."[3] The young man in question was the Duc de Vendôme, who accompanied the duchess to the Arsenal, holding

---

[1] Marie Charlotte Bonne Thérèse de Clermont-Tonnerre de Luxembourg. She had brought her husband the duchy of Luxembourg and a considerable fortune; "but she was ugly and infirm, and M. de Luxembourg could not endure her."

[2] *Déclaration de Lesage, Archives de la Bastille*, vi. 495 *et seq.*

[3] Letter of Madame de Sévigné, January 31, 1680.

her left hand, while the elderly husband supported her
on the other side, and a crowd of the nobility followed
to show their sympathy.   Madame de Bouillon, we are
told, entered the court "like a little queen," sat down on
a chair that had been placed for her, and instead of
replying to the first question, asked to be allowed to
enter a formal protest against the authority of the
Chambre, declaring that she had only attended out of
deference to the King's command and not to that of the
court, which she refused to recognise, "as she declined
to allow any derogation to the ducal privilege."[1]   She
refused to answer any questions until this had been taken
down by the clerk of the court; then she removed her
glove and "disclosed a very beautiful hand," and the
examination began.

"Do you know La Vigoureux?"[2]

"No."

"Do you know La Voisin?"

"Yes."

"Why did you want to do away with your husband?"

"I do away with my husband? Why, you have only
to ask him if he thinks so! He gave me his hand to
this very door!"

"But why did you go so often to La Voisin's house?"

"I wanted to see the Sibyls and prophetesses she
promised to show me; such a company would have been
well worth all my journeys."   Then, after denying that

[1] The ducal privilege consisted in being tried by all the courts
united in the Parliament.   Luxembourg had recognised the jurisdiction
of the Chambre Ardente and thus set a precedent, against which the
duchess's plea was of no avail.

[2] The question probably was, "*Did* you know La Vigoureux?"
La Vigoureux had died under torture some months before the Duchesse
de Bouillon's examination took place.

she had ever shown La Voisin a bag full of money, she inquired with a mocking and disdainful air?

"Well, Messieurs, is that all you have to say to me?"

"Yes, Madame," was the reply; upon which the duchess rose and left the court, remarking as she did so, "Really, I should never have believed that men of sense could ask so many foolish questions."[1]

Voltaire relates an amusing passage of arms between the duchess and La Reynie, in which the latter got decidedly the worst of the encounter.

"Did you ever see the devil at La Voisin's house, since you went there to meet him?" inquired the Lieutenant of Police.

"Monsieur," replied the lady, "I see him here at this very moment. He is disguised as a judge, and very ugly and villainous he looks."

The questioner proceeded no further.[2]

The charges against the Duchesse de Bouillon were, nevertheless, very serious, and it was certainly no fault of hers that the tiresome old husband was still alive to bore her. She had actually administered poison which she had obtained from La Vigoureux to the old gentleman, but without effect, after which, fortunately for him, she apparently came to the conclusion that he was poison-proof, and applied to Lesage to cause his death by magic. The King, hearing that she had had the temerity to boast of having baffled the judges, exiled her to Nérac, but she was allowed to return to Court some years later.

Less fortunate was her sister, the Comtesse de Soissons, who, as we have mentioned, was one of those at whose

[1] Letter of Madame de Sévigné *to* Madame de Grignan, January 31, 1680.

[2] Voltaire's *Siècle de Louis XIV.*

escape from justice Louis XIV. had connived. Evidence
was forthcoming that just before her exile in 1666 she
was in treaty with La Voisin for the purpose of having
both Madame de La Vallière and the King poisoned;
while there were other grave charges against her, among
them one of causing the death of a person in Savoy. She
was also suspected, probably unjustly, of having poisoned
her husband, who had died suddenly some years before.
The Chambre, no doubt influenced by Louvois, who saw
in the prosecution of the countess an opportunity of
annoying Colbert, whose friend she was, demanded her
arrest. The King, however, delayed sending the necessary
warrant for a couple of days, and, in the meanwhile,
despatched the Duc de Bouillon, her brother-in-law, to
the lady to offer her the choice between the Bastille
and exile. Madame de Soissons chose the latter alterna-
tive, and in the early hours of the following morning
(February 24, 1680) set out for Flanders, accompanied
by her friend and confidante, Madame d'Alluye, whose
apprehension had also been demanded by the court.

The news of the charges againt the countess had
evidently preceded her, for at Namur, Antwerp, and
several other towns she was refused admittance, the
people crying out, "We want no poisoners here." At
Brussels, the capital of the Spanish Netherlands, the
authorities did not dare to shut their gates against a
princess connected by marriage with the Court of
Madrid; but the populace evinced their hostility in an
unmistakable manner, and rendered the lady's stay among
them far from a pleasant one.[1] After remaining some

[1] Madame de Sévigné relates an extraordinary story, which she had
from the Duc de La Rochefoucauld, the son of the author of the
Maximes One day, soon after her arrival at Brussels, Madame de

years at Brussels, Madame de Soissons went to Spain, where Saint-Simon accuses her of having poisoned the Queen,[1] in a glass of milk, at the instigation of Count Mansfeld, the Austrian Ambassador.[2] But though the Queen's death certainly gave rise to grave suspicions, there is no evidence to connect the countess with it. Madame de Soissons's later years were spent at Brussels, where she died in 1708. To the end of her life she was kept under the closest police surveillance, and the leading members of the French colony were strictly prohibited from visiting her.

A more famous name than any of those which we have mentioned, at least in the eyes of posterity, was compromised by one of the depositions of La Voisin. In 1668, that is to say eleven years before the Chambre Ardente began its investigations, the actress Du Parc,[3] mistress of the celebrated poet Racine, had died under somewhat suspicious circumstances. The conduct of Racine on this occasion had aroused a good deal of

---

Soissons went to church. As she was entering the building, she was recognised, whereupon a number of people rushed out, collected all the black cats they could find, tied their tails together, and brought them, howling and spitting, into the porch, crying out that they were devils who were following the countess.

[1] Marie Louise d'Orléans, *Monsieur's* daughter by the ill-fated Henrietta of England. She married Charles II. of Spain.

[2] *Mémoires du Duc de Saint-Simon* (edit. 1881), xvii. 185.

[3] Marguerite Thérèse de Gorla, wife of an actor called Du Parc, whose stage name was Gros-René. Du Parc was perhaps the best, and undoubtedly the most versatile, actress of her time, equally successful in tragedy and comedy, and an accomplished and graceful dancer. She was also an extremely beautiful woman, and her toilettes were the envy and admiration of all the ladies of Paris. Before becoming the mistress of Racine, she had rejected the overtures of Molière, Corneille, and La Fontaine.

unfavourable comment among the relatives and friends of the lady, the poet having stationed himself at her bedside and refused admission to more than one person whom the dying actress had expressed a desire to see. Among those who by his orders were excluded from the sick-room was La Voisin, who had been on very intimate terms with Du Parc for several years. In her examination on November 21, 1679, the sorceress made a statement to the effect that " Racine, having secretly espoused Du Parc, was jealous of everybody, and particularly of her (La Voisin), and that he had made away with Du Parc by poison on account of his extreme jealousy ; that during her illness he never quitted her bedside ; that he drew a valuable diamond from her finger, and had also stolen the jewellery and principal effects of Du Parc, which were worth a great deal of money." She added that Madame de Gorla, Du Parc's stepmother, had been her informant.[1] Asked if Madame de Gorla had told her the manner in which the poisoning had been carried out, and who had been Racine's accomplice, she answered that she had not.[2]

M. Larroumet, Racine's latest biographer, dismisses this charge lightly enough as " the abominable invention of a ruined woman,"[3] and M. Loiseleur says much the same.[4] M. Funck-Brentano, on the other hand, for whose opinions we have a very great respect, takes a much more serious view of the matter, and remarks, and with reason, that it is inconceivable that La Voisin should have nursed a grievance against Racine for not having allowed

[1] Madame de Gorla had since died.
[2] *Interrogatoire de La Voisin, Archives de la Bastille,* vi. 50 *et seq.*
[3] M. Larroumet's *Racine,* p. 92.
[4] M. Loiseleur's *Les Trois Énigmes historiques.*

her access to his sick mistress to such an extent as to fabricate against him eleven years later so monstrous an accusation. If La Voisin had wanted to ruin Racine, she would have formulated precise and direct charges against him, instead of merely repeating rumours which had reached her ears. He adds : " The examinations to which La Voisin was subjected were very numerous. They brought to light innumerable details on a multitude of crimes, implicating a very large number of people. There were many confrontations. The declarations of the terrible sorceress were submitted to careful investigation by examining magistrates like Nicolas de la Reynie. All her declarations were found to be accurate." He further points out that La Voisin was not the only prisoner to bring this charge against the poet, as the following question, put by one of the judges to the sorceress, will show :—

" Asked if she was not aware that application had been made to Delagrange (another sorceress)[1] for the same purpose (the poisoning of Du Parc by Racine)." [2]

That Louis XIV. considered the charge of sufficient importance to justify a strict investigation is clearly proved by a letter from Louvois to Bazin de Bezons (January 11, 1680), in which he informs him that a *lettre de cachet* for the poet's arrest should be sent him whenever he applied for it. Bazin de Bezons, however, never did apply for it. Himself a member of the Academy, he was naturally reluctant to take any steps against his colleague until further evidence was forthcoming.[3]

[1] No trace of the examination of Delagrange remains.
[2] M. Funck-Brentano's *Le Drame des Poisons*, 291.
[3] *Archives de la Bastille*, vi. 95.

MADAME DE MONTESPAN

In spite of his interference with the course of the law in the case of the Comtesse de Soissons and other culprits of high rank, Louis XIV. continued to express his determination that justice should be administered without fear or favour. On December 27, 1679, he sent for Boucherat, the President of the Chambre, La Reynie, Bazin de Bezons, and the *procureur-général*, Robert, to come to Saint-Germain. "On rising from dinner," writes La Reynie, "his Majesty recommended us to do justice in extremely strong and precise terms, pointing out to us that he desired, on behalf of the public weal, that we should penetrate as deeply as possible into this abominable traffic in poisons, so as to cut its root, if this could be effected. He commanded us to do strict justice, without distinction of person, rank, or sex; and this his Majesty told us in clear and emphatic terms."[1] Then, on January 31, 1680, we find the Venetian Ambassador writing to the Doge: "His Majesty appears extremely affected at finding the first nobility of his realm sullied by these awful crimes. He is, therefore, causing the investigations to be pushed forward with the utmost rigour, and has declared that no person convicted of such grave offences shall have anything to hope from his clemency."[2] Finally, on February 4, Louvois informs the President of the Chambre that "his Majesty had commanded him to acquaint him with his Majesty's desire that he should assure the judges of his protection, and let them understand that he expected them to continue dispensing justice with firmness."[3]

On February 22, La Voisin "quietly surrendered her

---

[1] *Archives de la Bastille*, vi. 67.
[2] *Ibid.*, p. 124.
[3] *Ibid.*, p. 137.

soul to the devil,"[1] as Madame de Sévigné expresses it,
after which the investigations proceeded without anything of great importance being discovered until July 12,
when the sorceress's daughter, Marguerite Monvoisin,[2] a
girl of twenty-one, was brought before the examining
commissioners. This Marguerite Monvoisin had already
been examined, but without result. She appears to have
been much attached to her terrible mother, and, in the
hope of saving her, or at least of mitigating her punishment, had disclaimed all knowledge of her transactions.
Now, however, La Voisin being dead, she had no longer
any object in remaining silent, and, in fact, became so
communicative that La Reynie deemed it expedient to

[1] She was burned alive in the Place de Grève, and "merely passed
from one fire to another," adds the chronicler. Here is the death-
warrant :—

"The Chambre has declared and does declare the said Catherine
Deshayes, wife of Antoine Montabison, duly attainted and convicted
of the crimes of poisoning, abortion, seduction, impiety, sacrilege,
bribery, and other charges mentioned at the trial, as a punishment for which she is condemned to make *amende honorable* before
the principal door of Notre-Dame, whither she will be conducted in
a tumbril by the executioner, and there, on her knees, and holding
in her hand a burning torch, two pounds in weight, to say and declare,
in a loud and distinct voice, that, maliciously and badly advised, she
has done and committed the poisonings, abortions, seductions, impieties,
and sacrilege mentioned at the trial, for which she is repentant and
asks pardon of God, the King, and Justice. And, this done, to be
conducted to the Place de Grève, to be there burnt alive and her
ashes scattered to the wind, the said Catherine Deshayes having been
first put to the torture ordinary and extraordinary, in order to learn
from her mouth the names of her accomplices and to obtain information
in regard to the other charges mentioned at the trial.

"Given the nineteenth day of February 1680.

"Bazin, Boucherat, De La Reynie."

[2] This person is styled in official documents "*la fille* Voisin."

forward a report of her evidence and that of two other prisoners, Romani and Bertrand, who were examined about the same time, to the King, who was then in Flanders. In reply, Louis wrote to the Lieutenant of Police the following letter :—

Louis XIV. *to* La Reynie.

"Lille, *August* 2, 1680.

"Having seen the declarations of Marguerite Monvoisin, prisoner in my château of Vincennes, made on the 12th of last month, and the examination to which you subjected her on the 26th of the same month, I write you this letter to inform you that my intention is that you should devote all possible care to elucidate the facts contained in the said declarations and examinations ; that you should remember to have written down in separate memorials the answers, confrontations, and everything concerning the report that may hereafter be made on the said declarations and examinations (to the judges), and that meanwhile you defer reporting to my royal Chamber, sitting at the Arsenal, the depositions of Romani and Bertrand until you receive orders from me.

"Louis." [1]

Thus Louis directed that the declarations of Marguerite Monvoisin and those of Romani and Bertrand should be detached from the documents submitted by the examining commissioners to the court.

On September 16 Lesage was brought up for examination. He had been promised his life on condition that he should reveal all he knew, and related most horrible

[1] *Archives de la Bastille,* vi. 276.

things : how, some years before, Guibourg and another priest, named Tournet, had celebrated "black masses" and sacrificed children in the cellar of a house near the Invalides on nine successive nights ; how they had manufactured poison there, with which Madame Ridel, the wife of one of the King's *valets-de-chambre*, had made away with her husband ; and how they had afterwards removed to a house in the suburbs of Paris, where they said "black masses" on behalf of several ladies of the Court, whose names he mentioned, and the manufacture of poisons was carried on to such an extent that the wretches themselves were almost suffocated by the fumes. On the 26th he was again brought up, and made statements so amazing that at first La Reynie and Bazin de Bezons refused to believe him. But, four days later, the sorceress, Françoise Filastre, who had been condemned to death and the preliminary *question*, was put to the torture, and, in her agony, confirmed the testimony of her confederate. A report of her evidence and that of Lesage was immediately sent to the King, who had returned from Flanders at the end of August, and, on that very day (October 1), the sittings of the Chambre Ardente were suspended by royal edict.[1]

Now what were the reasons which had induced Louis XIV., who, a few months before, had exhorted the judges to do their duty, " without distinction of person, rank, or sex," and had publicly announced that no one convicted of these abominable crimes need have anything to hope from his clemency, first, to refuse to permit the depositions of Marguerite Monvoisin, Romani, and

---

[1] Although the sittings of the Chambre were suspended, it is important to note that the examining commissioners, La Reynie and Bazin de Bezons, were authorised to continue their private investigations.

Bertrand to be laid before the Chambre, and then, after perusing those of Lesage and La Filastre, to suspend the sittings of the court ?   The answer is that the evidence of the persons in question contained overwhelming proof that of all the ladies of the Court and the city who had been convicted of intercourse with the atrocious wretches awaiting the penalty of their crimes in the dungeons of the Bastille and Vincennes none had been more guilty, in intention if not in deed, than the woman who had been for twelve years the mistress of the King, the woman whose children had been made sons and daughters of France !

CHAPTER XVII

Madame de Montespan and the Poisoners—What happened
in the Rue de la Tannerie—Lesage and Mariette perform
incantations for Madame de Montespan at Saint-Germain—
Lesage and Mariette are arrested—But do not meet with their
deserts—Madame de Montespan consults La Voisin—The
"black mass" is said over Madame de Montespan at Mesnil
—And on two other occasions—Guibourg's story—La Voisin
gives Madame de Montespan "love-powders" for the King—
Their effect upon Louis XIV.—Madame de Montespan consults
La Voisin "whenever she fears any diminution in the favour
of the King"—La Filastre called into consultation during
the favour of Madame de Soubise—She brings "fine secrets
for love" from Normandy—The "black mass" again—
Mademoiselle Des Œillets and the English "mylord"—
Madame de Montespan determines to have Louis XIV. and
Mademoiselle de Fontanges poisoned—The conspirators meet
in the Rue de Beauregard—The plot—La Voisin goes to Saint-
Germain—She is arrested—Madame de Montespan com-
missions La Filastre to poison Mademoiselle de Fontanges—
Arrest of La Filastre—Mademoiselle Des Œillets the inter-
mediary between Madame de Montespan and the Poisoners—
Louvois refuses to allow her to be arrested—She demands to
be confronted with her accusers—Attempt to tamper with the
prisoners frustrated by La Reynie—Mademoiselle Des Œillets's
request is granted—Result.

By whom Madame de Montespan was first led to the
haunts of the witches does not appear to have been ever
discovered; but the following memorandum left by La

Reynie casts a strong suspicion upon the alchemist, Louis de Vanens :—

"To see La Chaboissière (Vanens's valet) again about his reluctance to have written down in his declaration, after hearing it read, the statement that Vanens had been concerned in giving Madame de Montespan counsel which deserves that he should be drawn and quartered."

What is certain, however, is that one day in the year 1667 the marchioness, who was then aspiring to the royal heart, met Lesage and one Mariette, a priest of Saint-Séverin,[1] in a house in the Rue de la Tannerie. (She had, it seems, already consulted La Voisin, and had by her been introduced to her confederates.) The lady was conducted to a little room, at one end of which an altar had been erected. Mariette, arrayed in sacerdotal vestments, uttered incantations; Lesage sung the *Veni Creator*; after which Mariette read a Gospel over Madame de Montespan's head, while she knelt before him and recited exorcisms against La Vallière, adding, according to the testimony of Lesage, various modest requests to the " Spirit," among them that " the Queen might be repudiated, and that she might espouse the King herself."

At the beginning of the following year, Mariette and Lesage were summoned to Saint-Germain, and there in the château itself, in the apartments occupied by Madame

---

[1] The Church came very badly out of this affair. "The clergy," says M. Ravaisson, "shared the general uneasiness in regard to the proceedings against the Poisoners. They feared that the great number of priests compromised would not add to the consideration in which the Church was held. Moreover, the confessors (of the prisoners), in spite of the care taken by La Reynie and Louvois in selecting them, exhorted their penitents to silence." One woman, named Dufresnoy, admitted at her examination that her confessor had told her " to forget everything that she had done."

de Montespan's sister, Madame de Thianges, they resumed their sorceries. The rough draft of a report drawn up by La Reynie for presentation to the King informs us of what took place on this occasion :—

" Mariette, wearing his surplice and stole, sprinkled holy water, and read a Gospel over the head of Madame de Montespan, while Lesage burned incense, and Madame de Montespan recited an exorcism, which Lesage and Mariette had given her in writing. The name of the King occurred in this exorcism and that of Madame de Montespan, as well as that of Madame de La Vallière. The exorcism was intended to obtain the favour of the King and the death of Madame de La Vallière : Mariette says it was merely to get her sent away."

From the same report we learn that before Madame de Montespan's visitors took their departure they asked for the hearts of two pigeons, " in order to say a mass over them and to pass them under the chalice." The marchioness gave them what they required, and, some days later, the mass was duly said by Mariette in the chapel of Saint-Séverin, to which he was attached. Madame de Montespan assisted at the ceremony, and afterwards repaired to Mariette's house, where further blasphemous rites were performed.[1]

Madame de Montespan was, of course, only one of many clients for whom Mariette and Lesage worked and a few weeks after the service at Saint-Séverin the sacrilegious practices of these worthies came to the ears of the police, with the result that they were both arrested and thrown into the Bastille, and subsequently brought before the Châtelet on a charge of sorcery. Unfortunately, the presiding judge, Président de Mesmes, was related by marriage to Mariette, and the investigation, in

[1] *Archives de la Bastille,* vi. 373.

consequence, was not carried very far. However, the little that could not be concealed sufficed to procure Lesage condemnation to the galleys and Mariette a term of imprisonment. But the former was soon liberated, thanks to the good offices of La Voisin's powerful friends ; while the latter made his escape and no attempt seems to have been made to rearrest him.

The success of Madame de Montespan's campaign against the royal heart must have greatly strengthened her belief in the efficacy of dealings with the devil; nevertheless, from 1668 to 1672 she would appear to have dispensed with the assistance of the sorcerers. Towards the end of the latter year, however, either because she was alarmed by some passing infidelity on the part of the King which has escaped the notice of historians, or because she was impatient to have her position more fully recognised, she again consulted La Voisin, who advised that recourse should be had to Guibourg and the " black mass."

To obtain the desired result from this horrible rite it was supposed to be necessary that it should be celebrated three times in succession. The three masses were said in 1673, at intervals of two or three weeks. The first took place at a château at Mesnil, near Montlhéry, where Guibourg had formerly lived as almoner of the Montgommerys. This château, a gloomy building, surrounded by deep moats, belonged to Leroy, governor of the pages of the Petite Écurie, who was a near relation of Mademoiselle Des Œillets, the favourite's confidential *femme-de-chambre* and the intermediary between her and La Voisin. We shall have a good deal to say about Mademoiselle Des Œillets presently. Leroy not only lent his house, but arranged matters with Guibourg, to whom he promised "fifty pistoles and a benefice worth 2000 livres."[1]

On the appointed day, there met at Mesnil, Madame de Montespan, "a tall woman " (presumably Mademoiselle Des Œillets), Guibourg, Leroy, and a man whose name did not transpire, but who was believed to be in the service of the Archbishop of Sens ; and there, in the chapel of the château, the abominable ceremony was performed over the body of the marchioness as she lay across the altar; a child, whom Guibourg had brought for the purpose, being as usual offered up to " Ashtaroth, Asmodeus, Princes of Affection."[2]

A fortnight or three weeks later, a second mass was performed at Saint-Denis, in a tumbledown hut, twenty pistoles being the price paid to the celebrant ; and the third took place in a house in Paris. Much secrecy seems to have been observed on this occasion. Leroy came to Saint-Denis and conducted Guibourg as far as the arcade of the Hôtel de Ville. Here, after they had been waiting some time, a coach drove up, in which sat the strange man who had assisted at the mass at Mesnil, and had, it appears, also been present at the second mass. Leroy told Guibourg to get into the coach, but did not himself do so. When they had driven a short distance, the unknown informed his companion that it was necessary for him to be blindfolded. The wretch submitted in fear and trembling, " as he was afraid that the man, who was armed with pistols, was going to kill him "; but his apprehensions were groundless and after he had

---

[1] No proceedings seem to have been taken by the Chambre Ardente against this Leroy. It is possible that he had fled from France at the first alarm.

[2] *Archives de la Bastule,* vi. 335.

performed his horrible office, he was again blindfolded and taken back to the Hôtel de Ville.[1]

The results of the " black mass " do not appear to have answered Madame de Montespan's expectations, and not long afterwards there was a temporary coolness between the King and his mistress, due probably to one of Louis's periodical fits of devotion.   The marchioness thereupon applied to La Voisin, who gave her " love-powders," which were mixed with the unfortunate monarch's food, it is believed, by Duchesne, an officer of the buttery, " who was always at Madame de Montespan's service."

The *Journal de la santé du Roi Louis XIV.* drawn up by d'Aquin, first physician to the King at this period, states that at the end of that year his illustrious patient suffered from violent headaches, and that on January 1, 1674, he was attacked by dizziness of such a kind that his sight became clouded and he was unable to stand without support.   In the opinion of M. Loiseleur, these head-aches and attacks of faintness, which recurred at intervals during the next few years, were the result of the powders prepared by La Voisin.[2]

In the summer of 1674, as we have seen, the difficulties with regard to her separation from her husband having been overcome, Madame de Montespan realised her ambition and became *maîtresse déclarée*, a result which she doubtless attributed in no small degree to the inter-vention of La Voisin, to whom henceforth she never failed to apply whenever matters were not progressing as smoothly as she desired.   " Every time that anything fresh happened to Madame de Montespan and she feared

[1] *Interrogatoire de l'Abbé Guibourg, Archives de la Bastille*, vi. 327.

[2] *Journal de la santé du Roi Louis XIV., écrits par Vallot, d'Aquin, et Fagon*, p. 119.   Loiseleur's *Trois Énigmes historiques*, p. 189.

some diminution in the favour of the King," said Marguerite Monvoisin, the witch's daughter, in the course of a further examination on August 13, 1680, " she told my mother, so that she might provide some remedy ; and my mother at once had recourse to priests, whom she instructed to say masses (*i.e.* ' black masses '), and gave her powders to be administered to the King." [1]

Questioned as to the composition of these powders, the girl replied that they were prepared in various ways, according to the different formulæ of witchcraft. Among the ingredients of those generally given to Madame de Montespan were cantharides, the dust of dried moles, the blood of bats, and other vile substances. (No wonder the royal digestion suffered !) Of these a paste was made, which was placed under the chalice during the sacrifice of the mass and blessed by the priest at the moment of the *offertoire*. Sometimes La Voisin took the powders to Versailles, Saint-Germain, or Clagny ; sometimes Mademoiselle Des Œillets would call for them ; and twice she herself had given them to the marchioness. The first occasion was in the church of the Petits-Pères, when, at a prearranged signal, she slipped the powders in a sealed packet into the lady's hand during the service. The second time she met Madame de Montespan by appointment on the road between Ville d'Avray and Clagny, and gave them to her as she was passing in her coach. [2]

The evidence of Marguerite Monvoisin leaves no

---

[1] *Interrogatoire de la fille Voisin, Archives de la Bastille*, vi. 288.

[2] *Ibid.*, vi. 297. At her examination on August 13, the girl denied that she had ever seen Madame de Montespan, but, two days later, she was again brought before La Reynie, and, probably under fear of torture, made a full confession.

doubt whatever that her mother was firmly convinced of the efficacy of the charms which she provided, and believed that she was giving her noble client good value for her money.

When, at Easter 1675, Madame de Montespan received orders to retire from Court, she, of course, at once summoned La Voisin to her aid. The witch again prepared powders for the King, taking them herself to Clagny on one occasion and bringing back fifty louis d'or, and again the result was such as to apparently justify the marchioness's confidence in the powers of sorcery.

For twelve months the lady basked in the rays of the royal favour, and then Madame de Soubise appeared upon the scene. La Voisin's powders were tried, but without effect, and, accordingly, the sorceress Filastre was called in. Filastre advised that application should be made to a certain Louis Galet, who was reported to have "fine secrets" in regard to poison and love, and, in company with a woman called Boissière, set out for Normandy, where the gentleman in question resided. Galet, urged on by the witches' assurance that their client would make his fortune if he were successful, prepared a most potent charm, the principal ingredients of which appear to have been dried plums and iron filings, and this was duly administered to the King.[1] But the Norman's prescription was no more effectual than La Voisin's had been, so again recourse was had to Guibourg and the "black mass."

The horrible ceremony was performed at La Voisin's house, as usual three times; once upon Madame de Montespan herself, with circumstances even more revolting than those which characterised the mass at Mesnil, three

[1] *Archives de la Bastille,* vi. 305.

years earlier, and twice by procuration, the witch acting as substitute.[1] This, as M. Loiseleur and M. Funck-Brentano point out, is a further proof that the sorceresses really believed in the efficacy of their abominable rites.

The " black mass" failed as the powders had failed ; to Madame de Soubise succeeded Madame de Ludres, and Madame de Montespan was beside herself with rage and jealousy. It was then that a very curious incident occurred. From a report drawn up by La Reynie, for the information of Louvois, we extract the following passage :—

"One day the Demoiselle Des Œillets, accompanied by a foreigner, who was said to be an Englishman and was addressed as ' mylord,' came to La Voisin's house, where Guibourg (the priest himself deposed to what follows), dressed in his alb, stole, and maniple, said a mass, which commenced at the *Te igitur*, and was what he called a *messe sèche*,[2] and to this he added an exorcism, in which the King's name occurred. The intention was to make a charm against the King ; *to cause the King's death*, so the wretch says. The design was common to Des Œillets and the ' mylord.' Des Œillets spoke with passion, complained of the King, said that he had caused her to be dismissed from Madame de Montespan's service.[3] The Englishman calmed her. He was her lover and had promised to marry her."[4]

[1] *Interrogatoire de la fille Voisin, Archives de la Bastille*, vi. 334.

[2] A *messe sèche* is a mass in which no consecration takes place. The *Te igitur* is the first prayer of the canon of the mass.

[3] Mademoiselle Des Œillets appears to have left the favourite's service about this time, and to have gone to reside with her relative Leroy. She was, however, still in constant communication with her former mistress, and continued to act as the intermediary between her and the witches.

[4] Various absurd hypotheses have been put forward by historians

La Reynie then goes on to relate that Guibourg gave a magic potion, " prepared according to the formulæ of La Voisin's book," to the *femme-de-chambre*, to be put upon the King's clothes, "or in some place where he was to pass." This, he said, would cause the King to die of a decline.[1]

Elsewhere the Lieutenant of Police observes that Mademoiselle Des Œillets, in order presumably to leave nothing to chance, applied to La Voisin, Lesage, a man named Latour, who went by the name of " the author," though he appears to have worked as a stonemason when he was not engaged in sorcery, and a woman called Vautier, who made a speciality of poisoned perfumes, from each of whom she demanded some charm to ensure the demise of the King.

M. Loiseleur is of opinion that the above facts clearly prove that as early as the end of 1676 or the beginning of 1677 Madame de Montespan had resolved to do away with Louis XIV., if he persisted in his infidelities.

In the following May, Madame de Ludres having been discarded, the Marchioness resumed possession of the royal heart, and for nearly two years these projects of revenge slumbered. But they awoke, " more ardent and more venomous than ever," when, towards the end of February 1679, she became aware of the relations

regarding the identity of this mysterious " mylord." One writer expresses his conviction that he was either the Duke of Monmouth or George Villiers, Duke of Buckingham, though what reason Monmouth or Buckingham could have had for desiring the death of Louis XIV. he does not condescend to explain ; while another sees in him a secret agent of Lady Castlemaine, who had come to Paris in search of some charm to cause the death of the faithless Charles II. Presumably, he meant to try its effect upon the French King first !

[1] *Archives de la Bastille*, vi. 421.

between Louis XIV. and Mademoiselle de Fontanges. No sooner had she satisfied herself of the guilt of her fickle lover than the infuriated woman took steps to put an end to both him and her rival.

"My mother," said Marguerite Monvoisin, in the course of her evidence on August 13, 1680, "told me that the lady (Madame de Montespan) wanted at that time to go to extremities, and tried to induce her to do things for which she had much repugnance. My mother gave me to understand that it was against the King, and after hearing what took place at Trianon's, I had no doubt about the matter."[1]

This Trianon was La Voisin's partner in her nefarious practices, and it was at her house[2] in the Rue de Beauregard that the plot was hatched. Two men named Romani and Bertrand were called into consultation by the witches. Romani, who was betrothed to La Voisin's daughter, was a *valet-de-chambre* in the service of a lady of the Court, a post which Mademoiselle Des Œillets had obtained for him ; "a very shrewd, crafty, determined individual, who had travelled much and tried his hand at all sorts of occupations," says La Reynie. Of Bertrand nothing appears to be known, except that he had formerly been employed by a silk merchant at Lyons. Both are described as "artists in poisons."

The King was to be poisoned first, and the *modus operandi* was as follows :—

---

[1] *Interrogatoire de la fille Voisin, Archives de la Bastille*, vi. 289.

[2] Trianon appears to have taken part in the affair with many misgivings, and to have endeavoured to dissuade La Voisin from proceeding with it. In order to frighten her, she cast her horoscope, and foretold that she would be implicated in a trial for a crime against the State. This document was found on La Voisin at the time of her arrest.

MADAME DE MONTESPAN

In conformity with the ancient custom of the Kings of France, Louis XIV., on certain days, was in the habit of receiving petitions from his subjects. Every one was admitted to his presence, and no distinction whatever was made; the rich merchant who arrived in his six-horse coach and the peasant who had trudged all the way from Brittany or Provence were equally sure of their Sovereign's attention. It was decided to prepare a petition and steep it in powders that had gone under the chalice; the King would take it in his hands and receive his death-blow. Trianon undertook the preparation of the petition, which La Voisin was to take to Saint-Germain, where the Court then was, and place it in the hands of the monarch. One hundred thousand écus was to be the price of success.[1]

To Romani and Bertrand were entrusted the assassination of Mademoiselle de Fontanges. The poison to be employed in her case was to be less active than in that of the King, "so that she might die a lingering death and that it might be said that she had died of grief at the death of the King." Their plan was to disguise themselves as travelling cloth merchants, obtain admission to the young favourite's apartments, and offer her gloves from Grenoble and stuffs "so rich that she would not be able to refrain from taking them." Both the gloves and cloth were carefully " prepared " according to the recipes of the magicians.

These proceedings seem grotesque and puerile to a degree; but, as we have shown, there can be no question that La Voisin and her confederates were absolutely convinced of the potency of their charms, and Marguerite Monvoisin stated that her mother kept the petition in an envelope and handled it with extreme care, saying that to

[1] Funck-Brentano's *Le Drame des Poisons*, p. 189.

276

touch it would be certain death. It was well for their intended victims that these wretches so often preferred to trust to magic instead of to arsenic and antimony.

The petition, which was to ask the King's intervention on behalf of an old lover of La Voisin named Blessis, upon whom the Marquis de Termes had laid violent hands and was keeping under lock and key in his château at Fontenay, was duly drawn up, and on Sunday, March 5, the sorceress, accompanied by Romani and Bertrand, set out for Saint-Germain. On the Thursday she returned very much annoyed. There had been a great number of petitions, and the King, instead of receiving each separately, as was his usual custom, had requested the bearers to place them on a table by his side. This, apparently, would not have suited La Voisin's purpose, so she had brought her petition back, intending to return to Saint-Germain on the following Monday, when she hoped to be more fortunate.

Marguerite Monvoisin's evidence went to show that next day the " missionaries " (members of a community founded by Saint-Vincent de Paul, who essayed the conversion of notorious sinners) called at the house to remonstrate with her mother on the error of her ways, upon which the sorceress became alarmed, and, early on the Saturday morning, gave the petition to her daughter to burn. All that day she remained in bed, but on the Sunday rose as usual, and went to the church of Notre Dame de Bonne Nouvelle to hear mass, after which she proposed to dine with Trianon, doubtless to arrange for the preparation of another petition.

As she was leaving the church, she was arrested.[1]

---

[1] *Archives de la Bastille,* vi. 234 ; Funck-Brentano's *Le Drame des Poisons,* p. 192.

MADAME DE MONTESPAN

We have seen that on March 15, 1679—that is to say, on the following Wednesday—Madame de Montespan suddenly left Saint-Germain and went to Paris, remaining there several days.[1] Great as must have been her terror at the arrest of La Voisin, and the knowledge that sooner or later her relations with the sorceress would inevitably come to light, her desire for revenge was greater still. To procure the assassination of the King now seemed hopeless, nor was it at all probable that, after the arrest of their accomplice, Romani and Bertrand could be induced to proceed with their designs against Mademoiselle de Fontanges. She, however, determined to try Filastre. This abominable hag, who, according to the testimony of five or six witnesses, had sacrificed one of her own children at a "black mass," after first having it baptized, undertook to dispose of Mademoiselle de Fontanges, and went to Normandy to find Galet, for the purpose, as she subsequently confessed, of obtaining powders "for poisoning without any sign appearing." From Normandy she went to Auvergne on a similar quest, though her movements there are shrouded in mystery. Returning to Paris, she endeavoured to gain admission to the apartments of Mademoiselle de Fontanges, but before she had succeeded in doing so she, too, was arrested.[2]

We do not propose to trouble the reader with even a brief *résumé* of all the evidence bearing upon Madame de Montespan's connection with the sorceresses which was collected between the suspension of the sittings of the Chambre Ardente on October 1, 1680, and their resumption in the following May, most of which merely served to corroborate the facts we have already mentioned,

[1] See p. 233.
[2] *Archives de la Bastille*, vi., *passim.*

and shall, therefore, confine ourselves to relating a single episode, which removed the last shadow of doubt as to the guilt of the marchioness.

On almost every page of the proceedings one name crops up. It is that of Mademoiselle Des Œillets, Madame de Montespan's confidential *femme-de-chambre*. She had been present at "black masses"; she had been seen in company with the mysterious Englishman, whose identity and present whereabouts were unknown, but whose movements had been highly suspicious; she had applied to Guibourg, La Voisin, and other magicians and witches for charms to cause the death of the King; she had been continually passing backwards and forwards between the Court and La Voisin's house, fetching "love powders," bearing notes, and so forth. Witness after witness bore testimony to these facts in the most positive manner, but still Mademoiselle Des Œillets remained at large. "The King will not allow me to be arrested," she said to one of her friends.

Madame de Villedieu, the person to whom this was said, was subsequently herself arrested. She appears to have been implicated in a plot to poison Louise de La Vallière; and M. Ravaisson thinks it possible that she had also accelerated the demise of her husband, who had had the bad taste to neglect her for a certain Mademoiselle Desjardins, a celebrated *bas-bleu* of the time, who wrote romances and had an unfortunate predilection for the society of married men. On being taken to Vincennes, she loudly protested against the injustice of imprisoning her, "when she had only been once to La Voisin's, while they left Mademoiselle Des Œillets at liberty, who had been there more than fifty times."

This remark naturally did not tend to allay the sus-

MADAME DE MONTESPAN

picions of the police ; and, towards the end of October, La Reynie wrote to Louvois, pointing out how imperative it was, in the interests of justice, that Mademoiselle Des Œillets should be confronted with her accusers. At first, however, the Minister would not consent. To take any steps against the waiting woman would, in his opinion, be tantamount to an indictment of her mistress. Louvois, it may be mentioned, had, next to La Reynie, been the mainspring of the proceedings of the Chambre ; he had seen in them an excellent opportunity for taking vengeance on his enemies, such as the unfortunate Luxembourg. But Madame de Montespan was his intimate friend, and had supported him against Colbert, while he had every reason to fear the growing influence of Madame de Maintenon, who cordially detested him. Moreover, he believed that by defending the marchioness he would ingratiate himself with the King.

At length, however, the case against Mademoiselle Des Œillets became so very black that, for Madame de Montespan's own sake, Louvois decided that something must be done. Accordingly, he sent for the *femme-de-chambre*, and subjected her to a private examination in his cabinet, hoping against hope that she would be able to clear herself. As a result of the interview, he wrote to La Reynie the following letter :—

LOUVOIS *to* LA REYNIE.

"VERSAILLES, *November* 18, 1680.

"MONSIEUR,—On the last occasion on which I was in Paris, I had an interview with the person whom La Voisin's daughter calls the 'go-between' (Mademoiselle Des Œillets). She admits having seen La Voisin once, and once only, ten years ago, when she was in company with five or six girls from her Quarter. She declares, with marvellous assurance, that not one of those who have named her know her, and, to convince me of her innocence, begged me to urge the King to allow her to be taken to the place where those who have deposed against her are confined. His Majesty has, therefore, been pleased to decide that I shall conduct her to Vincennes next Friday; that I shall cause Lesage, La Voisin's daughter, Guibourg, and the other people, who, as you inform me, have spoken of her to be brought down, under the pretext of asking them for explanations regarding a lady of quality whom they have mentioned; that, while I am questioning each of them, the person of whom I have just spoken shall enter and show herself to them, and that I shall ask them if they know her, without naming her."[1]

This letter occasioned the Lieutenant of Police considerable astonishment, as he himself had not the smallest doubt of the woman's guilt. A very little reflection, however, sufficed to convince him that there was something behind the "marvellous assurance" of which the Minister had spoken. He, therefore, lost no time in making inquiries, and discovered that, in spite of his vigilance, some one from outside was in communication with the prisoners. This "some one," needless to say, was Madame de Montespan.[2] La Reynie at once took

---

[1] *Archives de la Bastille*, vi. 575.

[2] It would be interesting to know when Madame de Montespan first became aware that her connection with the sorceresses had been discovered; but, unfortunately, we have no means of ascertaining. M. Ravaisson, M. Loiseleur, and M. Funck-Brentano all speak of a

extraordinary precautions to prevent any but those officials whom he could thoroughly trust approaching his charges, and the marchioness's little plot was nipped in the bud. On the appointed day Louvois and Mademoiselle Des Œillets came to Vincennes, and the latter was duly confronted with each of the prisoners in turn.

To the intense chagrin of Louvois, all immediately recognised the *femme-de-chambre*; and the last link in the long chain of evidence against Madame de Montespan was complete.

stormy interview between the King and the lady " about the middle of August," but their authority for this is a letter of Madame de Maintenon, which M. Lavallée unhesitatingly pronounces to be one of La Beaumelle's forgeries. However, it is extremely probable that some such interview did take place in August, for Madame de Montespan, in a letter, dated August 4, from Valenciennes, to her friend, the Duchesse de Noailles, speaks of herself as " having no heart for anything."

CHAPTER XVIII

Louis XIV. unwilling to allow Madame de Montespan or her accusers to be brought to trial—His reasons—Colbert and Louvois of the same opinion—The Chambre Ardente resumes its sittings—But on condition that the evidence against Madame de Montespan should be withheld from the judges— Fatuity of the proceedings under such circumstances—Trial of La Joly—La Reynie pleads in vain for justice—The Chambre Ardente is dissolved—Fate of Madame de Montespan's accomplices—Extraordinary precautions taken to ensure their silence —Louis XIV. destroys the incriminating documents—Death of Mademoiselle de Fontanges—Suspicions of poisoning—The King endeavours to prevent an autopsy being held—But the relatives insist on it—A natural death—The last ceremonies.

THE feelings of Louis XIV. when he learned of the terrible crimes of which the woman who had shared his life for twelve years stood convicted may well be imagined. Nevertheless, he speedily recognised that to punish her as she deserved, to allow justice to take its course, was absolutely out of the question. The investigations of the Chambre Ardente had already lowered the prestige of France to an alarming extent, and with the prestige of France that of its sovereign, who, by arrogating to himself absolute authority, had incurred and accepted undivided responsibility. What would be the result if the latest development of this most dreadful business were to become known? Moreover, there was a ludicrous as well as a tragic side to the affair. The former would, of course, predominate at home, but the reverse would in all probability be the case abroad ; and ridicule, as he well knew, cuts deeper than iron or steel. He pictured to himself the cynical amusement of his brother of England, the sneers of the hated William of Orange, the coarse jests of the German princes ; and the picture was not a pleasing one. How could a monarch hope to dictate the law to his fellow-rulers when he and his love-affairs were the laughing-stock of every Court in Europe?

Again, there were the children to be considered—the children whom he had legitimated, for whom he hoped to make great marriages. Would princes of the blood, would the proudest nobles in France, even at the bidding of their King, permit their sons and daughters to wed with those of the client of La Voisin, Filastre, and the Abbé Guibourg, of one who was in intention, if not in deed, a regicide? And what would the feelings of those children be if justice were done, and they learned, as some day they inevitably must, the iniquities of the woman who had given them birth? For his own sake, for his children's sake, for his kingdom's sake, he felt that, at all costs, the matter must be hushed up.

His two chief advisers were of the same opinion. Louvois, who, as the Venetian Ambassador wrote to his Government, "worshipped the French Monarchy, to which all things seemed to him subordinate," felt compelled to protect the prestige of the crown from the injury the condemnation of the ex-favourite would do it. Colbert, a sincere patriot, considered that the national greatness was indissolubly bound up with the greatness of the King. Besides, both had private ends to serve. Louvois's we have already explained ; while Colbert had recently betrothed his younger daughter to Madame de Montespan's nephew, the son of the Duc and Duchesse de Vivonne,[1] and naturally desired to avert the scandal which menaced the family she was about to enter.[2] Laying aside their antagonism for the moment, the two great Ministers united in urging Louis to quash the proceedings. "The King," wrote one of La Reynie's secretaries, "was strongly advised, even by persons in high places, to close the Chambre entirely, under various pretexts, the most specious of which was that a further investigation of the poisoning cases would bring the country into discredit abroad."[3]

With the views of Colbert and Louvois harmonising with the monarch's own, the result may be anticipated.

[1] The Duchesse de Vivonne (Antoinette de Mesmes) was also gravely compromised, and by the same prisoners as Madame de Montespan. The charges against her were, in a way, even worse than those against her sister-in-law. Not content with making compacts with the Evil One to surrender her soul to him on condition of receiving "a certain sum of money every month for a given period," "the power to make any one fall ill whoms he chose," and so forth, causing incantations to be said against her husband, and having "black masses" said over her, in order to secure the dismissal of Madame de Montespan and the love of the King for herself, she was accused of actually allowing, on the advice of Filastre, one of her own children to be sacrificed. These facts furnished both Colbert and Louis XIV. with an additional reason for preventing Lesage, Guibourg, and others being brought to trial.

[2] In February 1681, Colbert commissioned a celebrated advocate of the time, one Maître Duplessis, to draw up a statement designed to establish the innocence of Madame de Montespan. Duplessis fulfilled his task skilfully enough, and his arguments seem to have made some impression upon historians who had only a very partial acquaintance with the documents which M. Ravaisson has so ably edited ; but M. Loiseleur considers that they had very little effect upon the mind of Louis XIV.

[3] Quoted in M. Funck-Brentano's *Le Drame des Poisons*, p. 231.

MADAME DE MONTESPAN

On May 19 the Chambre Ardente reopened its doors, but on the express condition that no further steps should be taken in regard to the declarations in which Madame de Montespan was involved. The most damaging testimony against the marchioness was that of Marguerite Monvoisin and Filastre. Louis had already refused to allow the former's evidence to be laid before the Chambre, and on May 14 he directed that Filastre's should also be withdrawn from the cognisance of the judges, "for good and just considerations important to his service."

That the court was allowed to continue its investigations at all was entirely due to the efforts of La Reynie, who had gone to Versailles, and "on four different days and for four hours each day" represented to the King and his Ministers the imperative necessity of leaving no means untried to purge France of these horrible crimes, which were sapping the very vitals of the nation, and which, if not now checked, would speedily assume appalling dimensions. The King yielded on the conditions we have mentioned; but before the Chambre had been sitting long, it became evident to the Lieutenant of Police that its proceedings, hampered as the examining commissioners were by the necessity of withholding every scrap of evidence likely to compromise Madame de Montespan from their colleagues, were degenerating into a mere farce. The sorceress La Joly was brought before the judges—Louis having raised no objection, since her preliminary examination had revealed nothing to implicate the ex-favourite—found guilty of criminal dealings with persons in the Household of *la Grande Mademoiselle*[1]

[1] The composition of *Mademoiselle's* Household left a good deal to be desired ; her physician, Brioude, was a poisoner, and her almoner made compacts with the Evil One.

and various other offences, and condemned to torture and the stake. In the course of her trial she would appear to have *hinted* at relations with Madame de Montespan, for Louvois wrote in hot haste to Bazin de Bezons as follows :—

"I am in receipt of the letter which you had the goodness to write to me yesterday, from which the King has learned what La Joly said yesterday in the Chambre. His Majesty has commanded me to inform you that in case she speaks of *such things* when under torture, you must place her declarations in a separate portfolio (*i.e.* withdraw them from the cognisance of the judges)."

Next morning La Joly was put to the *question*, the "boot" being used with merciless severity; and, in her anguish, confessed to things which must have made the blood of the examining commissioners, hardened though they were after two years of such revelations, run cold with horror. After being tortured for an hour and a quarter, she was released, because, as M. Ravaisson explains, she was inclined to be "too communicative," and, later in the day, burned alive in the Place de Grève.[1]

This episode brought home to La Reynie and his fellow-commissioner the full absurdity of the situation. La Joly had been executed, it is true; but if by chance she had uttered Madame de Montespan's name at her preliminary examination, instead of when actually before the judges, the King would not have permitted her to be brought to trial, and one of the most abominable wretches in Paris—a woman whose crimes were surpassed only by those of La Voisin and Filastre—would have escaped her deserts.

La Reynie pleaded for justice in the strongest possible

---

[1] *Archives de la Bastille,* vii. 64 *et seq.*

terms. "There are one hundred and forty-seven prisoners in the Bastille and Vincennes," he writes to Louvois. "Of these there is not one against whom there are not serious charges of poisoning or dealing in poisons, and further charges of sacrilege and impiety. The majority of these criminals are likely to go unpunished." He then mentions a number of persons, including Trianon, Galet, the girl Monvoisin, and the infamous Abbé Guibourg—"of whom we hear every day new and execrable things, and who is loaded with accusations of crimes against God and the King"—none of whom would be able to be brought to trial if Louis persisted in his determination to suppress the whole of the evidence implicating Madame de Montespan.

But the arguments of the honest Lieutenant of Police fell on deaf ears at Versailles ; and at length, recognising the utter futility of the Court continuing to sit when it was impossible to bring the principal offenders before it, La Reynie decided to advise the King to dissolve the Chambre, which was done on July 21, 1682, by a *lettre de cachet.*

It is satisfactory to know that the wretches whose connection with the machinations of Madame de Montespan saved them from the gibbet and the stake were very far from going unpunished. None of them ever returned to the scene of their former crimes. At the same time that La Reynie had advised Louis XIV. to close the Chambre, he had suggested that, since the King would not permit them to be tried according to the rules of justice, they should be imprisoned for the rest of their lives, under *lettres de cachet*, in different fortresses ; and this course was adopted. Guibourg, Galet, Lesage, and Romani were sent to the citadel of Besançon, where the first-named miscreant died three years later; Marguerite Monvoisin was incarcerated in that of Belle-Isle-en-Mer; Bertrand spent the remainder of his life in the Château of Salces; Louis de Vanens, who is supposed to have been the person who advised Madame de Montespan to have recourse to the sorceresses, ended his days in the Château de Saint-André de Salins; Mademoiselle Des Œillets was imprisoned at Tours and died there in 1686; while Trianon saved all further trouble by committing suicide at Vincennes.

The most extraordinary precautions were taken to preserve the great secret. Louvois sent minute instructions to the governors of the different fortresses in which the prisoners were confined to prevent them from holding communication with other prisoners or with any one from the outside world, and to secure that only those officials in whose discretion the most implicit confidence could be placed should be suffered to approach them.[1] As, however, he thought it possible that the governors themselves might be curious to know something of the history of their new guests and be tempted to ask the

---

[1] On August 26, 1682, he wrote to Chauvelin, Intendant of Franche-Comté, as follows :—

" The King having thought fit to send to the Château de Saint-André de Salins some of the persons who were arrested in virtue of the decrees of the court which dealt with the poisoning affair, his Majesty has commanded me to inform you that his intention is that you prepare two rooms in the Château de Saint-André, in such a way that six of the prisoners may be kept safely in each of them, the which prisoners are to have each a mattress in the place prepared for them, and to be fastened, either by a foot or by a hand, to a chain, which shall be attached to the wall, the said chain, however, to be of sufficient length to allow of them lying down. As these persons are criminals who have deserved the

latter injudicious questions, he informed them that the prisoners were abandoned villains, who had invented the most infamous calumnies against Madame de Montespan, the falsity of which had been proved before the Chambre Ardente, and that if one of them ventured to open his lips on the subject, he was to be soundly flogged.[1]

So determined was Louis XIV. to guard against the smallest possibility of future scandal that, not content with incarcerating all who had been connected even remotely with Madame de Montespan, he likewise condemned to perpetual confinement several persons whose innocence had been fully established, but who had had the misfortune to be shut up in the same room with one or other of the marchioness's accomplices. Thus a girl named Nanon Aubert, who had shared Marguerite Monvoisin's cell at Vincennes, and "had been told everything," spent the rest of her days in convents, first, at Besançon and, afterwards, at Vesoul, with instructions to say that she was detained for dealings with a lady of quality accused of poisoning. "She was made to pass for a young lady of rank, and the King paid her a mention of 250 livres."[2]

As for the incriminating documents—the reports of the evidence of Marguerite Monvoisin, La Filastre, and

most extreme penalties of the law, the King's intention is that they be thus secured for fear lest they should injure the people set to guard them, or who pass in and out of their room to bring them their food.

" His Majesty's intention is that you prepare two similar rooms in the citadel of Besançon, so that twelve of the prisoners may be kept securely there. You will observe that these rooms are so situated that no one can hear what these people say."—*Archives de la Bastille*, vii. 112.

[1] M. Funck-Brentano's *Le Drame des Poisons*, p. 242.

[2] *Mémoire sur les Prisonniers de Besançon, Archives de la Bastille*, vii. 148.

the rest—they were locked up in a casket, which was then sealed and deposited with Sagot, the clerk to the Châtelet, who had acted in the same capacity for the Chambre. Twenty-seven years later, on July 13, 1709, Louis XIV. directed that this casket should be brought to his private cabinet at Versailles, and there, in the presence of the Chancellor, Pontchartrain, he burned its contents himself. " His Majesty in Council, after having looked through and examined the minutes and proceedings laid before him by the Chancellor, and having caused them to be burnt in his presence, has commanded and does command that Gaudion (the clerk to the Châtelet, in whose charge they then were) should be wholly and formally discharged of the same." [1]

Thus Louis XIV. believed that he had buried for all time the whole shameful story. But though much evidence had been destroyed, much still remained; and to-day, thanks to the indefatigable researches of M. Ravaisson, the great secret is a secret no longer.

Six weeks after the Chambre Ardente resumed its interrupted labours in the spring of 1681, Nature gave to Madame de Montespan the satisfaction she had sought from the magic of Romani and the poison of Filastre. Poor Mademoiselle de Fontanges did not remain long at Court after her return from Chelles in August 1680. Her chagrin at the indifference of the fickle monarch, who no longer visited her except to inquire after her health, greatly aggravated the complaint from which she was suffering, and early in the following spring she again retired to Chelles, " to prepare for her journey to

---

[1] *Procès-verbal du 13 Juillet 1709, Archives de la Bastille*, vii. 183.

Eternity." [1] As the death of a royal favourite in the midst of a community of nuns would have occasioned scandal, as soon as it was seen that the end was approaching she was brought to Paris, and there, at the Abbey of Port-Royal,[2] she expired on June 28, at the age of twenty-two, Bourdaloue administering the last sacraments.

The girl died convinced that she had been poisoned, and suspecting Madame de Montespan, a conviction which would appear to have been shared by Louis XIV., for, immediately on learning of what had occurred, he wrote to the Duc de Noailles, who had been present on his behalf at the death-bed,[3] as follows :—

LOUIS XIV. *to the* DUC DE NOAILLES.

"*Saturday,* 10 *o'clock.*

"Although I had been expecting for a long time the news that you have sent me, it has not failed to occasion me surprise and grief. I see by your letter that you have given all the orders necessary for carrying out my instructions to you. You have only to continue as you have begun. Remain as long as your presence is required, and afterwards come and render me an account of everything.

"You say nothing about Père Bourdaloue.

"In regard to the desire that has been expressed that

[1] Letter of Madame de Sévigné *to* Bussy-Rabutin, April 3, 1681.

[2] This monastery must not be confused with the famous Jansenist stronghold, Port-Royal des Champs, levelled to the ground in 1709, which was situated near Chevreuse. Port-Royal de Paris survived to the Revolution.

[3] Several writers have asserted that Louis himself was present, but this is quite untrue.

an autopsy should be held, *I think that the best course would be to avoid it if possible.*

"Present my compliments to the brothers and sisters, and assure them that, when occasion arises, they will always find me ready to give them marks of my protection.

"LOUIS." [1]

Noailles, acting on the King's instructions, used every endeavour to prevent an autopsy being held; but the dead woman's relatives insisted on it, and it was, accordingly, performed by six surgeons, who declared that the young duchess had died from natural causes, and, in spite of the statements to the contrary made by the Princess Palatine, Madame de Caylus, and other chroniclers, there can be no doubt that such was the case.

The body of the ill-fated Mademoiselle de Fontanges was buried in the church of the Abbey of Port-Royal; but, at the desire of her sister, the heart was deposited at Chelles. Here is an account of the last ceremonies:—

"*Presentation of the body of Madame de Fontanges to Port-Royal de Paris, the day of St. Peter and St. Paul,* 1681.

"This is the body of Madame la Duchesse de Fontanges which we present to you, Monsieur, and to which we pray you to give ecclesiastical burial in the interior of this monastery and repose in the midst of the spouses of Jesus Christ. We render thanks to this Jesus, who is the master of hearts, in that He has arrested on a sudden His creature in the headlong course of her desires and worldly

---

[1] Bibliothèque du Louvre, *MS. Correspondance de Noailles*; Clément's *Madame de Montespan et Louis XIV.*, p. 402.

prosperity, as formerly He did St. Paul, and keeping her cast down under His all-powerful hand and under the weight of a long and grievous malady, He has inspired her with a salutary remorse, and, awakening in her sentiments of faith and piety, has rendered her worthy, after great miseries, to experience great mercies, and to be a touching example for this age. You have had her with you a faithful servant of Jesus Christ. She has escaped from you and He has taken her to Himself: Behold, He has brought her back and gives her back to you! Offer for her, we beg of you, the sacrifice of praise and prayer, and do us the favour of giving us a part in it."

"Presentation of her heart to Chelles.

" . . . This heart," said the abbess, "was God's at first; the world gained it. God has at length recovered that which was his; *but it was not surrendered without difficulty. . . .*"[1]

[1] Bibliothèque Nationale, *MSS. Portefeuilles Vallant*; Clément's *Madame de Montespan et Louis XIV.*, p. 405.

CHAPTER XIX

To avoid all possibility of scandal, Louis XIV. decides that Madame de Montespan must be allowed to remain at Court —And be treated with the same consideration as before— Wonderful self-control of the King—Madame de Maintenon " on the very pinnacle of favour "—Nightly conferences between her and Louis XIV,—She brings about a reconciliation between the King and Queen—Her conduct in this matter not so disinterested as some imagine—" I am but too much extolled "—The conversion of Louis XIV. not yet complete —Madame de Maintenon in constant dread of a lapse from grace—Mademoiselle d'Oré partakes of *médianoche* with the King—Alarm of the devout party—Precautions taken by Madame de Maintenon and Madame de Montespan to disguise their antagonism from the world—Curious anecdote related by Madame de Caylus—Death of the Queen—An intelligent anticipation of events—The virtue of the King in jeopardy—Madame de Maintenon's agitation—Louis XIV. offers his hand to Madame de Maintenon—Probable reasons for this step—The amazing marriage.

THE same reasons which had prompted Louis XIV. to decline to permit Madame de Montespan's accusers to be brought to trial operated to save the marchioness from being driven from Court. Although the ex-favourite's connection with the Poisoners was known to but a handful of persons besides the King—Louvois, Colbert, La Reynie, Bazin de Bezons, the advocate Duplessis, and possibly one or two others—all of whom were, of course, pledged to the most inviolable secrecy, the charges brought against her by several contemporary writers in regard to the death of Mademoiselle de Fontanges show that it was strongly suspected ; and to exile her would undoubtedly have had the effect of raising these suspicions to the point of certainty. Louis, therefore, decided that she must remain at Court, and not only must remain, but that he must continue to accord her those marks of his regard which, as the mother of legitimated princes and princesses, the world considered she had the right to expect.

It was now that that wonderful self-control which never failed him even in the darkest hours of his reign, when France was well-nigh prostrate at the feet of her enemies and his very throne seemed tottering ; that calm and tranquil majesty which stamps him as the greatest actor of royalty who ever lived, and is perhaps his best claim on the admiration of posterity, came to Louis's aid, and enabled him, in spite of the horror and indignation which the crimes of this woman must have aroused, to receive her with smiles and compliments, to inquire with apparent solicitude after her health, to consult her wishes in regard to the festivities of the Court, to pay her daily visits, to treat her in every respect as if she had done nothing whatever to forfeit his esteem. But human endurance has its limits, and, though the King's conduct deceived careless observers, practised eyes were quick to note a change ; and, whereas, previous to the journey to Flanders, it had been Louis's invariable custom to spend an hour or two each day in his former mistress's apartments, Madame de Sévigné now reports that these visits seldom lasted more than a few minutes.

MADAME DE MONTESPAN

The proceedings before the Chambre Ardente, which dealt so deadly a blow to the pretensions of Madame de Montespan, naturally served but to augment the influence of her rival. For the first time in his life Louis XIV. realised to the full the terrible consequences of his lawless passions. Several of the ladies who had been most deeply compromised by the declarations of the sorceresses —Madame de Montespan, the Comtesse de Soissons, the Duchesse de Vivonne, and others—had resorted to these wretches, had taken part in these unspeakable abominations, chiefly, if not solely, for one purpose—to gain or to regain the love of their sovereign or to cause the death or disgrace of a successful rival in his affections. If he had listened to the exhortations of Bourdaloue, Bossuet, and Mascaron; if he had led a reputable and Christian life; if he had done his duty to his God and to his people, these frightful crimes would never have polluted his Court. It was to their King that the French nobility looked for an example; and what example had their King set them? Of all the high-born criminals whose misdeeds had been brought to light not one was so guilty as he. Deeply religious at heart, firmly convinced as he was that he held his throne as a trust direct from God, he shuddered when he reflected that one day he would be called upon to give an account of his stewardship—of the stewardship whose duties he had neglected and whose privileges he had so grossly misused.

Under these circumstances, one can well understand that Louis should have turned a willing ear to the pious counsels of the lady who "knew how to make virtue attractive," and should have sought her society more assiduously than ever. On September 11 the gazette Sévigné announces that "Madame de Maintenon is on the very pinnacle of favour "; and, a week later, we learn from the same source that the courtiers are whispering that Madame de Maintenon is now Madame de *Maintenant* (the lady of the present); that she spends every evening from eight o'clock till ten with his Majesty, and that " M. de Chamarante (first *maître d'hôtel* to the Dauphiness) conducts her thither and back again before all the world."

The first result of these nightly conferences was a *rapprochement* between the King and Queen. "I am informed that the Queen is very well at Court," writes Madame de Sévigné, " and that the complaisance and interest she has shown during the journey (to Flanders), visiting all the fortifications and travelling everywhere without complaining of heat or fatigue, have gained her a thousand marks of regard." [1] Louis, in fact, now paid his long-neglected consort such continual attentions that the poor woman declared that she had never been so happy in her life. "She was touched to the very verge of tears," says Mademoiselle d'Aumale, " and exclaimed in a kind of transport: 'God has raised up Madame de Maintenon to bring me back the heart of the King.' She took every opportunity of testifying her gratitude, and allowed the whole Court to see the esteem in which she held her." [2]

Madame de Maintenon's enthusiastic admirers affect to see in this circumstance a convincing proof of the

[1] Madame de Sévigné *to* Madame de Grignan, August 28, 1680.
[2] Quoted by M. Lavallée in *Correspondance générale de Madame de Maintenon*, ii. 259 note. M. Clément rather unkindly reminds us that Mademoiselle d'Aumale was Madame de Maintenon's most intimate confidante, and that these interesting details could only have been furnished her by the lady herself. "The one relates, the other holds

MADAME DE MONTESPAN

disinterestedness of the lady's motives ; but, to the impartial observer we venture to think this disinterestedness will not be so apparent. The King had returned to his consort, filled with virtuous resolutions ; but could this consort—this poor, weak woman, who positively trembled in the presence of her magnificent husband, who, Madame de Caylus tells us, was so overcome with terror when Louis happened to send for her unexpectedly on one occasion that she implored Madame de Maintenon to bear her company, lest she should be too embarrassed to answer the questions he might address to her—satisfy his need for companionship and single-handed keep him in the edifying path of conjugal duty ? If Louis were to carry out his good resolutions, if he were to remain proof against the wiles of all the light beauties who adorned the Court, a confidante, an *amie nécessaire*, a female confessor would be absolutely indispensable. And to whom should the King turn for the sympathy and support which he needed but to the pious lady who had so powerfully contributed to wean him from his wicked ways ? And was not this post of keeper of the conscience of the greatest monarch in Christendom one of exceeding honour, exquisite in its singularity, calculated to arouse the wonder and admiration of all the devout ? Let us listen to the enthusiastic M. Lavallée :—

"Louis XIV. was now in his forty-ninth year, and people saw with dismay that this prince had not yet abandoned the irregularities of youth, that he was

the pen." On the other hand, a letter from Madame de Maintenon to her brother, Charles d'Aubigné, dated December 1, 1682, informs him that "the Queen had done her the honour to give her her portrait at Chambord," which would seem to confirm Mademoiselle d'Aumale's story.

becoming more and more the slave of his pleasures, and that he was advancing towards a disgraceful old age, in which his own glory and that of his country would be tarnished. Now, the King was not only the head of the State but its very soul; he was the country incarnate, a sort of visible Providence and the lieutenant of God on earth; he was, in short, the man who was responsible for the happiness and the safety of twenty millions of men, of the fortune and the future of the first Christian nation. What would have become of this royalty of divine essence and its divine and glorious mission with a prince neglectful of his first duties, whose passions rose superior to all the laws of God and man, surrounded by women imploring a glance from him, and by courtiers who had built up infamous hopes on the future scandals of a licentious reign? What would have become of France if she had been afflicted by a Louis XV. before her time, at a moment when she was about to enter into the dangers and difficulties to which the English Revolution and the Succession in Spain gave rise? Out of this slough Madame de Maintenon drew Louis XIV.; she brought him back to his duties, to the assiduous care of his realm, to the good example that he owed his subjects; she dissipated the clouds of pride which enveloped him, and made him descend from Olympus to inspire him with Christian sentiments of repentance, of moderation, of tenderness for his subjects, and, above all, of humility . . ."[1]

Did ever devout lady secure so amazing a triumph? Madame de Maintenon, to give her her due, set but small store by the things to which other royal favourites attached so much importance; reasonable comfort in the

[1] *Correspondance générale de Madame de Maintenon*, ii. 147.

present, reasonable security for the future, was all she demanded. But she loved the praise of men, and especially the praise of the godly. It was to her what *tabourets*, and pensions, and resplendent toilettes, and flashing jewels, and eight-horse coaches, and royal guards were to the Montespans and the Fontanges. And the praise of the godly she now received; good measure, pressed down, running over. "All good men," says M. Lavallée, "the Pope,[1] the bishops, applauded the victory of Madame de Maintenon, and considered that she had rendered a signal service to the King and to the State." "I am but too much extolled (*glorifiée*)," wrote the lady with proud humility, "for certain good intentions which I owe to God."

It must not be supposed that the conversion of Louis XIV.—that remarkable transition from licentiousness to gloomy bigotry—was as yet complete; the habits of twenty years are not shaken off in a day, and, in the meanwhile, Madame de Maintenon lived in constant dread of a lapse from grace. She had nothing to fear from Madame de Montespan, for although it is extremely improbable that she knew anything of the revelations of Marguerite Monvoisin and her fellow-prisoners, she could not fail to discern that something had occurred which had rendered that haughty dame as harmless as

---

[1] Innocent XI. took the most lively interest in Madame de Maintenon's pious machinations. The relations between the Head of the Catholic Church and the Most Christian King had been exceedingly strained for some years past, and, doubtless, the Pontiff considered that the monarch's conversion might pave the way to a better understanding between them, and lead to Louis surrendering the absurd privileges claimed by the French Ambassador at the Vatican and other pretensions. He sent several briefs, relics, and so forth to the lady, and, on one occasion, a *corpo santo*, a martyr's body from the Catacombs, whom, as usual when the true name is unknown, he called St. Candida.

was poor Louise de La Vallière in her convent cell. But there was always the possibility of danger arising in a fresh quarter ; and from time to time some new star would make its appearance upon the horizon and for a moment shine with an effulgence which occasioned the worthy lady no little uneasiness. "I have been suffering terribly from melancholy *vapeurs*,"[1] she writes from Fontainebleau (August 5, 1681) to her friend, the Marquis de Montchevreuil.[2] "I never come here without getting them, but never have I had them so violently. I believe you already know Mademoiselle d'Oré. On Saturday she partook of *médianoche* with the King. They say that she has a sister even more beautiful than herself; but that is no concern of ours."[3]

This Mademoiselle d'Oré, or de Doré, who was responsible for Madame de Maintenon's *vapeurs*, appears to have been attached in some capacity to Madame de Montespan, and it was believed that her charms had been brought under the King's notice by the ex-favourite, with the object of arresting the triumphant progress of her rival. This is not improbable, but is of no consequence, for although his Majesty's attentions to the lady threw

[1] *Vapeurs* seem to have been the conventional name for hysterical complaints.

[2] Henri de Mornay, Marquis de Montchevreuil, *gouverneur* to the Duc du Maine. "A very worthy man," says Saint-Simon, "modest and brave, but most thick-headed and beggarly as a church rat." His wife (*née* Marguerite Boucher d'Orsay) was high in favour with Madame de Maintenon, and, in later years, according to the above-mentioned chronicler, acted as the head of that lady's intelligence department. "Without any understanding, she acquired such influence over Madame de Maintenon that she saw only with her eyes. She exercised surveillance over all the ladies of the Court ; and every one, even the Ministers and the King's daughters, trembled before her."

[3] *Correspondance générale de Madame de Maintenon*, ii. 196.

the devout party into momentary trepidation, the affair proved merely a *galanterie*—perhaps only a flirtation— and occasioned no scandal.

The attitude adopted by Madame de Montespan and Madame de Maintenon towards each other at this period is not a little singular. Bitter as was their antagonism, they took the most elaborate precautions to conceal their real feelings from the world, and when they happened to meet in public, invariably conversed with so much animation and cordiality that people who were not well informed in regard to the intrigues of the Court would have supposed them to be the best of friends. " Madame de Montespan and I," writes Madame de Maintenon to Montchevreuil, " took a walk together yesterday, arm-in-arm and laughing heartily; but we are on none the better terms for all that."[1] If we are to believe Madame de Caylus, these demonstrations of friendship were the outcome of an understanding between them. " I recollect," she says, " that, on one occasion during some journey of the Court, they found themselves obliged to travel in the same coach, and, I fancy, *tête-à-tête*. Madame de Montespan was the first to speak, and said, ' Let us not become the dupes of this affair, but converse as if we had no cause of quarrel.' ' Of course,' she continued, ' that will not necessitate our loving each other any the more, and on our return we can resume our former relations.' "[2]

Apart from the birth of the Duc de Bourgogne, eldest son of the Dauphin, the two years which followed were comparatively uneventful ones at the Court of *le Grand Monarque*, that is to say, from the courtier point of view.

[1] *Correspondance générale de Madame de Maintenon,* ii. 179.
[2] *Souvenirs et Correspondance de Madame de Caylus* (edit. 1889), p. 81.

Madame de Maintenon continued to keep watch and ward
over the morals of the King, a task which would appear
to have required the exercise of unsleeping vigilance, for
in one of her letters to the Abbé Gobelin she warns him
that "she had more than ever need of his counsels and
prayers."[1] But in the summer of 1683 an event of
great importance took place—an event which opened a
new destiny to Madame de Maintenon. The Queen
died.

On May 26 Louis XIV., accompanied by the Queen
and the greater part of the Court, including, needless to
say, his Majesty's female confessor, left Versailles to
inspect the troops stationed in Burgundy and Alsace. On
their return, at the end of July, the Queen, who had
greatly overtaxed her strength during the journey, was
attacked by an illness which rendered an operation—a
very simple one—necessary. Instead of performing it,
Fagon, her chief physician, recommended that she should
be bled, and, strongly against the advice of his colleagues,
this was done, with the result that on July 30, 1683, four
days after she had been taken ill, poor Maria Theresa
died at the age of forty-five.

A very significant incident occurred beside the death-
bed, where Louis stood shedding bitter tears—of remorse,
let us hope—and exclaiming, "This is the only grief she
has ever caused me." Madame de Maintenon, who had
been unwearied in her attentions to the royal patient,
seeing that all was over, was about to retire to her
apartments, when the Duc de La Rochefoucauld [2] took

[1] *Correspondance générale de Madame de Maintenon*, ii. 271.

[2] François VII., Duc de La Rochefoucauld, Prince de Marsillac
(1634–1714). He was the son of the author of the famous *Maximes*,
and a great favourite of Louis XIV.

her by the arm and drew her towards the King, saying,
"This is not the time to leave him, Madame. In the
state in which he now is he requires you."[1]

Truly an intelligent anticipation of events!

Immediately after the Queen's death Louis went to
Saint-Cloud, where he remained a few days, and then
to Fontainebleau, whither Madame de Maintenon, in
attendance on the Dauphiness, followed him. She
appeared before his Majesty clad in the deepest mourning and with an air so lugubrious that the King, who
had speedily recovered from the emotion he had displayed at his consort's deathbed, could not refrain from
laughing.[2]

Let us hasten to add that Madame de Maintenon's
grief at poor Maria Theresa's early death was perfectly
genuine, although it certainly did not proceed from any
feeling of affection for that long-suffering Princess. In
losing the Queen she had lost a very useful, almost
an indispensable, pawn in her game. So long as the
Queen lived and the King remained on good terms with
his consort, the work of conversion, and, with it, her own
glorification, might have been trusted to go on smoothly
enough. But her death had completely changed the
situation, and, notwithstanding the assertions of Madame
de Maintenon's enemies to the contrary, we firmly believe
that such a contingency had never been seriously taken
into account by that lady, and that it found her totally
unprepared.

The position of affairs indeed was one which might well
cause her anxiety. The King was very unlikely to marry

[1] *Souvenirs et Correspondance de Madame de Caylus* (edit. 1889),
p. 124.   [2] *Ibid.*

a foreign princess; the Treasury, depleted by constant
wars and ruinous expenditure at home, was in no condition
to support a second family, and, of course, it was impossible to guarantee that, if he did marry again, a second
family would not arrive. But, on the other hand, if he
were to remain a widower, was it not almost too much
to hope that his newly-acquired virtue would continue
proof against the assaults of all the ambitious beauties who
were already preparing for his subjugation, now that a
deviation from the straight path no longer necessarily
implied a breach of the Seventh Commandment, and
would undoubtedly be palliated by all but the most rigid
moralists on the specious pretext of political expediency?

Madame de Maintenon's conduct at this juncture
reveals the most profound agitation of mind. She scarcely
seemed to hear when people addressed her; she shed floods
of tears; she roamed about the Forest of Fontainebleau,
sometimes even at unseemly hours, with no other companion than her faithful henchwoman, Madame de
Montchevreuil, greatly to the astonishment of the ladies
of the Court. Her letters, too, are in keeping with her
conduct. "I implore you to pray for the King," she
writes, a fortnight after the Queen's death, to Madame
de Brinon, the superior of a home for little girls she had
lately founded at Noisy; "he has more need of grace
than ever to sustain a state contrary to his inclinations
and habits."[1] And to her brother, a little later, she
writes: "The longer I live, the more clearly I recognise
the futility of making plans and projects for the future;
God nearly always brings them to nought, and, as He
is hardly ever taken into account when they are made,
He does not bless them."[2]

[1] *Correspondance générale* ii. 307.   [2] *Ibid.*, p. 316.

MADAME DE MONTESPAN

But presently the clouds roll by, the sun shines forth
once more, and, on September 20, 1684, she writes to the
Abbé Gobelin—to the Abbé Gobelin, who had given her
so much good counsel and was now doubtless to reap his
reward : "Do not forget me before God, for I have great
need of strength *to make a good use of my happiness.*" [1]

The royal widower had offered his hand to the keeper
of his conscience !

Much has been written about the reasons which induced
Louis XIV. to take this step, but, in our opinion, the
Abbé de Choisy comes nearer the truth than any of his
contemporaries. Here is what he says :—

"He (Louis XIV.) was unwilling to marry through
consideration for his people, and wisely judged that the
princes of a second marriage might, in course of time,
cause civil wars. On the other hand, he could not dispense with a wife.[2] Madame de Maintenon pleased him
greatly. Her gentle, insinuating wit promised him an
agreeable intercourse capable of recreating him after the
cares of royalty. Her person was still engaging, and her
age prevented her from having children." [3] To which
we may add that Louis was sincerely desirous of leading
a regular life, and that, as Lamartine remarks, "an attachment to Madame de Maintenon seemed almost the same
thing as an attachment to virtue itself." [4]

Although of the marriage itself there is not a shadow

[1] *Correspondance générale*, ii. 307.

[2] According to the Duc de Luynes, Madame de Montespan, dreading
the final triumph of her rival, said, a few days after the Queen's death :
"We must think about marrying him again as soon as possible, otherwise, if I know anything about him, he will make a bad marriage rather
than not make one at all."

[3] *Mémoires de l'Abbé de Choisy* (edit. 1888), ii. 90.

[4] Lamartine's *Étude sur Bossuet.*

of doubt, no documentary evidence of it exists, and the
date is uncertain. All that is known is that at midnight,
some time in the early part of the year 1684,[1] seven
persons met in the private apartments of the King at
Versailles. These were Louis XIV. and Madame de
Maintenon; Père de La Chaise, who said mass; Harlay
de Chanvallon, Archbishop of Paris, who gave the nuptial
blessing; Louvois and Montchevreuil, who acted as witnesses; and Bontemps, the King's confidential *valet-de-
chambre*, last seen in a much less edifying rôle, who
prepared the altar and served the mass.

The daughter of the criminal François d'Aubigné the
widow of the needy poet Scarron, the head nurse of
Madame de Montespan's adulterine children, had become
the unrecognised consort of the greatest king in Christendom!

[1] Saint-Simon says the end of January; M. Lavallée thinks it was
during the first week in April; other writers place it as late as the
month of June. We are inclined to agree with M. Lavallée, who gives
two reasons for his selection. The first is a letter written by Madame
de Maintenon to her brother, Charles d'Aubigné, on April 7, in
which the following passages occur : " This journey (the Court was
about to accompany the King to Flanders) troubles me, *since we shall
not be long with the King*. . . . I do not like to inveigh against any one,
and less at this hour than ever." The second is the fact that Dangeau,
a most devoted henchman of Louis XIV. and Madame de Maintenon,
commences his famous *Journal* on April 1.

CHAPTER XX

Influence of Madame de Maintenon after her marriage with Louis XIV. considered—She decides to tolerate Madame de Montespan's presence at Court until she has consolidated her power—Madame de Montespan reconciles herself to the situation—Louis XIV.'s daily life at this period—Madame de Montespan leaves her old apartments for a suite more remote from those of the King—But makes Louis a magnificent New Year's Gift—And is still, to all appearance, high in favour—Revival of the antagonism between her and Madame de Maintenon—The latter determines to drive Madame de Montespan from Court—Madame de Montespan's *bon-mots* at her expense—Madame de Montespan excluded from a visit of the Court to Baréges—Her fury and mortification—The King spends all his time with Madame de Maintenon—But finally resumes his visits to his former mistress—Marriage of Mademoiselle de Nantes and the Duc de Bourbon—Marriage of the Duc d'Antin and Mademoiselle d'Uzès—Boyhood of the Duc d'Antin—His anxiety to push his fortunes at Court—Madame de Montespan's liberality to him—Her present to his wife—Madame de Montespan becomes a comparatively unimportant person at Court—Estrangement between her and her eldest son, the Duc du Maine, who is completely under the influence of Madame de Maintenon—Madame de Montespan's benefactions to the Convent of Saint-Joseph—She decides to retire from Court and make it her headquarters—And requests Bossuet to inform the King of her intention—She repents of her resolution, but too late.

THE amount of influence exercised by Madame de Maintenon after her marriage with Louis XIV. has been

the subject of almost as much dispute as the lady's
character, and is by no means easy to determine. But
we are inclined to think, as we have already said, that in
affairs of State it was really very small—infinitesimally small
compared with that wielded by Madame de Pompadour
in the succeeding reign. Louis never let the reins of
government out of his hands for a single moment, and if
he transacted business with his Ministers in her apartments; if he sometimes jestingly inquired, "What thinks
your Solidity on this matter?" he was quick to resent the
very smallest attempt on her Solidity's part to interfere
in matters which he considered outside the province of a
woman, as Madame de Maintenon's own letters abundantly
testify. "I did not please in a conversation about the
works now going on," she writes to Cardinal de Noailles,
"and my regret is to have given offence without profit.
Another building here will cost a hundred thousand
livres. Marly will soon be a second Versailles. There
is no help for it but prayer and patience." And again:
"The King will allow only his Ministers to talk to him
about business. He was displeased because the Nuncio
addressed himself to me. I should be well content with
the life of slavery I lead if I could do some good. I can
only groan over the turn that matters have taken." And
here let us again remark that the charge so often brought
against Madame de Maintenon of having urged upon
Louis XIV. the Revocation of the Edict of Nantes and
the persecution which accompanied that shameful and
disastrous measure is quite unfounded. Madame de
Maintenon approved of the Revocation itself, but so did
practically all her most famous contemporaries, Colbert
and Vauban excepted; while it was equally popular with
the bourgeoisie and the rabble of Paris, among whom the

passions of St. Bartholomew still smouldered. But if
she approved of the Revocation she certainly did not
approve of the steps taken to give effect to it, and, as far
as she dared, strove to obtain some mitigation of the
severities practised against the unfortunate Huguenots;
so much so that the King said to her on one occasion,
" I fear, Madame, that the mildness with which you
would wish the Calvinists to be treated proceeds from
some remaining sympathy with your former religion."
The Revocation was the work, not of Madame de
Maintenon, but of Louvois and his father, Michel Le
Tellier, the latter of whom declared on the day on which
it was signed that he could now sing his *Nunc dimittis*,
and had been resolved upon long before the lady reached
the " pinnacle of favour."

On the other hand, if Madame de Maintenon possessed
little or no political power, it is beyond question that her
influence in such matters as the distribution of honours
and pensions and places was very great indeed, and that a
word from her was sufficient to make or mar the fortune
of any courtier. How else are we to account for the
fact that, as she herself tells us, her apartment was like
a crowded church, and that Ministers, and generals, and
even members of the Royal Family were content to cool
their heels in her ante-chamber until it was her good
pleasure to receive them? How else for the virulence
with which chroniclers like Saint-Simon and the Princess
Palatine have assailed her?

Such being the case, it is not a little surprising that for
nearly two years after her marriage Madame de Maintenon
should have taken no steps to hasten the retirement from
Court of the woman whose presence must have served
as a continual reminder of the humble and decidedly

equivocal position she had once occupied, and of conduct
which those who were not of the elect and consequently
did not regard the ex-*gouvernante* as the chosen instrument
of the Almighty might conceivably be inclined to call by
an unpleasant name. But Madame de Maintenon, among
other admirable qualities, possessed that of patience in a
quite unusual degree, and, confident that she had little
to fear from the discarded mistress and anxious above all
things to avoid recriminations and give no occasion for
scandal until she had consolidated her power, she decided
to postpone the satisfaction of witnessing Madame de
Montespan's exit from the scene of her former triumphs
until a more convenient season. As for the lady in
question, we may be quite sure that she had not the least
intention of gratifying Madame de Maintenon and the
devout party by a premature retirement. " She was much
attached to the Court, not only on account of the ties
which bound her to it, but because she enjoyed Court
life." [1] Secure in the knowledge that her dealings with
La Voisin and her confederates were safe in the keeping
of the King, she had long since reconciled herself, in
appearance at least, to her position ; was still the life and
soul of the Court, still the centre of gaiety and wit,
organising boisterously, as was her wont, balls, lotteries,
masquerades, and the most sumptuous entertainments.

Nor for the first two years after the King's marriage
was there any ostensible reason for her quitting the
Court. As Dangeau tells us, Louis's union with Madame
de Maintenon had modified only insensibly his outward
habits. The following account which the chronicler
gives of the monarch's daily life at this time shows that
the untoward symptoms observed in the autumn of 1680,

---

[1] *Lettres historiques et édifiantes de Madame de Maintenon,* ii. 162.

when Louis was suffering from the first shock of the revelations of the Chambre Ardente and could with difficulty bring himself to pay Madame de Montespan visits of a few minutes' duration, had entirely disappeared, doubtless under the influence of that delightful conversation which caused even her enemy, the Princess Palatine, to declare that "it was impossible to feel *ennuyé* in her society" [1] :—

"He rises as a rule between eight and nine o'clock. As soon as he is dressed he shuts himself up with his Ministers until half-past twelve,[2] at which hour he leaves his cabinet, goes to inform Madame la Dauphine that he is ready to hear mass, and all the Royal Household proceed to mass, where the music is very fine.[3] Mass is generally over between one and two o'clock, after which the King goes to Madame de Montespan's apartments and remains there until dinner is announced. His Majesty then goes to Madame la Dauphine's ante-chamber to dine.[4] The gentlemen-in-waiting serve him. *Monseigneur*, Madame la Dauphine, *Monsieur*, *Madame*,

---

[1] *Correspondance complète de Madame, Duchesse d'Orléans*, ii. 127.

[2] Councils of State were held on Sundays, Mondays, Wednesdays, and Thursdays ; Councils of Finance on Tuesdays and Saturdays ; and on Fridays the King held a "Council of Conscience" with the Archbishop of Paris or Père de La Chaise.

[3] So fine that Madame de Caylus (then Mademoiselle de Villette) declared, after hearing it for the first time, that she was prepared "to become reconciled to the Church," provided she might be allowed to attend the King's Mass every day.

[4] To watch Louis XIV. dine must have been a truly awe-inspiring sight. Although he drank but sparingly, he was a most enormous eater. Here, according to the Princess Palatine, is one of his gastronomical feats : "Four platefuls of different soups, a whole pheasant, a partridge, a plateful of salad, mutton hashed with garlic, two good-sized slices of ham, a dish of pastry, and afterwards fruit and sweetmeats."

Mademoiselle, and Mademoiselle de Guise,[1] sit down to table with the King, and occasionally the princesses of the blood.[2] Dinner over, the King returns to Madame la Dauphine's apartments for a moment, and then again shuts himself up to work or goes out. At seven or eight o'clock in the evening he goes to visit Madame de Maintenon, with whom he stays till ten o'clock, which is his supper-hour, and then returns to sup with Madame la Dauphine. On rising from the table he goes for a moment into her apartments, bids her good-night, and then proceeds to Madame de Montespan's, where he remains until midnight; and the *petit coucher* is generally over by half-past twelve, or one o'clock at the latest.[3]

At the beginning of December 1684, Madame de Montespan quitted her magnificent apartments on the first floor of the château for a suite more remote from the King's life,[4] as Louis desired to join them to his own. This incident is regarded by some writers as the first sign of disgrace; but this is doubtful, and even if such were the case, the lady would not appear to have resented it, for on the following New Year's Eve we hear of her making a present to his Majesty of a book "bound in gold," containing miniature views of all the

---

[1] Marie de Lorraine, Duchesse de Guise, Princesse de Joinville, and Duchesse de Joyeuse, daughter of Charles de Lorraine, fourth Duc de Guise and Henriette de Joyeuse. In 1675, by the death of her great-nephew François Joseph, the seventh Duke, she inherited all the titles and fortune of her house, and when she herself died, thirteen years later, "the brood of false Lorraine" became extinct.

[2] The princesses of the blood never sat down to dinner with the King when the Dauphiness and *Madame* were present.

[3] *Journal du Marquis de Dangeau*, i. 87.

[4] The *Appartement des Bains*, on the *rez-de-chaussée*, underneath the King's State apartments.

towns of Holland taken by him in the campaign of 1672, with a description of the sieges and an *éloge* by those two most consummate flatterers of royalty, Racine and Boileau. This book was believed to have cost 4000 pistoles.[1]

The months went by and Madame de Montespan continued to all appearance high in favour. On February 15 she gave a grand masquerade in her new quarters, on which occasion the King graciously placed at her disposal the royal musicians. A few days later the lady prepared a surprise for his Majesty, who, when he came to pay her his usual evening visit, found that her apartments had been transformed so as to represent the Fair of Saint-Germain, with the booths in charge of the most beautiful ladies of the Court. This entertainment seems to have afforded the monarch much pleasure. Then we read of her being consulted by Louis on the choice of an opera for the ensuing winter; of her accompanying him on several excursions to dine or sup at Marly; of her riding with him in the same *calèche* at hunting-parties, and so forth.[2] But appearances, so often deceptive, were never more so than in that place of which La Bruyère wrote, "There is a region in which joys are visible, but they are false, and sorrows hidden, but they are known"[3]—the Court of *le Grand Monarque*.

Even while these marks of the royal esteem were being bestowed on Madame de Montespan, the antagonism between her and Madame de Maintenon, for a moment quenched, had gradually revived, and soon it became apparent to the ex-favourite that her rival, so far from

---

[1] *Journal du Marquis de Dangeau,* i. 87.

[2] *Ibid.,* i. *passim.*

[3] *Caractères et mœurs* ; chap., *La Cour.*

being satisfied with having supplanted her in the King's affections, was bent on driving her from Court, not by any overt acts of hostility—such would have been entirely foreign to the character of the discreet lady who liked not to let her left hand know what her right did, save in matters of religion and charity—but by subjecting her, or rather inducing Louis to subject her, to slights and mortifications, galling for any woman to bear, but doubly so for one as haughty as herself.

Powerless to counteract the sinister influence of her enemy, Madame de Montespan took refuge in biting *bon-mots*, which naturally only served to strengthen Madame de Maintenon's determination. " I recollect her coming one day," says Madame de Caylus, " to Madame de Maintenon's apartments, to a meeting on behalf of the poor which Madame de Maintenon used to hold at the beginning of every month, and at which the ladies used to present their alms, Madame de Montespan among the rest. On this occasion, she arrived before the meeting had begun, and observing, as she passed through the ante-chamber, the curé and the Grey Sisters of Versailles, and all the tokens of the devotion which Madame de Maintenon professed, she exclaimed on entering the room, " Do you know, Madame, that your ante-chamber is admirably prepared for your funeral oration ? "[1]

It was in the spring of 1686 that the first blow fell— the first of those cruel humiliations to her pride which were to end in driving the ex-favourite from Court. In May, the King, who had been for some little time under medical treatment for the malady which necessitated in the following autumn what is known as " *la grande opération*," was ordered a course of the waters at Baréges,

[1] *Souvenirs et Correspondance de Madame de Caylus* (edit. 1889), p. 152.

and "commands" were accordingly sent out to the favoured courtiers whom his Majesty desired to accompany him on his journey. Now, for a courtier who had hitherto occupied a high place in the good graces of the sovereign not to receive a "command" on these occasions was regarded as an infallible sign that the sun of the royal favour had ceased to shine; and Madame de Montespan's rage and mortification may be imagined when she learned that she was not to be of the party. "Madame de Montespan," writes the discreet Dangeau in his *Journal*, "was attacked with the most violent *vapeurs on learning that the King's health was not yet completely re-established.*"[1]

Furious with mortification, the marchioness rushed off to Paris and remained there some days. But the time for her final retreat had not arrived; she could not yet make up her mind to quit the Court she had loved so well, and where she had so long reigned supreme; and returned. The morning after her arrival, however, she again departed, Rambouillet being her destination; "wishing to avoid taking leave of the King or any one," says Dangeau, not so discreet this time.[2] The little Comte de Toulouse was preparing to follow his mother, to whom he was much attached, and was actually stepping into the coach which was to take him to Rambouillet, when he received a message from the King desiring him to remain and accompany him to Baréges. However, a day or two later, we learn that the King was feeling so much better that the journey to Baréges had been abandoned; that Madame de Montespan had returned from Rambouillet; and that his Majesty was

---

[1] *Journal du Marquis de Dangeau,* i. 337.
[2] *Ibid.,* i. 339.

visiting her as usual. But soon these visits, hitherto so regular, became less frequent; instead of going to the ex-favourite's apartments after mass and after supper, Louis turned his steps towards those of his unrecognised consort, and " Madame de Montespan gnawed her fingers with vexation." [1]

In her rage, she broke forth into bitter jests, not sparing even the King ; but still she remained at Court. " Her hour was not yet come," says the Abbé de Choisy, " and Providence, to punish her for the past, intended her to endure many further mortifications." [2]

In October the Court removed to Fontainebleau. Madame de Montespan, on some plea or other, remained behind at Versailles ; but a few days later followed, to find Madame de Maintenon installed in a magnificent suite of apartments on the same floor as those of the King, and his Majesty spending the whole of his evenings with her. On the arrival of the marchioness, however, Louis, perhaps considering that he had humiliated her sufficiently for the present, resumed his visits to her, and "gave her marks of his esteem." [3]

In the summer of the preceding year Madame de Montespan's elder daughter, Mademoiselle de Nantes, for whom, it will be remembered, poor Louise de La Vallière had stood sponsor, had married the Duc de Bourbon (*M. le Duc*), grandson of the Great Condé. The young duke was only seventeen, while his bride had recently celebrated her twelfth birthday. " It was ridiculous," says the Marquis de Sourches, " to witness the marriage of these two marionettes, for the Duc de

---

[1] *Mémoires de l'Abbé de Choisy* (edit. 1888), ii. 12.
[2] *Ibid.*, ii. 13.   [3] *Ibid.*, ii. 14.

Bourbon was absurdly short, and it was feared that he would remain a dwarf." The ceremony took place with great magnificence in the King's State apartments at Versailles, and " the Great Condé and his son[1] left nothing undone to testify their joy, just as they had left nothing undone to bring about the marriage."[2] The King secured to the duke the survivorship of all the offices held by his father, and gave him a pension of 90,000 livres, and to his daughter one of 100,000 livres.

Twelve months later, the Duc d'Antin, the son with whom Madame de Montespan had presented her husband " before she was translated to the arms of Jupiter to give birth to demigods," was married to Mademoiselle d'Uzès.[3] After his wife became the King's mistress, Montespan had taken his little boy away to Guienne, where he was educated by the Abbé Anselme, of whose eloquence as a preacher Madame de Sévigné speaks highly in her letters. In spite of the marquis's precautions, the child very early learned from the gossip of his nurses, to whom, such was the singular morality of the time, Madame de Montespan's position appeared wholly enviable, of his mother's adventures. "They were continually talking to me," he tells us in his *Mémoires*, " of the Court, the King, and of the great favours and fortune which awaited me," and to this he attributes the fact that he grew up with no other desire than that of making his way as a courtier. Montespan wished to send his son to continue his education in

---

[1] Henri Jules de Bourbon, Prince de Condé.

[2] *Souvenirs et Correspondance de Madame de Caylus* (edit. 1889), p, 157.

[3] Julie Françoise de Crussol, daughter of the Duc d'Uzès, and grand-daughter of the Duc de Montausier. Her father was strongly opposed to the marriage, and only gave his consent when the Duc de Montausier offered to provide the *dot*.

Paris ; but it was not until the boy was fourteen that permission to do so was accorded him. D'Antin and the
marquis then came to Paris, where poor Montespan had
to go about escorted by a certain M. de Fieubet, a Councillor of State, who had orders not to let him out of his
sight, and Madame de Montespan paid a surreptitious
visit to her son ; "but, for reasons connected with the
Court, she was unable to see any more of him, which
caused him extreme mortification." After completing
his education at the Collège of Louis le Grand, d'Antin
received a sub-lieutenant's commission in the Régiment
du Roi, and was presented to the King, who, much to
his chagrin, did not evince the slightest desire to cultivate
his acquaintance. However, when he was twenty, he
received the command of a regiment, and, shortly afterwards, Madame de Montespan obtained for him the post
of *ménin* (gentleman-in-waiting) to the Dauphin, an office
which carried with it a salary of 2000 écus. This,
according to the ungrateful d'Antin, was the only service
his mother ever rendered him, although he admits that
she was attached to him "in her way." On his marriage
with Mademoiselle d'Uzès, the marchioness gave him a
pension of 2000 écus and furnished a suite of apartments
for the young couple at Versailles. She also prepared a
charming surprise for the bride, who, on arriving from
Paris, where the marriage had been celebrated, found in
her boudoir "a great bowl, full of everything that a lady
could require—ribbons, fans, essences, gloves, and a very
beautiful set of emeralds and diamonds." [1]

These marriages, occasional visits to her sister at
Fontevrault, the nursing of the little Duchesse de
Bourbon and Mademoiselle de Blois, the future wife of

[1] *Journal du Marquis de Dangeau*, i. 374.

the Regent Orléans, through attacks of small-pox, both of which nearly proved fatal,[1] and the education of the latter were the chief incidents and occupations of Madame de Montespan's life during several years. The King continued to visit her in the interval between mass and dinner, and in the evenings, after supper, she generally went with the Duchesse de Bourbon to his apartments. But the time was now approaching when the Abbé Dorat was to write : " The King has become a saint. . . . All the ladies of the Court are compelled to cover their necks and arms, so that nothing but modesty is seen where they appear " ; and as Louis's bigotry and Madame de Maintenon's influence increased, his manner towards his former mistress became more and more cold and distant, while we have only to glance at Dangeau's *Journal* and contrast his references to Madame de Montespan with those during the years 1684 and 1685 to see how comparatively unimportant a person she now was.[2]

[1] " *Madame la Duchesse* was seized with the small-pox at Fontainebleau, and her life was in great danger. The Great Condé, much alarmed, left Chantilly, notwithstanding his gout, to go and shut himself up with her and render her all the cares not only of a tender father but of a zealous guardian. The King, on learning of the extremity of *Madame la Duchesse*, wished to go and see her ; but *M. le Prince* (Condé) placed himself at the door to prevent him entering, and there a great struggle ensued between parental love and the zeal of a courtier, very glorious for *Madame la Duchesse*. The King was the stronger and went in in spite of *M. le Prince's* resistance. *Madame la Duchesse* recovered ; the King returned to Versailles ; and *M. le Prince* remained with his grand-daughter. The change in his manner of life, the sleepless nights and the fatigue acting on a frame already so weakened as was his, brought about his death shortly afterwards."—*Souvenirs et Correspondance de Madame de Caylus* (edit. 1889), p. 158.

[2] Madame de Caylus says that during her last years at Court Madame de Montespan was " merely regarded as the *gouvernante* of Mademoiselle de Blois."

Another fruitful source of annoyance to the ex-favourite was the conduct of her son, the Duc du Maine. The Comte de Toulouse, as we have mentioned, was much attached to his mother, as were the Duchesse de Bourbon and Mademoiselle de Blois, but it was far otherwise with Madame de Montespan's eldest child. This boy had been Madame de Maintenon's especial care, and there can be no question that she now used the influence which she had acquired over him to gradually alienate the affection which he had once felt, or at least professed, for his mother. The task was not a difficult one. The young duke was, in his way, as consummate an egotist as his royal father, and, according to Saint-Simon, "an accomplished poltroon both in heart and mind." Mere boy as he was, he felt with the instincts of a born courtier that Madame de Montespan had become an embarrassing weight on his fortunes, while from his former *gouvernante* he could hope and expect all things; and it needed but a few disparaging smiles when the ex-favourite's name was mentioned, a few gentle hints that perchance the surest way to high favour might lie along a different road from that by which she was travelling, to establish a gulf between mother and son which was never to be bridged over. "I do not know," he writes on October 25, 1688 (he was then eighteen), to Madame de Maintenon, "if I ought to take this opportunity of asking you to tell Madame de Montespan that we shall soon require money. I have heard it said that she is sending us back M. de Malézieux,[1] a fact which does not surprise me, *for I know that she is always afraid that she will be robbed*, although M. de Montchevreuil

[1] Nicolas de Malézieux, tutor to the Duc du Maine. He afterwards became a member of the Academy.

has no inclination to do that."[1]   And, on another occasion, after losing money at cards at Marly, "where it is impossible to remain without playing, and where no one cares to play for small sums," he avows to "his confessor" that he fears her reprimands far more than those of Madame de Montespan, "because they are always guided by reason."[2]

For this unfortunate estrangement it is probable that Madame de Montespan was herself partly responsible. Her hatred of Madame de Maintenon was so intense that it extended to that lady's friends, and when she found that as the boy grew up, his regard for his former *gouvernante* increased rather than diminished, instead of endeavouring to gain his confidence and affection, she washed her hands of him, and declined even to undertake the management of his property, which the King wished to entrust to her.

In the spring of 1681, Madame de Montespan had enlarged the Couvent des Filles de Saint-Joseph,[3] a home for orphan girls in the Rue Saint-Dominique, parish of Saint-Sulpice, not far from the Hôtel de Conti, and liberally endowed it.   The community, out of gratitude for her benevolence, had elected her their *supérieure* and granted her "all the rights and privileges generally accorded to the founders of these kinds of establishments," among them that of residing there whenever she

---

[1] *Correspondance générale de Madame de Maintenon*, iii. 130.

[2] *Ibid.*, iii. 59.

[3] More than one writer speaks of Madame de Montespan having *built* this convent, but this was not the case.   The Congrégation des Filles de Saint-Joseph had been established in the Rue Saint-Dominique for more than forty years.   The society had been founded at Bordeaux in May 1638 by a nun called Marie Delpech de l'Estang, and removed to Paris the following year.

felt disposed. Towards the year 1690 the ex-favourite
gradually acquired the habit of spending at first a few
weeks, then entire months, at Saint-Joseph, and, finally,
on March 15, 1691, she sent for Bossuet and begged him
to inform the King that she had decided, with his permission, to retire from Court and make the convent her
headquarters for the future. Thus the illustrious prelate
who sixteen years before had endeavoured to break the
guilty chain which bound her to the King, was the one to
whom she now had recourse to sever its last frail link.

The Marquis de Sourches ascribes the lady's decision
to her anger and mortification on learning that Louis
intended to remove the Comte de Toulouse and Mademoiselle de Blois from her care. He says:—

"The Marquise de Montespan, learning that the King
was taking the Comte de Toulouse with him to the army
and that he was removing from her control her daughter,
Mademoiselle de Blois, in order to place her under the
charge of the Marquise de Montchevreuil,[1] conceived so
terrible a chagrin that she forgot all the wise resolutions
that she had made to give the King no pretext for dismissing her, and, in her first burst of anger, sent for the
Bishop of Meaux (Bossuet) and begged him to go and
inform the King that, since he was taking her children
from her, she saw clearly that he had no longer any consideration for her, and that she entreated him to permit
her to retire to her establishment of Saint-Joseph at
Paris. The prelate would, perhaps, have been very glad
to have escaped such a commission, but he could not
refuse, and, as soon as he had discharged it, the King
joyfully replied that he accorded Madame de Montespan
the permission she demanded, and immediately gave her

[1] Madame de Maintenon's henchwoman.

apartments in the Château of Versailles to the Duc du Maine, who surrendered his to Mademoiselle de Blois." [1]

Dangeau confirms these details :—

"*March* 15, 1691.—Madame de Montespan, who has been for some days at Saint-Joseph, has sent to inform the King, through M. de Meaux (Bossuet), that the decision which she has arrived at is to retire definitely, and that she intends to divide her time between Fontevrault and Saint-Joseph. The King has given the *Appartement des Bains* to the Duc du Maine, and the Duc du Maine's apartments to Mademoiselle de Blois, who will not accompany Madame de Montespan. She will remain at Court, and Madame de Montchevreuil has been placed in charge of her." [2]

The resolution hastily formed was almost as hastily repented of. Exactly a month later Dangeau writes again :—

"*April* 15.—Madame de Montespan, who has been at Clagny for several days, has gone back to Paris. She says that she has not absolutely renounced the Court, that she will still see the King sometimes, and that, in

---

[1] *Mémoires du Marquis de Sourches*, iii. 365.

[2] *Journal du Marquis de Dangeau*, iii. 300. Saint-Simon asserts that Madame de Montespan's retirement was not a voluntary one. It was, according to him, the result of an intrigue between Bossuet, Madame de Maintenon, and the Duc du Maine, who so worked upon the mind of the King that he sent the Duke to his mother with positive orders for her to leave the Court, a commission which the young gentleman discharged "*sans ménagement.*"—*Mémoires* (edit. 1881), xii. 114. Saint-Simon's hatred of Madame de Maintenon and the Duc du Maine is too well known, however, for much importance to be attached to such a statement, particularly when it is at variance with the account of the matter given by such impartial chroniclers as Sourches and Dangeau.

point of fact, *they have been a little hasty in removing the furniture from her apartments.*" [1]

But it was now too late; the Marchioness had been taken at her word. On the very day on which he was informed of her wish to retire from Court, the King, as we have seen, had given her apartments to the Duc du Maine, and that youthful egotist, having once got his embarrassing mother out of the way, was in no mind to allow her a chance of returning.

[1] *Journal du Marquis de Dangeau,* iii. 325.

CHAPTER XXI

Madame de Montespan in retirement—She pays occasional visits to the Court, but after a time these cease—And she is almost completely forgotten—Madame de Maintenon's protestations of friendship—Nevertheless, she informs Madame de Montespan that "correspondence with her will not be agreeable"—Madame de Montespan's chief consolation in her exile the society of her youngest sister, the Abbess of Fontevrault—Amiable character and accomplishments of this lady—Saint-Simon's appreciation of her—Her singular complaisance in regard to Madame de Montespan's connection with Louis XIV.—Madame de Montespan's eldest sister, Madame de Thianges—Her eccentricities—Her daughters, the Duchesse de Nevers and the Duchess Sforza—Madame de Montespan's brother, the Duc de Vivonne—His wit and imperturbable good humour—His children—Madame de Montespan's relations with her children by Louis XIV.— Her generosity to the Duc d'Antin and his family—His inestimable character—Madame de Montespan persuades him to give up play—Rebuff administered to him by the King— His servility to Louis XIV. and Madame de Maintenon—He is not received into favour until after his mother's death— Madame de Montespan's correspondence with the Duchesse de Noailles—And with Daniel Huet, Bishop of Avranches.

FOR some time after her retirement, Madame de Montespan continued to pay occasional visits to the Court. Thus, during the siege of Mons, when her daughters did not follow the King, she came several times to Versailles " like one of those unhappy spirits who return to their former haunts to expiate their sins"; [1] while, in September 1695, we hear of her being present at a supper-party given by Langlée, who, in the days of her splendour, had presented her with the gorgeous robe described by Madame de Sévigné, to the Duc and Duchesse de Chartres,[2]

[1] *Souvenirs et Correspondance de Madame de Caylus* (edit. 1889), p. 151.

[2] Mademoiselle de Blois, Madame de Montespan's youngest daughter, who had married the Duc de Chartres (afterwards the Regent Orléans) on February 18, 1692. This marriage was viewed with strong disfavour by *Monsieur* and *Madame*, though they did not dare to oppose the wishes of the King. The Princess Palatine was at no pains to conceal her fury and mortification at the *mésalliance* which had been thrust upon her son and at what she considered the latter's pusillanimity in consenting to wed the young lady. "*Madame*," says Saint-Simon, "promenaded the Gallery with her favourite, Châteauthiers. She strode along, handkerchief in hand, weeping bitterly, talking rather loud, gesticulating, and behaving just like Ceres after the abduction of his daughter, Proserpine. At supper, the King offered *Madame* nearly all the dishes which were placed before him, but she declined them in a very discourteous manner, notwithstanding which the King continued his attentions and civilities to the end of the meal. The following morning, everybody presented themselves at the apartments of *Monsieur*, *Madame*, and the Duc de Chartres, but not a word was spoken ; people contented themselves with bows, and everything passed off in perfect silence. Afterwards a move was made, as usual, to the Gallery (*des Glaces*) to await the breaking-up of the Council and the King's Mass. *Madame* came there, and her son, as was his daily custom, approached to kiss her hand. Thereupon *Madame* bestowed upon him so resounding box on the ear that it could be heard some distance off, and which, it was given in the presence of the whole Court, covered the poor Prince with confusion, and overwhelmed the numerous spectators, of whom I was one, with profound astonishment."

Curiously enough, Mademoiselle de Blois, aged fifteen, naïvely fancied that it was a great condescension on her part to wed the Duc de Chartres, "as he was only the nephew of the King, while she was his daughter." Duclos says that people laughingly compared her to Minerva, who, recognising no mother, prided herself on being the daughter of Jupiter

the Duchesse de Bourbon, and other members of the Royal Family. But after a while these visits grew fewer and fewer, and at length ceased altogether, and so short is the memory of courtiers that the once all-powerful marchioness became to the majority of the denizens of Versailles as if she had never existed, and had it not been for her children, the cause of incessant domestic difficulties, as later they were to become of political ones, no trace of her brilliant and dazzling reign would have remained save a few ballets and dedications of La Fontaine and other poets.

Madame de Montespan's successor in the royal affections continued to profess for her discomfited rival the most touching regard. "I am overjoyed, Madame," she writes to the marchioness's sister, the Abbess of Fontevrault (September 27, 1691), "to have received some tokens of remembrance from Madame de Montespan. I feared that she was annoyed with me. God knows if I have done anything to merit that and how my heart is hers!"[1] And ten years later, to the same correspondent: "You do not mention Madame de Montespan's name. She is too often present in my thoughts. I desire for her all that I desire for myself. Inform her, Madame, of the death of Madame de Brinon,[2] and believe both

[1] *Correspondance générale*, iii. 306. Commenting on this letter, the devoted M. Lavallée remarks with charming ingenuousness : " One sees with what tranquillity Madame de Maintenon speaks of her conduct so much criticised in regard to Madame de Montespan. She had never had the least intention of injuring Madame de Montespan in extricating her from her guilty intrigue."

[2] Madame de Brinon had been the first *supérieure* of Saint-Cyr. Madame de Maintenon caused her to be removed from her post because she brought up the young ladies in too worldly a manner, but she remained on friendly terms with her.

of you that the sentiments I entertain for you gives me a claim to your regard." [1]

In the face of these protestations of friendship, it is somewhat singular to find Madame de Montespan writing to her friend and confidante, the Duchesse de Noailles, as follows :—

MADAME DE MONTESPAN *to the* DUCHESSE DE NOAILLES.

"FONTEVRAULT, *November* 19, 1698.

"I wrote to-day to extol your merits to Madame de Maintenon and to felicitate her on the pleasure which she must find in your society, and in the sincerity and discretion that you possess in a supreme degree, to which, between ourselves, those who have approached her up to now, have not accustomed her. You will remember what I said to you about it at Saint-Joseph, and I repeated it to-day to Madame de Maintenon in the effusion of my heart which her letter [2] has provoked; for she has told me all that I desired of her, which consisted merely in showing me very plainly that inter-course with me is not agreeable to her. Such may very well be the case, and so well do I understand it that I ask nothing else to set my mind and heart at rest about a person who has made too deep an impression upon both not to retain her place there. Nor can I suffi-ciently impress on you, Madame, the good that you have done me by relieving me from so heavy a burden,

[1] *Correspondance générale,* iv. 425 ; Letter of April 18, 1701.

[2] This letter from Madame de Maintenon was in answer to one which Madame de Montespan had addressed to her, thanking her for having obtained from the King some favour for Mademoiselle de Vivonne, one of her nieces. Louis had requested the Duc du Maine to inform his mother that her request had been granted solely out of deference to Madame de Maintenon's wishes.

which to endure or to shake off entirely was always very painful. I can assure you that I feel greatly relieved, to an extent, indeed, which would have been impossible but for the explanation which you have procured for me. That is done; I thank you for it, and ask nothing more either of you or Madame de Maintenon. She has told me what could have been told by her alone, and which authorises everything that I shall require to tell myself in the future. I have only to conclude your letter, as I have concluded hers, by saying that silence between her and me becomes agreeable to myself when I know that it is so to her." [1]

Madame de Montespan's chief consolation in her exile was the society of her youngest sister, Gabrielle de Rochechouart-Mortemart, Abbess of Fontevrault, with whom she spent several months each year. This lady, whose appointment in 1670, at the age of twenty-four, had caused so much surprise and indignation, had, strange to say, proved herself from the very outset eminently qualified for the post, and the reputation of the famous abbey has never stood higher than when under her rule. All her contemporaries, with the single exception of Madame de Sévigné,[2] speak in the highest terms of

[1] *Correspondance générale de Madame de Maintenon*, iv. 268. A month after this letter was written, Madame de Maintenon wrote to the Abbess of Fontevrault : " I beg you to assure Madame de Montespan of the sentiments that you know I retain for her ; I can never cease to take an interest in everything which concerns her, from the most important matters to the most insignificant." M. Lavallée has the grace to acknowledge that this letter accords ill with that of Madame de Montespan quoted above.

[2] In her letters of May 13 and July 26, 1671, Madame de Sévigné, who, with all her virtues, had very small regard indeed for the

MADAME DE MONTESPAN

Madame de Fontevrault, as she was officially styled—of her beauty, of her wit, of her learning without a suspicion of pedantry,[1] of her wonderful aptitude for affairs, and real kindness of heart. Saint-Simon, who dubs her "the queen of abbesses," is especially eulogistic. "She was," he says, "the daughter of the first Duc de Mortemart, and sister of the Duc de Vivonne, Madame de Thianges, and Madame de Montespan, and was more beautiful than the last, and, what is of not less importance, more witty than any of them, with that same turn which no one but themselves, or those who were continually in their society, have ever caught. In addition to that, she was very learned, even a good theologian, with a remarkable talent for governing, an ease and a facility which made her regard merely as play the

Ninth Commandment, brings a very serious accusation against the abbess, namely, that she was carrying on an intrigue with that rather gay divine, the Abbé Testu. The Abbess defends herself from this charge in a letter to her friend, Madame de Sablé (August 23, 1671), which M. Clément has published in his interesting work, *Une Abbesse de Fontevrault au XVIIᵉ Siècle.* The author considers this letter, wherein the lady offers to appeal to the Bishop of Angers if necessary, and declares that she regards the charge against her as a trial sent her by God, a convincing proof of innocence. He thinks it not unlikely that Testu's frequent visits to the abbey were paid not to its superior but to a relative of his who appears to have been a pensioner there about this time.

[1] She was familiar with Italian and Spanish, and is said to have written and spoken Latin fluently. She had also some acquaintance with Hebrew and Greek, and undertook a version of Plato with the aid of a Latin translation. This she sent to Racine, who rewrote some part of it, and in 1732, twenty-eight years after her death, it was published under the title of *Le Banquet de Platon, traduit un tiers par feu Monsieur Racine de l' Académie française et le reste par Madame——.* She also translated a portion of the *Iliad,* and wrote a little treatise on Politeness (*la politesse*), which was published about the same time.

guidance of all her Order[1] and of many great matters
into which she entered, where, it is true, her position much
contributed to her success. She was very regular and
very exact, but with such sweetness, such graces, such
ways as made her adored at Fontevrault and by all her
Order. Her least letters were things to keep; her
ordinary conversation, even in relation to business or
discipline, was charming, and her addresses before the
Chapter on fête-days were admirable."[2] Madame de
Montespan was passionately attached to her, and, in spite
of her imperious temper, which her favour had increased,
always showed her real deference. Louis XIV. entertained for her the greatest esteem, which neither the fall
of Madame de Montespan nor the rise of Madame de
Maintenon could diminish, and when she died, showed as
much grief as he was ever known to exhibit. It is a
somewhat curious illustration of the morals of the time
that, although the abbess bore a high reputation for
piety, she never appears to have thought it necessary to
make the slightest protest against her sister's relations
with the King, and, when the affairs of her Order brought
her to Paris, generally took the opportunity of paying a
lengthy visit to Versailles or Saint-Germain. However,
if she failed in her duty in this respect, she now played
the part of comforter with the effectiveness which characterised everything she did, and probably the happiest
days of the ex-favourite's life after her retirement from
Court were those spent amid the peaceful cloisters of
Fontevrault.

Madame de Montespan's eldest sister, Madame de

[1] The Abbess of Fontevrault had jurisdiction over all the convents of
the Benedictine Order in France.
[2] *Mémoires de Saint-Simon* (edit. 1881), iv. 117.

Thianges, was a very different person from the abbess,
though, like her, she had her full share of the " *esprit de
Mortemart*," and in her youth her beauty was such that
poets were moved to sing her praises. " *Ange ou Thiange*,"
says La Fontaine in *Le Florentin*; while Benserade, in a
rhyming epistle to Bussy-Rabutin, speaks of snow as
being less white than her skin, and says a great many
other flattering things, which, however, we hesitate to
transcribe, even in the original. Madame de Caylus
asserts that she was *folle* on two points—her own personal
appearance and her family,[1] being equally proud of both.
" . . . As to her person, she considered herself a *chef-
d'œuvre* of Nature, not so much for external beauty as
for the delicacy of the organs that composed her body;
and uniting these two points of her insanity, she believed
that her beauty and the perfection of her temperament
proceeded from the difference which birth had made
between her and the world in general."[2] The King was
very fond of her, though he used to tease her unmerci-
fully, and the fall of Madame de Montespan made no
difference to her position at Court, where she occupied
a magnificent suite of apartments, had a standing invitation to join the Royal Family in Louis's cabinet in the
evening, and was treated with the greatest deference by
every one. She died in 1693 at the age of sixty. Of her
two daughters, the elder, upon whom the King had for
a brief moment cast a rather more than friendly eye,
married the Duc de Nevers, the brother of the famous
Mancini sisters. The younger, " who had a white skin,
rather fine eyes, and a nose pendant over a very red

---

[1] She would only admit that there were two really noble families in
France—the Mortemarts and the La Rochefoucaulds.

[2] *Souvenirs et Correspondance de Madame de Caylus* (edit. 1889), p. 64.

mouth, which made M. de Vendôme say that she resembled a paroquet eating a cherry,"[1] also married an
Italian, the Duke Sforza. He died a few years later,
when the lady returned to France, and, in her turn,
attracted the favourable attention of Louis, but Madame
de Maintenon's unceasing vigilance prevented any interesting developments. Saint-Simon speaks very highly of
the beauty of the Duchesse de Nevers and the intelligence
and amiable qualities of her sister.

The Duc de Vivonne, the ex-favourite's only brother,
had died in 1688. He had served his country with some
distinction on both land and sea, and in 1676, in conjunction with Duquesne, gained the Battle of Palermo
over the Spanish fleet, the greatest naval victory which
France had won up to that time. But he is chiefly
memorable for the countless jests regarding his extreme
stoutness, of the best of which he was himself the author.
On one occasion, the Chevalier de Vendôme challenged
him to a duel with pistols. The duke declined the
invitation, laughing heartily. " Why," he cried, " M. de
Vendôme might as well shoot at a *porte-cochère* while
he is about it." Another time, the King was rallying
him on his aldermanic appearance. " You are getting to
look very stout," said he. " You do not take sufficient
exercise." " Ah, Sire, that is a slander," replied Vivonne.
" Not a single day passes but what I walk round my
cousin d'Aumont " (who was even stouter than himself)
" at least four times." His good humour, like his wit,
never failed him. At the passage of the Rhine he
received a musket-ball in the shoulder, which compelled
him to wear his arm in a sling for the rest of his life;

[1] *Souvenirs et Correspondance de Madame de Caylus* (edit. 1889),
p. 67.

and, directly afterwards, his charger, Jean-le-Blanc, stumbled and threw him into the river. "Very fine, Jean-le-Blanc!" he exclaimed, as he was helped out and regained the saddle. "Do you want to drown a general of the galleys in fresh water?"[1] Vivonne had a genuine love of literature and frequented the society of men of letters as much as the salons of Versailles. He was on intimate terms with Molière and Boileau, and the latter mentions him in more than one passage in his works. Louis XIV., who never cared for books, asked him one day what was to be gained by reading. The duke pointed to his own well-complexioned face and answered : "Reading gives to the mind what your Majesty's partridges give to my cheeks." Madame de Sévigné speaks of Vivonne with a bitterness unusual in her ; but he is believed to have had some affair with her daughter, Madame de Grignan, at Marseilles, which probably accounts for her dislike of him. By his wife, Antoinette des Mesmes, who shared Madame de Montespan's immunity at the time of the Poison trials, he had a son, who predeceased him, and five daughters, two of whom took the veil and became abbesses, while the other three married respectively the Duc d'Elbœuf, the Duc de Créqui-Lesdiguières, and the Marquis de Castries.

Of her children by the King, Madame de Montespan saw very little after her retirement from Court. Their attentions were discouraged by their royal father, and they visited her rarely, and then only after having asked permission. The Duc du Maine, who had married in 1692 Mademoiselle de Bourbon-Charolais, daughter of the Prince de Condé, a lady who was in a large measure

---

[1] The Comte de Rochechouart's *Histoire de la Maison de Rochechouart*, vol. ii. ch. xii.

responsible for the troubles which befell her husband during the Regency, held completely aloof from his mother ; but the Comte de Toulouse, *Madame la Duchesse*, and the Duchesse de Chartres, continued to evince their affection, and always treated her with the utmost deference ; and Madame de Montespan used her influence over them to compose the frequent quarrels between her two daughters and between them and their husbands, for the Duchesse de Bourbon, if we are to believe Saint-Simon and Madame de Caylus, was far from an exemplary wife, while the character of her sister's consort, the future Regent, is well known.

The Duc d'Antin, Madame de Montespan's son by her husband, was, of course, under no such restrictions as his half-brothers and sisters, and it was he who now became the object of the ex-favourite's peculiar solicitude. As if desirous of making reparation for having so grievously failed in her duty towards him during the years when he had most needed a mother's care, it seemed that she could not do enough for him. "She occupied herself with enriching him," says Saint-Simon. In 1696 she purchased the estate of Petit-Bourg and entailed it upon the Duke and his heirs, and six years later acquired for 340,000 livres the beautiful Château of Oiron in Poitou, and settled it upon his children, although she retained a life interest in the property and resided there occasionally ;[1] while when his son, the

[1] Oiron in the middle ages was the seat of a *seigneurie*, which belonged to the House of Amboise, and afterwards to that of Sancours. Charles VII. confiscated it and gave it to one of his favourites, Guillaume de Gouffier, whose son, Claude de Gouffier, built the château, or rather part of it, for it was not until it passed into the possession of the Duc de La Feuillade in 1667 that it was completed. It contains a series of fine pictures

Marquis de Gondrin, married Mademoiselle de Noailles, the Marchioness presented the young couple with jewellery to the value of 100,000 livres, "half to be entailed on the eldest son and half on the eldest daughter."[1]

The Duc d'Antin, Sainte-Beuve's *parfait courtesan*, it may here be remarked, was quite unworthy of such generosity. Selfish to the core, he never appears to have shown the least gratitude for the favours which his mother heaped upon him, and regarded her as an impediment to his progress in the good graces of Louis XIV. Moreover, his personal courage was open to grave suspicion,[2] and it was rumoured that his extraordinary success at play was due to something more than good fortune.[3] In November 1700, Madame de Montespan, no doubt aware of these reports, and fearing that sooner or later an ugly scandal would ensue, persuaded her son to give up play, promising to increase the allowance she made him by 12,000 livres in return

representing scenes from the Æneid by the sixteenth-century painters, Pierre Foulon and Noël Jallier, while the windows are adorned with medallions by the sculptor Mathurin Bouberault. In 1568 the château was sacked by the Huguenots under François de Coligny.

Several writers state that Oiron was given to Madame de Montespan by the King. The error has probably arisen from the fact that Louis advanced part of the purchase-money to the marchioness, which, however, was in exchange for, or on the security of, a splendid pearl necklace which the lady had sent him.—*Journal de Dangeau*, vii. 278.

[1] *Ibid.*, xi. 287.

[2] His name was omitted from the list of lieutenant-generals selected for the campaign of 1707, a circumstance which was much remarked upon.

[3] Dangeau says that d'Antin confessed to having won between six and seven hundred thousand livres at play, "and it was even thought that he had gained a great deal more."

for his renunciation of the card-table. D'Antin considered that so meritorious an action on his part could not fail to earn the approval of the King, and accordingly requested the Comte de Toulouse to acquaint his Majesty with the fact. But, to his intense mortification, Louis coldly replied that the duke was at liberty to play or not as he chose, but he was at a loss to understand what it had to do with him.[1] The King, in fact, notwithstanding all d'Antin's suppleness, servility, and intrigue, remained impenetrable so long as Madame de Montespan lived, while Madame de Maintenon was equally disobliging, though to her also the duke paid the most assiduous court. However, as soon as he lost his too celebrated mother, the complexion of affairs changed; Madame de Maintenon smiled upon, the King visited him at Petit-Bourg, and not long afterwards he was appointed Governor of Orléanais. Saint-Simon says that, on receiving the news of his appointment to this post, d'Antin exclaimed, in a transport of joy, " *I am thawed at last !* "[2]

After her children, Madame de Montespan's principal link with the Court during her retirement was her friend, the charming Duchesse de Noailles, with whom the ex-favourite maintained an active correspondence until her death in May 1707. Her letters to the duchess chiefly relate to the affairs of common acquaintances of whom we know little or nothing or to family matters; but the following are of some interest :—

[1] *Journal de Dangeau*, vii. 410.
[2] *Mémoires de Saint-Simon* (edit. 1881), v. 339.

MADAME DE MONTESPAN

MADAME DE MONTESPAN *to the* DUCHESSE DE
NOAILLES.

"FONTEVRAULT, *July* 22, 1699.

"I am excessively annoyed by Fanchon's conduct.[1] I
strongly suspected, as you did me the honour to write
to me, that something would happen, and this very
day her sister has brought me a letter, from which she
learns of her marriage, and that it was a clandestine one.
These kind of adventures disincline one very much
from meddling in such matters. In good truth, I am in
despair over this affair; it troubles me more seriously
than such matters generally do, owing to the secrecy
which accompanied it.

"I have shown your letter to my sister, who thanks
you for having decided to send her your daughter. In
regard to that, everything that you can possibly desire
will be done. All you will have to do is to explain
everything clearly down to the smallest details and
communicate them through me. We have been accustomed this long while to discuss domestic affairs and to
calculate great and small matters. I believe that you
intend to send the furniture and all that she had at Saint-
Antoine. As for the vocation, I can answer for that.
This is a convent where no novice refuses to take the
vows, and with reason, for it is most holy and most

---

[1] Fanchon was one of the orphan girls at Saint-Joseph, who had
made a secret marriage, when Madame de Montespan had evidently
had other matrimonial intentions in regard to her. "Madame de Montespan," says Saint-Simon, "was very fond of marrying people, especially
young girls; but as, after all her charitable donations, she had very little
to give them, it was very often a case of mating hunger and thirst."

beautiful, and one where the nuns are a thousand times more happy than all the rest of the world.

"Two girls took the *habit* yesterday. Mademoiselle de Bourbon (her granddaughter) reckons that in seven years she will do the same. You can count on your daughter doing so also, if you are wise enough to consent to it.

"Convey my compliments, I beg you, Madame, to the archbishop and the marshal." [1]

MADAME DE MONTESPAN *to the* DUCHESSE DE NOAILLES.

"BELLEGARDE,[2] *October* 21, 1699.

"I have found my sister so weak after her course of the waters, having, indeed, a slight attack of fever, that I have not thought it advisable to speak to her of anything calculated to excite her. What you have written to me gives me the impression that you are aware that the King once offered her Montmartre,[3] in order to bring her nearer to Court. She declined from conscientious motives, believing that she ought to remain where she was. Since that time her charge has become a very heavy one; the edict of '95 and the manner in which the bishops have abused it render her yoke very difficult to bear.[4] Never-

---

[1] The Duchesse de Noailles's brother-in-law and husband. The former, Cardinal de Noailles, had succeeded Harlay de Chanvallon as Archbishop of Paris in 1696.

[2] Bellegarde-en-Gatinais. It was a château which the Duc d'Antin had inherited from his uncle, the Duc de Bellegarde. Madame de Montespan frequently visited her son there.

[3] The abbey of Montmartre, to the north of Paris. The post of abbess had just fallen vacant, and it was thought that the King might offer it to Madame de Fontevrault.

[4] An edict of April 1695, which gave the bishops increased powers over the religious houses in their dioceses.

341

theless, I do not think that she will be able to make up her mind to leave it, merely for the sake of an easier post ; and, for myself, I frankly confess to you that, apart from her interests, for which I would sacrifice everything, I much prefer Fontevrault to Montmartre.

"When one acts in good faith (*i.e.* in retiring from Court) one would rather be far away than near, and I have found, even in the short time I have spent in Paris, so much need for care and circumspection, especially in regard to appearances, that it seemed to me the pain greatly exceeded the pleasure. . . ."[1]

MADAME DE MONTESPAN *to the* DUCHESSE DE NOAILLES.

"BELLEGARDE, *November* 2, 1699.

"I am so little conversant with affairs at Court that I know not what sort of condolences I ought to offer on the death of Madame de Montchevreuil.[2] For my own part, I have grieved for her ; I looked upon her as a very good woman, and, besides, I retain an affection for all my old acquaintances. I have begged M. du Maine, from whom I learnt the news, to convey my condolences to her family and also to Madame de Maintenon. I ask of you the same favour and to convey them in the way likely to be acceptable. I am always embarrassed on these occasions to know what is the right step to take. My inclination very naturally leads me to show Madame de Maintenon what my feelings are for her ; but you know, Madame, that intercourse with me is not agreeable

[1] Clément's *Madame de Montespan et Louis XIV.*, p. 335.
[2] Madame de Montchevreuil had quarrelled with Madame de Maintenon shortly before her death.

to her. Let that be said without any intent to reproach
her, for I am more than satisfied with what I received
from her, through you, during the past year; but simply
to show you that, in point of fact, I am still endeavouring
to discover what I ought to do in order to please ; as
when I have followed my natural bent in allowing myself
to be forgotten, I found that I was being done more
honour than I thought, and that I was remembered for
my conduct to be found fault with. All this, joined
to my peaceful disposition, makes me fear all eventu-
alities. . . ."[1]

Another person with whom Madame de Montespan
corresponded during her exile was the learned Daniel
Huet, Bishop of Avranches, whose acquaintance she
had made many years before at the Court when he was
acting as *sous-précepteur* to the Dauphin. Few men in
the seventeenth century enjoyed a higher or more
extensive reputation than Huet, distinguished alike as a
theologian, a mathematician, and a philologist, and, with
all his learning, a pleasant and genial companion. A
contemporary describes him as " a true sage, loving the
world and pleasure, devoting himself in turn to society
and study, distressed on account of not having enough
piety, and, nevertheless, a good bishop." The correspondence between him and Madame de Montespan seems
to have begun in an argument which they had had about
the respective merits of conversation and letter-writing.
Huet had maintained that conversation was too often

---

[1] *Correspondance générale de Madame de Maintenon,* iv. 46. This
letter need occasion us no surprise. As we have already seen,
Madame de Montespan and Madame de Maintenon always professed
before the world the greatest regard for one another.

vapid, profitless, and even dangerous; that people spoke merely for the sake of doing so and without due reflection; that many of the best and cleverest things that were said fell on indifferent ears and were allowed to die with the moment that had given them birth; and that not infrequently persons were misunderstood and gave offence where none was intended. " Writing, on the other hand," says Madame de Montespan, summarising the bishop's argument, " is subject to none of these inconveniences; it is at once the safeguard of those who write and of those to whom they write. People express themselves without restraint, because their words are only addressed to the person whom they desire to hear them, and what they say becomes infinitely more agreeable to the recipient from the knowledge that he is not compelled to share it with any one. But what constitutes the great advantage of letters over conversation is that they do not consist of mere words which the wind carries away and the air dissipates; they render thoughts visible and as durable as the paper to which they are confided. We have the pleasure of recognising therein the hand of the person who writes to us, of following it along all the lines over which it has passed; we can seek even in the way in which the words are traced for what the most eloquent utterances would be powerless to make us feel."

The marchioness protested that letters lacked the sparkle and animation of conversation, and that even the most happy phrases left the reader cold and unmoved; but eventually pretended to agree with the bishop and writes to him :—

" You see, Monsieur, that I have profited very well by your instructions, and I hope that you will perceive it still more clearly in the future by the correspondence which I begin with you to-day."

The correspondence in question, in which Madame de Montespan was frequently assisted by the Abbess of Fontevrault or one of her nieces, is not of any historic interest, consisting for the most part of compliments, protestations, reproaches, and excuses, but it is distinctly amusing.

MADAME DE MONTESPAN *and* GABRIELLE VICTOIRE DE ROCHECHOUART *to* DANIEL HUET.

"We take the liberty of sending you these little New Year's Gifts which accompany the good wishes that we express for your prosperity and health. May God augment your cheerfulness ; may he preserve your good temper ; may he maintain the freshness of your complexion ; may he render your waters purgative, your perspirations abundant, the strawberries refreshing, and the peas more easy to digest. These are the good wishes of your very humble and obedient servants,—FRANÇOISE DE ROCHECHOUART ; GABRIELLE VICTOIRE DE ROCHECHOUART." [1]

Sometimes they expressed themselves in verse. One day the bishop having been invited to dinner by Madame de Montespan, gallantly excused himself as follows :—

"Un barbon frileux comme moi,
A perruque et barbe chenue,
Ne doit pas, ailleurs que chez soi,
Montrer sa mine morfondue.

[1] Clément's *Madame de Montespan et Louis XIV.*, p. 174. Gabrielle Victoire de Rochechouart was the eldest daughter of the Duc de Vivonne. In 1689 she became Abbess of Beaumont-les-Tours.

MADAME DE MONTESPAN

Votre palais est tout ouvert,[1]
   L'on y voit l'un et l'autre pôle,
Et l'on y sent, comme au Cap-Vert,
   Les trente-deux souffles d'Éole.

Quand la bise perce les os
   Des rigueurs de sa froide haleine,
Ni les bons mets, ni les bons mots
   Ne valent pas l'ouate et la laine.

Vos yeux, astres des beaux esprits,
   Font tout l'ornement de notre âge ;
Mais la martre et le petit-gris
   M'échauffent pourtant davantage.

L'on souffre plus d'une langueur
   Près de votre beauté divine :
Si l'amour attaque le cœur,
   Le rhume attaque la poitrine.

Quand je vous conte mes douleurs,
   Vous ne daignez pas y répondre :
Ce sont de nouvelles froideurs,
   Et vous me laissez me morfondre.

Vous en trouverez-vous bien mieux
   Si je reviens malade et triste
De ce repas délicieux
   Où vous souhaitez que j'assiste.

N'attendez donc plus mon retour
   Qu'au retour des chaleurs nouvelles ;
Je n'irai vous faire ma cour
   Qu'au premier vol des hirondelles."

To which the lady, anxious to prove that she had not
been the patroness of the poets for nothing, replied :—

[1] Probably Clagny.

MADAME DE MONTESPAN

Non, ne vous imaginez pas
    Me payer d'une vaine excuse :
Je ne sais si j'ai des appas,
    Mais je hais fort qu'on me refuse.

Quoi ! de fourrures tout armé !
    Lorsque pour vous la nappe est mise
Dans un lieu bien clos, bien fermé,
    Près de moi vous craignez la bise !

Voudrois-je mettre à l'abandon
    Votre santé qui m'est si chère ?
Vous souvient-il comme à Bourbon
    Mon secours vous fut salutaire ?

Là, vous receviez de mes mains
    Fruits, pois verts, artichauts, salades
Tandis que tous les médecins
    Les défendoient à leur malades. . . .

Vous viendrez, dites-vous, me voir
    Au retour de la primevère ?
Et moi je vous le fais savoir,
    Fuyez à jamais ma colère.

Las ! malgré moi, mon cœur trop bon,
    Me parle de miséricorde :
Si vous venez crier pardon,
    Je crains fort qu'on ne vous l'accorde."[1]

Occasionally, their correspondence took a more serious turn. Thus, one day Madame de Montespan propounded to Huet a question after the manner of the *Précieuses* of the Hôtel de Rambouillet: "Which is preferable—illusion or truth ? "

The good bishop replied at great length, examining closely the arguments of the advocates of illusion, and summing up, as might be expected, in favour of truth.

[1] *Revue rétrospective*, October 1833.

MADAME DE MONTESPAN

We give below part of his letter, which is too long for insertion in full :—

DANIEL HUET *to* MADAME DE MONTESPAN.

" December 17, 1691.

"To give a satisfactory answer to this question: 'Which is preferable—illusion or truth?' one must know what is illusion and what is truth. Illusion, that is to say, error, is a disposition of our mind which makes us see things as they are not. Truth is a contrary disposition, which makes us see things as they are. That granted, it is obvious that a person in a state of illusion would not be capable of deciding which of the two is to be preferred, since he would not know one from the other and would see them as they are not. This question ought not to be put except to a person who is free from illusion and capable of recognising truth.

"Now there is no one capable of recognising truth who could prefer illusion to truth; for if he preferred illusion to truth, he would prefer to be in a state of illusion than to know the truth; in other words, being sane, he would desire to become mad, for illusion is a passing madness, and from the moment that he had this desire he would be mad, since it is an infallible sign of madness to love folly and prefer evil to good. Further, those who take the side of illusion say, to support so extraordinary a contention, that illusion is an agreeable deception; that gaiety, pleasure, and hope accompany it; while truth, on the contrary, is sad, dull, and wearisome. They argue that, when illusion deceives us, it is always entirely to our advantage, inasmuch as it shows us our condition happier than it really is. But illusion can deceive us for evil as well as for good : avarice persuades the rich that they are poor, as intoxication persuades the poor that they are rich. If the illusion of pride makes us see in ourselves good qualities which do not exist, the illusion of humility prevents us from seeing those which do exist. If the illusion of temerity hides real dangers, the illusion of cowardice shows us imaginary ones. There is as much to lose as to gain in these diverse kinds of illusions, and it is a very poor reason for preferring them to truth to say that they are agreeable and fill the soul with hope and joy, since they as often have a contrary effect. . . ."

When, in June 1692, Henri Arnauld, Bishop of Angers, died, Madame de Montespan was very anxious that Huet should get himself translated to the vacant see, an event which would have brought him within easy distance of Fontevrault, and wrote to him as follows :—

MADAME DE MONTESPAN *to* DANIEL HUET.

" Sunday morning.

" My sister informed me yesterday of the death of M. d'Angers. If you have still the same liking for our neighbourhood, this would be a fine opportunity. It is needless for me to tell you how delighted we should be to have you so near us ; it would also be a great advantage for the abbess in her important charge at Fontevrault.[1] As I do not know whether the change would be an advantageous one for you, I dare not say any more about it I beg you, Monsieur, to send me news of your gout I am much troubled on account of your ill-health."

[1] The Abbey of Fontevrault was in the diocese of Angers.

Huet, however, was not appointed to the vacant bishopric, which was given to Michel Le Peletier; and not long afterwards his correspondence with Madame de Montespan ceased altogether, for what reason we are unable to say; and it is not a little singular that in his *Mémoires* [1] the bishop does not so much as mention the lady's name, though he speaks in the highest terms of her sister, the Abbess of Fontevrault.

[1] These memoirs were written in Latin, which Huet seems to have spoken and written almost as easily as his native tongue. There is a French translation by Nisard.

CHAPTER XXII

Madame de Montespan's conversations with Madame de Miramion—She becomes sincerely penitent—Her noble generosity—She founds the Hospice of Oiron—Particulars regarding this institution—She places herself under the guidance of Père de La Tour—And writes to her husband, entreating his pardon—Answer of the Marquis de Montespan—Death of her sister, the Abbess of Fontevrault—Madame de Montespan's secret macerations and penitent life—Her horror of death—She still retains her queenly manner—" *La chambre du Roi* " at Oiron—She has a presentiment of her approaching death—She is taken ill at Bourbon—Her last hours—Heartless conduct of the Duc d'Antin—A painful scandal—Louis XIV. receives the news of her death with profound indifference—His remark to the Duchesse de Bourgogne—Relief of the Duc du Maine—Sincere grief of the Comte de Toulouse and his sisters—Conduct of Madame de Maintenon—Madame de Montespan's sincere penitence and honest endeavour to atone for the past her best claim to our regard.

AT the beginning of her visits to Saint-Joseph, Madame de Montespan, says the Abbé de Choisy, had several interviews with the celebrated *dévote*, Madame de Miramion,[1] " to see if a conversation entirely about God could cause her to forget the world." These interviews

[1] Marie Bonneau, wife of Jacques de Beauharnais, Seigneur de Miramion. She founded two houses of refuge for fallen women, and, in 1661, a community of twelve nuns, who devoted themselves to the care of the sick and poor. This community, which was known as the

did not apparently have much effect upon the marchioness
at the time. " She wept much, but her tears were those
of weakness and despair, not yet of penitence." [1]   However, as the years went by, Madame de Montespan
gradually became sincerely penitent, and ended by throwing herself into devotion with the same passion which she
had formerly displayed in ambition and love.   Always
generously inclined, she now redoubled her benefactions,
and made a truly noble use of her wealth, building and
enriching hospitals and convents, pensioning members of
the poor *noblesse*, whom the ruinous wars had reduced
almost to the verge of starvation, and performing countless deeds of kindness with as much intelligence as
liberality.   We have spoken elsewhere of her foundations
at Paris, Fontainebleau, and Saint-Germain, and of the
munificent support she accorded for so many years to
the general hospital in the latter town; but we have
yet to speak of the last and most important of her
good works—the hospital which she founded at Oiron in
1703.

For some years the ex-favourite had maintained at
Fontevrault, entirely at her own expense, a kind of home
for aged persons and orphans of both sexes, which was
conducted by sisters of charity from the community of
Saint-Lazare de Paris. But when, in 1700, she purchased
Oiron, she decided to establish a hospice there which
might be more directly under her own supervision; and,
accordingly, three years later, removed her pensioners
from Fontevrault to a spot near her new château, where

Dames Miramiones or Miramionites, was afterwards incorporated with
the Congrégation des Filles de Sainte-Geneviève. Their principal
house was on the Quai des Miramiones, now the Quai d'Orsay.

[1] Bonneau's *Vie de Madame de Beauharnais de Miramion*, p. 304.

spacious buildings had been erected for their reception and "furnished with beds, linen, crockery, and everything necessary for the maintenance and lodging of poor people." The foundation deed, dated July 4, 1704, states that the hospice, which was to be placed under the name and invocation of the Holy Family, was intended for the support of one hundred poor persons of either sex, "professing the Catholic, Apostolic and Roman faith." The governing body was to consist of the bishop of the diocese (Poitiers) and his successors, the *seigneur* of Oiron and his successors, the dean of the chapter of Oiron, the curé of the parish, and the seneschals of Oiron, Cursay, and Moncontour. The Bishop of Poitiers, or some high ecclesiastical dignitary appointed by him, was to hold an annual visitation, when the governors were to meet and the accounts for the past year to be audited. The towns of Moncontour and Cursay were to have the privilege of nominating six pensioners, the parishes of Marnes, Vignolles, Saint-Chartres, Saint-Martin d'Ouzillé, Messe, Notre-Dame d'Or, Glenouze, and Montbrillais two each, the Abbess of Fontevrault six, and the Bishop of Poitiers three. The remaining places were to be reserved for the poor of Oiron. Provision was made for the spiritual needs of the inmates by the appointment of a resident chaplain; and the deed further states that "a person who did not wish his name known" had given the sum of 4200 livres for the special support of twenty-four old men, who were to form a separate body, "charged with the duty of offering up private prayers on behalf of Madame de Montespan."[1]

The Hospice of Oiron is still in existence and, as we have already mentioned, contains a fine portrait of

[1] Clément's *Madame de Montespan et Louis XIV.*, p. 415 *et seq.*

MADAME DE MONTESPAN

Madame de Montespan, which is believed to be the work of Mignard.

Madame de Montespan's endeavours to make atonement for the past were very far from being confined to philanthropy. She sought for some wise and enlightened *directeur*, and surrendered herself to the guidance of Père de La Tour, General of the Oratory, professing her readiness to follow his instructions in all things. The Oratorian took her at her word, and imposed upon her a terrible test of penitence—nothing less than that she should entreat her husband's pardon and place herself in his hands. After long agonies of hesitation, the haughty woman consented, and wrote to the marquis offering to return to him, if he would deign to receive her, or to live in whatever place he might appoint. "To those who knew Madame de Montespan," says Saint-Simon, "this must have seemed a most heroic sacrifice." It was, however, a vain one. Montespan, though the chronicler asserts that he had always loved his erring wife, and continued to love her to the day of his death, sent word, through a third person, that he would neither receive her, nor lay his commands upon her, nor hear her name mentioned so long as he lived.[1]

In August 1704 a great sorrow befell the marchioness. The Abbess of Fontevrault, that well-loved sister, in whose unvarying kindness and affection she had found her chief consolation in her exile, died suddenly. It is from this event that in all probability date those redoubled penances, those cruel mortifications of the flesh, that terrible and ever-present horror of death which only those who were aware of the revelations of Marguerite Monvoisin and her fellow-prisoners could have explained,

[1] *Mémoires de Saint-Simon* (edit. 1881), v. 261.

and of which Saint-Simon speaks in the following curious
passage in his *Mémoires* :—

"Little by little she proceeded to give nearly all she
had to the poor.[1] She worked for them several hours a
day at humble and rough tasks, to wit, shirts and such
like things, and she made those about her work at them
too. Her table, which she had loved to excess, became
most frugal ; her fasts were multiplied, and at all hours
of the day she would leave whatever occupation she happened to be engaged in to go and pray in her closet.
Her mortifications of the flesh were constant ; her chemises
and sheets were of the coarsest and roughest unbleached
linen, but concealed beneath ordinary sheets and under-
wear. She wore continually bracelets, garters, and a
girdle of steel with iron points ; and her tongue, formerly
so dreaded, had its penance also. She was further so
tortured by horror of death that she paid several women
whose sole employment was to sit up with her at night.
She lay with her bed-curtains drawn back, with her room
ablaze with candles, her watchers around her, whom,
whenever she woke up, she wished to find talking, playing
cards, or eating, to assure herself that they were not
drowsy."[2]

And yet, strangely enough, with all her bodily suffering
and moral subjection, she could never bring herself to
abandon that queenly air and manner which she had
assumed in the days of her favour, and which had
followed her into retirement. At Saint-Joseph, where
the most eminent persons of the Court came to pay their

---

[1] When, at the beginning of 1707, Louis XIV. reduced her pension,
she sent word to him that she was sorry for the poor, not for herself ;
they would be the losers.

[2] *Mémoires de Saint-Simon* (edit. 1881), v. 262.

respects to her, it was remarked that there was but one fauteuil in her salon, her own ; and even her children, on the rare occasions on which Louis permitted them to see her, had to be content with stools. She spoke to every one as if she were doing them an exceeding honour, and never returned a visit, however exalted the rank of her caller might be. At her château at Oiron, numerous portraits of herself, Louis XIV., and the Royal Family, hung on the walls as silent witnesses of her connection with the House of Bourbon ; while, although the King never entered its doors, nor, indeed, ever saw his former mistress again from the time of her retirement from Court till the day of her death, there was a room called "*la chambre du Roi*," magnificently furnished.

The hour which Madame de Montespan had so much dreaded at length arrived. About the middle of May 1707 she went, as was her custom at that time of year, to the waters at Bourbon. Although perfectly well, she had a strong presentiment that her end was near, and accordingly, before leaving Paris, paid all the pensions she was in the habit of giving two years in advance, and doubled her customary alms. Her fears were but too well founded. One evening, soon after her arrival at Bourbon, she retired to rest in her usual health, but in the middle of the night was taken suddenly ill. Her watchers awoke Maréchale de Cœuvres, one of the Duchesse de Noailles's daughters, who had accompanied the marchioness from Paris, and this lady, finding her friend gasping for breath, instead of at once summoning medical aid, proceeded to administer a powerful emetic, which effectually disposed of any chance which the unfortunate woman might have had of recovering.

Buffon has compared death to a spectre that terrifies

us from afar, but disappears when we approach it; and
Madame de Montespan's last hours, as Sainte-Beuve
points out, are a remarkable illustration of the truth of
this dictum. Now that she was actually in the presence
of the King of Terrors, her fears vanished and troubled
her no more. " She profited by a brief respite from pain
to confess and receive the sacraments," says Saint-Simon.
" Before doing so, she called in all her servants, even the
humblest, and made public confession of her public sins,
asking pardon for the scandal she had so long caused, and
for her ill-temper, with so deep and penitent a humility
than nothing could be more edifying." She then received
the last sacraments with the deepest piety. "Father,"
she said to the Capuchin who administered them, " exhort
me as an ignorant person, as simply as you can."[1] "She
thanked God before all present," continues the great
chronicler, "for permitting her to die far away from the
children of her sin, and she never spoke of them but that
once during her illness. Her mind was occupied only
with Eternity (though they tried to encourage her with
hopes of recovery) and with her condition as a sinner,
whose fears were tempered by a sure confidence in the
mercy of God."[2]

The Duc d'Antin, who was in attendance on the
Dauphin at Livry, learning of his mother's condition,
reached Bourbon three days after she had been taken
ill. The following afternoon a courier sent by him
arrived at Marly, where the Court then was, with intelligence that Madame de Montespan was at the point
of death, whereupon the King gave permission to the

[1] Letter of Madame de Maintenon *to the* Princesse des Ursins,
June 19, 1707.
[2] *Mémoires de Saint-Simon* (edit. 1881), v. 266.

Comte de Toulouse[1] to go to Bourbon. The young Count, who loved his mother dearly, started without a moment's delay ; but near Montargis was met by an equerry of the Duc d'Orléans, from whom he learned that he was too late.[2]

Madame de Montespan had expired in the early hours of the morning of May 27.

Doubtless thinking that d'Antin, as Madame de Montespan's legitimate son, had a better right than himself to make the necessary arrangements, and might conceivably resent his presence at Bourbon, the Comte de Toulouse decided to turn back, and went to shut himself up with his grief at Rambouillet. Though prompted by the best motives, this was an unfortunate decision, for, had he continued his journey, he would probably have been in time to avert a most painful scandal.

No sooner had Madame de Montespan breathed her last, than the worthy d'Antin, disappointed in his search for a will, which, it would appear, had been his main object in hastening to the marchioness's death-bed, started for Paris, to continue his investigations there, leaving his mother's remains to the care of servants, for Madame de Cœuvres had been so overcome by her feelings that she had been unable to remain in the house. The dead woman had left instructions that her heart was to be sent to the Convent of La Flèche ; "and her body," says Saint-Simon, "became the prey of the ignorant surgeon of some intendant from I know not where, who happened to be at Bourbon, and who essayed to open it, without knowing how to set about it."[3]

[1] The Duc du Maine was at Sceaux.
[2] *Journal de Dangeau*, xi. 377.
[3] Saint-Simon, *Notes sur Journal de Dangeau*.

Then, when he had at length blundered through his task, and the moment came for the body to be carried to the neighbouring church, whence it was to be conveyed to Poitiers for interment in the family tomb in that town, the coffin was allowed to remain for a considerable time at the door of the house, while the priests and canons who were to bear it wrangled about a point of precedence. The meanest peasant would have been treated with more respect than was the once dazzling mistress of *le Grand Monarque*.

The death of the woman who, for more than thirty years, had played so great a part at the Court, caused but very slight impression there. Louis XIV. received the news with the most profound indifference. Dangeau writes in his *Journal*:

"*Saturday, May* 28, *at Marly.* Before the King started for the chase, news arrived that Madame de Montespan died yesterday at Bourbon, at three o'clock in the morning. . . . The King, after hunting a stag, promenaded in the gardens till midnight." [1]

According to Saint-Simon, the young Duchesse de Bourgogne, the only member of the Royal Family who dared to speak her mind before the King, reproached Louis with his insensibility, whereupon the monarch replied that when Madame de Montespan quitted the Court, he had counted upon never seeing her again, and that from that moment she was dead to him." [2] Historians have often referred to this speech as a proof of Louis's egotism and heartlessness ; but to-day, when,

[1] *Journal de Dangeau*, xi. 378.
[2] According to Saint-Simon, Louis XIV. made much the same remark on hearing of the death of Louise de La Vallière three years later.

thanks to the researches of M. Ravaisson, we are better able to understand his feelings, it can occasion but little surprise.

As for Madame de Montespan's children, the Duc du Maine, like the estimable d'Antin, welcomed his mother's death as the removal of an impediment to his fortunes; but his brother and sisters, though peremptorily forbidden by Louis to wear mourning,[1] made no attempt to conceal their grief, a circumstance which does them much honour.

And Madame de Maintenon?

Madame de Maintenon, to whom every one thought the event would come as a relief, shed bitter tears! Her admirers see in this a proof of her exquisite sensibility; her enemies evidence of remorse. We prefer to express no opinion on the matter.

What can be said for Madame de Montespan—for this woman who was for twelve years the left-hand consort of the greatest monarch of his age, with the consequence that her blood runs to-day in the veins of half the Royal Houses in Europe? We might say that she was the patroness of artists and men of letters; that she founded and enriched hospitals and convents; that no good cause ever appealed to her in vain; that she was a devoted mother, an affectionate sister, a warm friend. But what would that avail? Remembering such things, it is conceivable that some might be found to

---

[1] Probably because Madame de Montespan had never been *officially* recognised as their mother. The letters of legitimation, it will be remembered, did not mention her name. The Princesse de Conti wore mourning for Louise de La Vallière, but La Vallière had been *officially* recognised.

overlook her infidelity to her husband, her treachery to her Queen, her insolent defiance of the precepts of religion and morality, the cruel humiliations she inflicted on Louise de La Vallière, her vindictiveness towards Lauzun, her spoliation of *la Grande Mademoiselle*, her prodigality, her arrogance, her ambition! But who can pardon that long connection with the most atrocious wretches in all the annals of crime? Who can pardon those unspeakable abominations—abominations which we have only dared to hint at in these pages—which took place in the gloomy château at Mesnil, in the tumbledown hut at Saint-Denis, in the unknown house in Paris, in the den of La Voisin?

The best, we think, that can be said for Madame de Montespan is, that if her sins were grievous, her expiation was grievous too ; that her repentance was no death-bed one, but one that extended over long, weary years ; that, after spending a considerable portion of her life in acquiring an infamous celebrity, she spent the latter part in an honest endeavour to make atonement, and that in so doing she gave cause to hundreds to bless her name

INDEX

ALBRET, Maréchal d', 177
Alluye, Marquise d', 251, 256
Amphitryon, Molière's, 57
Anne of Austria
regards Louis XIV.'s attachment to Olympe Mancini with complaisance, 4; rebukes the King openly for his attentions to Mademoiselle de La Motte d'Argencourt, 5; warns him that "he is wandering from the path of innocence," 5; sends Mademoiselle de La Motte d'Argencourt to a convent, 5; strongly opposed to the King's projected marriage with Marie Mancini, 11; avoided by the King, 13; supports the Princess Palatine's claim to wear a train to her dress, 20; tries to induce the King to break off his connection with Louise de La Vallière, 28, 29; persuades him to conceal his intrigue from the Queen, 29; undeceives him in regard to Mademoiselle de La Motte Houdancourt, 33; inspires him with an almost superstitious reverence for the rites and ceremonies of the Church, 150; her excessive partiality for perfumes, 230 note
Anselme, Abbé, 319
Antin, Duc d'
Madame de Montespan's son by the Marquis de Montespan, 4 note; his marriage with Mademoiselle d'Uzès, 319; his boyhood, 319; determined to push his fortunes at Court, 319; appointed *ménin* to the Dauphin, 320; his mother "occupies herself with enriching him," 337; his unamiable character, 338; his success at play, 338 note; rebuffed by the King, 339; his servility towards

Antin, Duc d'—*continued*
Louis XIV. and Madame de Maintenon, 339; his heartless conduct at his mother's death, 358
Antin, Marquis d' (father of the Marquis de Montespan), 41, 42, 59
Apologie de Marie Mancini, the, 7
Aquin, d' (first physician to the King), 270
Archives de la Bastille, M. Ravaisson's, 210 note
Arnauld, Antoine (cited), 163
Arnauld, Henri, Bishop of Angers, 349
Atys, Quinault and Lulli's opera of, 179 and note
Aubert, Nanon, 290
Aubigné, Charles d' (brother of Madame de Maintenon), 177, 232, 298 note, 306, 308
Aubigné, Constant d' (father of Madame de Maintenon), 88 and note, 308
Aubigné, Françoise d': *see* Maintenon, Madame de
Aubigné, Madame d' (mother of Madame de Maintenon), 88, 89, 90
Aubigné, Théodore Agrippa d' (grandfather of Madame de Maintenon), 88
Aubrey, John (cited), 223 note
Aumale, Mademoiselle d' (cited), 174, 298 and note

BADEN, Princess of, 48, 49, 56
Bazin de Bezons, 242 and note, 243, 260, 263 note, 287, 295
Beaufort, Duc de, 75 and note
Beauvais, Madame de, 5, 6 and note
Bellefonds, Judith de, 107
Bellefonds, Maréchal de
endeavours to persuade Louise de La Vallière to return from the convent at Chaillot, 78 and note, 79; arranges for her admission to

INDEX

INDEX

INDEX

INDEX

INDEX

2 A

INDEX

INDEX

Louis XIV.—*continuea*
marques de *piété,*" 159; his letters
to Colbert relating to Madame de
Montespan, 160–162; carries on a
clandestine correspondence with
the marchioness, 162; endeavours
to persuade Bossuet to consent to
Madame de Montespan's return
to Court, 162; finds Père de La
Chaise and the Archbishop of
Paris more complaisant, 163 and
note; refuses to listen to Bossuet's
remonstrances at Luzarches, 163;
returns to Versailles and resumes
his former relations with Madame
de Montespan, 164; his conversion resolved on by Madame de
Maintenon, 170–172; witness of a
"terrible scene" between Madame
de Montespan and Madame de
Maintenon, 175; corresponds with
the latter during her visit to the
Pyrenees, 178; receives her with
marked graciousness on her return,
179; pays her a pretty compliment, 179; joins the army in
Flanders, 179; affectionate reception of Madame de Montespan on
his return, 183 and note; in love
with Madame de Soubise, 184,
185; his conduct at this juncture
an interesting study for the moralist,
185; in love with Madame de
Ludres, 186–188; discards her and
returns to Madame de Montespan,
188; bestows a pension and a
gratification on Madame de Ludres,
189; "all eyes for Madame de
Montespan," 190; resumes his
correspondence with Madame de
Maintenon, 195 note; pleased at
the Duc du Maine's wish to go to
the war, 195, 196; compels the
Court to follow him to Lorraine,
197; enters Flanders, 200; takes
Ghent, 200; visited by Madame
de Montespan at Oudenarde, 201;
"still violently enamoured," 201;
refused absolution, 202; his generosity to Madame de Montespan,
203–205; annoyed by her losses
at hoca, 207; pays her gambling
debts and those of *Monsieur,* 211;
forbids bassette to be played, 211;
founds a convent for the Ursuline
nuns at Saint-Germain, at Madame
de Montespan's suggestion, 213;
summons Racine and Boileau to
read fragments of their contem-

Louis XIV.—*continued*
porary history to him and Madame
de Montespan, 215, 216; unable
to digest Racine's flattery, 215;
"on the brink of a deep precipice,"
220; his advances rejected by
Mademoiselle de Beauvais, 221;
transfers his attentions to
Mademoiselle de Fontanges, and
makes her his mistress, 221, 222;
resolves to finally sever his connection with Madame de Montespan, 222; performs his Easter
devotions, 223; appoints Madame
de Montespan Superintendent of
the Queen's Household, 224; and
gives her the rank and precedence
of a duchess, 224 and note; complains that "she is tormenting him
overmuch," 224, 225; "desperately
in love with Mademoiselle de
Fontanges," 225; loads her and
her relatives with favours, 225;
taking an increased pleasure in
the society of Madame de Maintenon, 227; creates for her the post
of second *dame d'atour* to the
Dauphiness, 227; "nothing but
perpetual conversations with her,"
228; has a child by Mademoiselle
de Fontanges, 228; becoming indifferent to her, 229; his heart
the object of a triangular duel,
229; quarrels with Madame de
Montespan, but reconciled by
Colbert, 230; his intense dislike
of perfumes, 230 note; spends
three hours in Madame de Maintenon's apartments, 231; goes
from Saint-Germain to Versailles
with Mesdames de Montespan, de
Thianges, and de Nevers, 232;
makes a royal progress to Flanders,
233; treats Mademoiselle de Fontanges with marked coldness on his
return, 234; shares the general
horror and indignation at the
crimes of the Poisoners, 242; his
private instructions to the examining-commissioners of the
Chambre Ardente, 243, 244; con-
nives at the escape of several culprits of high rank, 251, 252; exiles
the Duchesse de Bouillon, 255; con-
nives at the escape of the Comtesse
de Soissons, 256; urges the judges
of the Chambre Ardente to do
justice, "without distinction of
person, rank, or sex" 260; and

371

INDEX

Louis XIV.—*continuea*

assures them of his protection, 260; orders the evidence of Marguerite Monvoisin, Romani, and Bertrand to be withheld from the judges, 262; suspends the sittings of the Chambre Ardente, 263 and note; effect upon him of La Voisin's "love-powders," 270; the plot for his assassination, 275-277; orders Mademoiselle Des Œillets to be confronted with her accusers, 281; his reason for refusing to allow Madame de Montespan or her accusers to be brought to trial, 283-285 and note; permits the Chambre Ardente to resume its investigations, 286; but forbids the evidence against Madame de Montespan to be laid before it, 286-287; dissolves the Chambre Ardente, 288; takes extraordinary precautions to ensure the silence of Madame de Montespan's accomplices, 288-290; destroys the incriminating documents, 291; has suspicions that Madame de Fontanges's death is due to poison, 292; endeavours to prevent an autopsy being held, 292, 293; decides that, to avoid scandal, Madame de Montespan must remain at Court, 295; continues to give her marks of his regard, 296; his wonderful self-control, 296; turning a willing ear to the pious counsels of Madame de Maintenon, 297; nightly conferences between him and the lady, 298; reconciled to the Queen, 301; his conversion not yet complete, 301; partakes of *médianoche* with Mademoiselle d'Oré and alarms the devout party, 302; his grief at the Queen's death, 304; his virtue in jeopardy, 306; offers his hand to Madame de Maintenon, 307; his probable reasons for this step, 307; his marriage with Madame de Maintenon, 308 and note; does not tolerate Madame de Maintenon's interference in affairs of State, 310, 311; but permits her to exercise great influence in matters connected with the Court, 311; his daily life at this period, 313 and note, 314 and note; receives a magnificent New Year's gift from Madame de

Louis XIV.—*continued*

Montespan, 315; gives her marks of his favour, 317; does not invite her to accompany the Court on a visit to Baréges, 317; spends all his time with Madame de Maintenon, 318; resumes his visits to his former mistress, 318; his liberality to the Duc de Bourbon and Mademoiselle de Nantes on their marriage, 319; treats Madame de Montespan with increasing coldness, 321; informed by Bossuet of her resolution to retire from Court, 324; gives her apartments to the Duc du Maine, 325; his esteem for the Abbess of Fontevrault, 333; his kindness to Madame de Thianges, 334; admires her daughters, the Duchesse de Nevers and the Duchess Sforza, 334, 335; rallies the Duc de Vivonne on his corpulence, 335; discourages the visits of Madame de Montespan's children to their mother, 336; administers a rebuff to the Duc d'Antin, 339; refuses to receive him into favour during his mother's lifetime, 339; his conduct on learning of Madame de Montespan's death, 359, 360

Louis XV., 2, 123, 300

Louis, Dauphin of France (son of Louis XIV.)

the Duc de Montausier appointed his *gouverneur*, 61; and Bossuet his tutor, 108; makes his mistress observe fast-days, 149 note; warned by the King to avoid "these miserable entanglements," 153; betrothed to Marie Anne of Bavaria, 227

Louvigny, Madame de, 185 and note

Louvois

directs the intendant of Roussillon to institute proceedings against the Marquis de Montespan, 63-65; his curious instructions to the intendant of Dunkerque relative to a journey of the Court, 81, 82; "acknowledges an error that he has not committed," 125 note; seeks to induce the King to withdraw his consent to the marriage of Lauzun and *la Grande Mademoiselle*,136; intrigues with Madame de Montespan to ruin Lauzun, 139; precautions he enjoins on the governor of Pignerol in regard to

372

INDEX

Louvois—*continued*

Lauzan's imprisonment, 140; visits Madame de Maintenon on her return from Baréges, 179; letters which he receives from Saint-Pouange during the campaign of 1678, 198, 199; and from Villacerf, *maître d'hôtel* to the Queen, 200, 201; responsible for the proceedings against Maréchal de Luxembourg, 252; and the Comtesse de Soissons, 256; wishes to protect Madame de Montespan in the Poisons affair, 280; privately examines Mademoiselle Des Œillets, 280; his letter to La Reynie concerning her, 280, 281; brings Mademoiselle Des Œillets to Vincennes and causes her to be confronted with her accusers, 282; advises the King not to allow Madame de Montespan or her accomplices to be brought to trial, 284; his letter to Bazin de Bezons in regard to the evidence of La Joly, 287; his precautions to ensure the silence of Madame de Montespan's accomplices, 289 and note, 290; one of the witnesses to Louis XIV.'s marriage with Madame de Maintenon, 308; his responsibility for the Revocation of the Edict of Nantes, 311

Ludres, Madame de

her love-affair with Charles IV. of Lorraine, 186, 187; her amorous conquests at the French Court, 187; believed to be about to become *maîtresse en titre*, 187 and note; discarded by the King, 188; declines pecuniary compensation for her disappointment, 188; cruelly humiliated by Madame de Montespan, 188; retires from Court, 189; accepts a pension and a *gratification*, "in consideration of her services," 189; figures in Quinault's opera, *Isis*, 218

Luxembourg, Duchesse de, 253 and note

Luxembourg, Maréchal de

his trial before the Chambre Ardente, 252, 253

Luynes, Duc de; (cited) 307 note

MAINE, Duc du

eldest son of Louis XIV. and Madame de Montespan, 68 and note; entrusted to the care of

Maine, Duc du—*continuea*

Madame Scarron, 92; legitimated 100; pays a visit to the Court, 101; becomes lame, 102; goes to Antwerp with Madame Scarron, 102; established at Court, 103; obtains part of *la Grande Mademoiselle's* property in return for Lauzun's liberation, 142-144; sent to the Pyrenees in charge of Madame de Maintenon, 176; honours paid to him on the journey, 176, 177; returns in improved health, 179; goes again to the Pyrenees, 190; his letters to Madame de Montespan, 190-195; his letter to the King, 195 note; wishes to accompany the King to the army, 195; *Œuvres diverses d'un auteur de sept ans,* 220 and note; estranged from his mother, 322, 323; given her apartments after her retirement from Court, 325; accused by Saint-Simon of having intrigued against her with Bossuet and Madame de Maintenon, 325 note; marries Mademoiselle de Bourbon-Charolais, 336; holds completely aloof from Madame de Montespan, 337; regards her death as the removal of an impediment to his fortunes, 360

Maintenon, Château of, 170 and note, 185, 188 and note

Maintenon, Madame de

her description of the state entry of Louis XIV. and Maria Theresa into Paris, 21-24; recommended to Madame de Montespan as *gouvernante* for her children by Louis XIV., 84, 85; widely divergent views as to her character, 85; the probable truth, 85-87; her birth and parentage, 88; hardships of her early years, 88-90; her marriage with the poet Scarron, 90; her married life, 91; her husband's death, 91; her portrait by Madame de Scudéry, 91; granted a pension at the instance of Madame de Montespan, 91; declines to undertake the charge of Madame de Montespan's children, except at the King's request, 92, 93; difficulties of her post, 92, 93; removes with her charges to the Rue de Vaugirard, 93; precautions which she observes there, 93, 94; astonishment caused by her sudden

373

INDEX

Maintenon, Madame de—*continued*
disappearance from society, 94;
capricious treatment which she
receives from Madame de Montespan, 94, 95; the King's early
antipathy disappears on a closer
acquaintance, 95, 96 and note;
returns to society, 96, 97; takes
the Duc du Maine to Antwerp,
102; her letter to Madame de
Montespan, 102; established at
Court with her charges, 103; endeavours to dissuade La Vallière
from entering the Carmelites, 110;
advises Madame de Montespan
to oppose Lauzun's marriage with
la Grande Mademoiselle, 136; divided
between the conflicting claims of
religion and self-interest, 167; persuaded by her confessor, the Abbé
Gobelin, to remain at Court, 167,
168; her relations with Madame
de Montespan, at first friendly,
become strained, 168–170; buys
the Château de Maintenon and
takes the name of her property,
170 and note; resolves on the
conversion of Louis XIV. and the
discomfiture of Madame de Montespan, 170–172; warns Madame
de Montespan of the error of her
ways, 173, 174; remonstrates with
the King, 174; has a " terrible
scene " with Madame de Montespan, 174, 175; complains to Louis
XIV. of the favourite's treatment
of her, 175; her conduct at the
time of Madame de Montespan's
temporary disgrace, 176; her
journey to the Pyrenees with the
Duc du Maine, 176, 177; corresponds with the King, 177, 178;
her letters preferred by Napoleon I. to those of Madame de
Sévigné, 177, 178 and note; the antagonism between her and Madame
de Montespan an open secret at
Court, 178, 179; treated with increased consideration on her return
to Versailles, 179; compliment
paid her by the King, 179; with
Madame de Montespan at Maintenon, 188 note; declines to undertake the charge of Mademoiselle de
Blois or the Comte de Toulouse,
188 note; again takes the Duc du
Maine to the Pyrenees, 190; her
letters to the Abbé Gobelin, 190;
" spends all the day in spinning,"

Maintenon, Madame de—*continued*
193; resumes her correspondence
with the King, 195 note; her New
Year's gift to Madame de Montespan in 1679, 220 and note; im-
plores the Abbé Gobelin to pray
for the King, 221; high in favour
with Louis XIV., even during his
passion for Mademoiselle de Fontanges, 227; appointed second
dame d'atour to the Dauphiness,
227; " has perpetual conversations
with the King," 228; works to
detach him from Mademoiselle
de Fontanges, 229; her influence
increasing rapidly, 230, 231; cir-
cumvents Madame de Montespan's
attempts to overthrow her, 231,
232; accompanies the Court to
Flanders, 233; her schemes fur-
thered by the revelation of Madame
de Montespan's dealings with the
Poisoners, 297; " on the very
pinnacle of favour," 298; brings
about a *rapprochement* between the
King and Queen, 298 and note;
her conduct not so disinterested
as some imagine, 298–301; " is
but too much extolled," 301; receives a *corpo santo* from Pope Innocent XI., 301 note; in constant dread
of the King's lapse from grace,
301, 302; alarmed by his attentions to Mademoiselle d'Oré, 302;
her relations with Madame de
Montespan at this period, 303;
exercises unsleeping vigilance over
the virtue of the King, 304; accompanies the Court to Alsace
and Burgundy, 304; present at
the death of the Queen, 304; a
singular incident, 304, 305; rallied
by the King on her lugubrious
appearance, 305; greatly alarmed
at the change in the situation
caused by the Queen's death, 305,
306; her letters to Madame de
Brinon, her brother, and the Abbé
Gobelin, 306; the King offers her
his hand, 307; her marriage with
Louis XIV., 307, 308 and note;
her influence after her marriage
considered, 309–311; decides to
tolerate, for a while, Madame de
Montespan's presence at Court,
311; visited daily by the King,
314; renewal of the antagonism
between her and Madame de
Montespan, 315; decides to drive

374

INDEX

Mariette, Abbé (sorcerer)—*continued*
arrested and tried by the Châtelet,
267, 268 ; escapes from prison, 268
Mascaron, 171 and note
Maucroix, François (cited), 74 note
Mazarin, Cardinal
introduces his niece, Marie Mancini, to Court, 6 ; his project for
marrying Louis XIV. to the Infanta Maria Theresa, 8, 9 ; his
overtures to the Court of Savoy,
9 ; his proposals accepted by
Spain, 9 ; alarmed at the King's
infatuation for Marie Mancini, 10 ;
firmly refuses to consent to Louis's
marriage with her, 11 ; sends her
to Brouage, 11 ; goes to meet the
Spanish plenipotentiaries at Saint-
Jean de Luz, 12 ; his letter of
remonstrance to the King, 12-15 ;
marries his niece to the Constable
Colonna, 16 ; present at Louis
XIV.'s marriage with the Infanta,
19 ; the splendour of his House-
hold, 21 ; his death, 29
Mazarin, Duc de, 16 note
Meilleraye, Duc de : see **Mazarin,
Duc de**
Meilleraye, Maréchal de, 80
Mellot ; (cited) 117 note
Menneville, Mademoiselle, 31
Mesmes, Antoinette de : see **Vivonne,
Duchesse de**
Mesmes, Président de, 267
Mignard (painter), 67, 354
Miramion, Madame de, 351, 352
Molière, 57, 164, 336
Molina, Donna, 31
Monaco, Louis I., Prince de, 129 note
Monaco, Princesse de, 129 and note,
130, 133
Monsieur : see Orléans, Philippe Duc d'
Montausier, Duc de, 61, 159, 171
Montausier, Duchesse de (*dame
d'honneur* to the Queen)
inexpressibly shocked at La Val-
lière's conduct in following the
Court to Flanders, 47, 48 ; shares
apartments with Madame de Montespan at Avesnes, 50 ; loudly
protests against the charge of
" giving mistresses to the King,"
55 ; publicly insulted by the Marquis de Montespan, 61, 62 ; her
death, 62
Montchevreuil, Madame de, 302 note,
306, 324 and note, 342 and note
Montchevreuil, Marquis de, 302 and
note, 303, 308

Montespan, Madame de
comes to Court as *fille d'honneur*
to the Queen, 37 ; her birth and
parentage, 37, 38 ; her education,
38 note ; dances in the ballet,
Hercule amoureux, 38 ; officiates as
quêteuse at Saint-Germain l'Auxerrois, 38, 39 ; her praises sung by
Loret in *La Muse historique,* 39, 40 ;
her beauty described by her contemporaries, 40 ; her wit, 40, 41 ;
her marriage with the Marquis de
Montespan, 41 ; her children by
the marquis, 41 and note ; dishonourable conduct of her parents
and those of her husband in regard
to her dowry, 42 ; envious of
Louise de La Vallière, 42, 43 ; and
resolves to supplant her, 43 ;
erroneously believed by historians
to be the victim of Louis XIV.'s
desires, 43, 44 ; difficulties in the
way of realising her ambition, 44 ;
her duplicity towards La Vallière
and the Queen, 45 ; her pretended
indignation at La Vallière's conduct in following the Court to
Flanders, 48, 49 ; her suspicious
behaviour at Avesnes, 51 ; goes to
confession with La Vallière at
Notre-Dame de Liesse, 51 ; returns
to Compiègne, 52 ; accompanies
the Court to Flanders, 54 ; pleads
indisposition at Tournai and remains in her apartments, 54 ;
denounced to the Queen in an
anonymous letter, 55 ; indignantly
asserts her innocence, 55 ; generally suspected of being the King's
mistress, 57 ; threatened with ex-
communication by her uncle, the
Archbishop of Sens, 60 ; secret of
her ascendency over Louis XIV.,
67 ; her favour coincides with the
zenith of his reign, 67, 68 ; gives
birth to her first child by the King,
68 ; and to the Duc du Maine, 68 ;
list of her children by Louis XIV.,
68 note ; brings an action for a
separation from her husband before the Châtelet, 69 ; surrenders
the alimony granted her by the
court in favour of her children by
the marquis, 69, 70 ; occupies
apartments at the Tuileries communicating with those of La
Vallière, 74 ; cruelly humiliates
her fallen rival and compels the
King to do the same, 76 ; desirous

376

INDEX

INDEX

Montespan, Madame de—*continued*
liberality to her son, the Duc
d'Antin, 320; her present to his
wife, 320; nurses her daughters
through attacks of small-pox, 320,
321; becomes a comparatively
unimportant person at Court, 321
and note; estrangement between
her and the Duc du Maine, 322,
323; her benefactions to the Couvent des Filles de Saint-Joseph,
323 and note; decides to retire
from Court and make it her
headquarters, 324; and requests
Bossuet to inform the King of her
intention, 324; her apartments
given by the King to the Duc du
Maine, 324; repents of her resolution, but too late, 325, 326; pays
occasional visits to the Court after
her retirement, 327, 328; but soon
ceases to do so, 329; and is almost
completely forgotten, 329; her relations with Madame de Maintenon after her retirement, 329–
331; the society of her sister, the
Abbess of Fontevrault, her chief
consolation in exile, 331; her relations with her children, 335, 336;
"occupies herself with enriching"
the Duc d'Antin, 337; purchases
the Château of Oiron, 337 and
note; her correspondence with the
Duchesse de Noailles, 339–343;
and with Daniel Huet, Bishop of
Avranches, 343–350; her conversations with Madame de Miramion,
351, 352; becomes sincerely penitent, 352; her noble generosity,
352; founds the Hospice of Oiron,
352–354; writes to her husband
entreating his pardon, 354; loses
her sister, the Abbess of Fontevrault, 355; her secret macerations
and penitent life, 354, 355; her
horror of death, 355; still retains
her queenly manner, 355, 356; has
a presentiment of approaching
death, 356; taken ill at Bourbon,
356; her last hours, 356, 357;
scandal at her burial, 358, 359;
her death causes but slight impression at Court, 360; her best
claim to our regard, 361
Montespan, Marquis de
his marriage with Mademoiselle
de Tonnay-Charente, 41; his children by the marriage, 41 note;
only receives a portion of his wife's

Montespan, Marquis de—*continued*
dowry, 42; dishonourable conduct
of his parents, 42; finds himself
in debt, 42; refuses "to share
with Jupiter," 57; opinion of his
contemporaries in regard to his
conduct, 58 and note; has stormy
interviews with the King, 59; supported by his uncle, the Archbishop
of Sens, 59, 60; publicly insults
Madame de Montausier, 61; imprisoned in For l'Evêque, but
soon set at liberty, 62; his farewell
visit to the Court, 62; quarrel
between soldiers under his command and the under-bailiff of Perpignan, 62, 63; Louvois's letter to
the Intendant of Roussillon on
this matter, 63, 64; summoned to
appear before the Supreme Council
of Roussillon, 64; takes refuge in
Spain, 65; action for a separation
brought against him by his wife,
69, 70; correspondence between
Louis XIV. and Colbert respecting
him, 70–72; feared by the King,
76; still breathing forth fire and
slaughter, 97; refused permission
to have his son, the Duc d'Antin,
educated in Paris, 320; under
strict surveillance during a visit
to the capital, 320; his reply to
his wife's letter entreating his
pardon, 354
Montmorency, Madame de, 188
Montpensier, Mademoiselle de
styled *la Grande Mademoiselle*, 47
note; endeavours to dissuade La
Vallière from taking the veil, 106;
the richest heiress in Europe, 126;
her suitors, 126 and note, 127 and
note; her exploits during the
Fronde, 127 and note; conceives
a *grande passion* for the Comte
de Lauzun, 128; their amusing
courtship, 133, 134; "C'est vous!"
134; persuaded by Lauzun to
make a donation in his favour of
the bulk of her property, 134;
obtains the King's sanction to her
marriage, 135; "intoxicated with
love," 135; astonishment and indignation aroused by her proposed
marriage, 135, 136; Louis XIV.
withdraws his permission, 136,
137; her painful interview with
the King, 137; her despair, 137
and note, 138; inconsolable at
the imprisonment of Lauzun at

379

INDEX

Montpensier, Mademoiselle de—*continued*
Pignerol, 140; makes a conveyance of part of her property to the Duc du Maine in order to obtain his liberation, 141–143; present at La Vallière's taking the veil, 146; her physician and almoner compromised in the poison trials, 286 note
(cited) 47–51, 53, 59, 78, 116, 139 note

Monvoisin, Antoine (husband of La Voisin), 238

Monvoisin, Catherine, called La Voisin (sorceress and poisoner) her arrest, 238; her career, 238, 239; La Fontaine's verses upon her, 239, 240; her gorgeous robes, 240; her lovers, 240 note; her confederates, Lesage and the Abbé Guibourg, 240, 241; devotes herself to traffic in poisons, 241 and note; assists Madame Leféron to poison her husband, 250; promises to show the Duchesse de Bouillon Sibyls and prophetesses, 254; accuses Racine of having poisoned his mistress, the actress Du Parc, 257–259; " quietly surrenders her soul to the devil," 260, 261 and note; her death-warrant, 261 note; consulted by Madame de Montespan, 266; advises her to have recourse to Guibourg and the " black mass," 268; gives her " love-powders " to administer to the King, 270; firmly convinced of the efficacy of the charms which she provides, 272; receives fifty louis d'or from Madame de Montespan, 272; the " black mass " said over Madame de Montespan at her house, 272; and over herself, 272, 273; persuaded by Madame de Montespan to poison Louis XIV. and Mademoiselle de Fontanges, 275; conspires with Trianon, Romani, and Bertrand, 275, 276; goes to Saint-Germain to present a poisoned petition to the King, 277; returns to Paris and is arrested, 277

Monvoisin, Marguerite (daughter of La Voisin) disclaims all knowledge of her mother's transactions, until after the sorceress's execution, 261; her declarations, by order of the King, withheld from the Chambre

Monvoisin, Marguerite (daughter of La Voisin)—*continued* Ardente, 262; describes the composition of the " love-powders " provided by her mother for the King, 271; her evidence of Aug. 13, 1680, 275; given the poisoned petition to burn, 277; confronted with Mademoiselle Des Œillets at Vincennes, 281; condemned to perpetual imprisonment, 289

Moret, Comtesse de (mistress of Henri IV.), 22 note

Morison, Mr. J. Cotter (cited), 86, 87

Mortemart, Duc de (father of Madame de Montespan), 37, 41, 125

Mortemart, Duchesse de (mother of Madame de Montespan), 37, 38

Mortemart, Family of, 37 note, 334 and note

Motteville, Madame de; (cited) 4, 5, 6, 9, 12 note, 15, 24, 28

NANTES, Mademoiselle de second daughter of Louis XIV. and Madame de Montespan, 68 note; her birth, 93; entrusted to the care of Madame Scarron, 98; legitimated, 100; her baptism, 100 note; brought to Court, 102; Madame de Caylus's remark concerning her, 164, 165; "admired by every one," 196; accompanies her mother and the Court to Lorraine, 199 note; allowance made to Madame de Montespan for her maintenance, 204 note; marries the Duc de Bourbon, 318, 319; falls ill with small-pox, 320, 321 and note; much attached to her mother, 322; not an exemplary wife, 337; grieves for Madame de Montespan's death, 360

Nanteuil, Mademoiselle de, 187

Napoleon I., Emperor, 178 and note

Nass, Dr. Lucien (cited), 239 note, 241 note, 248 note

Navailles, Duchesse de (*dame d'honneur* to the Queen), 32, 116 note

Neuburg, Duke of, 127 and note

Nevers, Duc de

Nevers, Duchesse de

Noailles, Cardinal de, Archbishop of Paris, 310, 341 and note

Noailles, Duchesse de one of Madame de Montespan's most intimate friends, 117 note; Madame de Montespan's letters to her, 159, 282 note, 339–343

INDEX

RACINE, Jean (poet)—*continuea*
216; his ingratitude towards
Madame de Montespan, 218 and
note; writes a dedication to
Madame de Montespan for *Œuvres
diverses d'un auteur de sept ans*, 220
note; accused by La Voisin of
having poisoned his mistress, the
actress Du Parc, 257-259; writes
an *éloge* of the King for a book
presented by Madame de Montespan to Louis XIV., 314, 315
Raisin, Mademoiselle (actress), 149 note
Rambouillet, Hôtel de, 61, 347
Ravaisson, M., 285 note, 291
    (cited) 239 note, 240 note, 266
    note, 279, 281 note, 287
Rébenac, Comte de (cited), 210
Réflexions sur la miséricorde de Dieu,
Louise de La Vallière's, 109 note
Reuilly, Comtesse de, 207
Richelieu, Duc de, 249
Richelieu, Duchesse de (*dame d'honneur*
to the Queen)
brings about a *rapprochement* be-
tween the Queen and Madame de
Montespan, 160 note; receives
" kind and affectionate letters "
from the King, 160 note; enter-
tains Madame de Maintenon to
supper, 179; Madame de Dreux
seeks to put an end to her by
sorcery, 249
Rochechouart, Family of, 37 note
Rochechouart-Mortemart, Françoise
Athénaïs: *see* Montespan, Madame de
Rochechouart - Mortemart, Gabrielle
Victoire, 345 and note
Rochechouart - Mortemart, Marie
Madeleine Gabrielle, Abbess of
Fontevrault
youngest sister of Madame de
Montespan, 38 note; appointed
Abbess of Fontevrault, 125 and
note; her society Madame de
Montespan's chief consolation
after her retirement from Court,
331; serious charge brought against
her by Madame de Sévigné, 331
note; her amiable character and
accomplishments, 332 and note;
Saint-Simon's high opinion of her,
332; greatly esteemed by the
King, 333; does not take exception to her sister's relations with
Louis XIV., 333; her convent
" most holy and most beautiful,"
340, 341; declines the offer of the
Abbey of Montmartre from con-

Rochechouart - Mortemart, Marie
Madeleine Gabrielle, Abbess of
Fontevrault—*continued*
scientious motives, 341; highly
spoken of by Daniel Huet in his
Mémoires, 350; her death, 354
Rochefort, Maréchale de, 184, 191 note
Rochefort-Théobon, Mademoiselle de
185
Romani (poisoner)
his interrogatory, 262; his depositions, by the King's orders, withheld from the Chambre Ardente,
262; called into consultation by
La Voisin and Trianon, 275; " a
very shrewd, crafty, determined
person," 275; undertakes, in
conjunction with Bertrand, the
poisoning of Mademoiselle de
Fontanges, 276; goes to Saint-
Germain with La Voisin, 277;
condemned to perpetual imprisonment, 288
Roure, Comtesse du, 251

SAINT-CYR, Convent of, 218 note, 329
note
Saint-Evremond, 10, 86 note
Saint-Mars (governor of Pignerol),
139, 140
Saint-Pouange : *see* Colbert de Saint-
Pouange
Saint-Rémi, Madame de (mother of
Louise de La Vallière), 27 note,
105, 112
Saint-Rémi, Marquis de, 27 note
Saint-Simon, Duc de, 43, 177 note
    (cited) 40, 86 note, 128 note, 132
    note, 138, 139, 149, 257, 302,
    308 note, 325 note, 337, 339,
    354, 355, 357, 358 note
Sainte-Beuve ; (cited) 27, 338, 357
Scarron, Madame : *see* Maintenon,
Madame de
Scarron, Paul (first husband of
Madame de Maintenon), 89, 90,
91, 308
Scudéry, Madame de, 146, 155, 164,
224; (cited) 81, 91, 153, 154, 225, 233
Seignelay, Marquis de, 207
Sévigné, Madame de, 40, 94, 164, 178
and note, 336
    (cited) 34 and note, 67, 97, 101,
    110, 115, 116, 118, 122, 135, 137,
    159, 178 and note, 179, 181, 182,
    183, 184, 185, 186, 189, 207-209,
    226, 228, 230, 231, 233 and note,
    253, 255, 256 note, 296, 297, 298,
    331 note

INDEX

INDEX

Printed by BALLANTYNE & Co. LIMITED
Tavistock Street, Covent Garden, London

Lightning Source UK Ltd.
Milton Keynes UK
03 November 2009

145738UK00001BA/214/P